FROM A SUPER-SATELLITE
where a major snafu sent one man to his death
and annihilation tumbling to earth

TO A CALIFORNIA FIELD
where a couple of kids opened a high-tech
Pandora's box

TO A CLASSIFIED
GOVERNMENT LABORATORY
where a maverick scientist saw his brainchild
turning into a monster of destruction

TO AN
UNDERGROUND NETWORK
of Soviet agents who would do anything and kill
anyone for their nation's last chance of supremacy

TO THE WILD STREETS
OF NEW ORLEANS
where Mardi Gras turned into a carnival of
carnage on the eve of doomsday

DEATHFALL
There's no stopping it!

DEATHFALL

by

Robert E. Vardeman

AN ONYX BOOK

ONYX
Published by the Penguin Group
Penguin Books USA Inc., 375 Hudson Street,
New York, New York 10014, U.S.A.
Penguin Books Ltd, 27 Wrights Lane,
London W8 5TZ, England
Penguin Books Australia Ltd, Ringwood,
Victoria, Australia
Penguin Books Canada Ltd, 2801 John Street,
Markham, Ontario, Canada L3R 1B4
Penguin Books (N.Z.) Ltd, 182-190 Wairau Road,
Auckland 10, New Zealand

Penguin Books Ltd, Registered Offices:
Harmondsworth, Middlesex, England

First published by Onyx, an imprint of New American Library,
a division of Penguin Books USA Inc.

First Printing, May, 1991
10 9 8 7 6 5 4 3 2 1

REGISTERED TRADEMARK—MARCA REGISTRADA

Printed in the United States of America

PUBLISHER'S NOTE
This is a work of fiction. Names, characters, places, and incidents either are the
product of the author's imagination or are used fictitiously, and any resemblance
to actual persons, living or dead, events, or locales is entirely coincidental.

For Christopher Eric

1

The green light on the control console changed to amber and slowly blinked. After thirty seconds it grew tired of the inattention and became more insistent. Still not satisfied when another fifteen seconds passed, it started flashing an angry red until the senior space-systems analyst on duty noticed it. The Air Force captain yawned and tapped the indicator with his thumb. His board had experienced seven minor malfunctions in the past month, but this didn't bother him unduly. Other aspects of the job rankled him far more. Working buried under Cheyenne Mountain carried a cachet of respect from other officers and the public, but exile to the squat cinder-block Satellite Control Facility outside the mountain and far to the south of Colorado Springs amounted to little more than being a clerk. Worse, he decided. He was nothing more than a leper clerk.

He remembered better days in Sunnyvale, at the primary SCF everyone called the Big Blue Cube. The work hadn't been more interesting there than it was here. Being in Sunnyvale, so close to San Francisco and all those California babes, had been more to his liking than watching the slow orbit of junk from the Soviets, the Japanese, the EEC, and U.S. space launches. Hell, he had even developed a taste for wind-surfing. How was he supposed to do that in the middle of a mountain range where the only water came from spring runoffs?

Yawning again, the captain tapped the indicator light harder. It doggedly remained red.

"Will you clear your board?" came the aggrieved command in his headset. He adjusted the earpiece, turning down the volume. His supervisor rode him constantly for no good reason, and he resented it. Nobody gave the SSA's any respect. He had worked hard in training, and his technical degree had cost him plenty of sleepless nights studying. The hotshots under Cheyenne Mountain thought they ruled the roost, and to hell with everyone else. He couldn't even score with the local women; they were too wrapped up in the mystique of the Air Force Academy, just a few miles to the north, and all the prancing young pups there. A captain, and he was too old! Maybe he could wangle an appointment in the Pentagon. He'd heard the National Reconnaissance Office in D.C. was on the lookout for sharp SSA's. The NRO controlled all the birds in orbit, not just the junk he monitored.

He turned to his monitor to get a full readout on the problem.

"Colonel," he said into his throat mike after a minute of study, "there's trouble with one of the birds."

"Which one?" The colonel was terse. He disliked tending to real predicaments. His men stared at junk, and he reported in minute detail their findings. It was a dead-end job but one which suited the older officer, since he was waiting out retirement at the end of the year. A true problem might require him to find a different form to bounce it up the line—or worse. He might have to make a decision that would affect his limited tenure in the Air Force. "And what do you make the glitch out to be?"

The captain knew his supervisor was already switching his command circuit to multiplex. At any instant he might be overridden—and if he was, it would be entered on his service record in minute detail. He could kiss off any chance of the Pentagon if that happened and he made a wrong guess with all eyes on him.

"Sir," he said briskly, "a Keyhole bird is starting to tumble." He struggled with the slow-responding workstation. Why did the Air Force always go to the lowest bidder?

"Which one, dammit?"

"Uh, a KH-18 that lofted three months ago. A space-shuttle launch. It's got some NRO spy equipment on it."

"I know the capabilities of the Keyhole series, Captain. Don't teach an old hound dog how to suck eggs."

"I'd never do that, sir," the captain said, knowing he had made an error of judgment. Whenever the colonel fell back on the down-home homilies, all hell was out for lunch.

The captain saw his monitor flicker slightly. Every bit of data he had examined was now flashing across the colonel's terminal. The SSA started working harder, trying to pinpoint the problem. He tracked garbage, the spent boosters and other debris from launches around the world. Sometimes the debris held hidden spy satellites that would lie inert for months or even years before coming to full operational status. He had monitored one U.S. bird that had gone through an elaborate ritual of firing up and sending back a few microbursts of data communication, then going apparently dead. That particular Keyhole satellite had dipped down and picked up valuable intelligence on the Soviet complex at Tyuratum missile test site as they static-tested the engines for their new SS-34 booster.

But this was the first time he had watched a working satellite go out.

"Point failure, sir," he said with as much confidence as he could. He had made a snap decision. He hoped it was right. They were always watching senior SSA's for command ability. Making good decisions would bring him to the attention of higher-ups. He might parlay a transfer out of this hole yet.

"Dammit!" the colonel flared. "*How* did it fail?"

The captain couldn't even curse under his breath as his superior went ballistic. The throat microphone would pick up any small gurgle on his part, not to mention what he wanted to say.

"It's dipping down into the atmosphere and beginning to tumble. The data stream from it shows it's out of fuel."

"Impossible," the colonel snapped. "Its fuel supply ought to last at least six months. We haven't been using it; there's no maneuvering being done."

"It was spoofed, sir," the captain said, confident of this answer. He might be wrong, but if he was, they could never prove it. The Soviets played their games all the time. A coded signal turning on the KH-18's steering jets wasted fuel and improperly repositioned the bird, making its real-time image relay worthless. "All eighty-five hundred pounds of hydrazine fuel are gone. There's no way we can get it back into orbit."

"Dammit, dammit, dammit," the colonel swore. "What can we do to keep it aloft?"

"Sorry, sir, that's above my pay grade," the captain said. He bit his tongue the instant he realized the colonel was speaking rhetorically and hadn't expected an answer.

The answer was only too apparent. The KH-18 was lost. Without the fuel to boost it back into its usual near-earth orbit, it would drop lower and lower into the atmosphere. The growing frictional drag would cause the sophisticated satellite to tumble. As its instability increased and its orbital speed changed, it would plunge deeper into the atmosphere and eventually burn up.

A three-hundred-million-dollar bird the size of a Greyhound bus was swooping down to its death. The captain quickly calculated that it would blast a crater a quarter-mile in diameter when it hit. Impossible to figure where it would crash. The tumbling constantly altered the satellite's position and made precision impossible. It could fall in a week or a few hours.

He hoped his superiors wouldn't hold the KH-18's crash against him—and he hoped to be far from its point of impact. It would go off like a small atomic bomb when it hit.

2

Thomas Stevenson looked up from his screen when Jack Parkessian, his research assistant, entered the small cluttered office, removed his reading glasses, then rubbed his eyes. He had been working long hours on a complex molecular-biology problem for the Army Nuclear-Biological-Chemical Command. Reaching over, he blanked the screen of his computer workstation monitor. Jack was cleared for all their work, but Stevenson didn't think he had a "need to know" on this problem. It was above his pay grade, as the military were wont to say.

"What is it?" Stevenson asked. There was a glint in the young man's sharp eyes that Stevenson didn't like. He wished he could get another post-doc in, but Parkessian was good at his job—dammit.

"You been working all night?" Parkessian asked as he pushed some reference books off a chair and perched on the rickety back, his feet on the seat. Stevenson wished Parkessian would learn to sit normally rather than perching like some bird of prey waiting for dinner to stumble by and die. The monitor's dim blue light illuminated the high cheekbones, the deep-set dark eyes, and hawk nose, heightening Parkessian's predatory appearance. If Stevenson believed the scuttlebutt making the rounds, Jack Parkessian *was* waiting for the precise moment to swoop. He made no bones about what he considered his second-class position in the NBC biophysics division. Stevenson guessed Parkessian wanted his job. At the moment, he was willing to give it to him, no questions

asked. He was getting too old to spend entire nights hunched over a terminal, watching the simulated 3-D image of a crystalline biologic material precessing slowly on a VGA screen, stubbornly revealing its structure and properties to him. Deadlines crushed him as they always did.

He pushed his hands back through thinning sandy hair and wondered if that goop he had seen advertised on TV—minoxidil—worked. He might have to give it a try. If he lost any more hair, he'd be as bald as a baby's bottom.

"You haven't heard?" Parkessian took particular glee in delivering bad news. His dark eyes sparkled and his lips pulled back in a razor-thin gash of a smile.

"Have you seen the new regs?" Stevenson countered. "We're going back to the old Roman Empire traditions. We now kill messengers bearing bad news."

Parkessian's facial expression subtly changed. "It's the KH-18."

"What about it? More overflow readings from my experiment?" Stevenson muttered. The Air Force hadn't given him enough space for the bio-neutral replication, his "gray-gooey-gob" experiment aboard their damned spy satellite. He'd had to restrict growth to fewer than ten liters of nutrient divided into five equal units—and there had been no provision for expansion should growth exceed his upper-limit prediction. If the genetically engineered cells multiplied too quickly, they might explode from their tightly sealed environment and contaminate the innards of the KH-18.

Stevenson shrugged as he considered this. It was about the worst that could happen, and it wasn't *too* bad. The Air Force—and the CIA—might find some of the sticky gunk shorting out their circuitry, but it was designed to be biologically harmless. Unless they sent up the space shuttle to do an on-site inspection and deemed his experiment the cause, they could never blame him for a potential electronic point failure. Space was a hazardous

environment, even for expensive radiation-shielded, protected, *tough* military hardware.

"Worse, Tom, much worse." Parkessian hiked his other foot to the seat of the chair.

Parkessian smiled crookedly. Stevenson had never noticed the length of the man's canines before. He might be a vampire ready to suck his victim dry. "The bird is coming down. The SSA controlling it from the SCF out in Colorado Springs said the Soviets spoofed it."

"What? I don't understand—"

"The Russkies sent a signal to the satellite that made it waste its maneuvering fuel. It's starting to fall into the atmosphere. Friction will burn—"

"I know about friction," Stevenson said, irritated. "What about my experiment?"

"What does it matter? You said it's only a gray gooey gob. Even if it falls to Earth, there's nothing to fear—unless there's more to it than you're telling." Parkessian looked so smug Stevenson wanted to hit him.

Stevenson shook his head slowly. It didn't matter what happened to his experiment. It was a preliminary trial that ought to have been conducted quickly in a P-4 containment facility on Earth—and it would have been if an idiotic Midwestern congressman hadn't harangued the House about rogue genes and seven-headed mutated bugs. The man had even shown excerpts from a 1955 Leo G. Carroll movie about monster killer arachnids.

That session of Congress had been a full house.

"The experiment is harmless enough. If the satellite burns in the atmosphere, everything will be destroyed."

"The SSA says it will impact. He tried to figure out where, but couldn't do it."

Stevenson snorted in contempt. That ought to have been an easy problem in orbital dynamics, even with the KH-18 tumbling. The space-systems analyst had more computing power and information at his disposal than all the scientists who had lived and worked before the year 1980.

"How did you find out?" Stevenson asked. He studied Parkessian more carefully. This ought to have been highly classified, well above Parkessian's Q clearance and need to know. If anyone had been contacted directly, it ought to have been him. After all, his name was on the door as director of the biophysics division, and Project Big Hunk was completely his responsibility.

"The crypto expert picked it up. She and I are, well, let's say Sheila and I are real close." Parkessian leered, as if Stevenson hadn't caught his meaning. Stevenson didn't care if Parkessian knocked off a piece of ass on his own time, but did care that this Sheila had divulged privileged information to a subordinate in obvious violation of security rules. This would bear investigation later.

"She saw it coming in from Fort Fumble for you and handed it over to me."

Stevenson saved the data held in the workstation's memory and called up the files on Project Big Hunk. It took several seconds for him to enter the access commands unlocking the material hidden away behind veils of computer trapdoor codes. He knew he'd be on the road to the Pentagon within the hour. The destruction of a major spy satellite wasn't going to go down easily with the big brass at what Parkessian called Fort Fumble. If their military SSA's were at fault, they would hunt high and low until they found a sacrificial civilian goat to be roasted by one congressional committee after another.

Stevenson knew his experiment qualified as whipping boy. The National Reconnaissance Office had been forced by the Army to loft it. None of the research shuttle launches were adequate for such an extended experiment offering even a hint of possible genetic contamination. The Air Force had complained bitterly; the Army had shouted even louder. Age-old rivalry boiled over and made its way up the chain of command until the director of Central Intelligence had it dropped on her desk.

Stevenson had been there when Mildred Fenton had made her decision. She had walked the thin line between the DIA chief, the CIA analysts, and the need to maintain a modicum of cooperation between the various segments of the intelligence community. He had been allowed to loft Project Big Hunk and get back detailed telemetry from it on a weekly basis, but the experimental setup had to be contained within a one-meter cube and could not mass out more than fifty kilograms.

In a way, Stevenson had hoped the Air Force would prevail and he would be allowed to keep the experiment earthbound. Such preliminary work was better completed in a laboratory, where hands-on tinkering was possible. The flood of data he received was useful in designing more complex experiments, but it was somehow tainted by time, distance, and secrecy when gathered in orbit.

Besides that, he couldn't look at the gobs, poke them, move them, get a feel for the mechanisms producing genetically engineered neutral cells.

The congressman showing *Tarantula* returned to torment him. Big bugs. Rampant fear of recombinant DNA experiments. They were afraid of the dark and suspicious of the light. Neo-Luddites, all.

"Jack, how long will it take to do a chronological Pearl Harbor file?" Stevenson hadn't spent the last fourteen years in government research for nothing. He had learned the cardinal rule: CYA. Cover Your Ass. A Pearl Harbor file would permit a congressional oversight committee to track each step of the path to disaster, leading, hopefully, to the conclusion that Stevenson's insistence a year earlier on keeping the experiment in a tightly sealed lab was justified. He didn't enjoy the prospect of using the Challenger argument, either.

Whenever anything went wrong with a space mission, manned or not, it was always possible to find an ally in the "there are some things man was not meant to do" faction in Congress. Even the spider-hating congressmen might be useful, as hard as that was for Stevenson to believe.

"NASA has access to the design and launch parameters material too," Parkessian said. "I'll have to tinker with their computers, but that won't be too hard. Sheila showed me a neat trick to . . ." His voice trailed off when he saw the polar coldness in Stevenson's gray eyes.

"We're not doctoring the files. I want the chronology and references accurate. They just don't have to be complete. Do I have to spell it out for you?"

"No." Parkessian had turned sullen. Stevenson made a mental note to check the file before turning it over to the first committee to subpoena his records. Parkessian might be up for a little data sabotage to put Project Big Hunk in a bad light and himself in a better position. Stevenson took a deep breath and tried not to get too excited. It was *his* project. He was almost sorry he had insisted on such tight control now. Sharing blame always helped.

He shook himself hard. Nothing was going to go *that* wrong. And it wasn't right to foist off culpability on others, as appealing as the notion was. He had avoided it for three years since becoming head of the biophysics lab at Fort Detrick. His researchers knew he could take the heat, if necessary. But it was wearing him down. Too much time was spent putting out bureaucratic fires instead of doing real research.

"Get on with it. I'll alert the others to get their records in order. Basil Baker is still around somewhere. Elaine is on vacation, but that shouldn't matter. This wasn't her project anyway. All she did was design the containment vessels to my specs. I'll be back tomorrow, unless the shit really hits the fan."

He waved Parkessian from the office, then tapped the print key and started his antiquated laser printer. It moaned and hummed and whined as it loaded fonts. After almost five minutes it began flicking out the report he had dredged up from the computer's bowels. He entered a brief message to the rest of his staff on their departmental BBS, then added more bond to the printer's paper bin.

Stevenson sat and stared at the white sheets slipping

from the printer. After a few minutes the laser printer
clattered to a halt. From across his office he could feel
the heat billowing from the machine. Heaving himself to
his feet, he gathered the documents, slipped them into a
red-and-white-striped folder marked "SECRET" on the
cover, and dropped it into his battered briefcase. Stevenson made sure his workstation was secure, his files saved
and encoded, then turned it off. He usually left it on, but
he didn't think he would be back anytime soon. From the
hook behind his door he took down a heavy overcoat and
shrugged into it. He wasn't looking forward to the long
drive to the Pentagon in the lousy Middle Atlantic winter
weather.

And he sure as hell wasn't looking forward to the
meeting with the Air Force general responsible for satellite orbital surveillance. He touched the back of his neck,
more to assure himself that it was still intact than to
position the lamb's-wool scarf Elaine had given him. He
knew exactly what was going to be on the chopping
block.

Stevenson squinted as he tried to keep his eyes from
blurring. He had been lost in the seemingly infinite corridors of the 3.7-million-square-foot Pentagon for over
three hours. General Beaumont had rousted every one of
the twenty-three thousand employees in the Pentagon, or
so it seemed, to interrogate them one by one about the
satellite failure. Stevenson had stopped counting those
giving expert testimony when the number reached eigh-
teen. Or maybe nineteen. He had drifted during the
explanation of the SSA's wrong appraisal that the Soviets
had spoofed the bird.

That had been someone from the State Department,
he thought. They were always the apologists for the
Soviets, even though others with a technical bent appeared to share the opinion. Stevenson wondered what
they knew that the Air Force didn't.

Need to know. Always need to know. It put shackles and blinders on everyone.

"Dr. Stevenson, do you have any questions? You've looked thoughtful throughout Major Henley's report."

"Henley?" Stevenson fought to remember what the short, powerfully built black major had reported. Something about a rescue mission. All Stevenson wanted was to find a dark corner and go to sleep. He had no business sitting through interminable testimony.

"We are not giving this the mushroom treatment, Dr. Stevenson," the general said, barely containing his anger. "We are putting all our cards on the table."

"No mushroom treatment," Stevenson said. They weren't going to stick it down in the deep, dark shit and try to keep it from prying eyes. Edwin Beaumont wanted the Army NBC Command to take the heat in full view of the public and Congress. To do anything else jeopardized Air Force funding for future satellite recon work.

General Beaumont turned back to his shuttle astronaut. Stevenson tried to concentrate. This modern-day Inquisition had already lasted for hours. He was ready to confess everything, if only they would let him sleep a few hours. And he wasn't even guilty. A complex problem waited for him back at Fort Detrick, Parkessian was probably undermining his authority at every turn, and what the hell was *he* supposed to do about their damned satellite?

"It was not spoofed by the Soviets," Major Henley said forcefully. "There was internal failure—point failure caused by short-circuiting."

Stevenson sat straighter in the chair. "A proton event?" he asked casually. "Or do you think there is another cause?"

"It was not a manufacturing error," Henley said. The words hung in the air as if they had frozen. "We fully observed zero defects guidelines."

"And it wasn't caused by my experiment, either," Stevenson said softly, forcing them to listen. It had finally come down to fighting in the trenches, and he knew most of the tricks. "I've gone over the telemetry. There's no indication of excess pressurization in any of the five vessels."

"That was never considered," the major said primly. Dark eyes bored into Stevenson's gray ones. "You have not followed what General Beaumont outlined. We will launch a repair mission immediately."

"From the Cape? Can you launch the space shuttle that fast? The last mission took place last week."

"We have to try, Doctor," General Beaumont said. His bushy eyebrows wiggled like spastic caterpillars over the white, doughy flesh of his face. Beaumont had been in the fluorescent confines of the Pentagon too long and had taken on an unhealthy look. "The KH-18 is too important to abandon without attempting to repair it. It would take a year or more to obtain new budget authorization, and longer than that to manufacture a new bird. We don't have that kind of leeway in our current surveillance schedule. The Soviet hegemony is crumbling. We need complete and accurate intelligence reports on an hourly basis."

"You want to know what to expect *if* my experiment leaked," Stevenson said, suddenly relieved. They weren't any better informed than the others. Beaumont and Henley were both afraid they'd find ten-foot genetically engineered spiders inside their satellite.

"We need to know the details," Henley said. "We have to go into the bird to replace, uh, certain elements."

Stevenson tried to keep his eyebrows from matching Beaumont's in wiggling uncontrollably. They were going to do more than rendezvous and refuel the KH-18. He kept himself from asking what they suspected to be the trouble. He didn't have any reason to know what instrumentation was inside the satellite, or what its real mission was, or why they thought it had glitched on them.

"Truth to tell, General, repair in space is far too

dangerous. There's nothing in it that can't be done on Earth better, safer, and, after this fiasco, more efficiently."

"We won't return it, Doctor," Beaumont said. "That would violate the agreement we signed with the NRO and DCI Fenton to allow the Army to put your test in orbit. When Major Henley and the other EVA specialists pop the hatch, we don't want any nasty surprises."

"There's no indication that my experiment has broken out of its containment," Stevenson insisted. "Even if it had, the stuff is harmless. It's just a gray gooey gob."

"How's that?" Henley asked. "Gray gooey gob?"

Stevenson laughed. "We're practicing growing nondifferentiated cells. They are neutral cells and don't do anything. They just grow. You could eat a handful of the gunk and suffer nothing worse than bad taste on your tongue. The stuff is one hundred percent harmless."

Henley looked skeptical.

"Really, Major. Trust me. It's harmless."

General Beaumont dismissed his repairman-astronaut, then glowered at Stevenson. The meeting was over, at last.

And he had survived.

3

Colonel Arthur Jensen stirred when the others came into the ready room. He had drifted off to sleep. He smiled sheepishly. A hero of his, Gordo Cooper, three decades earlier had fallen asleep during countdown for an orbital flight in an antique Mercury capsule. Reaching that stage of relaxation was still beyond Jensen, but he was working on it. A veteran of eight shuttle flights over five years, there wasn't a great deal he hadn't experienced.

Even the solid-fuel-booster near-disaster on the *Invincible*'s maiden flight hadn't worried him. He yawned again, remembering how tiresome the medal ceremony at the White House had been for that bit of piloting on his part. All he had done was his job. Where was the heroism? He hadn't had time to be scared. That had come a week later, in private.

Jensen looked across the bare green-painted room at Milton Lefevre. The forty-year-old scientist was so obviously a rookie that Jensen wanted to take pictures and post them on a bulletin board. Huge arrows could point to the idiot grin and the wild look in the eyes—all symptoms of a civilian's first step off the Earth. Inside, Lefevre was undoubtedly churning, a high-school kid asking the girl of his dreams out for a first timorous date. Jensen smiled when he saw the scientist take a slug of antacid from a clear plastic bottle, then hide it to keep anyone from seeing. Jensen had never heard of anyone scrubbed from a mission because of nerves, but Lefevre couldn't know that. Throughout training, they had always been told that everything counted. The ones that cracked did it during training, where lives wouldn't be lost. Jensen didn't know much about Lefevre, but if he had passed muster at Huntsville, he was all right.

Jensen had taxied a couple dozen scientists up to orbit, in addition to the Air Force spooks like Major Henley, and he had always been able to spot the first-timers.

He hoped Lefevre didn't get worked up enough to puke, and if he did, that he'd do so inside his helmet. Cleaning up vomit in weightlessness was a bitch. It hung in small spheres that danced away when you tried to scoop them up. Some yahoo at NASA had designed a hand-held vacuum cleaner for use in the cabin, but the filter always clogged. Simple paper towels worked best, though none of the flight crews had ever had the heart to report this to NASA. The ridiculous vacuum cleaner had cost more than a quarter of a million dollars to develop.

"They're ready for us, Colonel Jensen," said the nameless, faceless civilian in charge of getting them out to the gantry. The guy was an astronaut wannabe. They all were. They all envied the men and women who packed themselves off to the shuttle cabin and blasted into space. Jensen took real pride in knowing that *he* was the one kicking free of gravity, not this civilian, not the people in the blockhouse, not the clever, expert controllers in Houston.

He was leaving. Let them eat their hearts out.

He nodded and picked up his portable air-conditioning unit. Earlier flights had required heavy compressor packs; he was glad some bright boy in a windowless room had come up with the new unit. It kept him ten degrees cooler with half the weight. Hefting it a couple times, he wondered what else they might add to the units. Scientists like Lefevre could never let things be. They had to change everything, put in new bugs, and let his kind work them out.

Jensen puffed with pride. *His* kind. He was more than a cabdriver, no matter what the others at the Cape said.

Jealous bastards. What did they know about sitting atop the three rockets as the fuse lit under their asses? The pressure wasn't much, but the thrill never quite went away. He might doze off now, but never during the actual launch. That made the bureaucratic drivel he put up with on Earth worthwhile.

"You ready for the ride of your life, Doc?" he asked Lefevre. The scientist stared at him with those febrile eyes. For a moment he wondered if the scientist was sane.

"A touch of indigestion," Lefevre admitted. "From nerves, I guess."

"Better men than you have gotten the weebles going up," Jensen said. "Just don't wobble." He had just insulted the scientist, but Milton Lefevre never noticed. Jensen headed toward the door, where Henley awaited him.

"He's looking a bit under the weather," Henley said, lifting his chin and indicating Lefevre. "Is he going to make it?"

"He checked out on preflight. Ask his medico." Jensen didn't have much time for spooks like Henley. They swooped down from the Pentagon bellowing orders and expecting everyone to jump to instantly. What they did was never discussed, on Earth or in orbit. A pox on all of them and their damned security.

"You're the flight commander. I'm asking you." Henley's dark eyes locked on Jensen's.

"You're just a paying customer, Major. If the flight surgeon says Lefevre is cleared for takeoff, then he's okay. Do you have any other questions?"

"Let's kick the tires and light the fires," Henley said. He spun and walked off, unable to storm off in the heavy flight suit.

Jensen snorted in contempt. Henley wasn't even much of a pilot. What kind of Air Force officer was he, anyway? Just a paper shuffler, not someone demanding to be put into the cockpit of a hot fighter just for the hell of it. Even worse, he was one of the spook computer jocks. What did he know about real work, riding a workstation's output and calling it progress?

The other three astronauts were sitting in the bus which would take them to the launch pad. Benjamin Nakamura, the solar-radiation specialist, muttered constantly to himself. Jensen wasn't sure if this was some ploy to irritate Henley or if the man just prayed a lot. The cargo-bay specialist, Harry Ellington, spoke into his dead microphone just loud enough for Henley to hear words like "Moscow" and "KGB" and "spies." This was going to be another boondoggle where a spook would huddle in the back of the hold and mutter to himself—all need-to-know classified monologue. But Jensen was mission commander and he had to know what was going on sometime along the way. Unlike the Soviets, U.S. flight crews controlled their shuttles directly. He might get advice from the ground in case of malfunction, but *he* was in charge, in complete command from the instant the solid-fuel boosters kicked him in the butt and put the *Invincible* into orbit.

"Do they pass muster?" he asked Henley. The black major scowled and settled down on the seat beside him just as the bus accelerated.

"I've never met any of them before. You can't be too careful. This is a very sensitive mission."

"You want to search them for weapons?" Jensen asked. "Don't forget to peer up their assholes. I've heard the Russky spies can hide an entire battalion up there. Something to do with using Iranian petroleum jelly."

"You've been briefed, Colonel Jensen. This is no time for levity."

"Sorry, Major. Thought you might enjoy the hunt."

Jensen leaned back, totally at ease. He closed his eyes and let the gentle rocking of the bus driving across the tarmac soothe him. He knew he shouldn't taunt the major. The man had a job to do and was doing it well.

The vagueness of his mission really annoyed him, though. His briefing had been unexpected. Launch scheduling had put him in rotation for the early-February flight—not one just days before Christmas. The emergency launch had angered his wife, Millie, but he had assured her he would be back before Christmas morning. Millie hadn't—quite—believed him. They both had had too much experience with military missions and the strict adherence to the FUBB principle: Fucked Up Beyond Belief.

It didn't matter as much as it once had; the kids were too old to believe in Santa Claus. For all he knew, it might give them more of a kick to see their old man showing up in the darkened sky as the star guiding the three wise men toward Jerusalem.

Jensen didn't think the mission would last until Epiphany, however. From the coordinates given at the briefing, the *Invincible* would go up into a polar orbit. That meant spy satellites. Having Henley aboard meant spooks; he recognized one of the other men giving the briefing as a Defense Intelligence Agency analyst; and he knew that Lefevre was on this jaunt because he was the only one available to perform his task on short notice.

"Hey, Doc," Jensen called out across the bus, "what's your orbital specialty?"

"Colonel, don't," Henley warned.

"I'm in command," he said in a low voice. "The civilian is uptight. If I get him talking about himself, he'll loosen up. If he doesn't, *you* get to clean up the mess. How many have barfed their guts out from sheer nerves?"

"Too many," Henley grumbled. The major huddled into himself even more, making Jensen think of a black hole sucking in all light and warmth within its Schwarzchild radius.

"I'm a university researcher in electro-optics."

"You design the fancy imaging gizmos that go into the birds?"

Milton Lefevre bobbed his head eagerly. He moved forward on the seat and bent over, hands on his knees for support. For a brief instant Jensen saw a flash of pain on the man's face, but it vanished as quickly as lightning in a storm.

"I'm going to check out the imaging system on the KH-18. It's developed a—"

Jensen thought Henley was going ballistic at this revelation.

"Doctor! You're violating security!"

"But—"

"That's all right, Doc. I was just trying to be friendly, and so were you. It's not your fault." Jensen heaved to his feet and hoisted the small air-conditioning unit. The bus had arrived at the base of the massive gantry holding the space shuttle. He exited quickly, leaving the major behind on the bus, fuming and muttering to himself about pissant pilots.

A shiver ran along Jensen's spine as he looked up. Feathery plumes of condensation boiled off the liquid-fuel tanks on the main shuttle engine. The solid-fuel candles on either side of the *Invincible* were silent and argent and looked more like grain silos from his youth on the southern Iowa farm than rockets capable of generating millions of pounds of thrust. Spotlights roved constantly over the craft. Jensen had never figured out what their operators looked for, but it gave the entire launch pad an eerie aspect, one removing it from the ordinary.

That was as it ought to be. A space-shuttle launch was never ordinary, not for the men and women inside or the tens of thousands who still gathered along cold, wet sandbars in Cocoa Beach to watch even the most insignificant mission depart.

As Jensen rode the dull aluminum cage up to the shuttle's cockpit, he wondered how many spectators had shown up to watch this dawn liftoff. It wasn't a scheduled flight; the *Invincible* hadn't been on the timetable until February, but it had come back from its November mission in good shape.

"Everyone inside. Buckle up, it's the law," he said,

making sure the others filed out of the elevator and found their stations aboard. He waited for Lefevre; Nakamura and Ellington were veterans of several flights and knew the drill. The scientist might have been trained, but he had no experience with the real thing. Nerves were always a factor for the rookies.

He frowned when Lefevre stumbled as he entered the shuttle's main compartment. Clumsy astronauts need not apply. Especially for any mission he commanded.

"Is there anything wrong, Doc?" he asked.

"No, nothing."

Boards were lighting up. Jensen had to begin the checklist soon or the elephants in the control bunker would shout and snort and threaten him with mayhem. He dropped into his command chair, and proceeded to calibrate and prepare the *Invincible* for space.

"Have you ever brought one back, Major?" he asked.

"Do you mean have I ever landed a shuttle? No. All I've done is go through the simulator."

"How many hours of flight time do you have?" Jensen started the automatics. In one hour the *Invincible* would launch. All decisions had been made. He was ready to go, no matter what.

"Nearly a hundred, mostly in trainers."

"If we get cleared for Edwards, you want to land her?"

Henley turned. His dark face broke into a huge ivory-white smile. This was answer enough for Jensen.

He heard a clicking in his headphones and switched to a private frequency used only by mission control at JSC.

"Art, this is Joe down in Houston. We're getting spotty readings on your civilian cargo. What's his condition?"

"Nervous as a long-tailed cat in a rocking-chair factory," Jensen said, mangling a Texas accent through his Midwestern one.

"We're getting static on his telemetry. Might be a short in his shorts. Keep an eye out and get back to me if you see anything."

"So what am I looking for, leprosy? Is an arm going to fall off? Do I check his diaper to see if he's peed on himself? I've got a mission to fly. I'm not a wet nurse."

"The hell you're not. I saw who all you got riding up this time. You got nothing but folks to wet-nurse."

Jensen laughed. Joe was right.

"Let me get on with it, will you?" The countdown now demanded his complete attention. He worked steadily to keep the onboard computer updated with a stream of information from the ground stations. He didn't need to know his destination, since the computer's silicon-chip brain contained all the information. He was glad, however, that Lefevre had confirmed his suspicion that they would connect with a spy bird.

Jensen remembered that he had launched a KH-18 a year or two back, and that his cargo had consisted of featureless boxes. Cargo specialists like Ellington had to worry about how to unload and jockey them into proper orbit. For him, being in space sufficed.

Time passed rapidly. Mission control started the inevitable countdown a 1930's German movie director had devised to make flicks more dramatic.

Colonel Arthur Jensen awaited kickoff into space.

4

"I resent being dragged down here like this, General," Tom Stevenson said. He glared at Edwin Beaumont, but the Air Force brigadier general had a lifetime's experience with lazy subordinates, haughty congressmen, and arrogant civilian scientists who thought they were beyond his control. Stevenson's tirade did affect the officer, however. Beaumont maintained his sangfroid, but his bushy ridges writhed with an eerie zombie life of their own.

"We must discuss things more fully, Doctor," the general replied. Both men entered the conference room and took the two free seats at the end of a huge oval table. The lights dimmed before Stevenson protested further. Being summoned like a flunky only two days after initially briefing Beaumont rankled. Stevenson was glad that Elaine Reinhardt was still out on the Coast and wouldn't be back from her vacation in San Francisco for a few more days. Explaining why MP's came for him at his home would be damned hard, even if she was cleared for the work he did.

The video began unwinding its pale image on the screen at the end of the long conference room, but Stevenson didn't pay attention; instead he peered through the darkness and examined the other men. Two Army officers had slipped in; he caught the reflection off their brasswork and saw the division patches on their shoulders.

Stevenson settled back. He wasn't going to swing by himself for whatever crime the Air Force had conjured up. One of the two who had entered was General Lucien

Morningside, in charge of the NBC research at Fort Detrick and Stevenson's superior. His presence meant this meeting wouldn't become an Air Force versus civilian scientist Star Chamber. Stevenson relaxed, even though the only one of his regular staff left on duty at Fort Detrick was Jack Parkessian. With the research staff on Christmas holidays, his assistant wouldn't get into excessive trouble or start too many rumors.

Stevenson considered sitting beside Morningside, then decided against it. Attracting attention was the last thing he wanted to do right now. He felt like a grade-school pupil who didn't know the answer and knew the teacher would call on him if he even blinked. He fumbled with the pencil and the yellow legal pad placed in front of him. Most of the others, all Air Force officers, scribbled notes. He didn't know whether he envied or pitied them.

Stevenson stirred in the hard chair. The military received billions of dollars each year and squandered most of it. Why couldn't they have wasted just a few dollars more on comfortable chairs? Once more he thought about going to talk to his superior. For all the bulldog bluster and rough exterior, Morningside was a highly trained scientist who knew Pentagon politics intimately. The general had gone through two years of medical school before dropping out to enter the Army. All his actions displayed toughness. He had enlisted as a grunt, worked his way through airborne training, then got the nod to go to OCS. Along the way he'd picked up a master's degree in chemistry. With his undergraduate training in biology, he was the perfect man to command the NBC division at Fort Detrick. He understood science and knew how to work within the system, even if he wasn't regular Army.

Considering the military's penchant for misassignment, Morningside had to be a top bear because he was too tenacious and clever to be steered away from the post he wanted. Otherwise, he would have ended up in charge of toilet-paper acquisition in the Far East command, or some other trivial job requiring the intelligence of a cucumber.

"That, gentlemen," Beaumont said, "was a space-view of the bird. We have studied it carefully, using the real-time capabilities of several other satellites."

"God, you mean we have a need to know something—finally?" Morningside sat with his loglike arms crossed on his chest. At the man's throat Stevenson noticed a pajama collar. Morningside often kept a scientist's hours rather than a military commander's, working late into the night and sleeping half the day.

"I didn't think the satellite could be retrieved," Stevenson said. "Your initial SSA report from Colorado Springs indicated—"

"We're not retrieving it," Beaumont cut in. "Major Henley is leading an emergency repair mission. There is no need to bring the bird back if it can be refueled and lifted to a higher orbit. We have every reason to believe this is possible."

"What caused the point malfunction?" Morningside asked.

"The mission will have to determine that," Beaumont said. His eyebrows began to wiggle furiously. "Colonel Jensen's mission has been shifted from the February schedule and ought to be ready for launch even as we speak." Beaumont made a show of studying his watch.

Stevenson took a perverse pleasure in the disruption of everyone's schedules. He needed to do critical work on his current project. Project Big Hunk might pay off in the future, but was too far away from results now to take up any more of his time. Again he damned nervous congressmen and their irrational fear of recombinant DNA research.

"We need to know if a malfunction of your experiment could have caused the circuit failure."

The question took Stevenson by surprise. His thoughts had been wandering. He shifted mental gears before Beaumont grew impatient.

"Impossible," he said firmly. "We've been over this before. The experiment ought to have taken place in an earthbound lab, not in space."

"This experiment was forced upon us," General Beaumont said harshly, glaring at Morningside.

"Putting it in the satellite was forced on *me*! I wanted it at Fort Detrick in a containment lab. If it wasn't for that jackass—"

"Calm down, Tom," Morningside said. He leaned forward and frowned mightily. "Assigning blame isn't appropriate right now. We all know what son of a bitch pushed this wrong decision down our collective throats. They didn't want our experiment in their spy satellite any more than we wanted it there. We're in this together."

"Thank you, General," Beaumont said. "We need to know the effect of a high radiation level on your experiment."

"Has it been exposed?"

"This is merely a hypothetical question, Dr. Stevenson. There is some chance a solar proton event may have damaged the bird's control circuits. There is also a chance the Russians blinded the KH-18 with a land-based laser."

"Their X-ray laser? Or a free electron laser?"

Silence followed his question.

He scribbled a dozen lines on the yellow pad, then scratched out the spurious solution he had created. "I don't know if I can give a good answer. I need more information. What wavelength radiation? Duration? Intensity? Were any of my five containment cylinders broken? If so, how many and when?"

"We don't know, Doctor. For a preliminary report and for Colonel Jensen's benefit, you must inform us of any eventual biologic hazard."

"You're asking for speculation beyond anything I've considered."

"All Beaumont wants to know," cut in Morningside, "is if the experiment will pose a risk if its containment is breached." The burly man leaned back and whispered to his aide. The major began making notes in a small spiral notebook, rather than on his legal pad. Stevenson thought there might be another meeting later, at Fort Detrick. Whatever Major O'Connors wrote down would come back to haunt him.

At that briefing, he had better be able to come up with the right answers to all the questions. Morningside wasn't inclined to let anyone get away with sloppy thinking or unjustified assumptions.

Stevenson shook his head as he tried to respond to Beaumont's question. "It's not inherently a dangerous experiment. We were merely growing neutral cells."

"More details," ordered Beaumont. He chomped hard on a cigar and puffed furiously.

"The genetically engineered cells—gengineered, we call them—are an experiment in replication. We wanted to see if we could grow cells that have no biologic purpose."

"These are new life forms?" Beaumont asked.

"Essentially. We took existing animal cells, mostly from muscle and viscera, and gengineered their DNA. None of the material used in the experiment can be identified as performing any true biologic function. We wanted to try out several new gene-splicing techniques, but not on viable genetic material. The cells cannot even reproduce on their own. That's not part of their new gengineered structure. They just . . . are."

"What happens if these so-called neutral cells are released?" Beaumont asked.

"Nothing, as far as I've been able to determine. I am somewhat worried about what might have happened to the experiment if, as you suggest, the containers have been exposed to high levels of radiation. Since these cells aren't a part of a living organism that controls them, radiation exposure might seriously alter their functions." Stevenson chewed at his pencil. The entire experiment might have to be scrubbed. The lost data didn't bother him as much as the hassles he had endured getting Project Big Hunk lofted. Hundreds of hours of testimony and deposition would have been wasted.

"What do these cells do?" Beaumont asked.

"Nothing except survive," Stevenson said, snapping back to the matter at hand. "That's all we wanted them to do. I could swallow a test tube of nutrient containing these cells and nothing would happen. They would pass through my body untouched, without harming me."

"They don't have a niche," Morningside cut in. "There's no place for them in the society of living organisms, and they aren't equipped to compete with other cells, out in the wild, you might say. Ecologically speaking, they are nonsurvivors."

"The human body's immune system would make short work of them," Stevenson added.

He heard Beaumont muttering back and forth with the Air Force captain at his elbow. He missed most of it but heard the end of Beaumont's angry statement: "We put *that* into our bird? Shit!"

"Dr. Stevenson," Beaumont asked, "what's the god-damned point of your experiment? What are you looking for?"

Morningside answered, motioning Stevenson to silence. "Replace a cancer cell with a neutral cell, and you've stopped the cancer. There are other reasons that fit in with the NBC command's stated mission."

Beaumont looked as if he had bitten into an apple full of maggots. Stevenson knew that the "nuke 'em from the skies" boys didn't appreciate the bio-weapons generated by both sides. The Air Force saw nothing wrong with killing millions of civilians with the touch of a button. That was a clean death. They all reacted like Beaumont at the notion of designing a weapon that could selectively kill a population. One of biological warfare's goals, and one Stevenson thought attainable, was to design a bio-weapon that would attack only one person. Get the tar-get's DNA pattern, custom-design the plague, and modern voodoo was possible.

Stevenson kept silent, following Morningside's lead. Specifically targeted bio-weapons were still in the future. One likely application of Project Big Hunk's "gray gooey gob" was the replacement of important nutrients in an enemy's food supply with biologically inert cells. The enemy would eat his usual crops and die from lack of protein and amino acid. It was a slower, different warfare technique, but one just as effective as a cruise missile—and much more precise.

And it didn't leave a patch of earth that would glow blue for the next ten thousand years.

"Thank you, gentlemen. You have answered our most pressing concern. It *is* safe to assume that no biologic hazard exists and that Colonel Jensen suffers no risk of contamination should he open the repair hatches on the KH-18."

"That is a fair assumption, General Beaumont," Morningside said. "All you will find, even if the containment vessels are shattered, is a bit of sticky goo."

Beaumont nodded curtly, an obvious dismissal. "We will keep you posted. The NRO, the Joint Chiefs, and the President's security adviser have requested a full disclosure of the contents of the experiment." Beaumont turned and glowered at the Army brigadier. "Thank you for your expertise, General Morningside." He cleared his throat and started a staring match with Morningside. "We've got several more hours of briefing ahead of us, and I am sure you have important work to do."

"It's a tough job, but someone's got to do it," Morningside said, heaving himself from his chair. His eyes locked with Stevenson's, and he made a slight gesture indicating that they should go. Morningside swung around and barreled out of the room. Major O'Connors shot to his feet and raced after him.

Stevenson caught up with the general and the notetaking O'Connors in the corridor.

"Sir, they're trying to hang their satellite's failure on my experiment, aren't they?"

"They've got enough scapegoats. Don't worry about it, Tom. Forcing us to put the experiment into orbit was a brain-dead idea." Morningside laughed and shook his head ruefully. "It might work to our advantage in the long run, though. Next time the congressional pencil dick tries to tell us how to do research, we'll point to the sky and ask him if he wants DNA to land in some voter's backyard." Morningside hurried on, laughing as he went.

Stevenson slowed to a more reasonable pace and let Morningside and his aide precede him down the deserted corridor. He had done what he could. Project Big Hunk was history.

5

It worked its magic once more on him. The candles lit. The liquid-fuel main engine on the space shuttle kicked in, and Arthur Jensen felt the *Invincible* shudder and begin to lift slowly. The engulfing black anvil of three gravities' acceleration dropped onto his chest, and he was on his way into near-earth orbit once more.

In space, where he belonged.

Jensen worked through the post-launch sequencing checklist. Green lights crossed his board. The *Invincible* was on its way into polar orbit, and he was going back to space!

"Everyone enjoying the ride?" he asked, his voice heavy from the weight still crushing down on him.

"Fine," came one voice—he thought it was Harry Ellington.

"Nominal," boomed Henley's response.

"Slicker than snot." That came from Ben Nakamura. Jensen waited for Lefevre's response. It didn't come.

"Hey, Doc, you still alive?" Even as the words slipped past his heavy lips, he saw a flashing amber light on his board. "I read you as having oxygen-uptake problems. Do you copy that?"

"I'm fine. Not used to it. Great ride, Colonel Jensen, great ride. Let's not pull the plug and go back because of me."

Jensen frowned. He hated ferrying the rookies. They never knew what to do or what they ought to be experiencing. No amount of training prepared an astronaut for this moment. Then the boosters cut off, and he had to ride herd on the shuttle's main engines, keeping everything in the groove. The onboard computer handled the transition smoothly. The buffeting at maximum dynamic stress hit and passed, a duck shaking off unwanted water from its impervious canvas back.

"We're almost up, gang," Jensen said cheerfully. "How's it looking? All stations report."

This time Lefevre chimed in when he was supposed to. Jensen tapped the amber light on his board. Vibration shook the life out of even zero-defects equipment.

"Mission control to *Invincible*, do you read?" came Joe's Southern drawl. "We're looking at a light. Do you copy?"

"I copy. It's on Lefevre's life-support circuit. He's reporting in at nominal."

"Rookie luck on this ride?" the Houston controller asked.

"Looking like, Joe. Run a quick circuit check for me, will you? I've got to maneuver to catch the bird on the first pass, over."

"The *Invincible*'s off just a tad," the controller reported. "Nothing an old sundog like you can't handle. Ride 'em, cowboy."

"You've been watching too many John Wayne movies," Jensen accused. Even as he spoke, his hands worked on the controls, fine-tuning and correcting. The shuttle's response was more sluggish than he liked. The amber light distracted him.

"You've got a problem in the attitude jets, Art. Can you correct, over."

"I'm finding this out the hard way," Jensen said. His pulse accelerated slightly as adrenaline pumped into his body. This was why they had pilots aboard instead of monkeys. No Spam in a can now. All the computers in the world couldn't do the job of flying he was performing instant to instant.

"Your orbit will be too low by fifty kilometers on the

first pass, Art," came Joe's measured voice. Jensen swore under his breath. That meant he had goosed the *Invincible* too much, gained speed, and had gone into an orbit lower than the KH-18's. He would have to recalculate, lose speed, and drift out to the higher orbit for the rendezvous. That might take up an extra day of jockeying, owing to the satellite's erratic tumbling in orbit.

"Recalculate for me, will you, Joe? I'm getting several ambers and a pair of red lights on my board now." Jensen disregarded Lefevre's life-support monitor. It had gone haywire on the way up. Vibration, probably. He was more concerned with the attitude jets. Lose them and he might as well kiss the KH-18 rendezvous goodbye. Getting back into space this fast had been a pleasant surprise, but it did his career no good if he tanked the mission. Jensen took it as a personal affront that the attitude jets were acting up. Equipment malfunction did not happen, not on his flight.

"Doc, check your circuits, will you? I'm still getting faulty readings. Ellington, you want to help him out? Or can you, Nakky?"

"Ellington's busy. A bolt on the cargo-bay door snapped during lift-off. What are they doing, going to the lowest bidder again? I swear my shoulder harness is made from rubber bands."

"You know it, Nakky. The doc's all right, isn't he?"

"Yes," came a wheezing agreement from Milton Lefevre. "I'm fine. Just didn't expect the takeoff to be so . . . intense."

Jensen snorted in disgust. Rookies never thought it would be bad—and their training prepared them adequately. Five g's in the centrifuge versus three on takeoff. A cakewalk getting to orbit, and they all bitched. He forgot about Lefevre when Joe came back with a readout on the *Invincible*'s woes.

"Hey, Art, do you copy? You've got circuitry problems in your starboard jets. The boys and girls down here are working on a rerouting. They'll pop it up to your onboard computer in a few minutes. Until then, sit back and enjoy the sights."

"That's a check on missing the bird on our first attempt, Joe. Don't get analysis paralysis on the fix-'em-up, over."

A chuckle sounded. JSC responded, "Never do that, Art. You go back to sleep now, you hear?"

Jensen settled down and let his eyes roam over the control console. Rushing the shuttle into space two months early hadn't been a good idea. Repairs from the last mission hadn't been properly inspected, but it could have been worse. This was no Challenger mission. Colonel Arthur Jensen would forbid that. He worked through the mechanical problems caused by takeoff, relishing each as a new challenge.

6

Stevenson rubbed his bloodshot eyes as he swiveled in his battered desk chair. The workstation monitor taunted him with its revolving image of a complex organic molecule. Impossible to get it to reveal all its secrets. He hated the idea of going back into the lab and running more tests, but he had to. If a problem was amenable to theoretical solution, it had to be worked out empirically.

"Hey, Tom, he wants us. Now." Parkessian's head came through the doorway. Stevenson had to put a lock on the damned door. Not only Parkessian but also everyone else barged in on him.

Stevenson heaved a sigh and shut down his workstation. When Lucien Morningside rumbled, the world shook around him. The summons hadn't been totally unexpected. He glanced at his screen calendar before hiding it behind a trapdoor code. Only fourteen hours until Christmas Day. He was actually working on Christmas Eve—and so were Morningside and Parkessian and probably Major O'Connors.

"The usual place," Parkessian said, already on his way out and heading down the hall. "See you there in ten minutes."

"Did Morningside want you there too?" Stevenson called after his research assistant. This didn't seem right. Parkessian didn't have anything to do with Project Big Hunk. It had been put together just before he was hired. What little his assistant might have done after the experiment was lofted couldn't matter one way or the other.

Stevenson strained to remember anything Parkessian had done and couldn't think of anything. He had told him to get the nonclassified details together for a Pearl Harbor file, but other than that, Parkessian had no connection to the project.

"He didn't say. I just thought—"

"Just me," Stevenson said. "This is sensitive stuff."

"Basil Baker is going to be there," Parkessian said, almost whining. He wanted to be included in the lab's innermost workings. Stevenson tried to figure out why he was so reluctant to let his hatchet-faced assistant join in the fun of being chewed out by the big boss. But that would have to come later. He had to put on a dog-and-pony show right now.

He grabbed the Pearl Harbor file on Project Big Hunk and slipped past Parkessian in the hall. "Basil's a full staff member. You're not. If you don't have enough work to keep busy, I'll be happy to supply some."

"There's the new botulism experiment, but it's taking longer to incubate than I'd thought. I'm just waiting."

"So wait more. See you." Stevenson forgot about his assistant as he trudged the half-mile of winding corridors leading to General Morningside's briefing room.

Stevenson settled down in a chair equally as uncomfortable as the one in Beaumont's conference room. This resembled any other military command post. The white-beaded projection screen at the end of the room would slip into the ceiling to reveal a wall-mounted television for videotaped presentations. At either of the far corners stood a tripod holding a chalk board for "dueling presentations."

"Glad you made it, Tom," Morningside said, glancing up from the stack of papers in front of him on the table. "Baker is on his way. This will be short and to the point."

"Did you want Jack Parkessian here too?"

"What the hell for? He doesn't know anything about your experiment, does he? Didn't think so. I wonder about that boy sometimes. He's always poking his nose into things that don't concern him."

Stevenson decided this wasn't the time to bring up possible security breaches between Parkessian and Sheila, the cryptographic expert. He opened his file. The first sheet held a chronological list of requests and authorizations. Then come the dates of congressional subcommitte hearings. Each carried a bibliographic notation that ran for pages and pages. The biggest hassle was putting Project Big Hunk into a spy satellite where it didn't belong. This was the public part; he had the classified details of the ridiculously simple experiment in the file too.

"Have you heard?" Morningside asked suddenly.

"No," Stevenson said, wondering what had happened. "I've been working on the—"

"The space shuttle developed problems on the initial rendezvous with the KH-18. Attitude jets malfunctioned, they said."

"What's this mean?"

"The jets took two full orbits to fix. The tumbling of the bird put it way out of their range. Their orbits won't meet until the twenty-sixth."

"Is that a problem, other than having to stay up in orbit a few extra days?"

"I don't think so. Beaumont was livid. I think he swallowed half his cigar stub when he called me. The *Invincible* pilot's experienced, and they only took four men. The shuttle was provisioned for a full seven-man complement. They can stay up until after New Year's, if they choose. Houston was getting antsy, and so is Beaumont. He wants his bird fixed before he loses it."

"So the SSA's guess that the satellite will crash might come true?"

"It's a possibility," said Morningside. He glanced at his aide. O'Connors pulled out a thick computer printout and shoved it across the table. "We've got a fifty-fifty chance now that they'll fail to reach it in time to refuel and boost to a higher orbit. Beaumont is betting they'll make it."

"And you, sir? What do you think?"

"O'Connors says no, but he's a damned pessimist." Morningside smirked at his aide, who dropped his eyes to the HP scientific calculator on the desk in front of him. "So I'm going to bet they'll make it. I met the shuttle pilot at a White House bash a couple years back. Art Jensen will rearrange every bird in orbit to get his mission done successfully. He's that kind of guy."

"There's no flak coming down about our experiment?"

Morningside fixed Stevenson with a cold stare. "That wasn't bullshit you dished out to Beaumont, was it?"

"The experiment is harmless, sir," Stevenson said.

"The cells are, but they can't reproduce on their own. What's creating them?"

Stevenson took a deep breath. He vowed never to forget that Morningside was a sharp observer and that, unlike most of the higher-ups, he *listened* when someone spoke. With his training he could even come to decent answers on his own without relying on "experts."

"We call them replicators," Stevenson said. "It isn't the point of the experiment."

"I know all about your reasons for trying Project Big Hunk," Morningside said, dismissing it with a wave of his hand. "Food-supply negation and all that."

"The replicators are gengineered cells that perform one function only. In this case, they manufacture the neutral cells. They live solely in the nutrient fluid and do nothing else. Even if they were released, they'd only replicate more neutral cells, and then they'd stop when they ran out of the specific nutrient."

"What if these replicators got out of containment?"

"No problem, General," came a high voice. Stevenson glanced over his shoulder. Basil Baker sauntered into the room. His nose was bulbous and bright red from blowing it. His normally dark complexion had turned sallow and his black hair looked like a fright wig, spikes going in all directions.

"Glad you could join us, Baker," Morningside said sarcastically. "I hope I'm not taking you away from anything important."

"Nothing, General, not a thing. I was just expressing my desire to lose dinner for the third time this week. The flu, you know. Beastly bad. Terrible."

"What about the replicators? You're doing work in a related field, aren't you?"

"They're something Tom conjured up at his marvelous workstation. The theory said we could custom-design biologic cells to act as constructors, and with my help, we whipped up a few milliliters of them."

Morningside said nothing.

"They can't do anything but manufacture neutral cells, sir," Stevenson said. He was angry at Basil Baker for taking any of the credit for the work. He had done both the theoretical and a good bit of the lab work required to form the replicatoring cells. Baker had come along during the last stages of the project and nosed in. Stevenson wasn't even sure Basil Baker understood the nature of Project Big Hunk.

"Even if they spill all over the country, nothing will happen? What if they fall into the ocean?"

"Nothing will happen, sir," Stevenson repeated. "The cells will die out when their carefully formulated nutrient is removed. They only reproduce when their environment is within prescribed limits."

"So to hell with the *Invincible* and the rescue mission," Basil Baker said. "We don't need those blokes going up to fumble about with *our* work."

Stevenson wondered how much Baker had been told and how much drifted around the lab on the gentle zephyr of rumor. He came across as knowing everything about the space-shuttle emergency mission. But then, Basil Baker always came across as knowing everything.

"They'll keep the bird upstairs," Morningside said,

again challenging the silent O'Connors to argue the point. "And I can, in full confidence, say that the project is harmless under all conditions."

Stevenson hesitated. Before he could respond, Basil Baker chimed in, "As harmless as believing in Santa Claus and the Tooth Fairy, General."

"Get the hell out of here," Morningside said. "I've got to finish this report and get it to the President on Christmas, for God's sake."

Stevenson quickly caught up with Basil Baker in the hall and grabbed the British researcher's arm. "Wait a second, Basil. I need to talk with you."

"Make it quick, old boy. I've got a hot date. She's promised me lots of bed time for the old flu."

Stevenson snorted. That was Basil Baker's problem. He spent more time between sheets than in the laboratory.

"Why did Morningside include you just now? You didn't have anything to do with Project Big Hunk. That was mine from beginning to end."

Baker shrugged. "I heard something big was happening. I included myself. O'Connors doesn't know." Baker smiled broadly. "It never hurts to have the brass know who you are."

"Big Hunk is my project. The replicators you're working on aren't even the same class as mine."

Stevenson paused. The expression on Baker's face told him he was saying things he ought not reveal. Baker knew nothing about Project Big Hunk—and it was a classified project. Stevenson was torn. It wasn't too late to get Baker included as a co-researcher. All he needed to do was brief the man. If anything went wrong, there'd be someone to take the heat with him. He shook off this notion. Too many of the research laboratories worked that way. No one shouldered the blame when something went wrong. They were always looking to cover their asses rather than get on with their work.

"Wouldn't think of stealing your thunder," Basil Baker

assured him. "You leaving for the day? It is getting toward Christmas and all that, you know."

"Yeah, Merry Christmas."

"Cheerio, mate. Have a good one." Baker went off down the hall, whistling. Stevenson wished he could be half as cheerful as Basil Baker appeared.

7

The dark figure stood patiently, waiting for Stevenson to power down his computer workstation. Even after the biophysics-department supervisor left, not a hint of movement came from the tiny niche down the corridor. The person watched and waited, showing immense patience. Only after the guard made his rounds, rattling doorknobs and poking his head into offices to check for classified material left lying around carelessly, did the silent watcher move.

The door to Stevenson's office opened easily. The dark figure flashed through light, then slipped in, closing the door silently behind. The workstation was quiet. A quick flip of the large red switch at the side turned it on. The screen took several seconds to light. Sharp eyes watched the image form. Hope died. Sometimes it was possible to get a quick look at the residual memory on the screen. The phosphor dots took long minutes to "forget" their last screen, unless refreshed constantly. Stevenson had turned off his monitor before leaving, and the time had been too great. The screen had relaxed.

Unperturbed at this tiny setback, the intruder dropped into Stevenson's uncomfortable chair, restrained the urge to adjust its height, then began working. The coded files paraded across the screen. The trapdoor codes hid their contents from prying eyes. The work went slowly, but there was no hurry. No one would come by all night; no one ever had before. Getting information wrung from the computer data banks on Project Big Hunk seemed important now.

If Morningside and Beaumont were agitated over Stevenson's project, it had to be important. Protest all he wanted, Stevenson could never lie well. He was agitated. Project Big Hunk was important. And its secrets would soon pop from the computer and into a waiting file in an unlocked section of the workstation's memory. A quick transfer, and another bio-warfare secret would be gleaned.

Hope flared that this one would open the golden doors to easy street. It was richly deserved after so long. No one at Fort Detrick appreciated real talent, especially Thomas Stevenson.

The computer gulped, beeped, and began revealing the carefully encoded files under Stevenson's password.

8

Nothing was going right. He had waited all day to use the telescope his mom and dad had given him for Christmas, and the sky was all clouded up. George Wyatt stared at the unrelenting clouds above Redding in northern California and shook his head in frustration. He had spent the entire day poring over the instruction book telling how to align the eight-inch Celestron telescope on the North Star.

He had read the pamphlet and a couple of his astronomy magazines and thought hard and decided he knew how to get everything into alignment, and then the sky stayed overcast and kept him from seeing anything. Dejected, he sat on a cold rock near the base of his tripod and wondered if he would ever be famous.

Discovering a comet was the most important thing in the fourteen-year-old's life. Find a comet and you get to name it. If the clouds kept the sky socked in like this, how was he ever to look into the depths of the solar system and see the tiny wisp of dust and carbon dioxide coming in from its birthing grounds in the Oort Cloud?

"It's not fair," George Wyatt grumbled to himself. He heaved a deep sigh that sent silver plumes of breath into the wintry night. George held a flashlight and reread the instructions for mounting, putting in the wedge on the tripod, sighting in on Polaris, everything. He didn't have a concrete slab to mount the scope for complete stability, but he wasn't going to take any astrophotographs. Without a computer to help track whatever he sighted in on, taking pictures was out of the question anyway.

But more than anything else, he wanted to find a comet—and to name it. George had thought about this at some length and he knew what he would name the comet.

"Comet Margaret," he said with determination. "After my mom. Then everyone will remember her when she . . . when she's gone." The thin, gangly youth swallowed hard and fought back the tears. He had been holding them in since he had arrived at his grandparents' house four days ago. In the dark, under the cloud-locked leaden sky with no one to see, he let some trickle out. They ran down his cheeks and turned to clinging icicles.

He wiped at them guiltily when he heard his grandmother calling his name from the house.

"Out here in the backyard, Grandma," he shouted. "I'm waiting for the sky to clear up."

"You'll catch your death of cold out there, George dear," she said. "Why not come back in now? You can watch the sky later when it's not so stormy."

"I'll stay out awhile longer," he said. "I'm not all that cold, and it looks like the overcast is breaking up."

He heard the kitchen door shut. He knew he didn't have much time. They were as worried about his mother as he was, and that made them overly protective of their only grandson. George wished his mother wasn't so sick. He missed her, he missed his dad, and he missed being home in New Orleans for Christmas.

He rested his hand on the short barrel of the powerful telescope. His folks had known he wanted the telescope. It was expensive, way too expensive when the medical bills for his mother piled up like they did. His grandma and grandpa must have helped out. They knew it wasn't easy going for any of the family, and he had been doing everything he could to help out.

Getting such an expensive gift strengthened his already firm resolve to find a comet. Comet Margaret. His mother would live forever in the astronomy books, even if the cancer ate her away inside and finally killed her.

"George, you want some company?"

"Sure, Grandpa," he said, watching the thin silhouette detach itself from the lighted kitchen door. His grandfather walked with a firm, confident step and joined him. In the darkness he saw a few strands of gray hair gleaming in the faint light from the house. George had never noticed them before. His grandpa didn't seem old, hardly any older than his dad. But his dad didn't have any gray in his hair, even if the past few months had added lots of worry lines to his forehead.

"The wind's kicking up. I feel it in my old bones. It's coming off the sierras. This time of year makes for the worst storms." Peter Stratton hunkered down next to his grandson, trying to make sense out of the complex tripod and the telescope mounted on it.

George looked back in the direction of the house. Miles and miles and miles of the continental divide rose up and split the country, separating him from the part with his home. On a good day, George could see Mount Shasta to the north and the Coast Ranges to the west. But he wasn't interested in them. He wanted to see stars; he wanted to find comets.

"Brought some coffee. You drink coffee, don't you?"

"Yeah, sure, I've had it. A lot of times." He took the plastic-cup lid from the thermos and sipped at the small amount his grandfather poured. George tried it and didn't much like it. The bitterness of the chicory-coffee mixture turned his mouth all funny. He hadn't much liked it at first, either, but the powdered sugar from the beignets at the Café du Monde turned it into a treat he missed. Almost as much as he missed his mother and dad.

He hadn't wanted to come to northern California for Christmas, but he saw how much his father needed to get away from just a little of the responsibility he felt. Without a young teenager around, he could concentrate even more on his wife. George had come, but he didn't like it, even if he had gotten a great Christmas gift.

"I put too much sugar in it," his grandfather said. "Sorry. I've got a real sweet tooth, just like your mother."

He paused. "The clouds aren't going to break up tonight. What do you say we pack up your telescope and go back inside? You can show me how to play that computer gizmo your grandmother and I got you. I saw it in the store, and . . ."

George Wyatt only half-listened as he silently relented and began taking the scope down for the night. But he would return the following night. There was a comet just waiting to be found.

9

"You're a slave driver, Tom," Basil Baker complained. "This is my day off. Worse! It's the bloody day after Christmas. Go away and let me die peacefully, in bed, with a lady of my own choosing!"

Stevenson motioned for the biochemist to be seated. He didn't like holding meetings the day after Christmas any better than the others did—worse. He needed to see Elaine Reinhardt for more than a few seconds as they passed in the hallway. She had returned from the West Coast late last night. Stevenson looked up when she came into the meeting room.

Her face, normally calm, was dark with anger. He didn't blame her. The Air Force was responsible, and General Beaumont was blowing this problem out of proportion.

"Good you could make it, Elaine." He motioned for her to sit beside him. She pointedly took a chair beside Baker. Arms crossed on her chest, legs tightly twined together, scowling hard, she was a perfect picture for a book on body language.

"I got back a few hours ago on the red-eye," Elaine said. Her voice sounded gravelly and coarse. She had a cold. "One A.M. That's in the goddamn morning, Tom. What can be so important?"

He said nothing. It was a quarter past seven. By eight o'clock Beaumont wanted a complete report from the team responsible for Project Big Hunk. Stevenson could have faxed up the Pearl Harbor file and let it ride at that, but this simple way out rankled. He wasn't the type to do things halfway. Basil Baker wasn't involved. Elaine, though, had designed the five containment vessels to his specifications. She might not know the details of what he had put inside, but she could make educated guesses.

Damn the military's need to know security.

"Have you heard what happened to the KH-18?"

"I spoke with Jack down in the cafeteria," she said, her dark eyes hot and accusing. She unwound slightly and ran her hands nervously through the tangles of her blue-black hair. "He filled me in on this fiasco. Let their damned satellite burn up. What's the difference?"

"They've got three hundred million tied up in it," Stevenson said.

"What's the difference to *us*?" she demanded. "I worked out a foolproof containment system for Big Hunk. The replicators aren't going anywhere, and the gray gooey gob surely isn't."

"I know—"

"Then why are we here? I'm tired. You know what it's like, visiting my family."

Stevenson did. Elaine got along okay with her father, but her mother presented entirely different problems every time they met. Elaine had never come out and told him why there was such rivalry, but Stevenson knew it was long-standing and deep-seated. For her to come back two days earlier than she had planned meant added friction with her alcoholic mother.

Thirty-seven years old and still dependent on the love of a mother who was a master at put-downs and game-playing. No one ever came out ahead with Alicia Reinhardt, especially her daughter. Stevenson marveled at the complexity of human relations. In a way, he was glad his parents had died when he was still in high school. It had been hard for him then, but there had never been a chance for a feeling of competition, of the son surpassing the father and the jealousy that entailed, to develop. They had been proud that he was doing well, and that was the way he remembered them before the drunk crashed head-on into their car, killing them instantly.

"I've got the report finished. I didn't want to add your name without letting you glance through it, to make any additions to the section on containment."

Elaine snatched up the folder on the table and quickly scanned its contents. She dropped it back and snorted in disgust.

"Do I take that to mean you agree to sign off on this?"

"You know I do, Tom. Damn, what a fucked-up mess this experiment has turned out to be. You could have done it in my lab. Hell, you could have done it in the kitchen sink for all the danger it presented. Isn't that so? Or have you put something else into it you didn't tell me about?"

"We've been over this, luv," said Baker. "The fly-boys are trying to corner us, that's all it is."

"Let them. Let them have my job, for all I care."

Basil Baker glanced from Stevenson to Reinhardt and back. He cleared his throat and asked, "What is the latest status report on the bird?"

"The *Invincible* matches orbit with it late this afternoon. Beaumont is confident of success, and so on. You know, the usual line of official bullshit. It's the standard press release. We don't have a need to know what's really going on."

"What's *your* opinion?" Baker stared hard at Stevenson, as if this would free any hidden bit of information.

Stevenson shrugged. "Since they missed the bird on their first orbit, I don't think the *Invincible* is going to be able to rendezvous in time. Going over the space-systems analyst's report, I think the satellite will crash."

"Where?" asked Basil Baker.

"What difference does it make?" Elaine snapped. "My containment will withstand any impact. More likely, it'll vaporize in the atmosphere during reentry."

Baker pressed the point. Stevenson said, "If we're

lucky, the pieces may come down inside the continental USA."

"Oh?"

"Basil, I'm no mathematician. The SSA said he thought it would be in California somewhere. That's only a guess, and from his record, it's not a good one. Beaumont isn't letting me see what his team's come up with."

"Guess where I'd rather be," Elaine asked, still angry over the meeting that had robbed her of precious sleep.

As Stevenson turned to her, Basil Baker rose and slipped out the door. Stevenson didn't bother to call after the biochemist to stop him. They all had work to do—and he had Elaine to soothe.

Baker wiped his forehead. He wished he had gotten over the flu, but it had returned to haunt him. It never paid to show weakness in briefings such as the one he'd just left. He cursed under his breath as he had to stop and put his hand against a wall for support. His knees threatened to buckle and send him to the floor. Several deep, slow breaths caused his barrel chest to expand to the breaking point but managed to revive him a little.

He wiped more sweat from his face, looked around the empty halls, and made his decision. Compromising his position like this was dangerous, but he had to move quickly. The number of meetings belied Stevenson's insistence that the KH-18 with the recombinant DNA experiment meant nothing. Something big was happening, and he had to alert his control.

Basil Baker checked to see if anyone watched, then ducked into Stevenson's office. From the expression on Elaine Reinhardt's face at the meeting, it might be hours—or even tomorrow—before Stevenson returned to work. Baker settled into Stevenson's chair and stared at the computer screen. Stevenson hadn't turned off his workstation monitor, since he hadn't intended to be gone long.

This suited Baker fine. He closed his eyes and recalled

the complex series of code numbers required to connect him with a special box on a distant electronic bulletin board. Stevenson's screen flashed as Baker activated the modem, got a cleared outside line, and then connected. He didn't know where the BBS was—and he didn't care. What he didn't know, he couldn't accidentally reveal.

The monitor flashed different colors to assure him of a secure connection. The color sequence and their frequency told him he had only five seconds to respond after the red bars appeared.

Hands shaking, as much from strain as from flu symptoms, Basil Baker waited. The red bars winked on. He began to type furiously, sending all the information he could about the tumbling KH-18 and its possible demise. Almost as an afterthought, he added the tidbit about debris falling in California.

Red bars raced across the screen again, looking like interference patterns. His message had been received. Basil Baker wondered for a few seconds what the KGB would do with the classified data; then he pushed it out of his mind. It didn't concern him; this BBS received little more than inconsequential intelligence. The real information, the top-secret material, was sent through more secure channels. He broke the connection to the electronic bulletin board and used his sleeve to wipe fingerprints he might have left on the keyboard.

Then he slipped from Stevenson's office. No one had seen him; he had done his duty. Now he could go home and rest, take aspirin, drink plenty of fluids, and do all the rest of the chicken-soup routine Americans followed so diligently.

10

"Of course I can maneuver closer, Major," he said angrily. "I'm a pilot." Jensen resented Henley's orders almost as much as the tone of the demand. The other officer assumed, once the bird was within radar range, that he was in command. Jensen had other thoughts. He not only outranked Henley, he was the damned pilot. *No*body outranked a space-shuttle pilot in orbit. His was the heritage of captain of an ancient seafaring vessel, not that of the namby-pamby commanders of modern-day naval vessels who were always being second-guessed by a DoD committee loaded with civilians hidden away in the Pentagon. He wasn't responsible to anyone for anything until he returned to base.

If the *Invincible* ever returned. Jensen muttered as red lights blossomed in madness across his board. The attitude jets had been improperly fixed. Ellington and Nakamura's kludging worked, but not well enough to assure easy sailing.

"Do it now, Colonel. We've got to rendezvous on this orbit. The two-day delay is making it impossible to get close."

"We'll do it when we can, Major," Jensen said coldly. He switched to backup circuits, but the jets refused to respond in a timely fashion. Misfiring was almost as bad as a delayed sequence. He hadn't relished the extra two days in orbit. Merely relaying his Christmas wishes to his family had galled him, too. A classified mission was prohibited from direct communication—everything went through JSC in Houston.

Jensen had reached the point where he didn't even trust Joe to talk to Millie. That smooth-talking Southerner might be making time with her.

Jensen shuddered and rubbed at his eyes to clear the blur forming there. He had been stressed out too long. Joe didn't care squat about Millie. Jensen doubted Joe even knew what city he and Millie lived in. Astronauts tended to be mobile people, moving from one town to another as the mood struck. In the past two years he and Millie had picked up stakes three times, once to be near her parents, once to get away from them, and the final time to be near the ocean.

At the memory, he looked up through the port and saw the unique blue of the Pacific dotted with wax-paper clouds. This was more ocean than even he could stand. He preferred maneuvering the shuttle so that he had a view of the stars.

"Colonel Jensen, we've got to do it now," Henley insisted.

"For your information, Major, I am in charge. If the bird dies a fiery death because we can't reach it, that's just too damned bad."

"You can't—"

"I won't risk the *Invincible* and the lives of everyone aboard. We pushed back into space too fast. The *Invincible* needed another week's checkout. Such amateurish maneuvering won't save the satellite, it will kill us."

"When? When are we going to match orbit? I've got it on radar." Henley stabbed a blunt finger on the circular screen showing the radar return winking as the KH-18 tumbled.

"The damned thing's radar cross-section is changing too rapidly to get a good fix on it. Look at it." Jensen was disgusted with Henley for thinking he could perform miracles on demand. Keeping the *Invincible* on track was all he could do at the moment.

"You knew it was tumbling when we came up three days ago."

"Want to tell me what's going on? Why is it dipping down so far into the atmosphere?"

"Just get us there, Colonel. You don't need to know the details. You don't want to know them."

Jensen knew he wasn't likely to get any more than need-to-know arguments from Henley. Their spy satellite had probably sprung a leak and they had to refuel. Jensen checked the altitude and decided that they had finally caught the bird at apogee. They were almost three hundred miles up. At perigee, the KH-18 must have skimmed across the atmosphere and begun its self-destructive tumble.

"Why did it run out of juice so soon?" he asked. "That's a new one in the real-time network. Pierre put it up not three months back." He recognized the satellite as being similar to one he had lofted for the NRO a year ago. The optics in the Keyhole series were reportedly so good they could read license numbers—and all the information was relayed back in real time, allowing the President and even company commanders in the battlefield to keep posted on enemy activity instantly.

"Did Colonel Gaudet talk to you about it?"

"Ease back, Major. Not everything is a security violation. Pierre and I are not stupid cabbies. I know you've got four tons of hydrazine riding in my cargo bay to refuel a thirsty bird."

"Did he speak to you about that mission?"

"Suck vacuum, Major, unless you want to tell me what we're supposed to do now that we've got a radar lock on it."

Henley muttered to himself, then somersaulted slowly in the cabin's micro-g environment and called back to Lefevre, "Get ready for EVA. The bird is tumbling badly. Getting to it is going to be tricky. Ellington, can you use the arm to catch it?"

"Not a chance, Major," the flight specialist said. "The

angular momentum on a KH-18 spinning that fast would rip the arm out of the bay. We're going to have to jet over to it, find the spigot, and put the juice in using the rotating nipple."

A mixture of apprehension and anticipation ran through Jensen. He had to bring the *Invincible* close enough to the spinning satellite to allow Ellington and Nakamura to unroll the refueling hose, then keep a relatively stationary position as the bird spun. Special rotary joints helped, but the danger of getting the hose twisted complicated the mission.

"It's not tumbling too fast," Jensen said, making a quick appraisal. "I can maneuver around, come up, and let you EVA over and do a quick connect."

"Lefevre has to examine the instrumentation before we start."

Jensen clucked his tongue as he thought. This was adding to their problems. Henley had extravehicular-activity experience. A novice trying to jet free and touch down on a tumbling bird the size of a freight car begged for disaster.

"You can go, then pull him over on a line," he said. "I don't want him out there without a lifeline."

"You don't care if I miss and keep on going, do you, Colonel?" Henley glared at him. A new battle for turf began. Jensen was only a truck driver; Henley was the hotshot spy from the Pentagon who fancied himself in command of anyone, military or civilian, who wasn't affiliated with a spook group.

"You've done this before, Henley. Don't be more of an asshole than necessary. Is there anything else we have to do on this mission?"

"No, just fix the Keyhole." The major stared at the radar display. The intensity of the radar return rose and dropped off, showing how fast the satellite rotated. He took several deep breaths, psyching himself up for the journey across nothingness to refuel the thirsty bird.

"Good. We can all be back home in time for the New

Year's party. My wife will appreciate it." Regret tinged Jensen's words. He had enjoyed his stardom in the west on Christmas Day, but quickly realized that it was no substitute for being with his family.

Jensen began feeding the radar data into the onboard computer to make his approach. He would do it with a little seat-of-the-pants flying, but it never hurt to see how the autopilot would have done it.

"We'll be ready for EVA in twenty minutes," Henley said. "It'll take that long to get buttoned up and give Ellington time to get the hose ready."

"Twenty minutes it is," said Jensen, already thinking about the approach and the subtle ways he could goose the shuttle's steering jets to give just the right amount of roll. He wasn't going to let them tangle up the hose. Not on his mission.

As it stood, he could always kid Gaudet about his toy breaking after only three months in orbit.

Milton Lefevre heard the command to prepare for EVA. His heart rate picked up. This was what he had trained for at Huntsville, but the actual work differed so much from the training. Another sharp jab coursed down his left arm and turned his wrist to a swamp of stabbing torture. Frightened, he spun—too fast—to check his life-systems monitor.

Lefevre swung past the monitor and smashed hard into the shuttle wall. He swore under his breath. He couldn't get the hang of weightless movement. Inertia still existed, even if most of his weight had vanished. He looked around, trying to determine the exact center of the space shuttle. There he would weigh exactly zero; anywhere else, there would be a small pull. He had been in the cockpit for almost an hour and had drifted noticeably toward the front, the effect of micro-g.

He worked his way along the webbing mounted on the wall and got back to the complex monitoring device hooked into his suit. Lefevre glanced over his shoulder to see if anyone saw him. Harry Ellington was busy at the airlock leading into the cargo bay. Ben Nakamura had settled down near a radiation-recording device and was lost in taking notes on a new solar flare.

No one saw him pry open the monitor and expose its electronic guts.

A simple adjustment, that was all it took. He used his fingernail to decrease the circuit's sensitivity until his readings were again in the green. Lefevre didn't know why they had set the limits so high, but they had. The pain in his arm wasn't important. It was just a nuisance, an effect of his nerves. Let him get down to his real work. Outside. In space. On the KH-18.

The spears of pain in his arm died down. He could tolerate ten times this level of discomfort. Lefevre reached for his antacid and swallowed hard, his mouth dry and cottony. He could do it. He could.

11

George Wyatt set up his new telescope and peered into the heavens. All day long he had read about 109 Messier objects, strange and wonderful gas clouds and nebulae and even distant galaxies cataloged starting back in 1790 by Charles Messier, using a telescope vastly inferior to his Celestron.

George sighed as he settled down near the tripod. He reached up and put his hand gently on the cold metal barrel. This afternoon he had spent taking it apart, looking at the insides, figuring out how the telescope really worked. Pictures were never enough for him. It had been fun, but he wished he had been able to spend his vacation at home. He knew how sick his mother was and what it was doing to his parents, but that didn't take away the feeling he had been exiled to Redding to get him out of their hair. He was big enough to take care of himself.

He looked up at the crystal sky and smiled slightly. Maybe it wasn't so bad after all. The skies here allowed for clearer viewing than in New Orleans. Even out near Lake Pontchartrain, away from the city lights, it seldom cleared up at night. Not like this. He bent over his small star chart and got the declination and right ascension off it to find Saturn.

"George?" came a hesitate voice. "Where are you?"

Billy Devlin lived four blocks over and had stopped earlier while riding his bike, curious to see what George was up to with the telescope in the backyard. George appreciated the company, since there were few kids in the neighborhood, but he wasn't sure he liked Billy. The kid didn't seem to have a true astronomer's devotion. He wouldn't freeze to death to discover a comet.

"Over here," George called. A bobbing flashlight showed as Billy made his way across the rocky ground. "Don't shine the light into the scope."

"Sorry, didn't know you were taking pictures."

"I'm not. Just don't want any extra light getting in." George knew he was being petty, but this was serious business. If he had been taking astrophotographs, the light would have ruined any shot. Always use a red-filtered flashlight when checking settings, the books had told him. Billy's flashlight was just a regular one, maybe a Boy Scout model, and he was careless about where he pointed it.

"You finding anything worth looking at?"

"I'm trying to get Saturn centered in the cross hairs of the sighter scope right now," George answered, fiddling with knobs at the side of the telescope. "I want to see the rings and the moons."

"That's neat. Can I look when you get it all set up?"

"Sure, I guess. Just don't go stomping around hard. It makes the telescope wobble." George hadn't noticed this, but it was something else he had read about. A concrete pad that damped vibration was the best, but he was just happy to get a good clear nighttime sky. Only a few occluding high cirrus clouds moved through the sky, promising immediate winter storms.

"I went down to Palomar Observatory once," Billy said, waiting for George to find the right coordinates and work them onto the setting rings. "They don't really look through the big scope there, not like this."

"I know," George said. "All they do is take pictures. Mostly they put it onto a television screen if they want to look. This is better. They can see galaxies farther away, but I want to *see* things, not wait for pictures hours later." He smiled in satisfaction. He had worried he wouldn't be able to get a good fix on Saturn because he had screwed up the polar alignment on Polaris, but the gas giant snapped into focus on the first try. He used the sighting scope to center it, then looked through the big lens.

The sight took his breath away. The rings were at an angle to the sun and reflected lovely pale yellow light.

"Let me see," asked Billy.

George reluctantly gave up his spot at the eyepiece, vowing to get it back soon. This was *his* scope and he had serious work to do.

"I've never seen anything so pretty," Billy said in an awed whisper. "You can even see Cassini's Divide."

This took George aback. He hadn't realized the other boy knew anything at all about astronomy. "The gaps don't actually exist," he said. "The Voyager pictures showed that. We just can't see the rocks and junk in them from here."

"I know. I saw all the pictures. And look! There's a moon. See, down in the lower-right corner. Which one do you think it is?"

George had no idea. As he stared at the ringed giant, he found two other moons. His heart was hammering so hard it made it difficult to keep still. When a chilly wind kicked up and disturbed his telescope, he was irrationally angry. He wanted to look longer, lots longer.

"Why not shift it over to Jupiter? That's supposed to be real close to Saturn right now."

"Yeah, it is," George said, not knowing where Jupiter really was but not wanting to show his ignorance. After all, he was the one with this nifty scope. He squinted at the sky, found the bright dot of Saturn, and tried to work his way along the plane of the ecliptic, hoping to spot the king of the planets.

"There, there it is," Billy said, pointing toward a spot far to the south.

"What . . . no, it can't be." George wasn't sure what Billy had located. Then he saw the quickly moving dot and knew it couldn't possibly be Jupiter. The dot was moving from the south to the north, an orbit totally at odds with a planet. "That must be a satellite."

"I thought they all stayed over the equator," Billy said. "It's hard to hit something moving that fast, and our TV signal doesn't fade."

"We've got cable," George bragged. "And there are a few comsats in polar orbit. The radio hams use one they call Oscar. They have to get a quick fix on it because it'll be gone in twenty minutes or so."

"Is that it?" Billy asked. The dot had climbed higher into the sky, looking as if it would pass directly overhead.

"No, I don't think so. And see? There's another dot trailing it."

The boys watched the pair of dots race upward across the dark vault of the cold, crystalline sky. Billy tried to swing George's big telescope around and get a good look at the satellites. They moved too quickly for him to do more than see blurs as he swung past them.

"If they're satellites, they'll be back in a couple hours," George said, planning to be ready for them.

"They won't be overhead, will they? Don't they move east or west or something with every orbit?"

"These were to the west, I think. But you're right. Why bother looking at a satellite? There's other neato stuff up there." He had finally found a dot he thought was Jupiter. He used the sighting scope and then homed in on the planet, seeing a tiny cup of moons at the lower corner and even making out the giant red spot of the chaotic storm whirling its way across the lower face of the planet.

The two boys alternated using the scope for almost an hour, until George heard his grandfather's call. He heaved a deep sigh. How would he ever get the feel of his new telescope? He had to monitor the area throughout the solar system if he wanted to find a comet, and he had a good chance. A damned good one. The majority of comets were found by amateurs.

"George, get on in here. Your grandma's made some hot chocolate for you."

"Let me stay out awhile longer, please," he called back.

"It's almost bedtime. Get down here right now!"

George looked at Billy and shrugged. He put his hand on the cold barrel of the Celestron, reluctant to give up viewing on such a clear night.

"Do you have to go?" Billy's tone convinced George of what he had to do. Great discoveries couldn't be put on hold because it was bedtime. Most astronomers worked all night and slept all day—they had to. Seeing the stars and galaxies during the day was impossible without a radiotelescope, and that was completely different.

"I got to," said George, "but why don't you keep looking? I'll be back in an hour or two."

"I can use it to look at whatever I want?" Billy almost glowed with anticipation.

"Why not? Here's my book. It's not an NGC, but it's got a lot of the good stuff to stare at. Too bad Sagittarius isn't up. There's a bunch of deep-space objects in it toward the center of the galaxy. You can get Orion and other constellations, and there's a double star in the handle of the Big Dipper."

"Alcor and Mizar, I know," said Billy. "I can see them with my naked eye."

"You keep looking and I'll sneak out later. Then we can get down to business."

"Business?"

George wanted to bite his tongue. He hadn't wanted to share his quest with anyone else, but he found himself spilling it all—about the comet he would name in honor of his mother.

"George! Do I have to put on a coat and come get you?" His grandfather's voice carried a snap of command to it he'd heard in his mother's when she got angry.

"Coming!"

George left his telescope in his newfound friend's care.

He might not discover a new comet tonight, but he wanted a better look at the two satellites that had spun across the sky so fast. When they came back, he'd be ready for them. And even if they didn't show up again, he had millions of stars to look at.

12

Milt Lefevre tried to still the tympani pounding of his heart. The sound of his pulse filled his head and made the vessels in his throat throb and pulse painfully. Every now and then he felt a twinge in the gut, but the uneasiness in his left wrist bothered him the most. He must have twisted it as he got into his suit. The bulky spacesuit was more difficult to don than he had imagined. Lack of gravity turned everything into a major task.

He ruefully smiled. He couldn't blame Colonel Jensen too much for considering him a liability. If the *Invincible* hadn't been called into emergency service, his name wouldn't have come up for a mission for over a year. Too many of the more highly trained and experienced astronauts had been on Christmas vacation and out of touch.

He peered up, over his head—and downward toward the Earth. A catch came to his throat. Lefevre had always heard how lovely the world was from orbit. He had assumed that these descriptions were exaggerations, but now knew that even the most vivid had been pale in comparison to the real thing.

Wisps of white clouds drifted near the terminator line and glowed with an inner vitality he had never imagined in water droplets and dust. Darkness covered the world below. He saw lights from the major cities twinkling as if they were protostars swirling their way into newborn galaxies. People rushed home from their Christmas holiday on highways unseen from a hundred-twenty-mile altitude, but Lefevre knew they were there. He turned his head and knew that they weren't quite over Ohio. Next orbit, or maybe two, they would be above his home. He didn't have time to work it out.

"Hey, Doc, you ready to earn your keep? We're going to overtake the bird in less than ten minutes."

"So soon?" Lefevre shook himself to clear his mind. A muzzy veil had dropped over his thoughts.

"Art told you five minutes ago to get ready." Ellington's voice carried more than a bit of irritation in it. "If you don't think you're up to the EVA, let me know right now."

"I'm fine. It . . . I've just never seen the Earth like this before."

Ellington softened a little. "Pretty, isn't it? But we can sightsee later."

"I looked at it these last two days, but from inside the shuttle. This is different."

"There's nothing between you and a hundred-mile fall except some angular momentum. It's special, yeah," Ellington said, already getting back to work. "Henley will be out in a second. He'll jet over to the bird and examine it. You'll be pulled over on a lifeline. No maneuvering for you."

"That's fine. I . . . I feel a little disoriented out here." Standing in the cargo bay made him dizzy. He reached out and clutched the nearest stanchion. Pain raced up his arm and dug dirty fingernails into his chest.

"Your life monitor glitched again, Doc. You doing all right?"

"All right," Lefevre said between clenched teeth. He sucked in deep drafts of almost pure oxygen. He adjusted the flow and eliminated some of the helium to give an even richer mix. The pain subsided. He wished he could take more antacid, but that wasn't possible once he had buttoned up in the suit. He contented himself with staring up at the Earth. So beautiful, so damned beautiful.

"There's the bird," came Ellington's sharp words. "See it, Doc? Up angle fifteen degrees, dead ahead."

Lefevre wasn't in position to look forward. He maneuvered around cautiously, remembering his problems inside the cabin. He made sure at least one lifeline was attached at all times to a safety ring.

"Colonel Jensen is bringing us around well," Henley said. Even through the compliment, Lefevre heard the major's contempt for Jensen. He didn't understand it. Jensen had tried to ease some of the flight jitters. Major Henley had gone out of his way to make him more nervous.

It was because of the overly critical Henley, Lefevre thought, that he had kept adjusting the life-systems monitor. Who had made it so sensitive, anyway? He stiffened his arms and felt small tingles up and down both of them from poor circulation. That was going to be behind him soon enough. He experienced a rush of adrenaline when he felt the *Invincible* begin to roll as Jensen brought the craft into position under the KH-18.

"Look at that son of a bitch tumble," Ellington moaned. "There's no way I can snag it, Art. Even the catcher's not going to work."

Static on the circuit almost drowned out the pilot's answer. Lefevre heard only the last portion of Jensen's command.

". . . the net and the arm. Use both, Harry. We're not getting another chance. That bird's going to fry within the hour if we screw this up now."

"Damn, damn, damn," Ellington swore to himself. With contemptuous ease he floated to the rear of the cargo bay and deployed a huge steel net. As the catcher rose, the cargo-bay specialist said, "Major, get the arm moving. We've got to kill one hell of a lot of momentum with this one."

"Check," Henley said in his brusque tone. Lefevre watched the two men go about their tasks with expertise born of long hours in space. He envied them their adaptation to this weightless environment. His stomach turned and tumbled faster than the errant satellite.

"Doc, get your gear ready. We've snared it. In fifteen minutes Henley will need you."

Startled, Lefevre looked up. The KH-18 had crashed into the steel net and had begun to rip away the wrist-thick strands, but this didn't bother either Ellington or Henley. Henley had swung the Canadian-made jointed arm out and gripped a protrusion on the side of the satellite. The incredible energy locked up in the bird's tumble broke off the jaws on the end of the arm, but Ellington had still snared the satellite.

"We've got it, Art."

"Can I report back to Houston that we've got it secured?"

"There's still some tumble, but it's under control," Ellington said.

Lefevre watched in fascination as the space-black satellite twisted in Ellington's steel trap. The sides were slightly curved, as if it were a giant metallic bug crawling around in orbit. These had been designed to deflect radar and laser defense systems. The antennas transmitting data back to Earth in microsecond-long bursts were hidden within the carapace, pulled in until they were needed. No extraneous sharp edge showed unless it was necessary. Keeping a small radar cross section was vital to the Keyhole series' mission.

Wiggling around until he was directly under the satellite, Lefevre tried to peer up the long axis of the forty-meter-long spy device. His electro-optic equipment was curled around in there. The SSA had been wrong about the Russians sending false signals to drain the bird of fuel. Cross-checking had also shown that external solar activity had not caused an electronic point failure.

The most likely area for failure rested in the atomic battery powering the electronics. A shield deficiency in the SPS-100 would leak low levels of radiation throughout the satellite's optical cavity. With the sophisticated equipment berthed there, the radiation might have been magnified inadvertently, the optical cavities turning stray radiation into a miniature laser of the wrong wavelength. It was Lefevre's job to find the cause and correct it, if possible.

"We're getting the refueling hose ready. Henley will start it, then drag you over, Doc. Ready?"

Lefevre said yes. In fascination he watched as Henley expertly used small hand-held jets to approach the huge KH-18. He didn't try landing on its still-moving surface, but instead brought himself to an abrupt stop meters from the black metal bird and waited, looking for the precise spot to land before applying another tiny squirt of energy.

"He's on!" Lefevre shouted, seeing the major surge forward. The jolt of a human docking with the satellite looked mild. The string of profanity erupting from Henley told Lefevre that it had almost knocked out the major.

"I'm grappled," Henley said. "Damn thing tried to shake me off. Putting in the nozzle will be hard. Still a hell of a lot of spin to this baby."

"Nakky, get your buns out here and help us," Ellington ordered. "We need another set of hands."

"No!" came Jensen's quick refusal. "You know regs. There must always be two men inside the shuttle when there's EVA."

"Give it a rest, Art. You're not going to screw up. We don't need witnesses for those bozos back in Houston. What we need is Nakamura's help. If we don't get it, we're going to lose the bird. Who'll tell them down there about it?"

"That's my job, and I say Nakky stays inside. If the three of you can't do it, it doesn't get done. Fuck the NRO and the CIA and all the rest of the alphabet-soup spooks."

"Colonel, your attitude isn't very helpful," Henley said coldly.

"Tough titty, Major. You want me to put all this on record from now on? I'm on five-minute delay to JSC right now."

"Do as you see fit. We need help out here."

"You should have asked for another crew member, Major. This is *your* mission, remember?"

"Colonel Jensen—"

"Wait, Major, Colonel, don't waste time like this," pleaded Lefevre. "I know I lack the experience, but I'm suited up and waiting around with my thumb stuck up my butt. Let me help."

"He's right, Art," Ellington said. "It'd take Nakky a half-hour to suit up and get over there."

"Use Lefevre however you want," said Jensen. "That's what he's here for, after all."

"Thanks," said Lefevre. "What do I do?"

Ellington issued a long series of orders. Henley moved slowly along the face of the rotating bird. Here and there, blunt radar snouts stuck out. Henley avoided the radomes the best he could, reaching the refueling port and pulling at its toggles. Lefevre felt the pressure of time working against him. He wanted to help, but everything felt so different through the heavy suit gloves and in microgravity. Inertia was still a problem, but nothing had any weight.

"Ready, Doc? I've got the port open and ready for the fuel."

"The KH-18 is still spinning, Major."

"Ellington's got a pivot joint fixed up. Jensen got us under the bird so that its rotation will be perpendicular to the hose."

"Are you sure? There is a small angular difference."

"Do it, Doc," Ellington snapped. "We're not going to let the hose get twisted. We've done this before, though not with a bird tumbling this hard." Lefevre saw him turn and check the steel mesh in the catcher. Two more strands had popped loose. Lefevre wanted to ask about the arm, but the tortured end with the pincers was useless. It had done its work and left the rest for the human touch.

"I've got the hose. I'm not going to be able to turn it on if Henley pulls me across," Lefevre said.

"We've got that covered. Nakamura can turn it on from inside. Not everything's done like a filling station."

"Yeah?" came Jensen's faint voice. "While you're out

there, check the antifreeze and clean the windshield. I've got a couple space bugs mashed against it."

"Right after we rotate the tires," Ellington shot back. He made wide gestures showing Lefevre where to stand and how to prepare himself.

Lefevre took a deep breath. His heart raced in excitement. He was going to step away from his only contact with Earth and float free in space.

"Now!"

He tried to hold back the scream but couldn't. His feet left the cargo bay and he was flailing wildly as he drifted toward the KH-18. Somehow, he clung to the refueling hose. The distance separating him from the satellite didn't seem to change. He slowly quieted, ignoring the tinges in his body. Too much excitement, too much sheer panic. Not for the first time, he wondered why he had ever volunteered for this torturous mission.

A quick glance at the Earth beyond the satellite told him why. He was a member of an exclusive club. The number of men and women who had ventured even this far into space numbered in the low thousands—and he was now one of them. Six billion men and women and children on Earth, and fewer than two thousand had ever left the planet of their birth.

"Get your feet under you, Lefevre," Henley snapped. "Land on your feet. Don't crash into the bird on your side."

He maneuvered around in a half-somersault. When he hit the satellite, it was both worse than he expected and a bit easier. The impact was feather-light. His bent knees readily absorbed the shock, but the apparent slipperiness of the surface took him by surprise. The composite material and the steady rotation caught him off-balance.

Lefevre grabbed wildly and almost sent himself sailing off tangent to the KH-18. Henley tugged hard on the line and held him in place until he could get his feet back under him.

"Glad you could make it," Henley said sourly.

"Sorry, I—"

"Never mind. Give me the hose. You start checking the interior electronics. We don't have much time before we have to relight the bird's jets and boost it back up."

Lefevre imagined the inside of his helmet growing warmer. He knew they were still at the fringes of the atmosphere, where there was little frictional heating. But the satellite had been lower. Colonel Jensen had caught it at apogee. Every second they stayed on the KH-18 took them "downhill" into the tenuous upper ionosphere.

"The wind's not whistling past your head, Doctor," Henley said, as if reading his mind. "Get inside. Evaluate, repair, do your job!"

"Yes, sir," Lefevre said, chagrined. He waited until Henley levered the hose into position. Without additional help from the arm in the cargo bay, the job took Henley longer than expected. Lefevre started to offer his assistance, then stopped.

He wasn't feeling well. Sickness grabbed at his belly and twisted hard. The free-fall trip from the *Invincible* had worn on him more than he cared to admit. He cautiously made his way to the inspection port. On hands and knees, he popped the toggles and dropped to his belly. Head sticking down into the satellite, he shone his light at the densely packed electronics modules that had caused the point failure.

"What do you see, Doc?" Ellington asked.

"Nothing out of the ordinary. I'm not picking up any unusual readings, either. The scintillator isn't showing any radiation leakage from the atomic battery. I . . . Wait. There *is* some. It's not much, hardly fifty millicuries."

"That could be natural," Henley scoffed. "Space is a hostile environment."

"There is something over expected background." Lefevre closed his eyes for a moment and swallowed hard. His mouth had turned to cotton and the satellite swung in crazy orbits under him.

"Give me a hand for a second, Doctor," Henley ordered. "The nozzle still hasn't seated properly and I'm getting leakage. The hydrazine does nasty things to the carbon-composite hull."

"Be right there." Lefevre hoisted himself to his feet. He looked at the Earth as it flashed by. The steel-mesh net from the catcher had pulled away to allow them to stand on the satellite's surface, but he could reach up and grab it.

"It's so close," he said, his voice sounding distant in his ears.

"The net? It's five meters away. Distances are deceptive in space. There's nothing to give you perspective. Will you help out, Lefevre? Now?"

"Coming, Major." Lefevre slid along the composite surface until he reached the hose. Henley had failed to get the bayonet fitting engaged. Hydrazine spilled from one side of the hose, formed tiny spheres, and went sailing off at a tangent to the KH-18.

"I see the trouble. Kill the flow for a moment, Nakamura," Lefevre said. "I can help guide it onto the port."

Lefevre and Henley wrestled the hose free.

"Tell me when you want the flow back on," Nakamura said, the circuit filled with static.

"I . . . I . . . No!" Lefevre cried. White-hot pain ripped into him with a ferocity he had never experienced.

"The fuel's coming your way," Nakamura said, misinterpreting the sounds as request for renewed flow.

Major Henley shouted incoherently as the large stainless-steel nozzle bucked and kicked free, spewing hydrazine in a heavy crimson mist all around him. The snakelike hose turned on him, its fiery venom catching him squarely in the chest. He tumbled off the satellite and went cartwheeling into space.

Milton Lefevre watched, sightless eyes seeing beyond infinity.

13

The wind turned the Redding, California, winter night frigid, but George Wyatt hardly noticed the cold as he slipped out the window of the spare bedroom. His grandparents had gone to bed a half-hour earlier, and he'd waited until he heard his grandpa snoring before raising the balky window. His grandmother had left the television on, but George knew she was probably dozing too.

He dropped to the hard ground and sneaked back to where Billy Devlin waited with the Celestron. The other boy was peering intently into the eyepiece. George held back a flash of envy. An entire hour wasted while his grandparents tried to get him to go to sleep, an hour he could have spent working the skies and locating the comet.

Comet Margaret.

George bit back tears. It wasn't in *memory* of his mother. She wasn't dead, not yet. No, she'd get better. George wiped his nose and dabbed at the frosty tears in his eyes.

The scope was a damned bribe, that's what it was.

"What's wrong?" Billy asked, looking up from the eyepiece. "You got a cold or something?"

"Yeah, I'm not used to cold weather like this. Back home in New Orleans it's still in the seventies." George wiped away the last traces of his tears and sniffed hard.

"What's it like, never having cold weather?" Billy asked. "It must be awful. I like winter. When it snows, my mom and dad take us skiing over in the Sierras."

"I've water-skied," George said, "or tried to. I didn't stand up too long."

He pushed Billy aside and peered into the telescope. He caught his breath. Billy had found a squidlike nebula. It didn't look anything like the pictures he had seen, but he knew those were photographs shot with special film and filters to enhance color. Still, the giant sprawling gas cloud was impressive.

"How long did it take you to find this?" George asked. He still had trouble finding stellar objects using the coordinates given in the star handbook.

"I found it in your book. It took about ten minutes. I've changed the position a couple times. You need one of those motor gadgets to keep the telescope aligned."

"Maybe by next Christmas," George said, remembering all the bills for his mother's hospital stay. He didn't know how much they were, but from the worried look on his dad's face every time he mentioned them, they were big. A pang of guilt flashed through him. His folks shouldn't have gotten the telescope for him.

"Let's see if the two satellites come back. I worked it out where they might show up. Just about there." Billy pointed at a spot low on the horizon and far to the east.

"How do you know that? They might be anywhere by now. We might not ever be able to see them again, at least no time soon. The Earth's turning and their orbits are—"

"I know," Billy said proudly. "My uncle is an engineer with NASA. He told me how to figure out stuff like this."

"Yeah? Show me."

Billy went through the simple calculations, stumbling a few times over places in the explanation where he wasn't too sure of himself. "Then there's the Coriolis force, but we don't have to worry about that because my Uncle Dennis says it's a fake force just made up to explain changes in rotating systems," he finished, repeating verbatim what he had been told.

George wanted to search for comets, but getting a good look at the two satellites also appealed to him. With the Celestron, he might be able to make out markings and decide whom the satellite belonged to. The Japanese had launched two satellites in the past week, and he had heard that the Chinese had fired a Long March IX rocket with a top-secret payload. He might be the first to see what they had sneaked up to orbit.

"Think we can track with the telescope?" he asked Billy. The other boy shrugged.

"We can try. We can take turns looking through the eyepiece. If the other one sees anything moving, we can try to swing it around."

George decided it was worth a try. The standard orbit was about ninety minutes, and it was getting close to that time for the two dots to return. He strained as he squinted into the rubber-ringed eyepiece. A pair of stars danced and bobbed around, but he didn't see anything worth mentioning.

Ten minutes passed, and he was getting a backache from hunching over. "Let's try to find something else," he suggested. "The satellites won't come back. Besides, there were two of them, and they were real close together. They don't launch satellites that way."

"You're probably right," Billy said. "I . . . There! There they are!"

George promptly worked his telescope into position. The gleaming dot moved slowly, but it was coming fast and would be directly overhead in a few minutes. It might vanish before he caught sight of it. Getting around the Earth didn't take long at all anymore.

"There *are* two of them. I can make them out," George said excitedly.

"Let me see. Come on, don't hog it," Billy protested.

With some reluctance, George relinquished the telescope and watched the dot climb into the sky. When it was almost forty-five degrees up the sky, he saw a dark red cloud surround the dot. He blinked, not sure what to make of it.

"It looks like it blew up or something," Billy said, moving away from the eyepiece. "You look. Be quick about it. I don't want to miss anything."

George eagerly pressed his eye to the sighting scope on the large telescope. The other view might give more magnification, but this would show him more of what was happening.

The red cloud caught sunlight high above them and shone with an inner luminance. Now and then he saw yellow flashes from two dots moving close together. Then the dots split, one showing a huge white-hot flare and the other appearing to come straight at him.

"Lemme see, lemme see!" cried Billy, shoving George out of the way to get to the telescope.

George started to protest. The words died in his throat as he looked up. One dot angled off at an even higher rate of speed than before—and the piece that had been wrapped in the red mist exploded like a green fireball. And George Wyatt watched it all until it vanished in the cold, crisp northern California night to the west.

14

"I'll have their balls for breakfast," Edwin Beaumont raged. "Those lying sacks of shit. I'll . . . I'll . . ." Words failed him as he reread the scrap of paper clutched in his hand. He crumpled it into a tiny ball and threw it across the room.

"Two points," someone behind Beaumont said *sotto voce*. The brigadier general spun in his leather desk chair and studied the assembled Air Force officers. No one moved. He could hear the sweat popping out on their brows. And that was the way it should be. He didn't tolerate such fuckups.

"What's the word from Henley? I'll send his ass to Greenland to freeze, I swear it."

"Uh, sir," said one aide, braver than the others. "Major Henley was injured in the mishap. No complete report has been filed yet. We may have to wait until *Invincible* returns to the Cape."

"Fuck mishap!" Beaumont roared. "The son of a bitch's ass is grass. He *promised*. He *told* me he could do it without any trouble. He should have lost the goddamned bird rather than put me through this. Dammit, he *promised*!"

"Colonel Jensen reports that Henley is in serious condition. He sucked in a fair amount of vacuum, and suffered ruptured blood vessels in his lungs. The hydrazine hose snapped around like a snake and bit him. Broke a seal on his suit, and he depressurized."

"Yes, sir," chimed in another aide. "If it hadn't been

for Captain Ellington's quick thinking, we'd've lost Henley too."

Beaumont glared at them. "He lied to me. He'll wish he had just stepped off that damned space shuttle and fallen to Earth, sucking vacuum the entire way."

"That's not really possible, sir. His orbital velocity would have been adequate to keep him in—" The lieutenant paled under Beaumont's fierce eyes and rippling brows.

"We've got to cover our asses. Figure some way of doing it," Beaumont said. He dismissed all the assembled officers but the captain. To the officer chosen to bear the brunt of his wrath, Beaumont said, "This doesn't go any farther than this room. Henley is a spook, and we can't admit publicly he worked for the CIA." He took a deep breath, but it didn't calm him. He fumbled in his drawer and found the tiny plastic vial with his blood-pressure pills. He popped two and didn't notice any difference.

Relax, he ordered himself. There's some way to salvage this abortion. There always is, no matter how black things appear.

He almost laughed. No matter how black. That's what had gotten him into this mess. Deep black spy satellites no one was supposed to know about—and that black bastard Henley. He had *promised.*

"There's always the civilian research project—Project Big Hunk, they call it. It may have caused the malfunction. That ought to be good enough."

"Dammit, Thomas Stevenson is well-respected, and he works under that hard-nose Morningside. If we tangle with the Army on this one, we've got to make it airtight and go public before they can. Everyone in Congress knows the Air Force is responsible for the Keyhole series. Even if we implicate them, the suspicion that we screwed up will remain. Congress budget hearings are scheduled to reconvene soon. This couldn't have happened at a worse time. Dammit!"

"Unless they've documented their every step, we can trip them up," the captain said confidently.

"Morningside isn't the kind to let his staff go around without ten pounds of Pearl Harbor file for every experiment. Those bastards. God, I *hate* NBC research. Bugs and poison and radioactive dust. Gives me the creeps."

"They ought to fight like we do, from a safe distance," the captain said, utterly deadpan. Beaumont glared at him, unsure whether his remark had been meant as sarcasm. Either way, it irked Beaumont. He was in trouble up to his ears. This wasn't the way to win a second star.

The KH-18 lost. An Air Force/CIA spy severely injured. Worse, a casualty in space. For the first time, a civilian had died in orbit. How the hell could he explain *that*?

"You don't have to stay with me, Elaine. I can take the heat alone. It wasn't your project. Hell, you don't even know what the five experimental cylinders in the satellite contained." It was three A.M., and both Tom and Elaine had been dragged out of bed. He paced endlessly, wearing a new path in the president's royal-blue carpet, while she sat calmly in an antique chair. The Oval Office looked nothing like it did on the news. The television reporters made it seem larger, more elegant, even posh. The carpet under his feet showed bare patches. The desk hadn't been polished in weeks, and dust accumulated at the corners. And in one corner stood a Marine guard who looked like a permanent fixture.

Heels clicked on the bare corridor floor outside the office.

Stevenson glanced over at Elaine, who still hadn't lost her composure. He knew her better than this, though. Her upbringing in the Bronx had given her a tough exterior: inside was another matter. Now and then he touched her, and it was special. And she always knew just the right ways to reach him. He was damned glad she had volunteered to come along when he had received the peremptory summons from the president.

"It's all right, Tom," she mouthed just as the door

opened and the president and his national security adviser stalked in. From their faces, Stevenson knew the meeting would be unpleasant.

"Good morning, sir," he said. Elaine remained seated. She wasn't going to be awed by anyone, even the man who ultimately approved and signed their paychecks.

"Sit down, Dr. Stevenson." Tall, thin, slightly hunched over, the president still commanded attention. Blue eyes so pale and watery they almost looked tear-filled turned toward Elaine. "This must be Dr. Reinhardt. You did the containment on the project, didn't you?"

"Is that why we're here, sir?" she asked. Stevenson closed his eyes and swallowed hard. He wished she hadn't started by questioning the president.

"Dr. Wyman will brief you. Go on, Fred." The president motioned to his security adviser. The aging Wyman scowled heavily, as if Stevenson and Reinhardt were responsible for the world's—and his—problems.

"The Keyhole satellite is down," he said without preamble. "Major Henley had an accident trying to refuel in orbit. The entire mission has ended in disaster."

"What's that mean to us?" Elaine demanded. She pursed her lips and scowled just as hard as Wyman. Stevenson relaxed a little. He let her speak; no one dealt with pompous bureaucrats and politicians better than she did. Elaine found just the right tack to take with the inhabitants of Fort Fumble. She was hell to play poker with.

He wished she had accompanied him when he'd been briefed by General Beaumont. Her presence might have made this meeting unnecessary.

"I thought you were project leader, Stevenson," Wyman said.

"I am. I'm a bit at a loss to understand why you requested us to drop everything and come here like this, Mr. President." He ignored Wyman and looked at the president. The man sat behind his desk and stared into the distance. Stevenson looked over his shoulder and tried to guess what the president saw.

"The president is most concerned over Project Big Hunk."

"We've discussed this at length with General Beaumont. It's *his* KH-18, after all," Stevenson said.

"It's not his. It belongs to the NRO. I read the report concerning your microbiology experiment, though having placed it aboard the satellite seems a bit odd to me."

"To us all, Dr. Wyman," Elaine said. "We didn't want it in space. We could have used a P-4 or even a P-3 facility at Fort Detrick and kept the world safe for motherhood and apple pie."

Wyman scowled even harder at her. His dewlaps quivered and Stevenson recognized the dawning of anger in the normally unflappable man. He didn't appreciate her flip attitude. Stevenson wondered whether he should intervene or allow Elaine to remain point man in the verbal duel.

The president made the decision. "You're wasting time, Fred. Get on with it. I've got the NSC meeting in ten minutes. I want their assurances by then."

"Our assurance about the experiment being harmless, sir? The containment vessels will not break open in space. I wasn't privy to what was placed in the vessels, but I know my job. Those five quartz cylinders are impervious to anything they're likely to run into in space. Project Big Hunk was *not* the cause of the satellite's malfunction," Elaine said firmly. She glanced over at Stevenson, who nodded in approval. Her tone was just right.

"That's not the problem now, Dr. Reinhardt. The KH-18 has broken apart due to the action of the refueling hose. The hose destroyed the satellite. The bulk of it is unable to maintain orbit much longer."

"What was the satellite's condition? What did Major Henley report?"

"Henley was seriously injured. The *Invincible* is returning to the Cape as quickly as possible. We believe we can save him if Colonel Jensen can get down on the next orbit."

"What happened?" Stevenson asked, taking the initiative from Elaine. She hadn't heard the briefing; he had to keep her from getting them into trouble.

Wyman cleared his throat and shook his head. The president slammed his hand down on the desk with a report that echoed like a gunshot. From the corner of his eye Stevenson saw a Secret Service man poke around a door to be sure nothing had happened to his charge.

"No more pussyfooting, Fred. If you're not going to tell him, I will."

"Sir, they don't have a need to know."

"They do too. We need information about their damned recombinant DNA experiment."

"Very well, sir." Wyman stiffened and pulled his shoulders back until he looked like a wooden soldier standing beside the president's desk. "An EVA specialist had a heart attack during the refueling."

"Not Henley. The man was built like a bull."

"Dr. Milton Lefevre. It was his first mission."

"You rushed a civilian into orbit without proper medical check? That's going to look great in the headlines," Elaine said. Stevenson motioned her to silence. There was a time to attack and a time to lie back and wait. He felt the chill winds of cover-up blowing in their direction—and the wind originated in General Beaumont's office.

"Dr. Lefevre tampered with his life-system-monitoring equipment. We can only guess at his motives. He had a fatal heart attack during the refueling, and Major Henley was struck when the improperly connected hose broke free of its bayonet fitting. It broke loose while under full pressure."

Stevenson pictured it all. A hose under as much pressure as the space-shuttle crews used during refueling would snap and jerk like a thing alive. The only way to stop it would be to turn off the fuel flow. If the steel fitting on the hose had hit Henley, he wouldn't be in any condition to examine the KH-18.

"What's really happening, Mr. President?" Elaine asked.

"We've filed reports with General Beaumont. Our experiment is harmless."

"Jurisdictional disputes," he muttered. "They wear me out. Endless disputes between the services, between the CIA and the FBI, between this group and that."

"Sir, this isn't the time or place to discuss such things," Fred Wyman cut in. The security adviser looked older by the minute. He turned to Stevenson and cleared his throat. "We need to know every detail about the replicators used in the experiment. I understand that the neutral cells you're generating are not viable outside their nutrient solution."

"Neither are the replicators. Not really," Stevenson said.

"Tell me about the 'not really' part."

Stevenson glanced at Wyman. He was beyond Stevenson's reading. It was up to Elaine to decipher motives. The filed report was plain enough, especially for a government research document. Wyman's face was still impassive; another person Stevenson wouldn't want to play poker with.

"I designed a special cell using molecular slice-and-splice techniques fairly common in recombinant DNA research now. The replicators have only one job: make neutral cells. They cannot even reproduce themselves."

"I understand that," Wyman said. He looked at the president, who slightly nodded. The one not speaking examined the others for weaknesses. Stevenson didn't understand the purpose of the questions. Everything had been answered.

"What will happen when your experiment is spattered over the countryside?" Wyman asked suddenly.

"What's left of the KH-18 won't burn up in the atmosphere, will it?" Stevenson said, getting a glimmering of the problem. This explained the president's comment about jurisdictional disputes too. The FBI would want to be in on the cleanup—and the KH-18 was a CIA bird.

"No. It is skipping along the outer atmosphere like a

stone across a lake. This has killed enough orbital momentum to allow it to come down mostly intact."

"There's nothing to worry about, Dr. Wyman," Stevenson said.

"Radiation," the adviser said.

"I beg your pardon? There's no radiation generated by these living cells."

"You misunderstand, Dr. Stevenson." Wyman took another deep breath, ready to launch into his explanation. The president waved him off.

"Can it, Fred. There is leakage from a radioisotope thermoelectric generator—an RTG. Big leakage, if Lefevre's equipment is reliable."

"We can't be responsible," started Elaine, sitting up and looking more alert than she had before. "Radiation can cause mutation, and mutation is beyond anyone's guessing. I never designed the cylinders to withstand—"

"There shouldn't be any trouble, Mr. President," Stevenson said, cutting her off. "The replicators are too complex a mechanism to mutate into viable organisms. The splicing done on their DNA structure took months of planning and hundreds of hours of computer time to design. Random accidental changes from radiation will likely produce more bio-neutral cells."

Elaine wasn't satisfied. "Why wasn't Tom told before launch that there was a radioactive source aboard the KH-18? This could have fouled up everything."

"Need to know," Wyman said in his tired voice.

Stevenson and Elaine exchanged angry looks once more. It wouldn't do any good getting angry. The damage had been done. If the plutonium core of the atomic battery had leaked, the replicators could have been turned into organically inactive mush.

"Most mutations won't survive on their own, Mr. President," Stevenson explained. "Why weren't we told of the KH-18's power source—"

"It is standard in this version of the Keyhole, sir," Wyman said.

"Perhaps, but we were not informed. We're biologists, not nuclear physicists or satellite designers."

"Your degree is in biophysics," the president said. "Doesn't that mean you understand these physics things?"

"I do as they relate to work for the NBC command. That's why I'm upset no one informed me of possible contamination hazards. Had I known—"

"Culpability is not the issue, Dr. Stevenson," Wyman said. He paused, then addressed both Stevenson and Elaine. "Just promise us that Project Big Hunk is harmless."

"The fall of a satellite with a leaking atomic battery will be your big concern, not lumps of gray glop that cannot survive on their own. And it's not Dr. Reinhardt's place to pass judgment. She didn't design the experiment. It is entirely mine."

"We're trying to isolate problems," Wyman said. "She designed the containment cylinders, and we need her thoughts on this. That concludes the briefing. Thank you both for coming at this early hour. Mr. President, we must now speak to the NSC."

The president heaved himself out of the leather chair and walked out, still slightly bent over. Stevenson doubted he had understood much of anything said. Fred Wyman was a trained researcher, but his aim had been to find a way to cover the president's ass, not to handle the KH-18's landing.

"What do you think?" Stevenson asked after the president and his security adviser had left the Oval Office.

"I think I can use a drink—and maybe a long soak in a hot tub."

Stevenson smiled crookedly. "Sounds good. Want company?"

She did.

15

"Naw, my folks don't care," Billy Devlin bragged. "My old man's conked out in front of the TV set before nine and my mother's too busy with selling her junk."

"Junk?" George Wyatt was only slightly interested in what Billy had to say about his home life. At times, his company was welcome, because it was lonesome out in the cold. At others, he rattled on with endlessly boring details. The telescope occupied most of George's attention, as it should. He was getting it ready again for a comet search. The night before had been fun. Finding all the deep-space objects, not to mention Saturn and Jupiter and the two satellites, had made standing around outside worthwhile. He just wished he could photograph everything he saw. But that would have to wait until he got a tracking computer and a good camera—and the thin emulsion, high-speed film and a darkroom for development.

"Yeah, she sells makeup and shit like that. She's trying to win some flashy car, but it won't be hers if she does sell a bazillion dollars' worth of that gunk. She'll just get to drive it around with the neon sign in the window and all that."

George shrugged. The scope was about set up for the night's vigil. "What's the difference if she owns it or she gets to use it? I'd give about anything to be able to use the Palomar telescope, but I'd never want to own it. Too much trouble."

"Well, yeah, you may be right," Billy admitted. "Don't your grandparents care if you stay out all night long?"

George hadn't told Billy he had sneaked out the night before. He hardly knew him and didn't think of him as a friend, but he had to admit Billy had taken good care of the ten-inch telescope while he was waiting for his grandparents to fall asleep.

"They thought I was in bed," George yawned.

"What would they do to you if they caught you sneaking out?" Billy sounded excited.

"I don't know. Never thought about it. Probably nothing."

"Yeah, same here. They'd shout a bit, but they don't care."

George didn't tell him that his parents did care. He changed the subject.

"I've got it ready to go. The best place to look for comets is in the plane of the ecliptic. Most of them come in from the Oort Cloud and pass the planets."

"I don't want to look for an old gas-ball comet," Billy said. "That's too much work. Let's try to find Neptune or Uranus or some other planet."

George didn't reply. Dozens of comets a year were found, and almost all were discovered by amateurs, because the professional astronomers were too busy photographing quasars and galaxies at the edge of the universe.

"We can't see them, even if we had a big enough telescope," George said. "They're in the wrong position right now."

"Let's look for something else, then. Your book's filled with neat things. Let's look for this Ring Nebula."

"We're watching for a comet," George said firmly.

"Ah, okay, if you want. It's your telescope, after all." Billy made it sound like a curse.

They waited in silence for almost ten minutes before George jerked back from the eyepiece. He rubbed his tired eye and looked into the dark winter sky.

"See something?" Billy asked.

"A meteor. Meteorite, I bet."

"What's the difference?"

"A meteor stays in space. A meteorite lands on the Earth. It'd be something to find a piece of one. They come in all kinds—rocky, iron-nickel, tektite."

"Tektite? What's that? It sounds like some kind of space alien you'd see in a movie."

"It's a special kind of meteorite. Bright green and glassy. They don't find many around here. Most are down in Australia."

"That's too far to go . . ." Billy started. Both boys were looking toward the west when they saw a huge green streak erupt in mid-sky.

"Wow," George breathed. He hadn't had time to move the telescope around to get it in his viewfinder. As fast as it had been traveling, he knew it wouldn't have been possible to locate and focus on it in time. "That must have hit somewhere nearby."

"Why? I didn't hear it hit."

"It was so big, some of it *must* have landed. And it was close. You saw how big it was."

"Just because it looks big doesn't mean that it was," Billy said. "My pa and I tried climbing to the top of a mountain once. It looked like it was a mile, two at the max. We hiked for three hours and didn't get anywhere close to the top."

"This was close, I tell you." George had never seen such a bright and beautiful meteorite before. "We can find it. Wouldn't you like a piece to put on your trophy shelf?"

"What trophy shelf?" Billy asked.

"So put it on your desk or use it as a bookend or something. It's got to be huge!"

Billy Devlin said nothing for a few seconds, his wide eyes scanning the darkness for another meteorite. "Do you think it might be one of those . . . ? What did you call 'em?"

"Tektites?" George wasn't sure, but he wanted to find out. "Could be."

"How about hunting tomorrow?"

"Let me take some readings so we'll know where to start." George scribbled furiously. Billy was right. Finding a comet was hard work, and it might take weeks. Bringing a meteorite chunk home might do as much to cheer up his mother as anything else.

A comet was the best, but a piece of rock from space would do almost as well.

16

"The attitude jets are responding only intermittently," Arthur Jensen said in a calm voice. The Mercury and Gemini and Apollo astronauts—his heroes—never let fear enter their speech with ground control. No one down below was going to think he panicked. It helped that Joe worked this shift at Houston. His easy Southern manner made it easier for Jensen to hold back the slavering beast of terror. Jensen lost track of time as he fought a dozen different disasters—and he was still in orbit.

"We copy that, *Invincible*," came Joe's measured tones. "The boys and girls down here are working on a good way around that problem. What's your condition in other departments?"

Jensen closed his eyes and leaned back. He let the acceleration couch hold him like a fine leather glove. Two deep breaths and he still hadn't composed himself. He was losing it. And why not? He had a corpse tucked away in a suit. Milton Lefevre was dead.

Colonel Arthur Jensen, USAF, first space-shuttle commander ever to lose a crew member in space. This was worse than the Challenger disaster. He had to return to the news-media vultures. He had to answer their double-entendre questions. The six-o'clock news would pronounce him guilty.

Dammit! It was Lefevre's own fault he had died. He had fucked around with his life-systems-monitoring equipment. What ought to have shown a heart condition read normal because he had recalibrated the sensors. But the news buzzards would pick at him until it seemed he, as mission commander, had been personally responsible. Suicide would become homicide.

Jensen opened his eyes and stared at the moving Earth above him. How easy it would be to change the attitude slightly and nose straight down. It would be quick. Let the bastards in the Pentagon and at NASA deal with the press scum. He and the others aboard the *Invincible* would be incinerated memories and nothing more.

He closed his eyes again and knew he couldn't do it. He was too good a pilot to simply let everything go like that. It would be hell for his kids if he did tank it. He remembered how everyone had poked and prodded and chivied Gus Grissom like a pack of hunting dogs after a fox; Jensen knew he could take it. Millie wouldn't like it, but she could deal with it too. But the kids! God, they would hear about how their daddy had murdered an innocent man in space and brought worldwide shame to the U.S. space program. And it would never end. That kind of stigma lasted a lifetime.

Resign. That was all he could do. He would resign in shame from the only job that had ever given him a moment's satisfaction. Jensen tried to remember a moment when he had wanted to do anything else but explore space. He had been five years old when Sputnik was orbited, and had immediately understood the Russians were ahead in the space race.

The thrill of Armstrong on the moon, the pain of Jack Schmitt and Gene Cernan becoming the last men to walk on that unsullied, dusty surface—he had experienced it all, had lived and breathed it and wanted it desperately for himself.

It was over. He had to resign because a son-of-a-bitch pencil-necked university type had tampered with his sensors and died during his mission. Beyond that, the Air Force's damned satellite had split apart and was lost too. A death and a mission failure.

"You there, Art? I said we're sending up a new program to circumvent the problem with your jets. You copy?"

"I copy, Houston," he replied, shaken out of his self-pity. "Standing by for reception. Fax it to me." He flipped on the computer and opened its guts to the rush of new programming being sent from the ground.

Such an insignificant tiny computer, he mused. His kids used bigger ones to do their math homework.

"Give it a try, will you, Art? The programmers are getting restless. You know how they are."

"Giving it a go right now, Joe." Jensen's fingers worked briefly on the keypad and loaded the program. Then he turned to his controls and waited for the red lights to blossom like weeds in his carefully tended lawn. The indicators that had resisted his every effort now shone a cheerful green.

The *Invincible* could go home safely.

He didn't know whether to laugh or cry. He could get the shuttle back safely, but one crewman was already dead and another was so seriously hurt he wasn't a good bet to make the trip.

"Nakky, Ellington, you got things tied down back there?"

"All systems go back here, Art. Did you get this bucket of bolts glued back together?"

"Really, Captain Nakamura, you shouldn't talk about this fine vessel like that. The *Invincible* is gonna carry us home."

"Swing low, sweet chariot," chorused Ellington.

For a brief moment Jensen felt camaraderie with the two men. They were professionals, experienced, tough, smart, sharp. They knew their limits—and how far to push beyond them.

If it hadn't been for Ellington's quick thinking and use of the damaged cargo-handling arm, Henley would have died too. Ellington had swung it around and used the magnetic portion to hold Henley firmly as his suit evacuated. If he hadn't done this quickly and on the first try, the major would be slowly somersaulting in an orbit a few klicks away from the *Invincible.* As it was, Ellington had barely been able to reach him and seal the crack in his helmet.

Another couple minutes and Henley wouldn't have had an unburst blood vessel in his body.

"How's the supercargo?" Jensen asked, referring to Henley.

"We've got him on ice. He's not looking good," Nakamura said. "I'm no medic, but my guess is that he ruptured blood vessels in his brain. What's that called? Aneurysm?"

"Something like it. Make him as comfortable as possible. We've got jets again, and we've got a reentry window coming up in less than ten minutes. We're going home."

Jensen prepared for the return to Earth. Too shallow an entry and the *Invincible* would skip along the top of the ionosphere like a hydrofoil. Too steep and they would look like the steak at his last outdoor barbecue. But he knew neither would happen. He was a good pilot. Damned good. Maybe too damned good for the Air Force.

He punched the buttons, causing the jets to kick in, reduce orbital speed, and allow the *Invincible* to slip back toward the planet of its birth.

"You're cleared for landing, Colonel Jensen," came the crisp voice over the headphones. Jensen cringed. He had been switched to field control at the Cape after a heat-generated ion cloud provoked reentry blackout around the *Invincible.* He wished he could have kept Joe and his continual banter on the line. That man had seen more bad movies than any five people Jensen had ever met and could talk about them for hours to anyone who would listen. Jensen needed all the distraction he could get.

"Thank you, Cape," he said in a stiff, mechanical voice. He was close to the end of his career. How long did he have left? Ten minutes? Less? He wanted to do everything by the book for the bears watching him from inside their concrete command post. Had they flown in from Washington just to see the *Invincible* return? Jensen thought that might be the case. He noticed more activity at the landing field at the far end of the sandbar, where his strip stretched for almost three miles. More Pentagon brass, more of the top staff from NASA, all come to skin him and hang his hide out to dry.

He'd show them all how a real pilot flew.

The touchdown was flawless. He taxied to a halt near the airtight stairway designed to get the astronauts away from the outgassing shuttle as quickly as possible. Friction heating of the tiles provoked toxic fume emanation. It would be days, even with the special chemical hose-down, before the *Invincible* was safe to be around.

He killed the internal power and watched as the indicator light flashed, showing the hatch had been opened.

"You ready for the major?" he heard Ellington ask whoever had entered the shuttle. "Get him the hell to a hospital and you might be able to save him."

Jensen didn't hear the answer. The heavy craft trembled as dozens of ground crew came and went, checking and poking and placing both injured and deceased on stretchers.

"They're waiting for you in the debriefing room, Colonel," came the cold voice of a suited ground crewman. The head didn't vanish when Jensen responded with a thumbs-up sign. "Now, sir. We'll take care of the power-down routine."

"I understand," Jensen said. And he did. The *Invincible* was no longer his. He swung out of the pilot's couch and pushed past to the stairway leading down to the tarmac.

His only thought as he descended was that a condemned man usually had to climb thirteen steps to the gallows. So much for progress.

17

Elaine Reinhardt rattled around in the bathroom, preparing for the party. Stevenson lay sprawled on the bed, eyes fixed on the small crack running several feet along the ceiling. He would have to get it plastered, he decided, but it could wait. Pressure from a settling foundation in an old and tired house had produced the crack; Stevenson's own psychic cracks were also due to pressure, though he was more and more willing to admit he was getting old and tired too.

"I'm glad you returned early from your trip," he said.

"I didn't have much choice, did I? When the president calls, no matter the reason, you answer." Elaine stuck her head out of the steamy bathroom. "Get me another towel, will you, Tom? I need one for my hair."

"You look just fine," he said. Moving off the bed required considerable effort on his part. Damned near everything did now. The hassle with Project Big Hunk sapped his strength as surely as if he had run a marathon. Worst of all, aches and pains he had forgotten about years earlier now reappeared.

All he wanted to do was forget the damned gray-gooey-gob experiment and get on with his other work, his important work. Deep down, he knew it wasn't going to happen that way. He felt like a last-place marathon finisher.

"You're mighty moody tonight. Talking to the president constipates you, doesn't it?" Elaine said, trying to kid him out of his bad humor.

He heaved himself off the bed, padded over to the linen closet, and pulled out the first fluffy towel he found. He had an eclectic, mismatched collection dating from his college days.

"Why don't you marry me?" he said suddenly.

"What? My absence made your heart grow fonder? I can't believe it." She grabbed the towel and began rubbing her long midnight-black hair dry with it. The other towel, the big green beach towel, enveloped her slender body. She came out of the bathroom and as usual, accurately read his mood.

"You're in the clear on the neutral-cell experiment," she said. "My containment vessel is good, and your design is flawless. Stop worrying."

"Do you want to go to Johannsen's party?" he asked her. "Really?"

"I'd miss Jo's Swedish meatballs."

"He doesn't make Swedish meatballs."

"I meant his current girlfriend." Elaine smiled broadly. The green towel began to slip slightly. Stevenson reached over to help it along. She slapped his hand and danced back, smiling wickedly.

"You've got to do better than that. Insincere offers of marriage, a crummy TV dinner, lukewarm bathwater, and cheap whiskey are not the way to this girl's heart."

"It wasn't a TV dinner, I've turned up the thermostat on the water heater twice for you since October, that was damned good Maker's Mark bourbon, and what makes you think the offer was insincere?"

"We're getting into a mid-life-crisis area, aren't we?" she said, sitting on the edge of the bed. He moved over and drew her closer to him. She tensed slightly, then relaxed and snuggled closer. He enjoyed the damp, sweet smell of her hair, the sleekness of her body, the way she managed to put him at ease.

"I'm thinking about cashing in my chips and leaving the lab. Government research is the pits. I spend more time worrying about idiotic things like this KH-18 business than I do on real work."

"And?" she prodded.

"Bio-weapons research hardly appeals to me anymore. Not that it ever did."

"You don't find it a noble pursuit, keeping the U.S. ahead of its enemies? What if there's a war?"

Stevenson said nothing for a few seconds. His hands caressed her flesh. Her presence distracted him from the question—or maybe it helped him come to decisions he had always postponed.

"You know the fuss over the DPT vaccinations in children?"

Elaine was taken aback by his abrupt change in topic. "Sure. Parents sue everyone from the pharmaceutical company down to the printer of the doctor's instructions because their kids have a bad reaction to the vaccine."

"Fewer than one in one hundred thousand have any significant reaction. Without the vaccination a few hundred in that group would get pertussis. And mandatory vaccination prevents a more widespread epidemic."

"What are you getting at?"

"This is an example of risk and reward. There is a small risk, but the reward is greater."

"You're saying your job has a reverse risk-reward ratio?"

"Right," Stevenson said, warming to his analogy. "When I believed that NBC weapons prevented war, I accepted the risk of having them around. Now, I doubt there remains any risk at all. The Berlin Wall has fallen, and the Communist nations are flirting with capitalism. Russia is economically bankrupt and would starve without our food shipments. We'd never use NBC weapons against a trading partner like Japan, even though commercial war is the real war."

Elaine finished for him: "To develop and keep stockpiling weapons is riskier than never developing them."

"Look at the hassles we're having with the gray-gooey-gob experiment. It's simple and might have applications in medicine. Replacing cancer cells with neutral cells could save lives, but that's not why we designed the experiment."

"Starve 'em into submission," Elaine said. "Replace the essential amino acids in their food crops with worthless gunk. Make them eat junk food and not know it."

He looked at her, a wry expression on his face. So much for classified material at Fort Detrick. She knew everything. He had merely told her about the neutral cells' nature, not the reason for the experiment.

"I'm tired of dealing with the military too," he said. "I'm tired of everything—except you."

"It's nice to be wanted," she said. She kissed him firmly, then wiggled free. "As much as you might want to stay here and get maudlin, I want to go to Jo's party."

"To see his latest bimbo?"

"You enjoy that as much as I do. Admit it. No, I want to get out. Christ, Tom, being dragged into the Oval Office to brief the president drained me too. I try not to show it, but I feel pressure."

"Pressure?" he said, reaching around her and tugging at the towel. "Everything I see looks nice and soft and in all the right places. No pressure packing anywhere."

She slipped away from him and shook her head. Stevenson eyed her appreciatively but saw that she wasn't going to relent. "You're right. Let's go to the party. This is still your vacation."

"Enlightened management. I like it. That's the way of the future." She dropped her large green towel, pirouetted, and gave him a tantalizing view of her entire naked body. Then she darted back into the bathroom, where it was warmer.

Stevenson lay back on the bed and studied the cracked ceiling again. What did he have to show for all his years of research for the government? The pay wasn't too good. Job security depended on the whim of congressional spending and who was rattling what saber around the world. His publications were limited because of security considerations. And his department coworkers were able scientists, but he didn't much like any of them.

Jack Parkessian was a good example of the bright, sharp, eager, and utterly ruthless son of a bitch he had to deal with. He sat like a giant spider in the middle of a web, listening to rumors, spreading them, maybe even creating them to see what effect they would have on others. More interested in promotion than production, Parkessian was likely to go far in government research circles. He had learned to play the paper and power games well. And Basil Baker was hardly any better.

Stevenson thought Baker's standoffish British accent was put on to impress the colonials and keep them in their proper, inferior places. Not that he wasn't British. His background as a researcher at Hanson Laboratories in England and his university work at Oxford before that proved he was ever so much the Brit. But he had lived in America for fifteen years and hadn't lost a bit of the accent. He managed to peer down his nose at anyone who wasn't of his social standing, and he was as much a rumormonger as Parkessian. Still, Stevenson preferred working with him. Baker was a chemist and looked at a project with a slight skew that led to quick results. Baker also saw his work through to the end, no matter what.

Stevenson heaved a deep sigh. He had to see Project Big Hunk to its conclusion, even if that was a cindered end in the atmosphere or a messy, splattered conclusion on the landscape.

"You're too quiet, Tom," came Elaine's cheery voice. "Stop worrying. It's the Air Force's problem, not yours."

"Don't you understand that I'm powerless? They put me in this position. Why did they ever place this experiment in a spy satellite?"

"Typical government compromise, that's why. No one wins, everyone loses something, and the project is lost. The way it's always been."

Stevenson laced his fingers behind his head and traced out the cracks in the ceiling. Elaine was right. The way it had always been. And he didn't see it changing after losing a man in space.

"Let's party," Elaine said, emerging from the bathroom. She pirouetted again to show off her black dress.

18

"You look like homemade shit, Tom," Jack Parkessian greeted him. Stevenson actually felt like homemade shit. "When did you leave Jo's party?"

"Before you did," Stevenson said, his head throbbing with a massive headache. He had gone light on the liquor at the party, but that hadn't stopped the hangover. Men with spiked hammers worked on the top of his brain and someone had substituted a dirty sweat sock for his tongue. Migraine threatened to kick out the insides of his eyeballs.

"A lobotomy is supposed to help. That and two aspirin tablets."

"I thought that was for heart attacks. What can I do for you, Jack? You're obviously out cruising the halls hunting for me. Or will anyone do to torment?"

Parkessian slipped closer and lowered his voice to a conspiratorial whisper. "What did you think of Jo's new girlfriend? Isn't she a knockout? I heard she was a topless dancer outside Georgetown."

"Someone told me she worked at some sleazy dive in the Block in Baltimore." Stevenson really didn't care about Jo's love life. The man was old enough to take care of himself. With Johannsen's medical connections, he could take care of damned near any socially transmitted disease, and Stevenson didn't consider Johannsen a candidate for really pernicious diseases.

"I've heard that too," Parkessian admitted. "I was talking with Basil at the party, and he said that he thought she was cockney. I didn't talk to her at all."

"Oh? You were so stunned by her beauty that you just admired her from across the room?" Stevenson wished his research assistant would run down, but this wasn't likely. When it came to gossip, Parkessian always had fresh batteries installed.

"In case you weren't watching, I was making time on my own. And was she a looker. She came with Basil, though she wasn't *with* him, if you get my drift."

"You stole Baker's date."

"No, no, Tom, nothing like that. Lisa came with him, but she was just a casual friend. She wasn't really his date." Parkessian smiled and nudged Stevenson in the ribs with his elbow, reminding the biophysicist of a Monty Python vignette he had seen years earlier. He almost expected Parkessian to say, "She's quite a goer, know what I mean, know what I mean?"

"You scored," Stevenson said dryly. "How nice."

"You're getting to be a real stick in the mud in your old age, Tom. But then, you and Elaine are still quite an item, aren't you? How does that work out for you, her being one of the staff? I saw the way she looked at you at the party. Bet you scored too."

"We can compare notes at half-time during the Super Bowl. Excuse me now, I must check my mailbox. The trip to the White House yesterday for a chat with the president took me away from work too long."

Stevenson garnered some small pleasure at watching Parkessians' face melt when he mentioned his small soiree with the president. Apparently this trip hadn't entered the rumor mill yet. Parkessian wasn't sure if he was joking, but he would find out quickly enough by asking anyone he could buttonhole.

Stevenson settled into his chair and fired up the workstation. The usual demands for paths and security passwords crossed the screen. Stevenson responded mechanically until he got to the department BBS. The amount of electronic mail waiting for him was enough to keep him busy for a week. He sorted through it quickly, discarding a few notes as time-wasters, forgetting others until he could deal with them, and finding only two of any importance.

Basil Baker had requested full information on Project Big Hunk for his files. Stevenson considered the chemist's insignificant role in the project up to this point, then typed in the disapproval for Baker to access classified and locked files relating to the gray-gooey-gob experiment. Everyone had to look over his shoulder in such perilous times. A lost astronaut could bring anyone down. Let Basil Baker work out his own defenses.

Stevenson smiled at the other message, a note from Elaine asking for a lunch date. He didn't know if she checked her electronic mail through her modem at home, but left a message agreeing to meet her. If he hadn't heard from her by noon, he would call her at home.

He had just settled down to work on the complex molecule problem when his screen winked at him. He straightened, then pressed the Save button. A top-priority message waited for him.

When the program had saved his current data, the screen flashed emerald green and a message began to wiggle and crawl like a spastic caterpillar across the bottom. Stevenson had seen this only a few times before, and always during a test of the computer system. He read the message twice before pushing himself away from the workstation monitor and grabbing a notebook and pen. General Morningside wanted him, and he wanted him now.

"What's the ruddy hurry, Tom?" came the British-tinged words from Basil Baker, who was just coming in to work. Despite his tardy appearance for work, he didn't look any the worse for giving up his date to Parkessian the night before. If anything, he was disgustingly bright and chipper for any time before noon.

"Got a flash from Morningside. Top-level stuff."

"What about? The *Invincible* boondoggle?"

"Probably. What else would rattle his cage so much to break in on my workstation while I'm doing a computation?"

Baker shrugged. "Busy holidays for us all. If you need any support, let me know. Be glad to back you up."

The offer surprised Stevenson. "Thanks, I will." He didn't bother telling Baker that he had just turned down his request for access to the Project Big Hunk files. He would find this when he checked his own E-mail.

He wondered if he had misjudged Basil Baker. The offer of support sounded genuine. He shook his head. He could think about it later, when he knew what Morningside wanted. He hurried on past a security post manned by MP's, went through a metal detector and explosives sniffer, up two flights of stairs, and came to the wardroom Morningside used for his briefings. Stevenson was already thinking of excuses for being late, when he noticed that Morningside wasn't present. His aide, Major O'Connors, sat silently thumbing through a thick volume with red-and-white classified markings on the cover. He didn't look up when Stevenson came in and took a seat at the opposite end of the table.

Odd things raced through Stevenson's mind. The Japanese used seating as an indicator of rank and position in a company. Was sitting here a high- or low-status position for him? Did it matter as much as the material Morningside wanted to discuss? Was he a peasant below the salt? Stevenson then did the ultimate; he worried about worrying too much. Did anything matter anymore?

O'Connors looked up and said, "The general will arrive shortly. The techs have to finish stringing the cable first."

"Cable? For what?"

"A direct satellite broadcast from the president. I understand you and Dr. Reinhardt spoke with Fred Wyman two days ago."

"And the president," Stevenson added, watching the major carefully. O'Connors' expression didn't waver until the three men in overalls walked into the room with heavy video equipment. The major silently pointed to an empty corner. The men spent the next ten minutes hooking up with DBS system, ran a test pattern, and then left.

"Security is important," O'Connors said, as if reciting his catechism.

"Loose lips sink ships." Stevenson grew tired of waiting.

"It's ready. Good." Lucien Morningside bustled into the room. Stevenson expected him to trail a dozen other aides, but he was alone.

"The link is secure, sir," O'Connors said. "We can begin whenever the president is ready."

"I'm ready, Stevenson is ready, you'd damn well better be ready. Where is—?" Morningside cut short his tirade when the screen flickered. Red and white stripes around the border indicated that a classified message would soon be transmitted on the direct broadcast system uplinked to a comsat. The president appeared, a talking head bolstered by his national-security adviser behind him to the left, where he could hear the whispered advice.

Stevenson wondered if Wyman had aged ten years in the last two days. He looked grayer and more haggard. The president seemed ageless.

"General Morningside, Dr. Stevenson," the president acknowledged. "We've got a secure link." The last was directed to someone out of the line of sight of the camera. The president seemed assured with whatever answer he received. "Good. You both know the seriousness of—"

"Sir, sorry to interrupt, but *I* haven't been briefed." Stevenson hesitated. This made it sound as if Morningside was at fault—which he was. "I just arrived. I'm sorry I'm so late that the general didn't . . ." He let his words trail off. Wyman pushed past the president and became the new talking head.

"The KH-18 came down. A major section failed to burn up during reentry. The damned thing scattered itself over northern California. What more do you need to know?"

"What about the leaking radioisotope thermoelectric generator aboard? What's the condition of the atomic battery *vis-à-vis* my experiment?"

"You'll have to find out. We're sending you and a containment team out to the site. Clean up the mess."

Stevenson turned to Morningside. The general blinked,

as if this were news to him. He cleared his throat discreetly and got Wyman's attention. "Dr. Wyman, Stevenson and his research team aren't equipped to do cleanups."

"Especially not radioactive spills, sir," cut in Major O'Connors. "There are strict guidelines concerning the agencies to be involved. We are not among them. This is a research facility, not a contamination and storage—"

"Screw that," the president hissed. "I want it done. You had an experiment in that damned satellite, and you will clean it up. Radiation won't be spread around like cream cheese. Do I make myself clear?"

"Yes, sir," Morningside said. He exchanged a quick glance with Stevenson. The president lacked scientific acumen, but there wasn't any mistaking his vehemence. "We can get a nuclear team to go with Dr. Stevenson. Is that acceptable?"

"Send every damned janitor at Fort Detrick, for all I care," the president snapped. "Just get it cleaned up and don't talk to the news people. Fucking parasites, the lot of them. They'll be all over this like maggots on decaying meat . . ."

Wyman pushed back into view. "The president is late for a cabinet meeting. He has authorized me to complete preparations for him in this matter."

"Very well," Morningside said. "Give us a complete rundown. The last I heard, you'd lost one of your astronauts and the *Invincible* was on its way home. What about the bird?"

"It's dead," Wyman said, as if his tongue had been dipped in acid. Every word came out as if he spat hard. "Pieces rained down, but the main portion of the KH-18 crashed in northern California."

"Where? Northern California is a big place," Stevenson said.

"Near Mount Shasta. We're doing air recon now. Other KH-18 satellites are working to locate the wreckage. We must contain the plutonium fuel packs from the atomic battery and be sure Project Big Hunk won't contaminate the countryside."

"Tom?" Morningside raised one eyebrow as he looked at him.

"There won't be any problem with my experiment. Worry about the plutonium. I can leave immediately."

"Who do you want with you?"

Stevenson thought for a moment. Basil Baker had been marginally involved, but he hadn't played that large a part in anything after the experiment was lofted. He considered and discarded Jack Parkessian in one second flat. There was only one in his section that he wanted along.

"Elaine Reinhardt, sir. She designed the containment vessels. No one else worked on it enough to involve now."

"Good suggestion, Doctor. Keep your personnel to a minimum," Wyman said. "That's the way to maintain the tight security the president desires. We'll have an Air Force command team out to Fort Detrick by noon."

"I can't—"

"Noon, Dr. Stevenson. I'll personally arrange a flight to the Coast." Wyman's gray, drawn face vanished from the screen. The red and white stripes winked out a few seconds later, indicating a break in the satellite security link.

"You heard the man, Tom. Get Elaine ready. I'll find a cleanup squad for the nuclear debris. You're responsible for the rest—and you will be in charge. Understood?"

"Yes, sir." Stevenson felt as if he'd entered the men's room and blundered onto a roller coaster by mistake. He forced his stomach back into place and stood.

At least Elaine would be going with him, though he wondered if she would appreciate such involvement. It was—had been—her vacation.

19

"I'm freezing to death," Elaine Reinhardt complained. "Why can't we let the satellites do their reconnaissance work and pick up the mess when it gets warm? I've heard northern California is pretty in the springtime."

"You know the military," Stevenson said, trying to joke her out of her foul mood. "If they can't do things the hard way, they won't do them at all."

"We should be so lucky." She slapped her hands around her body in an attempt to stay warm. The cold wind blowing off the nearby Atlantic cut through even the warmest of coats. Neither of them had had time to think about clothes. They had been given less than three hours to pack equipment and formulate a plan for taking care of any spill from Project Big Hunk.

"This is a wild-goose chase," she said suddenly. "The containment cylinders held. They're tougher than any crash landing. I can't say what might have happened to the atomic battery, or if it leaked more radiation than the cylinders could accommodate. Dammit, I've got work to do. Damn them all."

"For what? Getting us to fly cross-country just before New Year's or for letting it happen?"

"They didn't just let it happen," she grumbled. "Nobody wanted the satellite to come crashing down. This is a PR nightmare. They should never have put nuclear material into space. Remember the Russian Voskod a couple decades back? It crashed somewhere in the Yukon. We all deemed it terrible, a menace, and what did we do? We ignored the precedent and put an atomic battery into orbit built from off-the-shelf parts."

Stevenson knew nothing about the RTG used in the KH-18 and was surprised Elaine seemed to.

"What difference does it make how it was designed and built?" he asked. "It failed. I think I'd rather have a gizmo assembled from spare parts than one costing millions of dollars. Both will fail sooner or later."

"When did you start caring about costs? Except for Big Hunk, you've never come close to an estimated budget."

Stevenson frowned. How did she know he had come in far under estimates on the project? That was classified material. He had told her some of the experimental details, but not many. He was still considering it a liability for her to know too much. If the press got hold of the downed satellite—and they might easily do so—anyone connected with the fiasco would be tarred and feathered publicly. Stevenson wanted to shield Elaine.

Need to know might actually prove beneficial this time.

Elaine pointed to the landing strip. Sno-Cats had been plowing the main runway for twenty minutes. The cold wind promised another snow flurry within the hour, and the vestige of the last storm was barely cleared off.

"Ironic," Stevenson said. "You're right about being under budget for the experiment. I come in with a lowball, and the entire platform comes crashing down on top of me."

"Do you have any experience handling radioactive material?" Elaine asked. "I did some post-doc work at MIT using cobalt sources. That was some time back, though, and I didn't have to sweep up every night." She shivered again. Stevenson put his arm around her and pulled her close. There wasn't any warmth to be gained from it, but he felt better. From the look in Elaine's eyes, she felt better too.

"Why do they make us stand outside like this? It's

warmer in there." She pointed toward a Butler building at the edge of the small field.

"We don't have a need to know what's going on in there."

"What is?"

"Top-secret coffee brewing. Classified Penthouse reading. Confidential placement of feet on desk."

"Oh, the usual," she said. Elaine looked up when a loud roar echoed across the field. An MC-130A transport dropped from the cloudy sky.

"We're being honored," Stevenson said dryly. "A Combat Talon transport like the ones used for the Special Operations Forces. They must consider us commandos in the name of science, dropping from the sky to battle the evil forces of gravity and stupidity."

Elaine snorted at this bit of melodrama on his part and sent long, silvery plumes of condensed breath into the air. The wind caught the frosty puff and immediately changed it into a swirling kinetic sculpture. The roar from the airplane's engines drowned out anything she might have said.

The side hatch opened and an officer dropped down to the ground. He marched over, back stiff and eyes ahead. Stevenson tried to tell himself this wasn't their military commander for the mission, but he knew it had to be. They didn't rate higher than a major, even if he was Special Operations Forces.

"Zamora, Major, USAF," the officer snapped out crisply. He held back a salute when he saw that only civilians huddled in the cold wind. "Are you the passengers?"

"Tom Stevenson, Major," Stevenson said, thrusting out his gloved hand. The officer shook it hesitantly, as if this might be a violation of protocol. "We're more than your cargo. I'm the mission commander."

"Oh, no, sir, you can't be. *I* am military—"

"I know you are, Major Zamora, but technically this isn't a military mission, is it? I'm in charge. Those four dragging their equipment out are part of a radioactive-garbage-collection team. Have you been briefed on what we're trying to accomplish?"

"Well, yes," Zamora said, his facade showing cracks at this terrible turn of events.

"Without radiation-hazard suits and proper handling equipment, your SOF team can't clean up the radioactive spill." Stevenson took a small amount of pleasure in defining their roles. Most military men assumed they had authority simply because they wore uniforms. Establishing the chain of command early would eliminate future problems. In his years of government service, Stevenson had found that the military mind hated uncertainty more than anything else. Zamora would take orders from him, if that was the proper chain of command.

"We're to furnish isolation and deal with possible area penetration of undesirables," Zamora said.

"Good. And my team will handle the radioactive gunk and eventual biological contamination in the countryside." Stevenson watched the reaction on the major's face at the mention of biological danger. Biologic hazards weighed on most soldiers' minds. They understood disease better than radiation poisoning and hated it.

"You don't have biohazard suits, so obey orders without delay when given. We can't have unfortunate accidents."

"This was not made clear at my briefing, sir."

"Sorry. This is an emergency mission."

"Yes, sir. Have you loaded your equipment?" Zamora glanced over his shoulder at the four men struggling with their supplies. "They must hurry and get aboard. We're ordered to spend no less than ten minutes on the ground."

"Better have a few from your squad help them, Major," Elaine suggested.

"Of course, sir. Right away." He trotted off to get a half-dozen camo-uniformed men to help load the last of the bulky equipment aboard the MC-130.

"Looks as if you've put yourself in the chain of command too," Stevenson said.

"Over or under you?"

Stevenson smiled crookedly. "I rather like both. Take your pick."

Zamora made sweeping motions with his arm to indicate that they ought to board the plane. Stevenson and Elaine trudged across the snow-packed field and scrambled up the aluminum ladder into the bowels of the transport. To his surprise, Stevenson found comfortable seats lining the walls. When the Air Force moved their SOF teams, they did it in style. Stevenson settled down next to Zamora.

He started to speak, but the roar of the engines revving for takeoff drowned out any chance of conversation. Stevenson waited until they were airborne and on their way to California before trying again.

"Where are you stationed, Major? I don't recognize your insignia."

"Twenty-third Air Force, First Special Operations Wing, Hurlburt Field, Eglin Air Force Base."

"No wonder your men have nice tans," Elaine said. "I envy them being stationed in Florida."

"That's not a cushy assignment, ma'am. We're the toughest unit in the Air Force. We transported the first Ranger unit into Grenada."

"Grenada?" Elaine asked.

"A quick in-and-out about ten years back," Stevenson explained. "Someplace down in the Caribbean."

"Yes, sir," Zamora said, not happy that his passengers didn't know the intimate details of the operation.

"What's that gizmo at the back of the plane?" Elaine asked. "It looks like a winch, but it's nothing I've ever seen before."

"Fulton Recovery System, ma'am, designed for surface-to-air retrieval of personnel and matériel. A balloon is floated and the Combat Talon snatches the line with 'whiskers' on the nose. The winch reels in the payload."

"What's a likely catch?" Stevenson asked.

"It can pull up two men and up to five hundred pounds of gear. Early next year we're installing a six-man unit."

"Impressive," Stevenson said. "Are you anticipating use of the system?" He was on a fishing expedition of his own to find out what Zamora had been told.

"No, sir. We stay ready for delivery anywhere in the world. We've got a cruising range of forty-two hundred miles."

Stevenson counted seats. "You can carry a squad of twenty-six men?"

"Exactly," the major said, proud of the transport's capabilities. Stevenson tried to think of more to say to the officer but failed. He turned to Elaine, who was dozing off, her arms wrapped tightly around her body.

"We'll be there in about six hours," he said softly. Elaine stirred and muttered something he missed, then went to sleep. Stevenson disengaged gently, unstrapped, and moved to the back of the plane where the four men in the nuclear-containment-and-disposal team played poker.

"Want to join us, Dr. Stevenson?" asked the team leader, Will Gorton. "None of the grunts have money to lose."

"Neither do I," Stevenson said, smiling.

"We're not actually betting money. The loser gets to scoop up the plutonium dioxide when we find it."

"Another reason not to play," Stevenson said. "I'm not very lucky, and poker was never my game." The four civilians probably played the game with the *winner* retrieving the deadly plutonium. Stevenson liked it better this way, even if it was less macho.

He chatted idly with the men while they played, getting a feel for their abilities and opinions on the cleanup. He was pleased with them by the time he worked his way back to the front of the passenger compartment and took his seat beside Elaine.

He watched her for a few minutes, then curled up and tried to catch a few hours of sleep too.

20

"It's more in that direction." Billy Devlin looked at the crude map George Wyatt had drawn after watching the meteorite come crashing to the Earth. He pointed with a straight arm and extended finger to emphasize his opinion. The area was rugged, slightly forested, and mostly rocky ravines and sharp rises. An army could get lost in there for a week before anyone noticed.

"No, I've got it lined up right. See?" George pointed at a saddle mountain in the Coast Ranges miles and miles to the west. "I sighted on them. We keep going just like we were trying to walk through the middle of the peaks."

"You've got the map turned around. It's more in that direction," Billy insisted, shifting off to the north.

The two stared at each other, waging a battle of wills. George was sure of his map and had aligned the telescope. Billy was equally sure of his directions; he had lived in the neighborhood his entire life.

"We could split the difference," George suggested. "Go off in that direction." He tried to be as fair as he could in choosing the northwesterly direction, though his arm wavered a bit and moved like a compass needle back toward the saddle peaks.

"That's dumb," Billy said. "That way neither of us can be right."

"So why don't you go off to look where you think, and I'll keep going where the meteorite really crashed. Whoever's right will come home with a meteorite."

"A tektite?" Billy asked hopefully.

"Yeah, maybe. It might not be anything more than a chondrite." He had spent the day reading about different kinds of meteorites.

Billy studied the sky to the west. The sun had already begun dipping lower in the sky. Less than an hour of sunlight left. With the cold wind blowing down from Oregon carrying more than its share of sleet, it wasn't too smart staying out past sundown. A major storm had been predicted to rip through Redding before midnight.

George studied his map again and took another look at the terrain. "We could swing toward the ravine, then head back. It's not too much out of the way."

They trooped along in silence for twenty minutes before dropping down into the rocky gorge. George shivered as the sheer walls rose up on either side of him. He imagined the torrents of water that rushed through every spring to cut such a deep arroyo. Getting trapped would be pure death, no escape.

"Look, George, look at the face of the ravine." Billy stood and stared at a long gash in the stone. "What do you make of it?"

"Don't know," George said, not liking the sensation of the walls toppling over onto him. This was worse than being in a big city with its massive skyscrapers, all straining on tiptoe and leaning out, on the verge of falling.

"If we follow the bottom of the ravine, we can make better time. The trees of the ridges would keep us from . . . Holy shit!!"

Both boys stood and stared at what Billy had found. Sticking up in the sandy ravine was a long shard of metal. They circled cautiously, looking at the dull black spear.

"What is it?"

George didn't know. He picked up a dried tree limb and poked at their find. He couldn't move it, no matter how hard he shoved with the stick. He moved closer, daring to reach out and touch it.

"Don't," Billy said. "It . . . it looks sharp. You'll cut yourself."

George gingerly touched the carbon-black piece. It was cool like metal, and slick, but had a different texture to it, one he couldn't quite put into words. Bolder, he stroked the edge and then stared at it closely.

"It's one of those composite materials they use in the space program," he said. "My dad showed me some— and some tiles from the space shuttle—when we went to a museum." He stroked it confidently.

"Wow, a piece of a spaceship," Billy marveled. He came over and grabbed the spear with both hands and began wiggling it to and fro, trying to wrest it free. He gave up after several minutes of futile effort.

"Whatever's down below, it must be big. We can dig it up," George said. Was this the meteorite they had seen, or some other great new discovery on their part? He couldn't tell. The bright flare of light had looked like any other shooting star, but it might have been part of a space shuttle.

"I don't remember when they were launching the next shuttle," he said.

"So what? It's not part of the space shuttle," Billy said. "Maybe it came from a rocket engine." His face dropped when he said, "It might not even be from space. It might have fallen off an airplane."

"But this is composite material," George protested. "They don't use it much in commercial planes."

"There are Air Force bases all around here. There's no telling what they're testing. The B-2 was tested around here."

"That was down in Palmdale," George scoffed.

"This might be part of a B-2. You don't know that for sure. You can't. I bet you've never even seen a B-2."

"Of course not. Nobody has. They're invisible. Even to the naked eye."

"You don't know what you're talking about," Billy said, getting angry. "I've seen one."

"Where?"

"On television," Billy admitted.

"I bet it was a fraud, just a model and not the real thing. You don't know if you can really see it or not. It's invisible and the Air Force just showed you something to confuse the Russians. Nobody's ever seen one, because you can't."

As they argued, the boys dug in the sand. Some of the area had fused into glass from intense heat. George sat cross-legged in the sand and stared at those patches. Something had come crashing into the ground and it had been *hot*. That didn't sound like any airplane. He didn't know if he was excited that he had seen something coming down from orbit rather than a real meteorite.

He turned slowly and looked around. Billy concentrated on digging away at the base of the composite strut and didn't see the larger piece of metal sticking out of the bank almost twenty yards away. George got to his feet and walked the distance slowly.

Alien space monsters cloned from Elvis? The thought made him smile almost shyly. There weren't things like that. The SETI project had listened for intelligent life in space for years and hadn't found anything. Then there was the Fermi Paradox: if intelligent beings lived in space, why hadn't anyone ever seen them? This metal wasn't made on another planet. Whatever it was came from Earth.

"What did you find?" came Billy's aggrieved cry. "Wow, it's huge. Ten times bigger than this." He came running up to join George. "Look at that, will you? It looks like a big box."

"I see stuff inside. Electronics and antennas and mirrors." George's curiosity took over. He recognized the mirrors used for a telescope, even if he couldn't figure out exactly where the scope was inside the huge container. It looked as if a very long telescope had been folded repeatedly. He started poking around. Most of the circuitry he yanked out was useless, fused beyond any chance of restoration. The lenses were cracked, and one box holding something that looked like a glass sandwich made with layers of shiny silicon had spilled out inside the bigger cavity.

"Look at this, will you?" George poked a metal rod. He dropped it. "Damn, it burned me."

"Be more careful," Billy said, standing back. He edged around to get a better look inside this treasure trove. He picked up the tiny metallic rod George had dropped. It was warm to touch, but not as hot as George had made out. The metal case was dented but not breached.

"Sissy," Billy said. "That didn't hurt you. Look." He closed his hand around the chunk of metal and ignored the smarting, which was not as bad as a bee sting.

"It's still hot from landing. Look at how everything's been burned and turned to slag."

"Yeah. Wonder if anything still works." Billy opened his hand and stared at the tiny rod. He began digging around and found a graphite block, split open, holding three more of the small rods.

"What do you figure this is? All of them feel kinda warm. It's nice, in this cold weather. I forgot my gloves."

"Me too," George said, not caring what Billy did. There were a half-dozen of the carbon blocks with the shiny metal rods embedded. He couldn't decide what their purpose was, nor did it much matter. He was content to let Billy play with the two-inch-high-by-four-inch-square carbon blocks as long as he could dig inside the large module. This was his find. He avoided touching the silvery metal and found another box with a huge split running its length. He tugged and pulled and finally scooted it out to the edge of the larger container.

"Help me. This looks like a Wells Fargo strongbox. It might have all kinds of great stuff inside."

"Just a second. I want to get this open and see what's inside." Billy put one of the tiny rods on a rock and pounded hard with another. The silvery dust inside spewed up into his face when he finally broke it open.

Billy lifted the silvery powder from the rock anvil and sniffed at it. "There's hardly any smell to it." He sneezed.

"Help me dig here. That doesn't look like any fun."

"Well, okay," Billy said, eyeing the pellets still inside the graphite block. He left it reluctantly and helped George lower the large module to the ravine bottom. George tried to pry open the door at the front of the box, but it had been fused shut. Then he spotted a huge fissure running along the side, which proved to be the best way of getting at the paraphernalia inside.

"Look at this, will you? There are metal tubes with spigots on them. What do you think they were used for?"

Billy shook his head. He pried out a second tube and shook it. "It unscrews. And look. The metal opens like this, and there's a clear glass tube inside. How many of these things are there?"

"Four," said George, "and one that has cracked open." He struggled to get the broken tube's top off. The threads resisted turning, but he kept at it until the contents gleamed in the setting sunlight. The cylinder was ten inches long and half that thick. The thick sides convinced him this wasn't ordinary glass—it was something special to have endured the crash that had torn open carbon-composite panels. The spigot that had come from the outside of the metal cylinder proved to be part of the glass tube. He tried to turn it, but a complex system of valves prevented anything from coming out.

"That's pretty," Billy said, staring at the glass cylinder in George's hand.

"What? Oh, the stuff inside? Yeah, it is, isn't it?" Bright green flecks floated in a clear liquid. "I've never seen anything this color before." He upended the tube and let the green dust inside turn into a miniature snowstorm. It reminded him of a paperweight his mother had broken when she was cleaning a year or two back. He remembered how she had loved that tiny snow scene, turning it over and watching the snow fall endlessly. She had said it was as close as she was likely to get to seeing snow like she knew when she was a child in Maine.

"Let me see if mine's as neat."

Billy got the top off his tube and pulled out a glass cylinder similar to George's, but his contained only the clear liquid and dismal gray specks. He hid his disappointment as he grabbed for another tube. This one disgorged only gray matter too.

"The others are like yours," George said. "There's only this one with the bright green pieces. Isn't it pretty?" He held it up to the fading sunlight again. Sparks of gold reflected off the kelly-green slivers floating in the solution. He shook it up. The specks divided into a finer powder. Even as he watched, more formed, leaving a dusty green residue on the bottom of the tube.

"I don't want these," Billy complained. "I want that one."

"What?" George's eyes went from the intriguing tube to Billy. The boy stood with his hands on his hips and his mouth set. "I found this. It's mine."

"Is not. If I hadn't told you to come this way, you'd be halfway to the ocean by now and you wouldn't have found anything."

George tapped the glass and watched the verdant motes do their silent Brownian dance.

"Maybe this doesn't belong to anybody," he said slowly, wanting to keep this tube. The rest of the stuff was junk. The lenses were cracked, and he didn't know the point of electronics. It was all burned up and not worth dragging to a flea market. "Whoever lost all this might want it back."

"No," Billy said sullenly. "It's ours."

"Why?"

"Right of salvage! And I should share in it. I ought to get half. At least half."

George saw that Billy's claim was fading as he realized whose tube this really was. He picked up all five tubes and held them together.

"It's mine," he said, "but you can have first dibs on anything else. There's got to be a lot of neat stuff here.

There are a couple dozen of those carbon bricks scattered around, the ones with the metal rods in them."

"Okay, let's keep looking," Billy said, slightly mollified.

Another hour of scrounging produced a set of uncracked, heat-discolored lenses that Billy accepted as a fair trade for his disputed half of the glass cylinders.

21

Major Zamora was in his element at McClellan AFB outside Sacramento, directing the small SOF squad off the MC-130 and preparing everyone for the foray against the unknown. Stevenson, on the other hand, worried that the equipment brought by Gorton and his men was damaged. The other three members of the contamination team complained as they pulled heavy paraphernalia from the airplane.

"What do you think, Will?" Stevenson asked Gorton.

"Good weather will help us find the bird. Or has the Air Force recon already located it?"

"I can't say. I'm not sure we have a need to know."

Gorton laughed. "For those bozos, everything's classified. I heard that even the Pentagon's brand of floor wax is confidential."

"That's to keep the Russians from putting slow-acting poison gas in it. Trust me, Will," Stevenson said in a conspiratorial whisper. "The technology exists. We can do it."

Gorton shook his head sadly. "There are things man was not meant to know."

"Well, men, listen to this," Elaine said, coming up with a small FM radio in her hand. "I decided to tune in to NPR and find out what's going on in the world. Guess what made the top of the broadcast."

"The First Lady's lost basset hound?" Stevenson suggested.

Elaine looked at him with a quizzical expression. "Wait, here it comes again. Tell me what you make of it."

Stevenson and Gorton listened to the newscast with limited interest. Stevenson perked up when he heard mention of the *Invincible* and Colonel Jensen. As the story unfolded, he became angry.

"That's nothing but a lie from beginning to end," he cried. "The *Invincible* wasn't on a routine mission."

"And I don't think there was an unfortunate accident involving an unexpected solar flare cooking an astronaut. They're sweeping it under the rug to avoid congressional wrath," Elaine added.

"More than a few senators would get their noses out of joint if they heard that a scientist-astronaut died from a heart attack. The training at Huntsville and the medical checks along the way are supposed to root out any physical flaw."

"I don't understand why Jensen didn't notice something was wrong," Elaine said. "From what they told you at your briefing, he's a top-notch pilot. This was not his first trip."

"It was Lefevre's first," Stevenson said. He smiled wryly. "His last too."

"Is there a direct connection between Lefevre's death and the KH-18 crashing?" Elaine asked.

"You don't need that information to do your job, Dr. Reinhardt," Stevenson said with mock sternness. He had effectively told her what she wanted to know. From Morningside's briefing, from all Wyman had said, from the president's wrath, nothing had proceeded according to the *Invincible*'s mission plan. Stevenson felt some sympathy for those concerned, including the feckless Lefevre, but he needed to protect Elaine—and himself.

Nothing had gone right since the satellite had lost its fuel and started tumbling back into the atmosphere. They wanted to be sure he wasn't hiding dire experimental results.

Stevenson heaved a big sigh. On this score, he and the

Army's NBC command were in the clear. The bio-neutral-cell experiment was probably gone, vaporized as the KH-18 fell through the air. If that hadn't permanently removed it, the crash and any resulting fire would have. Sterilization from friction and fire efficiently ruined both the neutral cells and the replicators forming them.

"Major!" he called. "Have you heard the news?" Stevenson saw Zamora turn cagey. He might not have heard the news, but he'd certainly discussed it during his Pentagon briefing. Stevenson read it in every line of the major's weathered face.

"No, sir, can't say that I have."

"Jensen will become the fall guy in this fiasco, won't he?"

"Jensen?"

"Colonel Arthur Jensen," Elaine supplied. "The *Invincible*'s pilot. The report said there had been a single casualty during the refueling attempt."

"What refueling?" asked Zamora, genuinely perplexed. "The *Invincible* went up to repair several comsats. The KH-18 was on a routine maintenance schedule, if time permitted. Colonel Jensen tried to squeeze in the checkup, even though solar flare activity was picking up. He gambled and he lost a life." As Zamora spoke, his voice turned as chilly as the wind blowing down from Oregon.

"So they hinted at on NPR. I thought better of them. They usually check their facts."

"That's unfair, Elaine," Stevenson said. "The government can be very efficient when it comes to 'leaking' information they want released without official sanction."

"Disinformation." She spat out the word and glared at Zamora, as if he were personally responsible. Stevenson thought the eager Air Force major was only following orders and had no clear idea what had happened in orbit or after.

"Let's get on with our jobs," Stevenson said, breaking the ugly silence forming like hoarfrost between them. "Major, have you located the site of the crash?"

"NORAD tracked three pieces. The largest section landed near Redding. We've got a bus coming to take us there. We'll arrive on the scene within three hours." As he spoke, Zamora's spine stiffened until he stood at full attention, reporting to his commanding officer.

"Very good, Major. Carry on." Stevenson almost laughed when Zamora executed a snappy about-face and marched off to muster his troops. In a way it was sad. They all operated in a bubble of silence, floating along on a river of information. If the bubble broke, they might all drown. Stevenson had a fleeting glimpse of what it meant to be inundated with information; then it vanished.

"We know how they're going to railroad that astronaut Jensen. We'd better do a good job of playing CYA," Elaine said in disgust. "We'll be next on their hit parade if this gets out."

"I'll play CYA with you anytime you want," Stevenson said. He got an uncharacteristic scowl in reply. Elaine swung around and went off to check on her equipment. Stevenson shook his head. Let Gorton and his team sweep up the plutonium residue. A few sweeps with a Geiger counter, and that was it. In this hilly-to-mountainuous terrain, the background radiation level might be higher than in Maryland, but it wouldn't mask the high-level activity of high-grade plutonium 238 from the atomic battery.

His part in the cleanup was going to be easy. Elaine had designed the containment vessels to his exacting specifications, but he had not planned on the experiment crashing back to Earth. He saw no way for the bio-neutral cells to have survived such a fiery return in their quartz tubes. The RTG's had been designed to withstand such punishment. Let the others dig and freeze as they hunted their atomic battery. All he had to do was watch, his experiment a victim of atmospheric friction.

"There's the bus. Let's get going," Gorton shouted. "The sooner we finish, the sooner we can find a motel room with cable TV. I don't want to miss the *Gilligan's Island* rerun."

"That'd be a fate worse than death," Stevenson said. He helped Elaine with her equipment, climbed into the bus, and sank into the seat beside her. In ten minutes the bus driver ground the gears and the vehicle started north and east for Redding along I-5. Hunched over a field radio, Zamora looked as pleased as the cat who'd scarfed up the canary.

"What happened, Major?"

"Good news, Dr. Stevenson. An aerial pass turned up a smear of radioactive debris in Redding."

"In Redding? The bird crashed inside the city?"

"Not exactly. We have it pinpointed near a group of middle-income-family houses just to the west—I can't call it a suburb, the town is so small."

"We have to deal with civilians," Stevenson mused. "Any UFO-sighting reports?"

"There were several reports to the CHP, but they were ignored. We have sent investigators to Sacramento to go over the full reports."

"And make them vanish, just as the solar flare appeared so conveniently to cook Lefevre's goose," Elaine grumbled. "Bureaucrats."

Zamora looked at her as if she were an alien life form. "We can deal with the civilian population. My men are trained for it."

"Yeah, spray a few hundred rounds into the houses and we've got the place to ourselves," Elaine said. Stevenson couldn't understand her sarcasm. They were free of blame, after all. The Air Force or NASA's story had little to do with reality; to admit that the downed satellite had contained a Nuclear-Biological-Chemical warfare experiment, and that Lefevre had died trying to rescue it, would rip funding from every military and federally funded research department.

Too much was at stake for the truth to get out.

"We might not even have to cordon off the neighborhood while you work," Zamora said stiffly.

"How nice," she said as she leaned back. Stevenson hated to watch her collapse into herself, but she needed time to think. She was in a shaky position. Elaine might be held accountable for a project which hardly concerned her.

"I should report to General Morningside," Stevenson said. "Do you have a satellite link?"

"This is—" Zamora started, but the radio operator suddenly shoved headphones in his direction. Zamora listened intently for a moment. Stevenson thought the officer was going to faint. His face turned pasty and he wobbled.

"Are you all right?" Stevenson asked.

"They sent in an Army unit. They got there ahead of us."

"What do you mean?" Stevenson cried out.

"Morningside double-crossed us," Elaine said. "I never trusted the old bastard. He sends us out with the fly-boy here, then calls out an Army commando unit. We show up, and we're in the spotlight. We get nailed for everything, and he's off scot-free."

"That's ridiculous, Elaine." Stevenson thought hard. Morningside had much to lose from stories about an experiment aboard the Keyhole satellite. It wouldn't take a reporter ten minutes to determine that they had just flown in from Fort Detrick—Morningside's territory.

"Someone else did this to us."

"I hope they won't pick up plutonium-dioxide ceramic pellets with their bare hands," Gorton said. "The damned stuff is radioactive, chemically poisonous if you swallow it. If it gets in your lungs, you're one dead son of a bitch."

"There's nothing anyone can do if you just touch it or breathe it in?" Zamora asked, still pale. For the first time he may have realized the seriousness of the mission he had wanted to command. Stevenson studied him closely, wondering just what the hell the officer had been told in briefing. It was obviously not the truth.

"Terminal, kaput, cashed in, dead." Gorton was firm in his appraisal of misadventure with plutonium. "Don't worry, Major," Gorton said when he saw Zamora pale. "The plutonium is encased in a platinum-rhodium-alloy rod and there are only four rods in each graphite block."

"How many blocks does a radioisotope thermoelectric generator contain?" Elaine asked.

Gorton shook his head. "They didn't give me the specs on this one. Usually there would be one hundred and forty-four pellets total. The entire unit might weigh upwards of a hundred and twenty-five pounds, have a four-foot length, and a foot-and-a-half diameter. Not big, but I don't expect the RTG to have remained intact after crashing."

Gorton went on with detailed discussion of what he expected to find. Zamora shoved himself to his feet and went forward to speak with the bus driver. Stevenson glanced at the speedometer: almost eighty miles an hour on a poorly maintained road.

"They're throwing the lot of us to the wolves," Elaine said, more to herself than to Stevenson. "God, they're slime, the entire government full of them."

Stevenson didn't have any good reply. She might be right.

22

"What's the fuss?" Tom Stevenson asked, peering out the mud-splattered side window of the bus. Everywhere he looked, soldiers patrolled with rifles at port arms and flashed red lights. "I thought this was supposed to be a quick in-and-out operation, Major."

Zamora looked as if he had eaten something that disagreed with him. He wiped his lips, then got to his feet and rocked forward to the radioman sitting behind the driver. Stevenson couldn't hear what was being said. The radioman shook his head several times as Zamora grew angrier.

"Is there a falling-out in the ranks?" Elaine asked, one eye opening slightly. She had slept most of the bumpy trip up from McClellan. "I told you we should have put on chutes and dropped in on the site."

"You just want to play commando," Stevenson said, pressing his face against the window to get a better look outside. There were more than a hundred soldiers on patrol. Something had gone wrong. The soldiers should have drawn reporters like shit attracts flies. It was exactly what Morningside, Beaumont, and the others up to the president had wanted to avoid.

"He really hates them," Stevenson said. "Reporters."

"Who? The president? He has every reason to," Elaine said, stretching mightily. She yawned and then settled down, arms still wrapped tightly around herself. Stevenson had seen Elaine like this before when she was under great stress and trying to make difficult decisions. Extroverts tended to seek out others and draw energy from them like emotional vampires. Introverts like Elaine—and himself—retreated behind a wall of quiet and tried to build up their own energies. Being forced to deal with matters outside those introvert walls drained them. Stevenson knew he turned surly until he could deal with his problems in his own way, in his own time. He respected Elaine's need to contemplate now.

"What's wrong?" he asked softly. "Is it something I said or did?"

"What? Nothing's wrong." Elaine drew even more into herself, a flower closing its petals at sundown. Stevenson wanted to tell her about body language, about the nonverbal ways she communicated. Over the years, he had learned how to read others. It was the only way he could cope with the military commanders, most of whom were extroverts who didn't understand that even their simplest demands were outrageous to outsiders.

"You don't like Zamora. Is that it?"

"No, I don't like him. So what?"

"You're talking in circles." Stevenson tried to concentrate on Elaine, but his attention kept straying to the soldiers outside. They were even more numerous than he'd thought. Glancing to the back of the bus, he saw that the Air Force SOF team wasn't pleased to see their comrades in arms either. They preferred the scalpel to the meat-cleaver approach, and these soldiers would prevent them from finishing their mission.

"I've got work to do back at Fort Detrick. I don't need to be here. There aren't any pieces to pick up."

"I know," he said. "I've got a month's work ahead just to synthesize my new project. My computer projections aren't accurate enough, and I can't get supercomputer time to do the calculations right."

"Why won't the Mary Cray ladies help you?" Elaine asked. "They owe you at least a few hours' time on the big machine."

"Wrong security classification. I'm not allowed to run

anything secret on it without getting clearance from the assistant secretary of defense.''

"What a crock. They don't let us do our work, and when we don't deliver, it's our fault." Elaine closed in on herself a bit more.

"I'll see that you don't lose your vacation time," he said. "Thanks for coming along with me on this wild-goose chase."

"Don't worry about fighting the big bears over it," Elaine said. "But you could take me to that new French restaurant."

"The one with the cartoon-character name?" Stevenson laughed.

"Le Smurf is *not* a cartoon-character restaurant," she said haughtily. She uncurled from her tight position and started looking around. The bus ground to a halt and Zamora boiled out the door.

"Let's see what the trouble is," Stevenson suggested. "I just love it when the right hand doesn't know what the left is doing."

"Are we sinister?" she asked.

"Considering who we work for, I think that's a good assumption." Stevenson and Elaine followed Major Zamora and two of his junior officers to the front of the armored column.

"What the hell's going on, Captain?" Zamora bellowed. "My recon tells me you have ten APC's, two tanks, and fifteen jeeps on patrol."

"That's supposed to be classified information," the fuzzy-cheeked captain said. Moving to the side, Stevenson peered at the insignia on the officer's sleeve. Once he identified the captain's unit, everything came clear.

"National Guard," he told Elaine.

She let out an incredulous laugh, which she quickly bit back when Zamora turned a stormy face in her direction.

"This is not *your* mission, Captain. We have come from . . . back east." Zamora finished lamely. He couldn't reveal the route they had taken without also disclosing sensitive information to the weekend warrior. "This is an Air Force mission."

"We got the call from civilian sources. It took us four hours to mobilize, but by damn, we did it, and we're here. If that goes against your orders, Major, contact Colonel Feerman."

Zamora motioned to his radioman. The man trotted forward with the heavy rig, put it down, and worked to set up the uplink to a comsat hidden somewhere in the sky. Indicator lights flashed when the uplink was established.

The National Guard officer watched in appreciation at such high-tech equipment. His own outmoded radio unit sat on the hood of his Vietnam-era jeep—his unit didn't even rate a Hummer. Zamora's fingers tapped on a small keypad until the transmission codes were established and the link was untappable. Somewhere in orbit, two or more Milstar satellites bounced the signal around, changing frequencies hundreds of thousands of times a second, blending and stripping the signal to prevent enemy interception.

Stevenson smiled wryly at the thought of enemy expropriation of the signal—the enemy might be AP or Reuters or even the U.S. Army.

"General Beaumont?" Zamora cleared his throat. Stevenson could only speculate on what he heard in the headphones, but it must have been blistering. It was getting late back in Washington and it was a Friday. The general might have been on his way out to a holiday dinner party or entertaining his mistress.

Zamora was silent for almost a minute.

"Sir, the National Guard field commander claims authority to handle the . . . mission. Should I turn my duties over to Colonel Feerman?"

Zamora flinched when he got his reply. His dark eyes darted to the bus where his SOF unit waited, fingers moving restlessly on their weapons. Stevenson hoped the major wouldn't take Beaumont's remarks too literally. An SOF squad with full weapons could take out the entire National Guard armor company, if ordered.

"I don't think you're supposed to be here," Elaine said to the Guard captain. "We've come from Washington. It's been a long day. You could just slip off and no one would know."

"Sorry, ma'am, we cannot. My orders are clear."

"Oh?" Elaine said softly. "What are your orders?"

The captain told Elaine everything he'd learned in his briefing. There wasn't a secret safe anywhere once the young officer started.

"So you really don't know why the governor activated your unit for this maneuver, do you, Captain?" Stevenson asked.

"No, sir, but the colonel promised—"

"Captain!" Zamora barked. "Here. It's for you. Listen hard."

The captain accepted the headset and put it on gingerly, afraid that he might break it and have the cost taken out of his pay. "If you say so," he said.

"Who's on the line?" Elaine asked Zamora. "It can't be the president. He'd be having a conniption fit."

"The only one at the party General Beaumont could find was the secretary of defense."

Stevenson laughed. Beaumont was attending a high-level Washington function. Not only did his aide troop in with a request to speak to peons out toiling in the field, but he probably had been raked over the hot coals by the secretary for losing the KH-18. A simple salvage job was turning into a national mobilization boondoggle.

"Are you really the secretary?" the captain asked. "How do I know?" He pulled the phones away from his ears and shook his head. He handed the rig back to the radioman.

"Well?" Zamora demanded.

"I talked to someone who claimed to be the secretary of defense. But I don't know if he was. You could have connected to anyone."

"Dammit, do you want a full visual? Donner, get this asshole a full visual link with the secretary."

"Sir, wait a minute." The captain frowned. "That's not going to do any good either. I've seen what they can do with computer images."

"Where do you work when you're not out . . . in the field?" Stevenson asked.

"Sir, I'm a data-processing manager for Mr. Bucky's. It's a California-based retail chain."

"Captain, there's a message for you. From the colonel."

"Excuse me." The captain went to his own radio and spoke for several seconds. Stevenson knew the fun was over. After failing to get the guardsman to relent, Beaumont had sent orders down through Pentagon channels. The secretary of defense wouldn't enjoy an interruption of his party any more than Beaumont had. These orders would be definitive.

"Sir," the guardsman said, eyes wide. "Colonel Feerman has ordered me to comply with your orders."

Zamora was almost beyond words. He knew the path that command had taken. It would be his neck because of it. He was more than an Air Force major. He was in command of a Special Operations Force unit. They were supposed to deal with overwhelming odds and triumph—and he had been stymied by a National Guard company.

"Start by telling us why you were ordered out," Stevenson suggested. He looked to Elaine. She nodded slightly. She already knew the answer from her brief conversation with the captain.

"We were to cordon off the area and initiate a search for a UFO."

"What?" Zamora's eyes widened.

"You know, flying saucers. Space aliens. There have been a dozen or more reports. I assume that's why you're out here. These people are scientists, aren't they?" He stared at Stevenson and Reinhardt.

"We are, Captain," Elaine said. "We had hoped to keep this field investigation quiet, but maybe you can help. If Major Zamora approves, you can ring the area and keep the curious back."

Stevenson continued: "The major wants you to deal with any PR connected with this too. I'm certain reporters will show up. Newspaper, TV, radio—you handle them. Can you do that?"

"Certainly!"

"Major, let's get into the area. We have triangulated on the source of the alien signals, haven't we?" Stevenson nudged Zamora. The Air Force officer shot him a savage look, wheeled around, and stalked back to the bus.

"You'll do a great job, Captain," Elaine said, patting him on the arm.

"I'm sure you will too," Stevenson said. "Don't bother telling the reporters that Air Force scientists are here, though. We work better in the dark."

"Yes, when we're kept like mushrooms." Elaine smirked. "In the dark and up to our knees in shit."

The captain blinked. Stevenson made sure the captain would deal with the press. When journalists showed up, and they would, they'd get a better story than the real one.

"UFO's," Zamora muttered. "I'll be damned."

"Won't we all, Major, won't we all." Stevenson settled back in the bus, his arm around Elaine's shoulders. She snuggled closer and was asleep in minutes.

Stevenson was glad this snipe hunt was coming to a conclusion soon. He had had more excitement than he could stand. National Guard. Flying saucers. It was more than he ought to have to put up with.

23

George Wyatt lay on his bed holding the clear cylinder with the pretty green flecks above his head, turning the tube slightly so that light from his reading lamp caught the planes and refracted off most of the rainbow colors. He shook the cylinder harder, and the dust came off the bottom to give a snowstorm effect.

"Green snow, wow," he said softly as he marveled at his find. This was almost as good as a comet. He couldn't name it after his mother, of course, but it would still make a great gift. She would never get tired of looking at the tiny bright green dust motes turning and twisting inside the glass tube, trying to change colors as they drifted around. It might not cure her cancer, but it would help take her mind off the disease.

George heard a scratching noise at his window. He jerked around, sure that his grandparents had caught him with his treasure. He didn't want to explain to them where he had gotten it.

"George!" the wind whistled. "George, let me in!"

He jumped out of bed and peered around the chintz curtain. Snow formed gentle catenaries at the exterior corners of the window, and the humid warmth inside frosted the windowpane. He peered into the darkness, but could only figure out dim shapes moving in the darting snow.

"George, dammit, it's me!"

He struggled to pull up the window. A gust of frigid air took away any hope of heat in his chest. George twisted to the side and let a fresh northern blast enter the room.

"Get in, Billy. Fast! If you don't, my grandma and grandpa will come to see what's wrong. They keep this place like a furnace and feel the slightest cold draft."

"My folks are the same way," Billy said, scrambling through the window. He doubled over, kicked, and landed on the floor amid a small heap of pure white snow. George struggled to get the window closed before the temperature in the house dropped ten degrees. As it was, the central heating kicked in again, futilely blowing hot air against the torrents of wintry wind coming inside.

"Why'd you come over? It's past midnight."

"I saw your light. My mom and dad are arguing again. He came home drunk." Billy Devlin sat on the edge of George's bed, his head down a little. His chin lifted and a sneer crossed his lips. "It doesn't matter. They do it all the time when he's drunk."

"That's too bad," George said, thinking about his own parents. His dad had to work two jobs to keep them going since his mother had entered the hospital. George couldn't remember seeing either of his parents take a drink.

He frowned, then remembered. They had drunk champagne at his aunt's wedding, but that had been years and years ago. He'd been six, maybe seven then, and Aunt Lita had insisted.

"Yeah, I guess I know how it can be," he said, without a clue of what Billy was enduring.

"I got bored. Those lenses from the wreck weren't too good. They curved the wrong way to use as magnifying glasses."

"They were concave, not convex," George said. "But that doesn't mean they aren't any good. You can look through them and—"

"I know, I know. Everything's all twisted around, tiny and upside down and like that. Big deal." Billy pulled a pair of the lenses from his pocket and tossed them onto the bed. They were still cold and fogged over slightly.

"I might be able to use them," George said uncertainly. He had what he wanted from the wreck and didn't want to give it up. The green snow scene would replace the more traditional one his mother had broken years ago.

"Did you see all the soldiers?" Billy asked suddenly. "There must be a million of them everywhere."

"Soldiers?" A cold lump formed in George's stomach. They had called out the Army to search for them.

"Well, not really soldiers. Not exactly. They're National Guards. My dad says they aren't worth shit, even when it comes to directing traffic and pulling people out of rivers."

"This isn't a good time to be outside," George said, peering through the curtains. He imagined a tank pointing its huge cannon directly into his bedroom and a soldier popping out of the hatch demanding that he return the cylinders stolen from the wreckage.

"They can't find their asses with both hands and a flashlight," Billy went on. "My dad said that too. He served over in Vietnam. You should see his medals."

"He was a hero?"

"Sure was. He's got a Purple Heart and a Bronze Star and even a Good Conduct medal. Before he was all shot up, he made it to sergeant."

"Wow," George said, impressed. His father had been too young to serve in Vietnam. His awe passed quickly as he remembered the soldiers patrolling outside. They'd probably turned Redding into an armed camp, with checkpoints and searchers. How could he hide the cylinders he had stolen?

Was it best to turn himself in and take whatever prison sentence they gave him? George shuddered at the thought of going to jail. It would kill his mother.

"They might be looking for this shit. We should have taken more," Billy said.

"If they're looking for it, they want it back. We're thieves."

"Bullshit," Billy said. "We have salvage rights. They

let it fall out of the sky. We *deserve* anything we can get." He started to elaborate, but a coughing fit bent him over. He wiped his nose and muttered something about a bad cold.

"Are you all right? You're coughing up blood," George said, worried.

"I'm all right." Billy's tone cut off any further conversation for almost a minute.

George took the time to think about what Billy had said. George wasn't sure about salvage rights, but he wanted to believe his friend. Having to explain why they had taken the equipment from the wreckage would be hard, and George knew they would be put into a concentration camp for questioning if caught. He had seen enough shows on TV to know how the Army responded. Hadn't they shot half the students at a campus in Ohio years and years ago?

"Maybe we should call and ask, you know, anonymously, so they won't know who we are and—"

"Are you going to turn me in for the reward?" Billy demanded. "What kind of friend are you?"

"Reward? I didn't know there was a reward."

"There must be. They don't call out the National Guard for bank robberies. They don't even get them up here anymore to bust the guys growing pot."

"There's too many of them, maybe," George said weakly.

"We're all right. You're a real chicken, you know that?" Billy lounged back on the bed. He rolled one cylinder back and forth. The gray gunk inside moved sluggishly. His attention shifted to the tube with the green particles. He was as captivated by it as George.

As he watched his friend turn it over and over, stirring up fresh clouds of kelly-green rain, George wondered if he should let Billy take the cylinders. If the Army was out hunting him down, he could always deny everything, claiming that Billy was responsible.

The thought revolted him even as it rose in his mind.

He had stolen them and had to pay for it if they caught him. Billy might be guilty too, but that didn't change anything. He, George Wyatt, had ripped off the equipment in the crashed pod. Nothing he did would change that. He was guilty.

"Do they have any clues?"

"Why are you getting so uptight, George? They're National Guardsmen, not Magnum P.I." Billy looked confident. George wondered if his friend really felt that way or was just putting on an act.

"They wouldn't be here unless something serious was going on."

"Of course something serious is going on." Billy turned the crystal tube over and over, watching the light work into rainbows. "Whatever it was we found fell from up there." His thumb jerked toward the ceiling. "They won't know this junk didn't fall out somewhere else. How can they know *we* took it? Stuff must be scattered all over northern California." Another coughing fit hit him. He wiped his lips and glared at George, daring him to say anything about it. George didn't.

"Someone might have seen us," George said, trying to keep his worry on the real problem.

"No one was around, and I didn't tell anyone where we were going. Did you?" A sly look crossed Billy's face. "Some of the stuff we took is better than the rest."

Right now George was so sick with worry he couldn't think. His vision blurred a little, but he forced that away. His hand burned, down deep inside, where he had touched the part of the wreck buried in the sand. He tried to get hold of himself. It was all in his head. The government didn't know what had happened to their equipment. How could they? It had burned up, just as Billy said, and must have spilled its guts across half the country.

"Real pretty stuff. Not like that in the other tubes." Billy held up the green-flecked solution and swirled it around in the thick quartz cylinder.

"You want to split it? You take half and let me have

the rest?" George wiped the sweat off his forehead. He held down his rising gorge. Outside, in the wintery weather, the entire army looked for him. He ought to give it all to Billy, let him take the rap for stealing it. But if he did, what would he have to show for his trip to northern California?

."You'd do that?" Billy shot to his feet. "How are we going to divvy it up?"

"I don't know. Wait, yes I do. Pour out the gunk in one of the other tubes. I was fooling around and figured out how to use those faucets on the sides of the tubes. It's a screwy setup, only letting stuff in or out when you hold it right, but I can get around it." He showed Billy how to connect two cylinders at their valves.

"Yeah, this gray stuff isn't real interesting to look at." Billy went to the window, opened it, and struggled with a small valve on the side of the tube. It hissed and almost erupted like a rocket when he got it open. The solution inside dropped into the thin snow outside the window, hissing as it cooled.

"Be careful. Here, you do it," George said. His stomach had knotted until it felt smaller than his fist. Funny blurry amoeba swam in front of his eyes, and he almost lost his balance. He propped himself up against a dresser as Billy took the prized tube from him.

"You won't regret this, George. You'll be my friend for life. This stuff is great!"

Billy worked open the valve on the side of the tube. It sputtered and hissed as if it were under pressure, but he didn't lose any of the contents. He siphoned off half the solution into his empty tube, then turned off the spigot.

"Got it," he said. He held up the tube and frowned. He had left George with most of the green substance in the cracked cylinder. He reached over and ran his finger around the tip of the valve, getting off a few drops of the solution he'd missed. Billy fastened his newly filled cylinder to a second and split the difference. The way the green flakes multiplied so fast pleased him. He could always decant from his two green-filled tubes into the third later when he got rid of the gray grunge in it.

George took his tube back, hardly noticing he still had most of the green flakes. He wiped off the fluid spilled in the transfer on his shirt sleeve. Sudden weakness forced him to his knees.

"You all right, George?"

"Dizzy," the boy said. "Want to . . . want to throw up."

"Don't, you'll wake your grandparents. God, we can't let them know what we've been up to. This is our secret. They'd turn us in to the Army."

"No, no, they wouldn't," George said without much conviction. Sweat popped out on his forehead. He wiped it off with his sleeve. He wished he wasn't such a wimp. Nerves turned him inside out. Billy sized him up, a cruel smile crossing his lips.

"I'll give you back the lenses," he said. "It's only fair."

"You keep them," George insisted. The less he had from the wreck, the better off he would be if they caught him.

"No, no," Billy said. "You can have them, but let me borrow the telescope. Just for a day or two."

"No!"

Billy went to the window and rubbed away the frosted patch and peered into the darkness. "I can see the soldiers out there. They're coming down this street. What do you think they're looking for?"

George knew blackmail when he heard it. "Keep the lenses," he said. "And you can borrow my scope, but only for the night."

"Great!" Billy crowed.

"What do you want with it, anyway? The weather's terrible. You won't be able to see any stars."

Billy hesitated, then said, "I just want to study it." The look in his eye told George his friend was lying, but he wasn't going to press him on what he wanted the telescope for.

"You won't hurt it?"

"I've watched you use it. It'll be like new when I bring it back, honest. Cross my heart." Billy had to put down the three glass cylinders he had taken, the one with the decanted green motes and the other two with the gray gobs, to make the huge X over his chest. "Trust me, George. I'll take real good care of it. You won't be sorry."

George's stomach churned even more. Nerves tore him up inside. "Go on, take it. But just for tonight. I want it back tomorrow."

"It's a deal!"

Billy sneezed, then wiped his bloody nose with his fingers. "I'd better get home. My old man's likely to be passed out by now. See you in the morning." He struggled to get his treasure trove of cylinders and telescope out the window.

" 'Night, Billy."

George watched his friend vanish through the window and into the blustery night. He sat and stared at the fraction of the green flakes he had left in the cracked tube. His eyes kept blurring on him; that may have been why they seemed to multiply back to their original number.

24

"What a farce," Stevenson grumbled. His back against a stony ravine wall, he sat staring into the distance. The wind whipping down from the north carried more than a hint of the arctic. Snowflakes danced in the flashlight beams and an occasional wet spot formed on his eyebrows. It melted and froze almost instantly. If the wind changed and came off the Sierra Madres to the east, the entire of northern California would turn into an icebox. As it was, Stevenson desperately needed defrosting.

"Why won't they let us back there?" Elaine asked. She pushed back the hood of her parka and ran her fingers through dark hair in a gesture Stevenson wished he could duplicate. His hair had been falling out in clumps for the past few days. Arriving in Redding had been stressful enough, but dealing with the National Guard unit had about undone him. After two hours of heated conversation, he still hadn't been allowed to search for his experiment.

He watched as Elaine paced. Her shoes crunched on the cold sand in the ravine bottom. Did the spy satellites high above their heads pick up their activity? The Keyhole series relayed data in real time. The president could watch her pacing and Stevenson steaming, if he wanted. Why hadn't they been allowed to go through the wreckage of the KH-18?

"There's another piece," Elaine said, pointing into the snowy gloom. "Looks like a strut for the solar arm."

"That would have come off during reentry," Stevenson

said. "And I didn't think the bird even had a solar power system. Why put an RTG inside if it's going to get its juice from the sun?"

"Redundancy." She spat out the word as if it left a bitter taste on her tongue. He knew what she meant. He said "need to know" the same way.

"Where is Zamora? This is getting to be ridiculous. We're freezing our asses off, and he's off somewhere playing tin soldier." Stevenson had to agree. He heaved himself erect and went off looking for the Air Force officer. He didn't get ten feet before one of the SOF corporals blocked his path.

"Sorry, sir, no one beyond this point."

"You're wrong." Stevenson started to go around. The commando moved and blocked his path again.

"I am sorry, sir, but Major Zamora gave orders. No one past this point."

"I'm in command of this mission."

This had no effect on the soldier. Taking a different tack, Stevenson asked if he could talk with Zamora.

"He's busy, sir."

"Tell him I'm pulling my team back. Tell him we'll be in a motel in Redding if he's interested in letting us do our jobs—and that he should contact General Morningside, not me." Stevenson spun and stalked off. He stumbled slightly in the hard sand and hoped his exit wasn't as ludicrous as it felt. He had reached the end of his patience. Morningside had said he would be in charge. Either Zamora was running this boondoggle or he was. Let the military take full authority for this mess. Hell, let the National Guard do the cleanup. They had beat everyone here, and all because of a UFO sighting.

"Well?" Elaine looked as if she wanted to spit fire. He was in the same mood.

"Get Gorton. Tell his team to pack up. We're going to find a warm place to go to ground for a while. Zamora won't even talk to me, and I can't get by his trained gorillas."

"That's guerrillas," Elaine said, trilling the RR properly in the Spanish pronunciation.

"I said what I meant. If they want us to work, we'll work. I won't waste my time freezing in the dark."

They made their way down the ravine to a small mound of cleanup equipment. Two of Gorton's team slept. The remaining one and Gorton played gin rummy, keeping the cards pinned down against the gusty wind with heavy rocks. Gorton looked up when Stevenson stormed past.

"We finally ready for work?" he asked.

"Get your team out of here, Will. Zamora won't let us see the site. I don't know what orders he's received, or from whom, but there's no need for us to play games. We're scientists, not buck privates."

"I no longer have any privates," said Gorton. "They froze off well nigh an hour ago." He glanced at his hand, smiled, and put them into the deck.

"How are we going to get into Redding, Tom? We're two miles off and this equipment is heavy. I helped them unload it." Elaine dropped down on a tarp-covered pile.

Stevenson considered leaving it, then quickly discarded that notion. This was their equipment, and they were responsible for it. Zamora was likely to bury it or give it to the National Guardsmen as souvenirs. From the bulk, it was too much for the six of them to carry without making several trips. The weather worsened by the minute, and Stevenson wasn't in any mood to play pack animal.

"I'll get the Guard captain to give us a hand."

"Zamora told him to stay back two miles," Gorton said. "I can go and talk to him and see if they'll send a couple jeeps. That's all we'd need. We came here light."

"Three jeeps," Stevenson decided. "There's no need for us to rough it any more than we have."

"There's no need to rough it at all, Doctor," came Zamora's hoarse voice.

"Oh? Have the gods descended from Olympus? Are mere mortals being honored with a visit?"

"There's no need to be sarcastic, Dr. Stevenson. We had to scout the area and determine the extent of the . . . problem. We're ready for your decontamination team."

"Will, get your men into suits." Gorton jumped to, waking the two sleepers and digging through the piles to prepare the heavy radiation-hazard suits. Stevenson turned back to Zamora. "What took so long?"

"The plutonium spill was greater than anticipated. Aerial surveillance didn't show the minute traces scattered along this ravine. The KH-18 must have bounced and skidded for several hundred yards before crashing into a bank. The entire area is moderately hot."

"How hot? Why didn't you let us do the scouting work?" Gorton asked.

"A good question, Major. We're equipped for this. Why not let us do our jobs?" Elaine moved to let two of Gorton's men rummage through the equipment under her. "Your men aren't dressed for plutonium chasing, are they?"

"Orders, Dr. Reinhardt."

"From Beaumont? Wyman? The Director of Central Intelligence? Who gave the orders?" Stevenson asked, still angry at the delays.

"I can't tell you, sir."

Stevenson was sick to his soul with this secrecy. He tried to calm himself. It wouldn't do anyone any good to blow up now.

"You win, Major. Where is the main compartment? Prelim photos showed it was near here."

"It's been broken open and is badly damaged," the major said. "We haven't approached it. The level of radiation is too high."

"It's too damned high only if you don't have suits," Stevenson said. "I'm beginning to wonder why I volunteered for this."

"You volunteered for the same reason I did, Doctor," Zamora said. "You were ordered to come."

The officer turned and faded into the night.

"We're about suited up, Doc. You want to come along? If you do, you two might want to put on the spare suits. The readings Zamora's boys took must be a lot higher than I'd've anticipated. That's unusual for plutonium 238. The stuff's a strong alpha emitter, not gamma." Gorton saw his puzzled look. "The stuff's only got an eighty-eight-year half-life. It's not all that bad to clean up, unless they lied to me about what they sent up."

"Anything's possible," Stevenson allowed.

"So?" Gorton pointed to spare suits on the pile of supplies.

"You want to let them clean up before we go in?" Stevenson asked Elaine.

"The suit's got to be warmer than this parka," she replied, and began to wiggle into the heavy radiation-hazard suit.

Stevenson had done this before and knew how to get in with a minimum of effort. He sat down on the hard ground and got his feet into the bulky legs, then pulled. Suspenders over his shoulders held up the weighty trousers. He rolled over and got to his knees, then burrowed forward, arms over his head, and worked into the jacket. Lifting, he got upright, then stood. The leaded-glass helmet was the final touch to make him look like the UFOnaut the National Guardsmen sought.

"I'm already hot," he shouted. His voice was muffled by the heavy lead-treated canvas hood. He pushed it back until he got a better view out the glass window. Gorton and his men were already around the bend in the ravine.

Elaine hitched her trousers, adjusted her suspenders, and then got her hood into place. Like the wagon master signaling his train, she lifted her arm and motioned Stevenson forward into the growing snowstorm. The snow dancing beyond the leaded picture window further muffled sound. They might have been lost on an alien world.

Lanterns in the niches along the ravine gave some

illumination. Stevenson still found the walking hard. The suit weighed more than eighty pounds, and he was out of shape. Panting, almost winded, he hiked up a low rise and came to a sandy-bottomed stretch. Zamora's men had positioned lights to shine directly on the sundered compartment from the KH-18. He started forward, but Zamora's shouts held him back.

"High radiation. Let your team sweep up some of it first. No risks."

Will Gorton and his three assistants were already on hands and knees, working with small lead-lined boxes and scintillators. Two men located the plutonium-dioxide debris and Gorton and the man he had been playing gin with scooped it into their containers.

"I caught a look at a Geiger-counter readout," Elaine shouted. "Every gram of the damned plutonium must be spilled here."

"Our experiment must have been in the same module."

Stevenson fumed at the wait. Gorton and his team worked methodically, and Stevenson knew they weren't dawdling. His real anger turned toward those in the Pentagon, at NASA, the NRO, and interservice rivalry. It also turned against the illiterate son of a bitch in Congress who had insisted on lofting an experiment that belonged in an isolation lab such as the one at Fort Detrick. It was nothing more than a gray gooey gob, neutral and harmless. The only problem had been in presentation. The words "recombinant DNA," and alterations of basic reproduction mechanisms, had frightened the ignorant.

"Levels are down fifty percent, Doc," came Gorton's loud voice. "We've got most of the pellets from the atomic battery. Less than a couple hundred grams, total." He held up a silvery pellet the size of a pencil eraser. "Zamora's men got spooked by the radiation levels. They aren't much. Christ, the background radiation gets worse at high altitudes near uranium tailings from old mines. This was a cakewalk."

"Glad to hear it," Elaine said. She pointed toward the main body of wreckage and called out, "Can I go check the wreckage now, Major?"

Zamora stood behind her, eyes on Gorton and his men. Radiation didn't hold the terror for him that the biohazards did, Stevenson decided. Zamora had marched right up to this spot without a protective suit, more to show his courage to his men than anything else. Stevenson wondered if he could get the officer to join him at the KH-18 module.

"Go on," Zamora said. "I'm having my men pull back to a safer distance while you poke through the wreck."

"That won't be necessary. Project Big Hunk was destroyed in the atmosphere. I don't expect to find even the quartz test cylinders, much less any spillage from the experiment." Stevenson motioned for Elaine to join him.

"Go on. We'll patrol the perimeter. The Guard might let in a few curious reporters."

"We wouldn't want that, would we?" Stevenson and Elaine followed the path Gorton had cleaned. He dropped to his knees and shone his flashlight inside. The heavy gloves made handling the light difficult. He frowned as he studied the structure revealed to the bright white beam.

"I should have insisted on a blueprint for this section of the bird," he told Elaine. His nose started to itch, and sweat ran into his eyes. Only willpower kept him from lifting his hood and wiping away the moisture. He didn't share Gorton's contention that the radiation levels were minimal.

"I can't make heads or tails of it. What are we looking at, Tom?" Elaine half-crawled into the module and whipped her light around. Everywhere lay fused circuitry and burned areas, some going through to the KH-18's exterior.

"About one percent of the total payload was inside," he guessed. From other sources he knew the size of the Keyhole satellite series. "We have the atomic battery over there . . ." An entire section had been ripped free. The heavy metal case remained in place, but the silicon-germanium sandwiches with their graphite-contained plutonium-dioxide pellets were missing.

"This looks like the mount I designed to isolate vibration during liftoff."

"Don't get your hopes up. They might have pirated your ideas for something else." Stevenson crawled farther into the module. He had to agree with Elaine after examining the mounting more closely. "The mounts are intact. You designed them well, but . . ."

"What's wrong?" She scooted up beside him.

"The latches have been opened."

"You mean sprung."

"No, opened. The experiment was removed."

"You mean it fell out?"

"I mean"—a cold knot formed in Stevenson's stomach as a hot flush raced across his forehead—"that it was removed. There's no way it could have fallen out. Someone beat us here."

25

Once the pressure had been released inside the cylinder, George Wyatt managed to transfer the green-flaked liquid from one container to another. He did this several times, dividing his take evenly after throwing out the gray gunk in the other tube, as Billy had done with his. George marveled at the way the green leaves fluttered in suspension and multiplied to fill the new tube. He tasted the clear liquid to see if he could tell what it was. The salty taste indicated it wasn't just water.

Billy had taken his share of the booty the night before, and George hadn't seen him since. The sky had been heavily overcast with the winter storm hammering away at the countryside, keeping him inside all day. The lousy weather made viewing impossible, and George didn't mind that Billy hadn't returned the fancy telescope as he had promised. He had painful stomach cramps, and his vision blurred. Try as he might, he couldn't rub away the gauzy veil that dropped over him, sometimes for hours.

"George dear, are you in there?" came his grandmother's voice. He hastily hid the two tubes with the green flakes. Explaining to her how he had found them was still too big a hurtle to jump.

"In here," he said. His voice almost broke. He coughed, and it felt as if his guts were going to come up his throat. Deep down inside, a grinding motion tore at him. He coughed again, and specks of black-red blood came up.

"What in the world?" His grandmother bustled over and looked at the tissue he had spat into. "Are you sick?" She thrust her hand against his forehead. He was burning hot. "I do declare. You're just like your mother. She never took good care of herself. I knew we shouldn't have allowed you to stare at the stars all night. Certainly not in a blizzard."

"I'm fine, Grandma. Honest. It's nothing but a cold."

"We'll see. Those soldiers ran a tank down our street. The very idea!"

"I didn't get a cold from them. I didn't even go out to look at them." George's head turned into a rotted melon, ready to explode at any instant. He clutched it when the room started to spin. And now that she had mentioned it, he was hot. Damned hot.

"There's no telling what germs they brought into town. You know how an army lives."

"They weren't living off the land. Besides, it's cold. No germ's going to survive long outside."

"You aren't used to this awful weather. Why, I saw on the weather that it was almost sixty degrees in New Orleans. That's your idea of winter, not this."

George said nothing. His throat was scraped raw. He'd had colds before, but not like this. His guts were churning and grinding together painfully; he felt as if everything inside him had been turned into sandstone.

"I—" He tried to talk, but nausea overcame him and he vomited right there in the middle of the room. Blackish blood came up with it. Bent double, he tried to apologize. He could hardly croak.

His grandmother rushed out, presumably to call a doctor. George curled up on his bed in a fetal position. Another bout of coughing seized him. He wondered if he had caught his mother's disease. He had never heard if cancer was contagious. He tried to think, but the pain was unbearable.

George wiped off his mouth. Small drops of bright red blood dotted the mucus on his hand. Groaning, he reached for a clean handkerchief on his nightstand.

"So, we've got a cold, do we?" asked his grandfather.

"Your grandmother's calling the hospital. Damned doctors don't make house calls anymore." Peter Stratton focused through the top of his bifocals; more snow was piling up outside from the savage storm. "It's colder than a well digger's destination out there."

"Just a cold," George croaked.

"Spitting up a bit of blood, are we?" His grandfather studied the bright specks. "That's a sign of a bad throat. We'll get you something for it."

"Aw, Grandpa . . ."

26

Stevenson was bone tired. He had hustled around in the eighty-pound hazard suit all night, until every muscle in his body ached and he was ready to collapse. The day hadn't brought any light or heat to the crash site. He thought there was a faint brightening in the east, but Gorton assured him that the direction he had indicated was south. The storm kept the area socked in and buried under an increasing blanket of snow.

"How are we supposed to find the experiment under all this?" he lamented. An inch of new snow covered the ground. The plutonium pellets were easily located with Geiger counters; Gorton and his men made sweep after sweep of the area, hunting for the deadly metal pellets at ever-increasing levels of sensitivity. He had heard Will say that they were down to background levels, which made it impossible to find more plutonium bits.

At that level it hardly mattered; the health danger was quasi-nil. Stevenson was past caring anyway. That part of the cleanup had gone perfectly. What tore at him was his inability to find any part of Project Big Hunk.

"There's some hope for the search, Doctor," Zamora said. "A KH-18 satellite will make another pass over the area in an hour. We have real-time capability on it."

"So what? An aerial recon won't spot anything buried under snow."

"The satellite can find objects buried at depths of several feet," Zamora said.

"Synthetic aperture radar," Elaine told Stevenson. "Archaeologists used it to find Mayan ruins in Belize and the ancient aqueducts in the Sahara. I remember seeing photos when I was on the Earthwatch dig in the Negev a few years back."

"And the Navy uses it to track Russian submarines," Zamora finished. "It is very efficient. We can pinpoint objects less than a meter square. Believe me when I say the satellite that'll be doing the search is *very* efficient in this regard."

"All right, it's efficient," Stevenson said, "but it'll find any piece of buried garbage." He looked around hopelessly. "This area must have been used for years by teenagers working on their cars. See the oil patches in the sand? What was left behind? Bumpers? Fenders? Your radar is going to find all of that."

"True, Dr. Stevenson. Then your team will investigate every target located by the bird. You know what you're looking for."

"Peace," Stevenson blurted. "I'm looking for fucking peace of mind."

"Calm down, Tom," soothed Elaine. "We're all tired."

He allowed her to pacify him. They took turns with each other.

Zamora called out, "We're getting the first pictures from upstairs, Doctor. We're recording at this end even as Adviser Wyman receives similar photos in the White House."

Stevenson took several seconds to decipher what appeared on the small video screen. The angle was acute and interpretation should have been done by space-reconnaissance intelligence experts. In spite of the perspective problems, he got his bearings and detected a pattern in the pictures. Locating Redding was easy from the IR display showing heat sources and lights. The asphalt streets shone in a dull red glow, and individual auto engines looked like cigarettes in the darkness. But this display was used only for alignment and did not give the pictures they needed.

"Here's our position," Zamora said, indicating a tiny glowing dot. "We've got a special beacon turned on for the skycom work. The bird sights in on it and gives a picture of the terrain around us. Every ten seconds a new radar pic comes down."

"You're recording this in your computer?"

"I can blow it up to greater detail after transmission," the major said. "It's useful for battle operations."

Stevenson saw that it would be. No enemy position would go undetected, even tunnels—especially tunnels. The infrared display showed the storm drains and sewers under the Redding streets. The synthetic-aperture radar went even farther, giving a distinct picture of tubes and arches hidden under the streets.

"Can you reset the depth of visual penetration to only a few centimeters? I doubt our missing experiment dug deeper than that. The radar looks 'through' the snow."

The major worked a few seconds and changed the picture's attributes. Anything buried at a depth of ten centimeters shone in the purest orange on the display. The satellite passed over and left them with a computer memory filled with images.

"I'll retrieve them," Zamora said. The small computer began slowly disgorging fax-quality hard copy from an auxiliary printer. Stevenson took the pictures as they popped out, and stared at each one until he had decided there wasn't anything more to learn. Then he passed it along to Elaine. If he missed a detail, she would be sure to pick it up and let him know.

An hour later, the storm broke and the dim blue disk of the sun poked out feebly. A shadow crossing his space-recon photo was the first he noticed of the change. Stevenson still hadn't found anything resembling the missing experimental setup.

"We're going to have to bring in more personnel," he said. His eyes blurred. He couldn't remember the last time he hadn't been tired and cold and hungry. This was combat. "We'll comb the area inch by inch. It's the only way we'll find what happened."

"I don't want to do that," Zamora said. "There's been enough publicity. The press is curious about why we're still in the field. They spent hours grilling the Guard captain about his UFO."

"That sighting was the satellite coming in, wasn't it?" Elaine asked.

"Must have been. We've found six modules from the other KH-18's pass-by photos. All grounded modules were ruined internally, circuits fried from overload and reentry. We can account for ninety percent of the bird now."

Stevenson shook himself to full wakefulness. He had been poring over the photos too long. He hadn't realized Zamora and his SOF had been out locating the parts of the downed satellite while he frittered away his time staring at the photos.

"There was no trace of my experiment?"

"Trust me, Doctor, I'd have let you know."

"Sorry," Stevenson said. "We have to retrieve the experiment. It was *removed*. Someone's grubby fingers popped those snaps, removed it, and then carried it off."

"Are you sure it was aboard the satellite? It might have never reached orbit."

Stevenson stared at Zamora, thinking hard. The major had a point. Then tiny facts slipped into place and Stevenson's left brain kicked into high gear. "That's impossible. We received telemetry on cell growth and replicator function over the past few weeks. There might be a case made for recorded, faked reports, but that's stretching the limits of credulity. No one except that idiot Midwestern congressman cared about the experiment, and the restraining box wasn't even scorched during reentry. The experiment was in place when the satellite came back. Someone took it out after it crashed."

"Other items, notably the optical-systems lenses from the same module could be missing," Elaine said. "I took pictures of the inside, but we'd have to send them to the NRO for verification."

"You can't be sure," Stevenson said. "It could have happened in orbit, during the repair and refueling of the bird. We'd have to ask Colonel Jensen what was done, if he knows." A momentary pang of regret seized Stevenson. The space-shuttle pilot had already caught the flak for the bungled mission; it meant his career. Stevenson wasn't going to let the same happen to him.

He had to recover the quartz cylinders holding his neutral-cell experiment. The press would crucify him for turning loose recombinant DNA monsters on the country if he didn't.

"There were fresh scratches, scratches cutting through the surface burn to bare metal," Elaine said. "Someone yanked out the lenses."

"We'll check," Zamora said.

Stevenson rubbed his eyes again as he watched Zamora march off. The man appeared just as fresh and crisply military as when they had arrived. Perhaps the SOF training turned out supermen after all, as the PR hinted. At the moment, Stevenson was glad Zamora and his men were on his side.

"The atomic battery definitely split open," he said.

"Gorton has cleaned up that mess."

"Whoever yanked the experiment and lenses must have come into contact with the plutonium," Stevenson said.

"Assuming someone did steal the equipment and test cylinders, are you saying we can track them down by looking for radioactive traces?" Elaine chewed on her fingernails as she considered this. "They must be falling ill. Such contact . . ."

Stevenson shut his eyes and inhaled deeply. The cool air wiped away some of the exhaustion. And this was merely the beginning. The atomic battery's plutonium 238 was now loose, and no one knew how quickly it would spread.

27

"I don't know, dear. This doesn't seem like a good idea to me. One of us should go with him."

"There's no reason for us to keep arguing about it. He'll be fine during the trip. It's only four hours, and the stewardesses will watch over him," Peter Stratton said. He shared his wife's concern over George, who sat on the hard airport bench twenty feet away. The boy radiated agony. He was pale, drawn, and had spent much of the night throwing up. At the moment, the symptoms had died down, but a slight fever remained.

"Go with him, dear. The ticket won't cost that much more."

He shook his head and moved George's heavy bag along the floor, one step closer to the ticketing agent.

"We don't have enough money. We're going to have to pay an extra fifty dollars to get him on a flight as it is. Damn the airlines and their no-change rules."

Stratton grumbled more to relieve the tension of his worry than anything else. The drive to San Francisco from Redding had been dangerous because of snow-packed roads. I-5 had been slick in patches, but from Sacramento to the San Francisco airport, the roads had been free of snow. Stratton wasn't used to driving such long distances anymore, and the trip had tired him.

"He'll be okay. And we *don't* have the money, dear."

Only four days earlier, the doctor had come and had only been able to advise George to stay in bed; sending him home wasn't the best solution, but they had talked with his father and had reached the decision.

"Margie is out of the hospital. Seeing her again will do as much for him as anything. It'll perk him right up."

"You'd like to see her too, Peter. Please. Go with him."

"You're treating him like a child."

"He is. He's only fourteen."

"He'll have much more than a bellyache to deal with soon," Stratton said tiredly. George was gradually coming to grips with the notion that his mother wasn't going to survive her bout with lymphatic cancer. Such knowledge turns a boy into a man fast—too fast.

Peter Stratton was sixty-six years old, and he wasn't sure he was able to cope with it. It wasn't fair, outliving your only child.

"May I help you?" The ticket agent looked up from the winking computer screen.

"We called ahead. A ticket for George Wyatt to New Orleans."

The agent looked down the listing on his computer screen. "Only a first-class upgrade is available. The rest of the flight is filled." The agent played with the computer keyboard a few seconds. "Upgrade from San Francisco to New Orleans, nonstop, will be four hundred and sixty-four dollars."

"But you said—"

Stratton cut off his wife's complaint. "Here." He pushed his credit card across the counter. He almost regretted spending so much for the boy's telescope now.

"Suitcases?"

"Just the one," Stratton said, hefting the heavy, dilapidated bag. It gurgled strangely. He had asked George about it, but the boy hadn't given him a straight answer. He was more interested in his grandfather's promise that he would ship the Celestron later. They had agreed not to trust the precious telescope to the airline's baggage handlers. Stratton frowned when he thought of the telescope. Something hadn't been right, but he couldn't put his finger on it. He shrugged it off and decided the fatigue was wearing him down—that and the heavy bag. George had insisted on taking back every single one of his unwieldy astronomy books. He had more of them than he did clothing.

"Boarding begins in twenty minutes," the agent said, already looking to the next customer.

The Strattons joined George. He was staring into the concourse.

"Are you doing okay, George?"

"Sure, Grandpa. Feeling a little woozy, but I'm not that sick. Not like last night." He remembered the waves of nausea that had come and gone repeatedly until he felt like a boat ready to sink into the ocean. "The headache's the worst right now."

"We all have headaches. That's nothing to worry about. Any more blood coughed up?"

"No," George lied. He wasn't up to traveling, but the idea of going home gave him added strength—to see his mother, who was now home from the hospital.

He might not be feeling good, but he was going to see his mother and give her his present. Giving away three cylinders to Billy hadn't been too much of a loss. He still had two tubes with green stuff. He could give one of the kelly-green-flake tubes to her and keep one for himself.

"You checked the suitcase?" he asked his grandfather. "It's not too strong."

"Don't worry, dear. That old suitcase of mine has been around the world several times. It's forty years old and no airline has smashed it yet. And we did add a nylon webbing strap around it."

"But it's got those cloth sides. Anything inside—" He stopped short of telling them about the two glass tubes.

"You're acting as if it contained your telescope."

He almost told them that Billy had his telescope, then decided against it. Explaining how the other boy had blackmailed him for it would take too long. He covered his confusion by saying, "The sky's always cloudy at home."

"There will be clear nights so you and your dad can go out and look at the stars," George's grandmother said.

He fell silent. His head was going to explode. He remembered a movie in which everyone's head blew apart. George felt like that now. Even breathing was a chore. His guts were aching, and every time he breathed, his insides ground together painfully.

"The wind's kicking up again," Len Passmore complained. He adjusted his ear protectors against the wind. The cold, damp breeze came down from San Francisco to the airport. He slapped his hands against his arms.

"You're always bitching. If you don't like the weather, why not move to Phoenix? I hear it's always over a hundred down there, even in winter." Jackson—he never used a first name—grabbed the plaid cloth bag as it came down the chute off the escalator. He took a quick look at the tag and then heaved the bag over his shoulder and onto the flatbed truck going out to Flight 23 to New Orleans.

The bag landed with a dull crunch, which neither of the bag handlers heard over the whine of taxiing aircraft and the rush of wind down the peninsula.

"I like it here, except on days like this," Passmore said. He rubbed his hands together, then put his work gloves back on. He finished loading the last-minute arrivals for Flight 23, then waved to Jackson. The small cart wheeled around and shot between the planes. Passmore was an expert at driving the cart and getting the bags to the loading conveyor. Other drivers missed and had to back up, always a hassle when you pulled a half-dozen baggage-laden carts behind you.

"Got a few last-minutes for New Orleans," he called out to the crewman getting ready to button up the cargo hatch. The man swore under his breath. Passmore didn't care. He jerked the wheel around and came to a halt. A skidding noise sounded behind him. He glanced over his shoulder and saw the plaid bag bouncing along the tarmac.

It was his turn to swear. Sometimes the passengers watched from their two-story perches inside the big planes. Sometimes they saw mishaps like this and complained. He kept his head down, hoping no one would see his face or read the employee-identification card dangling from his pocket.

Passmore jumped out, scooped up the bag, and hurled it toward the conveyor. It landed with a liquid squish. Something wet stained the cloth exterior, but Passmore wasn't interested. He wiped off the fluid on his front and forgot about it right away. He started working on the dozen other bags, wrestling them off the carts and onto the conveyor going up into the bowels of the silver plane.

"That's it," he called to the crew chief inside the hold. He looked down and saw that that one bag had leaked more than a little fluid. He brushed the wetness off the bottom of the cart. A sudden gust of wind blowing from the north tickled his nose. He caught the sneeze before it ripped out his lungs.

"Put it over there and lash it down. We don't want the load shifting like it did on the last flight." The crew chief's sharp eye studied the way the baggage had been loaded. His men had done better in the past. The last flight out had had the pilot ripping his hair out as the luggage shifted every time he banked the plane. It wouldn't happen this time.

"All set," came the report.

He ducked down and motioned for the driver on the conveyor belt to back off. His foot slipped a little on some liquid. Distracted, he glanced down, trying to find where the leak was. Sometimes a hydraulic leak would ground the plane, and it was his job to look for it.

The dampness came from a passenger's bag. He smiled wryly. Someone's clothes were going to reek of after-shave after the four-hour flight. But that wasn't his problem. Whoever unloaded in New Orleans would have to deal with it.

He reached up and pulled down the cargo hatch. Twisting agilely, he took one last look at the load in the hold. Everything was strapped and secure. He slammed the cover and went to see about the flight coming in from Chicago. It was hell during Christmas.

A small puddle formed under George Wyatt's suitcase, then began to spread as the engines revved and sent vibrations throughout the aircraft.

28

It was New Year's Eve, and Stevenson still had no idea what had happened to his bio-neutral-cell experiment. Will Gorton and his team had undertaken the tedious job of marking off areas in a grid pattern, then had worked through them, hunting for signs of the container holding the five experimental cells. Stevenson and Elaine had repeatedly gone over the photos taken from the spy satellite—to no avail. He had demanded a second pass and had received it after speaking directly with General Morningside.

He was almost frantic when he called back and couldn't get the general. He needed more personnel in the field. Someone had stolen the experiment.

Stevenson almost yelled into the phone at Major O'Connors. "Send out Basil Baker, send out Jack Parkessian, send out my entire damned department, if you won't give Zamora more troops."

"I'm sorry, Dr. Stevenson, this is impossible. Congress is adjourned, the president is on vacation until January 6, and frankly, I have no idea where the general is. You were lucky to get him when you called two days ago."

Stevenson forced himself to remain calm—as calm as he could get. But what about the five quartz tubes? What if a child broke one open and swallowed the nutrient fluid? It wasn't poisonous—far from it. But the kid could get one hell of a stomachache and probably be reported to a poison-control center. When that hit the six-o'clock news, Stevenson's career would be over.

He worried about the innocuous nature of the gray gooey gobs. The replicators were designed to produce the neutral cells in solution. Every computer run showed how difficult it was for the quasi-living gunk to live outside the special nutrient fluid. But what would it do if someone swallowed it? The nutrient, the nonreproducing cells, maybe even a touch of plutonium from the crushed atomic battery. He would be responsible if anything went wrong.

"Call Fred Wyman. Get me authorization. Someone must send more troops."

"I'm sorry, Doctor. I'll put your message in the top-priority bin when the general returns. That's all I can do."

"The DCI. What about going directly to the Director of Central Intelligence?"

"I don't have the authority. You know that," O'Connors said.

"In that case, tell me how I can."

"I've never done it. With everyone gone for New Year's, there isn't anyone left in the office who knows how."

Stevenson was beside himself. "The experiment is missing. Someone *took* it. Someone *has* it who shouldn't. It was classified secret. Whom do I report that to?"

"No one. The general, as commander of your research division, knows. It is his responsibility to decide."

Stevenson hung up in a cold fury. He didn't know what to do. Zamora had finished his cleanup of the satellite's pieces. Unmarked Air Force trucks came into the area, one or two at a time to remain inconspicuous, and removed the larger hunks of the downed satellite. With his chore at an end, the major was preparing to move out his SOF unit and return to his base in Florida. What would he do once Zamora was gone?

"Nothing?" Elaine Reinhardt asked. "I didn't think O'Connors would be able to do much. He's a real wimp. How he made it to major is beyond me."

"Making decisions like this is above his pay grade," Stevenson said. "I'm here. I've got to figure out what to do."

"You didn't ask O'Connors to pass along the trouble to Basil, did you?" Elaine asked. "He's such a gossip. Between him and Jack, everyone at Fort Detrick will know what happened out here."

"That might help," Stevenson said glumly. He perched himself on a rock near the pay phone he had used to call O'Connors and stared into the distance. Haze formed over Redding, a smoggy layer that belied the rural setting. Somewhere out there lived the person who had stolen his experiment.

"It wouldn't help," Elaine said. "Jack would make you the villain in the piece. And Basil? He sometimes listens but doesn't hear. What he'd pass along is anyone's guess."

Stevenson slammed his hand down hard against his thigh. "This is drivel. We're talking about the shortcomings of others instead of dealing with our problem." His gray eyes worked around the landscape. The snow had partially melted from two back-to-back days of sun, but the forecast was for more snow after New Year's.

"Zamora had done a good job of keeping this quiet so far." Elaine paced back and forth, hands working inside her gloves to keep them warm. "The UFO thing was all the rage for a couple days. Anything else we've done after the Guard left is being chalked up to stupid government orders. The reporters are busy with the usual New Year's drunk-driving stories."

"We might have to go public with this," Stevenson said suddenly.

"We can't—"

"Someone out there has a potentially dangerous box containing our experiment. We might not have a choice."

"The gray gooey gobs aren't dangerous. You said so, and nothing in your re—" Elaine snapped her mouth shut. Stevenson paid her little attention. He knew his reports said the experiment was harmless, but anything could be turned into a deadly item if used improperly.

"Any unusual sickness will be attributed to them if we don't recover the test tubes soon. Government cover-up, public panic, the whole nine yards."

Elaine didn't respond. She turned and looked down the road toward the town, a few miles away. A small cloud of snow and mud was kicked up, marking the progress of Zamora's vehicle up the hill.

"Perhaps he found something," Stevenson said.

"He'll tell us soon enough. He's driving like a madman."

Zamora skidded to a halt and motioned them over. "I've got a lead. I went to the hospitals and nosed around, asking if anything unusual had happened in the past weeks."

"And?" Stevenson wanted to hope, but hardly dared himself this luxury. Still, the major was excited. That had to mean something.

"Get Will Gorton. He's the closest you have to an expert on radiation exposure, isn't he?"

"Yes." Stevenson's eyes narrowed as he stared at Zamora. "What did you find?"

"Trinity Hospital has a case, a young teenager, they're having trouble classifying. The symptoms are plutonium poisoning."

"Chemical or radiation?"

Zamora shrugged, ignorant of the symptoms in either case. "It might be both, or it might just be that he's got a new strain of the flu. The doctors have tried a half-dozen different treatments and he's not responding."

"Any burns?" Elaine asked.

Zamora nodded. "On his hands. I think he touched fragments from the atomic battery."

"Let's go," Stevenson said. "Will isn't the one to call in on this. Elaine and I know as much about radiation effects as he does."

"What's the boy's name?" Elaine asked.

"Billy Devlin," Zamora answered. He slammed the

vehicle into gear and retraced his route toward Redding. "He lived less than five miles from here, in a small housing subdivision."

"Better and better," Stevenson mumbled. For the first time in a week, his spirits rose. At last, a lead.

"This is most unusual," the resident, Dr. Crane, said. "Are you physicians?" He eyed Stevenson and Reinhardt and their disheveled dress. They had been prowling the hills for five days and looked more like homeless transients than successful medical doctors.

"We heard about the case while we were snow-camping up near Mount Shasta," Stevenson lied. "We're from Maryland, out here on vacation. We encountered something similar a few months back."

"Yes," Elaine cut in, "it was an isolated instance, and it puzzled us. But this case sounds so close . . ." She let the hint of solution to a mystery feed the resident's imagination.

"What were the symptoms?" Crane asked.

Stevenson took a deep breath. This was the test. If they failed, the resident would call an administrator, who would demand credentials, who would call their supposed hospital back in Maryland, who would have them arrested.

"Bloody sputum, coughing, chills, high fever," he said.

"What of the sputum?"

"Dried blood. There was hemorrhaging in the lungs, caused by ulcerated tissue. As the ulcers progressed, bright red blood was spit up along with the dried blood."

The resident began to nod. Stevenson knew they had him—and they were describing a fatal condition. Billy Devlin had inhaled plutonium. His life was to be measured in days or hours. The chemically poisonous element hadn't killed him outright, but the specks in his lungs would cause fatal cancer.

"What about the trauma on his hands?" Stevenson asked, taking a long shot. "Any dark brown spots?"

"Yes," Crane said, startled at the accuracy of Stevenson's prediction. "We didn't think anything about them. I asked if he had been working around electronics, but he said no."

"An RF burn wouldn't cause visible injury, and it would have manifested itself by now," Stevenson said. "This is something else."

"What happened with your patient?" the resident asked.

Stevenson and Elaine exchanged glances. Stevenson took a deep breath and said slowly, "We couldn't do a thing for him. We made him comfortable, tried to treat the lung condition, but . . ." He shrugged eloquently.

"I was afraid that might be the case. Billy has weakened progressively since being admitted. His parents let him linger for several days before bringing him in."

"Could we talk to him?" Elaine asked. "It might give us a clue about the cause. We have so little to go on."

"I understand. Nurse, take the doctors to Room 707."

The nurse turned, adjusted an off-white cap, and looked curiously at Stevenson and Elaine. "Very well, Doctor." She spun and marched off. Stevenson watched her, thinking something was wrong. He tried to put into words the gut-level feeling, then pushed it from his mind. He had to get as much information as possible from the boy, and he knew how difficult that would be. Billy had to know that he was dying.

He also had to know that he had provoked his condition. That, more than anything else, might seal his lips about the Project Big Hunk experiment.

"Do I know you, Nurse?" Elaine asked. "You look familiar."

"No, I'm new here." The woman strode even faster to the door. She turned to open the door to Billy's room. Stevenson caught a glance at the woman's nametag.

He almost laughed. "Nurse Ratched? Is that really your name?"

"Yes, Doctor, it is," she said coldly as she raised a hand to her cheek and partially hid her face. "I am not supposed to leave him alone if he has visitors. Those are my standing orders."

"Very well," Stevenson said, "but we must ask some questions I'd prefer you didn't hear."

"Why is that?"

Stevenson floundered for an answer. Elaine came to his rescue. "They are confidential about his family and background. They'll go into our report."

"This is most unusual. I'd better ask Dr. Crane."

"Please do," Elaine said. She waited for the nurse to leave, but the woman held back.

"I'll ask later, after you've gone. Ask whatever else you need to while I am here."

Stevenson was already at the boy's bedside, while Elaine kept Nurse Ratched occupied with trivial requests. The boy's pallor was undercut by a grayness that foretold death. If Billy had developed Cheyne-Stokes breathing, his immediate death couldn't have been more certain.

"Billy, my name is Tom."

"Who are you? You're not my doctor."

"No, I'm not, Billy. I'm . . . I'm a specialist and I want to help you."

Billy's eyes seemed to glaze over and wander. Stevenson knew he might be having a difficult time focusing, and his attention span would be short because of the inexorable death gnawing away at his guts.

"What did you take from the crashed satellite?"

This brought the boy's eyes wide open.

"Did you remove a box with five quartz cylinders?"

"Who are you?"

"I'm responsible for those test tubes. That was a secret satellite you found."

"How do you know? I didn't do anything!" Billy tried to sit up. The IV tubes and monitors fastened to him prevented easy movement. Stevenson pushed him back down to the bed, but warning lights flashed everywhere.

"You took something from the satellite."

"I didn't know it was a satellite."

"You also contaminated yourself with plutonium dioxide from a broken atomic battery aboard. Where did you put the box with the five tubes?"

"I don't know anything about any satellite!" He shouted loud enough to draw the nurse's attention away from Elaine.

"You're disturbing him. You must leave immediately."

"We've got a few more questions," said Elaine. "Just a couple and then—"

The nurse shoved past Elaine and into the corridor.

"Better hurry. She's going to get the resident. We'll have years to explain—from inside a jail cell."

"I know, Elaine, I know." Stevenson turned back to the boy. "Where did you put the experimental cylinders? How long were you in contact with the plutonium? When did—?"

Elaine's grip on his arm tightened. Billy coughed hard. The fit didn't end. Warning buzzers and lights flashed all across the bank of monitoring equipment by his bed. Stevenson knew the nurse's station received the identical warnings.

The nurse slid out of the room, paused for a moment as she looked up and down the hall, then hurried for the fire stairs. She took the steps two at a time as she raced down. She slowed and came to the ground floor hardly winded from her swift descent. She patted her hair into place, then pushed on the door's panic bar and stepped out. The gust of wind caught at her cap. She ignored it as it fluttered back into the stairwell. She had more pressing matters to attend to. A pay phone hung on the wall to her right.

She reached into a pocket and dropped a quarter into the slot. She dialed a recently memorized number and waited for the answer.

"Stevenson and Reinhardt interrogated him," she said without preamble. "They mentioned a fallen satellite.

The boy's response displayed his guilt. Our information was correct. Act now."

The connection was broken. She hung up and studied everyone in the hospital lobby. No one took notice of her. Head high and shoulders back, she walked through the front door and to the parking lot. She didn't feel the cold wind cutting at her bare arms. Her assignment was completed. The other operatives now had to find what the satellite had contained.

29

Stevenson grabbed Elaine's arm and pulled her from the room. From the nurse's station came an orderly and a nurse, neither running but both walking with determination.

"General Morningside will have a litter of kittens if we have to explain how we questioned a sick kid until he passed out. Let's contact him rather than take the rap for this ourselves—it's better to let someone across the country cope with it," Stevenson continued, looking for the stairs.

"We didn't do anything," Elaine protested.

"We didn't, but the plutonium killed him—*will* kill him," he corrected himself. "The doctor didn't recognize the symptoms. He's going to wonder why we did—and just who the hell we are and why we're in Redding. Do you want to answer these questions in front of the police and the press?"

"News is the public's way of finding out what the government is hiding," Elaine said. She opened the door to the fire stairs and slipped past him. She wasn't arguing, she was just talking to keep herself calm. Stevenson glanced back and saw Dr. Crane and another white-coated man with a stethoscope hung around his neck. They were calling in the big guns now.

"We can get Zamora working on this. He has contacts. Maybe the CIA can get us out of this mess."

"Fat chance of that happening anytime in this century, at least aboveboard. They aren't supposed to work inside the U.S. We'll have to go through the DCI and rattle cages in the Justice Department. This is FBI territory."

"Whoever." Stevenson raced down the stairs. He paused at the landing to catch his breath. As he bent over, hands on his knees and vowing to get into better shape, he noticed a nurse's off-white starched cap on the floor. He wondered how a nurse could lose part of her uniform and not know it. Shoving this from his mind, he exited into the lobby and walked at a steady clip for the front door, intending to be away as quickly as he could without attracting unwanted attention. Elaine trailed behind like a child's captive balloon. She ran into him when he stopped abruptly.

"What's wrong?" she asked, irritated at his insistence on running, then his sudden halt.

"Look at the nurses' caps. See anything unusual about them?"

"No."

"They're different from the one Billy's nurse wore. And they're the same as those of the nurses going into his room after we left."

"So what?"

"The cap back in the stairwell is unique among the ones we've seen. I think our Nurse Ratched lost her cap."

"I still don't—"

"Nothing," Stevenson said, a growing tension urging him to action. "Let's go to the Devlin house before the shit really hits the fan."

"What do you think you can get out of Billy's parents if you do go there? The phone call's already been made and the Devlins are on their way to the hospital. The kid was in bad shape. Crane didn't strike me as the kind to let a boy die without trying to get the parents here."

"We'll see. Maybe someone stayed behind. We need to get *some* information. He cooked his lungs handling plutonium, that much is for sure. That means he was digging inside the KH-18 module. It could also mean he has my experiment."

"Or has a friend who kept it," Elaine finished. "In either case, we've got to talk to the parents." She pointed toward the jeep, where Major Zamora sat impatiently. "Let's get our chauffeur moving. He's likely a law-and-order type who'd want to stick around and discuss the matter with the hospital's doctors."

Stevenson cursed under his breath as Elaine told Zamora where they needed to go. They had to stop at a phone booth to get a telephone listing and address for the Devlins—Stevenson tried to hold a city street map flat as Elaine read off the addresses. He picked the Devlin listed closest to the crash site.

Stevenson knew that if the matter was made public, he would be thrown to the media wolves. He wasn't sure if this wasn't the least of the punishment that could be inflicted. He would be made responsible for the radioisotope thermoelectric generator in the satellite; he would be the one the finger pointed to for civil lawsuits and outrageous monetary damages. The boy dying from handling the plutonium from the atomic battery was unfortunate, but, dammit, it wasn't his fault.

The jeep ride was rough and cold and wet. Stevenson huddled down, his arm around Elaine. Together in the back they tried to keep from being thrown out into the muddy, icy streets. He thought about the approach to take with the Devlins. He didn't know what kind of people they were, but they would be worried about their son. That was human nature. He could play on that for a few minutes, if the hospital hadn't already called.

And if the Devlins had already left for the hospital, he had to break into their home and look for the Project Big Hunk test tubes. The thick quartz cylinders meant nothing now, but they were the only pieces missing from the downed satellite. Hushing up their existence would focus the eventual probe solely on the use of atomic batteries and not on the straw man of recombinant DNA research.

It was always CYA.

"That must be the one," Zamora said, slowing down. "Their car's still in the driveway. You're in luck."

"Looks like it," Stevenson said. He didn't know if he wanted Elaine and Zamora with him for support or if he should approach the boy's parents alone. Elaine might be able to sneak a look in the bedroom windows, and Zamora could patrol the area with a Geiger counter. Splitting forces would be better than presenting a unified front.

But he couldn't do it. Billy Devlin's sad, tortured face kept returning to haunt him.

"Will you both come with me?" he asked. Elaine looked at him closely, frowned, and then understood the problem. She fought the same demons of conscience.

"I'm in uniform. I don't think that's a good approach right now," Zamora said. As if he had read Stevenson's mind, he said, "Let me scout the area for traces of plutonium. If we find it, we'll call Gorton and his team in right away. This isn't a heavily populated area, but there are more people here than up in the hills."

"Do it, Major. Thank you."

"Are you all right, Doctor?" Zamora fixed him with a penetrating stare. Stevenson reminded himself that Zamora was highly trained and competent. "You've been acting strange since we left the hospital. What's the boy's condition?"

"Stable," Elaine volunteered. "He's likely to be as we left him for quite some time."

Zamora nodded, then fumbled under the seat for a Geiger counter. He put it under his heavy jacket and started off on foot. Stevenson watched him go, wishing he could swap jobs with the Air Force officer.

"Do you think we ought to let them know why their son is dying?" Elaine asked.

"The experiment comes first. Nothing will bring Billy back. Retrieving our gray gobs will keep the confusion to a minimum."

Stevenson stared straight ahead as he marched to the

door. He was aware of every piece of gravel under his boots. The cold wind across his face chapped his lips and turned his mouth to cotton. Tears ran down his cheeks, and he wasn't sure the brisk wind was the cause. He reached out, his finger poised over the doorbell, then stopped.

Something was wrong.

"The door's ajar," Elaine said in a low voice. "This is a nasty, cold day. They're losing all their heat."

Stevenson pushed the door open. Unoiled brass hinges creaked and protested loudly. The blast of hot air from inside turned him weak in the knees.

"Should we go in?"

"No," Elaine said.

"Mr. Devlin? Mrs. Devlin?" Stevenson looked over his shoulder. The battered green 1982 Chevy Malibu in the driveway had seen better days. Rust had destroyed most of one fender and worked at another, but from the puddles of oil under the car, Stevenson knew this was the family vehicle. It was moved often enough to let the dripping oil pool in different places. He doubted from the cheap, threadbare furnishings he saw inside that they had a second, fancier car.

"Mr. Devlin?" he called again. He stepped inside, one huge raw nerve ending. He jumped when Elaine put her hand on his arm.

"Something weird is going on," she said. "Take a deep sniff. What do you smell?"

Stevenson almost panicked at the coppery, metallic tang in the air.

He took two more steps into the living room. The television set was turned on but only static came from it. Stevenson rounded the corner and stared at the screen. The set had been turned to an off channel.

"Why?" he asked, more to himself than to Elaine.

"They like white noise? Some people can't go to sleep without something to blot out other sounds."

"This is the middle of the day—and why was their

front door open?" Stevenson was speaking in whispers, as if he had stepped into a library. He raised his voice to a normal tone. "I don't get it. Where are they?"

He left the living room and went into the den and almost vomited. He had found Mr. and Mrs. Devlin.

The woman had been stripped to the waist, then tied to a straight-backed chair with electrical tape. Her husband had been similarly fastened to another chair facing her.

Then someone had taken a knife and begun to skin her. Strips of flesh less than a quarter-inch deep and two inches wide had been peeled back along her arms and upper torso. Stevenson blinked and tried not to stare, but the woman's breasts had been savaged. Amid the bloody ruin of what had been a human being were tiny patches of skin the psychopath had missed in his torture. Her face showed white cheekbones sticking out starkly, and her eyes had been gouged at. From the way the chairs were placed facing each other, Stevenson guessed that the torturer had wanted to make the man talk. Mr. Devlin's body was free of signs of trauma other than a few bruises on the upper arms—as if he had struggled while someone forced him to watch his wife's slow death— and a prodigious amount of blood.

Holding down his gorge, Stevenson moved closer. A single slash had opened the man's throat from ear to ear. A rubbery hunk of severed esophagus protruding from the cut gave mute testimony to the savage fury of the single death cut.

"Oh, my God," Elaine whimpered. Stevenson tried to speak, to warn her back. His voice wouldn't even croak.

"I'll call the cops. This is getting out of hand, national security or not, CYA or not."

She went to the living room to use the phone. Stevenson tried to collect his thoughts and slow the hammering of his heart. He failed on both counts. All he could do was stare at the pair and wonder what animal would do this to other human beings.

Stevenson forced himself away from the grisly scene. He pulled out a rag from his pocket and spat into it. This removed some of the bile from his mouth and kept him from vomiting. He heard Elaine's voice in the living room. She spoke slowly and distinctly, but there was a hysterical edge to her voice.

He drifted toward the other end of the house, passing Elaine but not looking at her. The mere presence of another human being in this death house seemed a violation. *His* presence was a violation of the sanctity of the death. Stevenson glanced into the master bedroom. A few drawers had been opened, but the search, if that was what had happened, had been perfunctory. Mrs. Devlin might have just been a sloppy housekeeper. He knew Elaine was always chiding him about not closing the dresser drawers when he took clothing from them.

Stevenson glanced into the second bedroom. It was almost bare of furniture and had been used as a hobby room. Fly-tying equipment stood on a small bench. A three-legged stool had been turned over. Again he couldn't tell if the room had been searched or if the occupant had been careless.

The third bedroom was a complete disaster—obviously a teenager's room. A poster of a heavy-metal group was thumbtacked on one wall. On the far wall a pinup calendar, tame by most standards, faced it. Stevenson guessed it was all Billy's mother would allow. Clothes were strewn everywhere and the dresser drawers were open. To one side of the room, near the window, stood a large telescope, but what caught Stevenson's eye was the sun reflecting off a discolored lens on the floor.

He knelt and examined it, finding a second lens. The discoloration came from heating a special lens coating, one not commonly available. Stevenson wasn't sure, but they might have been used in the KH-18's electro-optics system—the one Elaine claimed had the lenses popped out, just as his experiment had been removed. He dropped them into his pocket. Sirens blared outside. It hadn't taken the police long to arrive.

Stevenson screwed up his courage. It was going to be a long afternoon and a longer night before the police let up on their questioning.

30

"I don't like this. I don't like this one damned bit," the police lieutenant growled. Stevenson watched the huge hairy man and wondered if he had an ursine ancestor to account for the appearance of a grizzly, or if it was all an act.

"Who does? We can get to the bottom of this by beating the hell out of him, right?" said the FBI agent whose name Stevenson couldn't remember. The other one—Larry Bartholomew—stood at the side of the interrogation room scratching his balls. In spite of the toothpick hanging from the corner of his mouth, the gut hanging over his belt, and his unkempt look and crudities, Stevenson pegged him as the brains of the pair. The one played the bad cop, badgering and threatening, and Bartholomew waited to come swooping in as an avenging angel. Stevenson was then, out of gratitude, supposed to spill everything he knew.

He just wished they would bounce this up the chain of command, contact Morningside, and get word from their bosses in the Justice Department to lighten up.

"I'm going to book 'im," the police lieutenant said, growling deep in his throat. Stevenson had never heard his name mentioned. It hardly mattered because this was an FBI project, not a local-police incident to be solved by conventional means. And unless Stevenson missed his guess, the Redding police were more than willing to turn this hot potato over to the feds. Having two citizens killed, one skinned alive, the other with a slit throat, while their son died mysteriously didn't make for good headlines. There was always a new police bond issue coming up at election time. The better the police looked, the more likely they were to get their pay raise or new precinct station or whatever they wanted to spend the taxpayers' money on.

Stevenson looked past the tall, thin, intense FBI agent straight at Bartholomew. The man yawned widely, as if he didn't have a care in the world. The toothpick slipped out of his mouth and dropped to the floor. He didn't notice.

"Agent Bartholomew," Stevenson said, "can we speak alone? Or at least with your partner?"

"I reckon that can be arranged. Lieutenant, you mind steppin' out for a cup of java? Make it a ten-minute cup."

The police officer glowered at Stevenson, then shoved back angrily. As much as he wanted the FBI to take responsibility, he didn't like being ordered around in his own precinct—and this was precisely what Bartholomew had done. Out, little boy, and let the men talk. He crashed out of the room.

"This better be good, Doc," said the FBI agent whose name Stevenson couldn't remember. He wished he could see Elaine for a few minutes. She was always better at names and faces than he was. She wouldn't have forgotten this quickly, no matter what pressure they put her under.

"This is a national-security matter. I told this to the lieutenant at the outset."

"The Devlins don't look like the sort of folks to be keepin' national secrets, now, do they?" Bartholomew said. He heaved a chair around and sat in it, resting his forearms on the back of the chair. He leaned forward and balanced his chin on his crossed arms. "Why don't you just fess up and tell us what happened 'fore the lieutenant gets back from his coffee break? It'll make this a mite easier on all of us."

"Have you contacted either General Beaumont or General Morningside?"

"That's a stickin' point, Doc. Seems they're both out on a New Year's hoot-'n'-holler mission. Getting a tad soused, 'less I miss a guess. Don't need to spoil their New Year's celebratin', if you'd talk some to us."

Stevenson stared straight ahead at the large mirror. It was a two-way mirror. The police lieutenant was undoubtedly on the other side with a psychiatrist, recording every word in the room.

"The National Secrets Act prohibits me from discussing the details of what's happened. I have no knowledge about the Devlins' death. Contact Major Zamora—"

"We've been trying to find this elusive Air Force major," the tall, thin FBI agent said. "There doesn't seem to be anyone in the area by that name. We've put in a search-and-find request with the military. They ought to get back to us around the third or fourth." He didn't have to add that Stevenson was likely to stay locked up until then. The threat hung in the air like a heavy L.A. smog.

"Dennis here is a mite impatient," Bartholomew said. "Can't say I blame him much. You're tryin' *my* patience, and I'm known far and wide as a real patient fellow."

Bartholomew found another toothpick and stuck it into his mouth.

"Have you verified my employment?" Stevenson asked.

"Reckon not. This Fort Detrick place is all shut up for the holidays. We're trying to get in touch with someone in Washington, D.C. but they're slippery there too. Tell us about the Devlins."

Stevenson had been grilled for more than two hours. He had repeated his story more times than he could remember. Either the police lieutenant or the FBI agent named Dennis would leap on the slightest variation in tellings, but Bartholomew had always remained aloof. Stevenson took it as a good sign that the stocky agent was assuming a greater role in the questioning.

"I'll cooperate fully, but only in a secured area. Mc-Clellan Air Force Base must have such a facility. Major Zamora and his team landed there almost a week ago."

"You keep comin' back to this Zamora fellow. He wouldn't be that wetback Lennie Zamora who's all the time tryin' to organize the melon pickers, would he?"

"He's an Air Force major, Special Operations Force. I forget the unit. First Special Operations Wing out of Eglin Air Force Base."

"Now, that's a long ways to come. Redding's not exactly on a flight path between Florida and much of anywhere, now, is it, Doc?"

"They wouldn't have pulled the FBI in if there hadn't been a national-security angle. You must know what's going on. Charge me with a crime or let me go. I've made a full and accurate statement concerning the Devlins."

Stevenson had reached the end of his patience. If they charged him, he got a phone call. He'd make it to the largest local newspaper affiliated with a press service. Beaumont and Morningside and Fred Wyman and the president would hear about this on the morning news. If he was going to swing for his crime, he'd make life hell for all of them. But he wasn't going to put up with another minute of this harassment.

"You're in no position to give orders," Dennis said. Stevenson wondered if that was the man's first or last name. As casual as Bartholomew was, it might be a given name.

"You're in no position to hold me, either," Stevenson snapped. "Whoever cut up Mrs. Devlin spilled a hell of a lot of blood. The only blood on my clothes was on shoes and pants legs. Neighbors must have seen Dr. Reinhardt and me drive up. You *have* asked around if anyone saw us enter the Devlin house? And I'm sure Dr. Crane at Trinity Hospital will confirm that we were with him less than a half-hour before we called in the murders. I'm no expert, but I doubt anyone can skin a person like that in only a few minutes."

"Shows what you know, Doc," Bartholomew said, his face somber. "As to holdin' you, we can do that for forty-eight hours. Questioning and all that, but it's messy. We wouldn't go doin' that 'less you made us."

"I've said my piece. Charge me, let me get a lawyer, or believe me when I say I don't have any idea at all who killed the Devlins."

"You want us to believe that," Dennis said, "but you won't tell us what you're doing in Redding?"

"That's classified. Show me a clearance and get me authorization of your need to know, and everything I know is yours for the asking—but it won't do you a damned bit of good."

"We'll be the judge of that." Dennis shoved his face to within an inch of Stevenson's. The biophysicist didn't flinch. He didn't blink. He didn't move a muscle, and the FBI agent backed down.

Stevenson locked eyes with Bartholomew. Neither man said anything. Stevenson was damned if he was going to break now. He had endured grillings as difficult as this. Talking with the president about the bio-neutral-cell experiment aboard the Keyhole satellite had frightened him. He had never met anyone with so much power over him before—and the president's power was vastly greater than that of the FBI agents.

A rap sounded on the door and the lieutenant stuck his head in. "I want a word with you. Now!"

Bartholomew confirmed Stevenson's estimation of who was senior agent. He pushed back from his chair and motioned that Dennis was to stay with their prisoner. The overweight agent returned less than a minute later.

"This is your lucky day, Doc. We're releasin' you."

"Just like that?" The suddenness of it startled Stevenson. He wondered what had been said outside the interrogation room. Whatever it was, it had come down from the mountaintop like the Ten Commandments.

"Just like that. We thought over the passel of things you said and it sounded good to us. Good-bye."

"What about Dr. Reinhardt?"

"She's a real pretty lady, isn't she? She's waitin' for you out in the lobby." Bartholomew dropped an envelope with Stevenson's belongings onto the table.

Stevenson didn't press his luck. He stuffed his possessions into his pockets and left without another word. He had the gut-level feeling that he hadn't seen the last of Special Agent Bartholomew.

"Elaine!" He crossed the dirty lobby of the precinct station and hugged her.

"They finally let you go. I didn't think they would ever stop asking questions."

"They let me go too fast. Did Zamora get through to Morningside?"

"I haven't seen the major. I think he and his team have been pulled out. They might be back in Florida by now."

"Great," Stevenson said in disgust. "We're cut loose for no good reason, and are on our own until we can contact someone in the Pentagon about this. I can't believe Zamora would strand us at the Devlin house like he did."

"His orders must have been specific on the point. I didn't care much for him, but the major seemed a decent-enough fellow," Elaine said.

Stevenson took Elaine's arm and guided her out of the police station. He doubted they had been cut loose, not entirely. When they had gone a half-block, he said in a low voice, "They're probably following us. I didn't divulge anything about Project Big Hunk."

"Or the satellite," Elaine said. "Me neither. I can't believe they thought we killed those two. My God!"

"We were convenient and the only lead they're likely to get. Whoever killed the Devlins did so for a reason."

"But what?"

Stevenson fumbled through his pockets and came out

with the lenses he had found in Billy Devlin's room. He held up the discolored glass lens and shuddered.

"I think they wanted the experiment." Even as he said it, Stevenson wondered who had known it was aboard the satellite.

31

George Wyatt didn't enjoy the luxury of riding in first class. He was sick to his stomach during the entire trip to New Orleans. The stewardess was nice and tried to help, but nothing stayed down. Soda pop, fruit juice, nothing. And George couldn't bear the thought of eating the airline food, even though it looked better than he had gotten on the trip to his grandparents'.

Head pressed against the cool window, George stared down and saw the once tiny spots growing in size. The airplane was descending. His ears usually popped, but they hadn't this time.

He was glad to be home, but he wished his grandma had talked his grandfather into coming with him. The man in the seat next to him when they'd taken off from San Francisco International had asked for another seat, even one in coach. George didn't blame him much. Who wanted to sit next to a kid vomiting for five hours?

Somehow, the plane landed and George didn't notice. The stewardess gently touched his shoulder and brought him around with a start.

"We're on the ground. Would you like to be the first off? We'll hold back the other passengers."

"Thanks. My dad ought to be waiting for me. I appreciate everything you've done."

The dark-haired woman smiled weakly and muttered something about hoping he would be over his flu soon. George wiped sweat from his forehead and tried to get his wits about him. Just standing proved to be an unexpected chore. He steadied himself on a seat, then made his way forward just as the door opened.

"You take care of yourself," the stewardess said. The other two stewardesses said nothing.

George thanked her as he walked haltingly along the jetway. Twice dizziness hit him, and he thought he was going to be sick again. He kept walking and saw his dad waiting outside the chained-off walk.

"Dad!" For a moment his sickness vanished. He ran forward and threw his arms around his father.

"You're looking puny, son," said Hank Wyatt. "Let's get you home."

"How's mother?" George tried to concentrate on the answer. A roaring in his ears wouldn't go away, and his guts felt as if they were coming loose as he walked.

"She's home and waiting for you. We'll all be together again." Hank Wyatt stopped and looked hard at his son. "George, you're not feeling good at all, are you? I know Peter said you were sick, but I thought it was just the flu."

"It is the flu." That was the worst sickness George had ever endured other than a bout with the mumps. This was worse, but the symptoms were close.

"There's nothing you need in your bag. I'll come back for it later. I want to get you home and into bed."

"My suitcase has got stuff in it," George said, his mouth drier than a desert. "A present for Mom."

"She can do without it for a day or two. I want the nurse to check you out. Come on. We can be home in an hour. Let me have your ticket and the claim check."

George reluctantly passed over the ticket with the purple-and-black stub stapled to the envelope. He wanted to give his mother the shining crystal tube with the bright green snow in it. She could set it on her bedside table and let the sun shine on it and make the rainbows that had so intrigued him.

She could do that, but later. Sickness washed over him once more and he had to lean more on his father than he liked. George was unconscious during the entire trip home.

32

Lisa Taylor finished stripping off the nurse's uniform in the backseat of the car. She scowled when she couldn't find the cap, then pushed it from her mind. The uniform was rented; what did she care? All she had wanted to do was blend into the faceless mass of nurses at Trinity Memorial, and the uniform had worked. She had changed the schedule when the duty nurse wasn't looking, and had assigned herself to Billy Devlin.

She slithered into a jumpsuit. The weather had turned cold once more, and slipping around on the freezing vinyl seat sucked up her body's warmth. Running her fingers over her legs and up her sides, she vented a long animal sigh of sheer pleasure. She was damned good-looking, she thought, even if she had a face no one remembered for long. She might not have the facial looks, but she had the body, and that was what mattered.

"It was stupid to do this," the man in the front seat said as he took the turns in the narrow road leading away from Redding.

"What was that?" she said, angry at any criticism. The mission had gone perfectly.

"This." He tossed her nametag back. "Someone will remember it."

"No one in America reads anymore," she said haughtily. "They will not remember. They won't get the joke."

"The movie, the movie, you . . ." He hesitated to call her a stupid bitch. He still needed her and her contacts.

"There was a movie, and Louise Fletcher won an Academy Award in 1975 for this role. It's memorable."

"John, shut the fuck up. You can quote all you've memorized and it doesn't mean shit. I don't care about baseball scores or old movies or any of the other crap they've forced into your head. No one noticed." Even as she said it, Lisa Taylor remembered how Stevenson had commented on her name. It *had* been foolish vanity on her part.

"You are native-born. You think of the others around you with contempt. There are some here who are not stupid." The man settled down and stared at the winding dirt road in front of him. The mud made driving treacherous, but he took the turns skillfully, doing the four-wheel drifts with just enough flare to get the adrenaline pumping in his arteries. His controllers in Dzerzhinskiy Square had prepared him well, no matter what the bitch said.

And he could recite all World Series winners, batting averages, and the other trivia Americans doted on.

"You got their experiment. That is what matters," she said. She smoothed the wrinkles in her tight-fitting jumpsuit, then stretched languidly. For this mission they would pay her well. She could buy the house down in Monterey she had been eyeing for so long.

"There is the check-in point," John said. He took his foot off the gas and coasted. Only after some of their forward speed had diminished did he apply the brakes, and then he did so gingerly. The dirty, nondescript car slowed to a halt just a few feet from the covered porch jutting out from the rustic cabin.

"Your equipment is in there?"

"Yes." He had almost given himself away by saying "*da*." His instructors had drilled this single point into him repeatedly and, for all the memory work he had accomplished, some reflexes were difficult to extinguish.

Lisa Taylor jumped from the car and dashed to the porch. The cold wind sucked at her body, strangely invigorating her. She preferred warmer weather, or more moderate temperatures. Monterey was frequently chilly and wet, but it was seldom as freezing cold as this. The ocean, the lovely, powerful ocean, mediated the temperature. She could sit and watch its primal movement for hours.

"I will need help," John said. "I removed much of interest from the house." He opened the car's trunk and rummaged inside. "I would handle the containers with great care." He pulled out long-handled tongs to use on the pair of cylinders.

From her vantage on the porch, Lisa watched. Her lips pulled back into a tight, thin line of disapproval. She had discovered a couple weeks earlier that her country was dabbling in biological warfare again. This proved it and confirmed the truthfulness of her informant. She was glad she had sold out the capitalist pigs in Washington. Thinking of her spying and betrayal as treason pleased her in an odd way. She wasn't able to vote them out of office; they continued to do whatever they pleased. Once elected, they were in for life—or at least ninety-eight percent were, thanks to the immense sums of money pumped into their campaigns by political-action committees. Her work for the KGB was profitable both financially and politically.

Vote them out? She could do more. She could counter the worst policies and leaders in the century. The two containers John wrestled from the back of the car were proof that the U.S. plotted terrorism. Why else would a nation with such a prodigious stockpile of nuclear weapons develop biological weapons?

She had no desire for the contents to be released on the country of her birth—or anywhere else. If the Kremlin could use the cylinders to shame the U.S. into cessation of their experimentation, all the better.

"There are two varieties," John said, swinging one around and balancing it on the trunk lid. "This is gray. The other contains green particles."

"What are they?"

"Our scientists will have to find out."

Lisa swung open the cabin door for him. As a nurse, she had worked in too many ICU's; she had seen the result of military experiment and "war games" too many times. Hating it all did nothing to stop it.

John carried the tube with the gray gluey substance in it up the steps and into the cabin, then returned for the cylinder with the green matter. Sweat poured down his cheeks.

"It is nerve-racking work," he said, "dealing with such deadly material."

"You said you didn't know what it did."

"It is killing the Devlin boy by inches. You saw him. He had the two cylinders in his room. Is it not obvious he exposed himself to the bio-war reagent?"

Lisa Taylor sat across the room from the holder John had used for the gleaming twin quartz cylinders. She stared at them as if this would make them yield their deadly secrets to her.

"Why did the boy have them? Why were they even on the satellite? That model is a spy satellite, one equipped with optical gadgets."

John shrugged. It didn't matter to him. Lisa had received only the briefest of explanations for the deadly presence. Her informant had said the experiment was too important to conduct on Earth. He mentioned concern over it escaping and contaminating the entire country, so they placed it in space.

"The green one is so pretty. It's hard to think it might be dangerous." She craned her neck to get a better look at the dancing motes in the tube. Their motion in the sunlight was brilliant and almost hypnotic. She could understand why the boy had stolen the experiment from the crashed KH-18.

"If I must venture a guess, it is the dangerous one. The other tube has not been breached. Seals on its valve are intact. Whatever infected the boy came from that tube."

John indicated the one with the green dust floating in solution.

"It's amazing that something this pretty can be so dangerous. How did his parents react when you said you wanted to search his room?"

John smiled winningly. She was so stupid. "They obeyed quickly when I showed them my credentials. The golden badge is powerful. They did not ask to see other ID."

"Wouldn't have mattered," Lisa Taylor said. "You had it, didn't you?"

"I have several different kinds of identification, but in assorted names. They might not have noticed." His nose wrinkled slightly at the memory of the man he had killed with the single quick cut across the throat. The man's blood had spewed forth like a geyser. "The man had been drinking heavily, and it was not even midday." Things had been more difficult with the woman. Torture had proved necessary to break through the alcoholic fog and make her confess to knowing nothing about the tubes. They knew nothing about their son's link to the American experiment.

John trusted his skills in torture and truth extraction. They had never failed him.

Before Lisa could bother him further, a distant humming sounded. John leapt to his feet and rushed to the wall, fingers searching beside the chimney. He pried loose two weathered planks and exposed a compact short-wave radio set recessed in the wall. He checked frequencies, then transmitted a short message. He waited, verified the code, then turned off the radio.

"Well?" asked Lisa. "What's the good word?"

"Good word?" The idiom caused him to falter for a moment. He had studied three years, and still American phrases caused him problems. "Ah, yes, the good word. We are to make it to the coast, between Eureka and San Francisco, where there is an old Russian settlement."

"Fort Ross," she said. "Dates back to the days of the czar."

"Ross Counter," John said. "An outpost in America in the early portion of the nineteenth century. It was—"

"I don't need a history lesson. What are we going to do? Will I get my money then?"

"We'll go to Ross Counter and wait for the signal from a sneak boat. A rubber raft will come ashore, bringing a senior KGB officer empowered to pay you. I will take the American bio-war experiment and return with him to a submarine."

"Good," Lisa said. "There wasn't any quibbling over my price for this mission?"

"You have earned it. They are pleased with your work, and your contact's."

Lisa beamed. She was getting rich off a brief affair with a man who thought he was a better lay than he really was. What other information might be hers from inside Fort Detrick if she returned and continued balling Stevenson's assistant? Whatever it might be, the Soviets would continue to pay well for it.

33

Tom Stevenson and Elaine Reinhardt sat in the twenty-two-fifty-a-night motel room. The small television was on, more for the low level of noise comfort it provided than for entertainment. Stevenson stared out the window. In the far distance to the west rose the Coast Ranges. The snowcapped mountains would have been postcard beautiful if he hadn't been so absorbed in his own troubles.

"I never thought I'd be spending the first days of the new year like this," Elaine said, sprawled on the hard bed. She had kicked off her boots and laced her hands behind her head. The pillow was too lumpy for comfort and the thin blanket hadn't been any match for the cold creeping in past windows and doors.

"We're in a real predicament," Stevenson said. "It's a good thing we both brought credit cards with us. I'm out of cash."

"So we wait for a bank to open and get an advance," Elaine said, knowing this wasn't what troubled him the most. She sat up and crossed her legs. "There's no way to find Zamora?"

"I've tried everything I know. It's as if the Earth opened up and swallowed him. He's been pulled back now that the satellite pieces have been recovered."

"What of Will?"

Stevenson shook his head. "Gorton and his men must have gone back with the SOF team. I tried calling Fort Detrick to get through to his division, but there's no one on the switchboard. We're cut off."

"Worse than cut off, Tom. We might be accused of two murders."

"The FBI agent—Bartholomew was his name—knows we didn't do it. Who would call the police after committing such a crime? Anyone with a lick of sense would have hightailed it out of town. And there's no motive, no weapon, no—"

"You're starting to sound like Bartholomew," she said. "But that's logical about getting away. The rest isn't, though."

"What do you mean?" He looked at her and saw she wasn't joking.

"If they dig deep enough, they'll find a motive: the experiment. We killed them to keep Project Big Hunk from being discovered and to avoid getting implicated in bio-warfare research gone wild."

Stevenson felt sweat beading on his forehead. "You're right," he said after thinking about the case that might be woven against them. "Especially if they find someone took my experiment from Billy's room. The entire house had been expertly searched, but the most careful attention was paid to the boy's room." He took out the lenses he had found there and bounced them in the palm of his hand. It was too bad the murderers hadn't taken these and left the tubes.

"Why did they want the experiment?" Elaine asked. "Come clean, Tom. You've never told me what it contained."

"There's nothing to tell, Elaine. I'm not pulling a need-to-know scam on you. Whoever killed the Devlins must have thought it was a bio-warfare project. Putting it into that damned spy satellite makes the experiment seem more important than it really is. What bothers me is that they knew the experiment was there. It was classified secret."

Elaine was silent for several minutes, allowing Stevenson to stew in his own ideas. They both came to the same conclusion.

"Well," she said, "who is it? Someone at Fort Detrick leaked this."

"To the Soviets? Would they kill two innocent people for a gray-gooey-gob experiment?"

"Maybe someone heard of the experiment and deemed it bigger than it is."

"There's still a leak. Who outside our department even knows about it?"

Stevenson worried that he had gone to the cafeteria one day and complained about putting an experiment into orbit. If that was the case, there was no telling who had known about Project Big Hunk. Still, everyone in the security area was supposed to be cleared. If he was right, there was a security leak.

"Jack," Elaine said, starting to tick off the people on her fingers. "How much did you tell him?"

"Very little. Most of this happened before he arrived."

"Basil was always poking around, but he didn't know too much about it, either."

Stevenson snorted. Basil Baker was adequate as a researcher but he lacked motivation. As long as he did an average job, he wasn't likely to be canned.

"Others drift in and out, but there's no way to check on them. I wish Morningside would get back in the office. I tried calling a few minutes ago and I couldn't even reach O'Connors. We've been cut adrift."

Elaine chewed on her knuckle for a moment, then said, "We'll get through to Beaumont or Morningside or somebody. They can't let us rot out here forever."

Stevenson snorted again. He wasn't sure about that. They might use them both as scapegoats if things really went to hell. He didn't have any illusion that the FBI had forgotten them. If anything, Bartholomew was the sly kind who would follow them until they compromised themselves.

There was even a word in FBI parlance for this: dangling. The agency would dangle a suspect, blatantly trailing him and trying to force him to panic and make an incriminating mistake. Stevenson wished he could do something to draw the attention of the DCI or even Fred Wyman. The higher the official noticing his predicament, the better off he was likely to be.

"We've got two choices," he said, coming to a decision. "We can let this run its course or we can try to force the issue. We're agreed that the Soviets are probably involved and that their agents have the cylinders from the experiment."

"It doesn't make any sense for the CIA or FBI to kill a citizen to seize something so easily. Whoever killed the Devlins did so to be sure they had all the information." Elaine grimaced. "As much as I dislike some of the CIA analysts I've met, I can't believe they'd do what was done to Mrs. Devlin."

Stevenson couldn't either. Under other circumstances, he might slip toward thinking they were sons of bitches who would callously murder, but not this time. All government officials needed to do was to ask General Beaumont for the files on Project Big Hunk. It wasn't even a *big* experiment, and full disclosure was theirs for the asking.

"We must ask Billy some questions about the experiment. He might have seen something more than the tubes with the gray gobs."

Stevenson clenched his fists and shook. He was a scientist, not a criminal investigator. Until he could get through the red tape and to Morningside, he had to do something. And it wasn't out of patriotism that he did it, either.

CYA. He had to protect himself and Elaine, avoid becoming scapegoats dragged through a public scrutiny that would ruin their careers. He wasn't proud of it, but the U.S. government should have tended its own business better. And why had Major Zamora been pulled so fast? Why had he disappeared without warning?

"To the hospital," he said firmly.

He pushed out of the chair and looked out the motel

window. The mountains were hidden once more behind thick billows of white clouds that promised snow. He saw no sign of an FBI tail. He tried to work meaning into the conundrum and failed. A dangle required them to conspicuously tail their suspect; Stevenson didn't see anyone out there. That didn't mean Bartholomew and his partner, Dennis, weren't secretively on the job.

"Let's do it," Elaine said, "but we're going to have to use the bus. I only have two dollars left."

Stevenson checked his wallet and pockets and came up with less than ten dollars. They hadn't come to Redding thinking about money; the government supplied everything during assignments.

"We can just make it if we stiff the driver," Stevenson said. He used the room telephone to call for a cab, then stewed for twenty minutes until it arrived.

Pooling all their change allowed them to pay the driver—barely—to drop them six blocks from Trinity Hospital. Stevenson saw this as a plus. The driver's logbook would show them at an address far enough away from the hospital for them to make alibis, if needed. But he didn't know if anyone was interested in what they did. He was working in a complete vacuum.

"What do we say?" Elaine asked. "We can always do a divide-and-conquer. Find the nurse and—"

"She won't be there," Stevenson interrupted. "She was a fake."

"What?"

His mind flashed through the possibilities. "She is tied in with the Devlins' deaths. I'm not sure how. I've seen her somewhere before, but I can't remember where. Nurse Ratched, indeed," he scoffed. A new idea occurred to him that turned him cold inside. Could his visit to Billy have triggered the Devlins' deaths? Had Nurse Ratched phoned an accomplice after she overheard him mention the downed satellite?

"We've got to find out the condition of the quartz containment cylinders," he said. "No matter how we get it from him, we've got to find out."

"Skin him alive, like his mother?"

"Not that," Stevenson said, but he was ambivalent on the amount of force to use. This was escalating into something beyond his capacity to understand. "There must be something about the experiment worth killing for."

"Come on, Tom. There's no chance for that. What could have happened?"

Together they retraced their path up the fire stairs. He looked for the discarded nurse's cap but didn't see it. The janitor had made his rounds in the stairs and had swept up all debris. The cap was probably in the garbage by now.

As he climbed, Stevenson tried to remember where he had seen the bogus nurse before. It fluttered just beyond recognition and bothered him like a buzzing mosquito; he was acutely aware of its presence but couldn't pin it down and kill it.

At the floor, he opened the door and peered down the hall. Matters had worsened. He saw a policeman slowly patrolling the hall. An empty chair stood beside the door leading to Billy's room. After his parents' death, he had been placed under protective custody. Whether the local lieutenant or the FBI had ordered the surveillance didn't matter. Getting to Billy was now almost impossible without creating a ruckus.

Stevenson pulled back and muttered to himself. Elaine asked what the problem was. After he told her, she said, "This might be a trap. They've probably moved the kid to an ICU, where the nurses can have him under visual observation."

"You're right," Stevenson said. "The monitoring equipment was good, but his condition was deteriorating rapidly. Dr. Crane had no idea what was wrong with him. They'd have him under close observation."

"I'll get some coffee and doughnuts and bring them to the nurses' lounge," Elaine said. "I've never known anyone to turn down free food. They'll drift in and out. You might have a minute or two to talk with Billy if I can distract them."

It wasn't much, but it was all Stevenson could hope for. "How will you pay for the food?"

Elaine pulled a credit card from a pants pocket. "Never leave home without it."

"Go on," he urged. "I'll get past the cop and find the ICU. I want to be ready when you bring in the coffee."

"It'll be a while," she warned. "At least ten minutes."

Stevenson gave her a quick kiss, then turned to worry about the police officer. The man was alert, too alert. Stevenson climbed up another flight of stairs, found a directory near the elevator, and found the intensive-care unit listed on the third floor. He retraced his path, going past the fifth floor, where Billy had been before, and stopped before the door with the big white-painted numeral three. He took a deep breath, peered out and down the corridor, and saw a half-dozen nurses at a desk in the center of a circular area. Their patients were behind glass. There were too many nurses for Elaine's ruse to work.

He slipped into the corridor and darted into a linen room. The pungent smell of cleaning solution hit him like a hammer, but Stevenson saw what he needed. A lab coat hung over the edge of a laundry hamper. He put it on, making a face when he saw the blood stains on the front. Whoever had worn it earlier had wisely put it here for cleaning. No patient liked to see his doctor looking as if he had just butchered a steer.

Stevenson picked up a clipboard and tried to look official as he walked down the hall. He glanced at the empty clipboard several times, as if performing useful duty. All the while, his gray eyes shot back and forth, looking for Billy Devlin. He found the boy in an ICU with a nurse beside him. She checked his vital signs, entered notations, and started out.

Stevenson moved so that they collided. He gave her a quick glance, saw that he had been right about the nurses' caps being different from Nurse Ratched's, then said, "Pardon me. Wasn't looking where I was going."

"That's all right," she said, more irritated than curious.

"How's the boy?" he asked, hoping this wasn't pushing his luck too far. The nurses at the central desk must be staring at him by now. He was an invading bacterium, and they were the white cells waiting to flock and crush him to death.

"He won't make it through the night," she said bluntly. Before the nurse could ask what his interest was—and who the hell he was—Elaine bustled onto the floor.

"Coffee, doughnuts, all yours for the taking. Come and get it before it's gone."

The nurse beside Stevenson pushed past him to see what this strange offer was. Stevenson never hesitated. The instant her back was turned, he stepped into the alcove where Billy was hooked up to IV's, monitoring equipment, and devices Stevenson couldn't even guess at.

"Billy," he said urgently. "Can you hear me?"

"Sorta," Billy whispered. "Who're you?"

The boy didn't remember him from the earlier visit. Stevenson took that to be a good sign—and a bad one. The boy's mental alertness was fading fast.

"Tell me about the crystalline tubes you found in the satellite."

"I didn't take them. He did."

"Who?" Stevenson didn't get an answer. He wanted to shake the boy, but knew better. The electrodes glued to his body would set off a cacophony of signals that not even the deaf and blind could miss. Stevenson felt time running out on him.

"Are the cylinders in your bedroom, Billy?"

"They're so pretty. Such a pretty green. Got three, but only poured the green into another one."

"What are you talking about?" Stevenson asked. He picked up the boy's chart and glanced at it. He couldn't make out most of the medical arcana there, but he did see that they had tried to X-ray him. Radiation had burned a small hole in one negative of his chest. The microgram of plutonium was firmly lodged in a lobe of the left lung. Stevenson was glad to see that Crane had somehow diagnosed the boy's illness as radiation damage, but couldn't decide what course of action the doctor was taking. Opening Billy up and taking out the left lung might have saved him.

As it was, he had sustained too much physical and chemical damage from the poisonous speck caught inside his chest.

"What is pretty green?" Stevenson repeated.

"The stuff in tube. Green flakes. Like green snow. Green snow."

"It isn't gray? There isn't gray sludge in the tubes?" Stevenson realized that his brief interview was over. From a brain-wave trace, he understood that Billy had slipped into a coma.

He had pushed his luck to the limits—and he wasn't sure what he had found. Stevenson left just seconds before a nurse came from the lounge, coffee cup in hand. He kept walking even when she called after him. By the time he got to the stairwell, alarms were ringing.

Billy Devlin had died. But from what? The plutonium caught in his lung? Or a miscalculation in Project Big Hunk's design?

34

"Hello, Dr. Stevenson. How is the boy doing?"

Stevenson swung around guiltily. Standing just inside the hospital lobby, Larry Bartholomew picked his teeth with a battered toothpick. He looked more the part of a ragtag homeless person than a special agent for the FBI.

"Not too well," Stevenson said, seeing no point in lying. It would take only a few seconds for the agent to verify that Stevenson had been in the intensive-care unit and that Elaine had decoyed the nurses away with her coffee and doughnuts. "He won't make it. He has a speck of plutonium in his lungs."

"I spoke to the boy's doctor about that. Where could such a radioactive material have originated? Could you enlighten us all, Doc?"

"All right," Stevenson said. If Beaumont and Morningside and the Pentagon and all the rest back in Washington were going to strand him in the field, he saw no good reason to fall back on the need-to-know and national-security arguments. Lives had been lost.

What worried him was Billy Devlin's odd statement about the green snow in the cylinders. Had the boy opened them and replaced the gray gooey gobs with something else? Or had the experiment gone crazy in space due to some unforeseen factor? The radiation from the atomic battery? Stevenson needed time to sit and work it out.

"Good, glad to hear you're goin' to tell us some more things we never heard before. Let's wait a second. Den-

nis is bringin' your friend down in a few minutes."
Bartholomew scratched himself. Stevenson wondered if
this was a down-home country-hick act to make his victims underestimate him. If so, it wasn't working in Stevenson's case. He saw the sharpness in Bartholomew's
eye, the intelligence boiling inside his pumpkin-shaped
head.

"There's the little dickens now. Come on over here,
Dennis. Bring the little lady with you."

"That's a good way to get your balls handed to you
one at a time," Stevenson said under his voice.

"Do tell. Most womenfolk are like that now." Louder,
for Elaine's benefit, Bartholomew said, "This way, Dr.
Reinhardt. We're going to have a little conference where
we won't be disturbed."

"By whom?" she asked coldly. Elaine jerked her arm
free of Dennis' grasp. "By the people who cut up the
Devlins?"

"That's what I want to talk about. I reckon we can
come back here in an hour or two and tidy up this end of
the mess. The boy didn't suffer much toward the end, did
he?"

Elaine shot Stevenson a quick look. He shook his head
slightly, indicating that the FBI agent had figured this out
alone.

Bartholomew led the way outside into the cold air.
The sun was setting and the mountains, both east and
west, had vanished into the bluster of a newly forming
snowstorm. Stevenson pulled his jacket tighter around
him, wondering how Elaine was faring. She was always
cold, even in the summer. How she could eat, metabolize
her food, and still have cold hands, feet, and nose escaped him.

"That flea trap of a motel you holed up in is probably
the best for asking and answering questions," Bartholomew
said.

Stevenson sat in stoic silence as Bartholomew drove
through Redding. He skidded to a halt at the motel just

off I-5 and let them out. "You two go on in. Dennis and I'll be along in a second. We got some stuff to fetch from the trunk."

"They've wired our room," Stevenson said on the way in.

"So what do they think they're going to learn? That you talk in your sleep?"

"They still believe we killed the Devlins. That's the only explanation for their presence." Stevenson fell silent when he pushed into the small, barren room. He noted that the television set that had been on when they left was now off. Maid service at this dump was almost nonexistent.

"Here, now, you folks just set yourselves down and let me tell you what's what." Bartholomew's eyes darted from the silent TV set to Stevenson and then to Dennis. In that instant Stevenson knew who had forgotten to turn the set back on. As he had thought, Dennis wasn't the brains of the duo.

Bartholomew dropped a report on the bed between Stevenson and Elaine. "Take a look at that and tell me what you think."

Stevenson picked it up. The top sheet told him Bartholomew was showing them the report on the Devlin murders. He scanned the report and saw mention several times of his part in reporting the crime, but no hint that either he or Elaine was a suspect.

"So?" Stevenson dropped it on the bed. If Elaine wanted to look at it, she could. She let it lie where it had fallen.

"I've been tryin' my damnedest to find out how you got here. This story of yours about a commando Major Zamora from Florida seemed too farfetched to believe."

"It's true." Stevenson wished he had a few minutes to speak with Elaine. He hadn't had a chance to tell her about Billy's dying statements.

He needed an ally. If help wasn't forthcoming from

Fort Detrick or the Pentagon or the president, it had to come from the FBI.

"He died from plutonium inhalation," Stevenson said, taking a deep breath. Elaine looked at him, eyes wide. She started to speak, then clamped her mouth shut.

"That's what Crane said. I don't know how he could have found any radioactive debris out here. Why, that nuclear plant—Arroyo Seco, they call it—is miles from here."

"It doesn't use or produce plutonium," Stevenson said. "It's not only shut down for years and empty of fuel rods but it only had uranium inside."

"Plutonium?" Dennis looked confused. He scribbled in a spiral notebook, then looked up, hoping someone would tell him what was going on. Stevenson thought he might not be as dense as he seemed. Like Bartholomew, he might have his methods for making a suspect underestimate him and make a mistake.

"The Air Force lost a satellite," Stevenson said.

"Tom, wait. They don't have a need to know. We should clear this with General Morningside."

"Or Beaumont or Fred Wyman?" he asked. Stevenson shook his head. They were cut loose and on their own. Whoever called for Major Zamora's return to Eglin AFB was responsible for their predicament. Their very careers— their freedom—were on the line. Need to know served no good purpose now. People had died who shouldn't have.

"Would that be General Edwin Beaumont and the president's national security adviser you're talking about?" Dennis asked. Bartholomew shot him a cold stare that quieted him.

"Put down that I'm cooperating," Stevenson said. "I know a couple murders isn't FBI territory. You would let the local police handle this if there wasn't a national-security angle in it."

Bartholomew picked at his back teeth with the broken toothpick but said nothing. From the alertness in his eyes, though, Stevenson knew he was on the right track. The FBI didn't care about a few deaths, even grisly ones like the Devlins'. Something else had kept them interested.

"A KH-18 spy satellite crashed a few miles outside Redding. That was where the UFO sightings originated. We came to clean it up. A radiation-hazards team from Fort Detrick came with us—we're with the Army NBC command—the Nuclear-Biological-Chemical Command. General Morningside is in charge of our research group."

"You're a biophysicist and she's a biologist. Unless I miss a guess, you're her boss, and you're saying this Morningside is *your* boss?" Bartholomew waited for an answer, but Stevenson saw that the agent watched for body language. Bartholomew got more information that way than he ever could from simple verbal responses.

"That's right. We came out because an experiment of mine, a minor experiment, really, was aboard the satellite."

"Wait, wait, what's an Army-employed biophysicist doing puttin' an experiment into an Air Force spy satellite?"

"Just accept that it happened," Stevenson said. "The bird crashed and the contents of the atomic battery used to power it were scattered across a few hundred square yards."

"This is where the plutonium came from that killed the boy?"

Stevenson nodded. "Billy must have been poking around in the debris, maybe following up on the reported UFO sighting. He had these." Stevenson pulled out the cracked, discolored lenses and put them on the table beside Bartholomew. "They're part of the satellite's optical system."

Stevenson tried to sort out what he had just said. A tiny clue to something bigger nudged and prodded but refused to come full-born into his head.

"Billy scrounged around and sucked in some of your plutonium—"

"It's not *our* plutonium," Elaine snapped. "We had

nothing to do with the radioactive source inside that bird. We thought they powered it with solar cells."

"Reckon this is a sore point," Bartholomew allowed. "You folks might be liable for the boy's death if it was your doing to put this atomic battery inside the satellite."

"She's right. We didn't know they were furnishing it with a radioisotope thermoelectric generator power source." Stevenson saw that this went by both men. He hurried on. "The plutonium dioxide scattered when the power module hit the ground, and Billy was contaminated—and he took our experiment."

"You willing to tell us the nature of this here experiment?"

"It wasn't supposed to be anything important," Elaine cut in. "It wasn't!"

"The experiment might have been . . . altered," Stevenson said slowly. Elaine shot him a look of pure fire. "Billy said the cylinders with the nutrient solution and the gray gooey gobs contained green snow."

"Green snow? What is this, Larry? We're getting a fairy tale from them." Dennis snorted in disgust and tossed a torn sheet from his notebook toward the trashcan with fair accuracy.

"Don't play good-cop/bad-cop now, Dennis," Bartholomew said gently. "The time's passed for that game. I'm hearing the truth. Don't much understand some of it, but what the doc's saying is the gospel."

"I've tried to call my superiors and there's nobody home."

"I've thought that for years," Bartholomew chuckled. "Go on, Doc. Don't let me interrupt you. What happened to your green-snow experiment?"

"Whoever killed the Devlins must have it," Stevenson said. "Elaine and I have discussed this part of the whole mess, and there must be a spy at work at Fort Detrick. It's the only way we can explain all that's happened."

"Great," Dennis grumbled. "We got dead bodies, we got goddamn spies now."

"There's nothing more we can give you," Stevenson

said. "I shouldn't have told you about Project Big Hunk, but something's got to be done fast to get those quartz tubes back. If something has altered the contents, they might be dangerous now."

"Radiation," Elaine said. "Mutation from exposure to the plutonium-dioxide pellets from the atomic battery might have done it."

"Elaine, please. Later."

Bartholomew looked back and forth between them. He scratched his crotch, then folded his hands on his protuberant belly. "We might have a KGB agent involved," he said. "The torture aspect of the killing struck a chord when I saw it on the wire. At first, the locals thought it fitted the MO of a serial killer back in Minnesota, which is the reason I got the call over in San Francisco. I ran it through the computers in Washington and came up with a surprise. Sure enough, there was a similar mutilation killing, but it was laid at the doorstep of a Soviet agent, code name John."

"John? How imaginative," Elaine said sarcastically. She settled back and crossed her arms, eyes staring straight at Bartholomew.

"Don't get me wrong, Dr. Reinhardt. The man's damn dangerous. We had less than an hour's hint that he was even in the area. He moves quick and quiet and seldom makes a mistake. He is a real pro. Would he be able to turn this experiment of yours into any kind of political hay?"

"You mean, did the U.S. violate any biological-warfare treaties? No," Stevenson said firmly. "What happened must be considered an unfortunate accident. The experiment—we call it a gray-gooey-gob experiment—was intended to be absolutely harmless."

"I'll believe you on that point, Doc. Now, see if you can make me believe you on another point. Who leaked all this to the Russians? They didn't send John out here for his health, and he must have arrived here before you made it out from Fort Detrick. The KGB *knew* something heavy was going down. *How did they know?*"

Stevenson started to answer, but the details fled before they slipped from his tongue. He sat numbly on the bed shaking his head. He had the answers—almost. He just couldn't put it all together properly.

35

"I don't feel too good," George Wyatt said. His voice rasped out and the nurse had to bend over to hear the boy's words.

"Your temperature spiked again," she said softly. He knew that his condition had turned for the worse. The nurse spent more time with him than with his mother.

"Get me some orange juice?" he asked.

"I'll be right back." The nurse left his room and heaved a sigh of relief that she was away from the boy. She worked with terminal patients, but watching them sink closer and closer to death wore her down. Margaret Wyatt was resting quietly. The nurse had the unexpected burden of a sick teenager in the same household—and he was fading faster than his mother.

She sought out Mr. Wyatt. The man sat, as he did most of the day now, staring at the television. He stared to hypnotize himself into believing everything would work out for the best.

"Mr. Wyatt, your son is getting worse. His temperature went up to one-oh-one again and it's going higher. It might peak at one-oh-three by midnight."

"It's not the flu, is it?"

"It's not like any flu I ever saw. It'd be best for you and him if he checked into University Hospital, where the doctors can watch him."

"The cost," he mumbled, his mind forced back into action. "We've already used everything for Margie."

"Sir, he's dying too." The nurse bit her tongue as she

spoke. This wasn't the proper bedside manner. A nurse or doctor never came right out and said something like this without careful preparation. She stared at Henry Wyatt's drawn face and decided he was as prepared as anyone might be, but it was for his wife's death. The loss of a son and a spouse might be more than he could handle, and she hated herself for being so blunt. But the nurse had no other choice. She wasn't able to do anything for the boy.

She watched his face for a reaction, certain now that she had done the right thing. He was in shock and needed a hard jolt to get him thinking again. Later, when he had taken care of his responsibilities, he could wallow in self-pity.

"He needs a doctor," Wyatt said, stating what had been obvious since the boy had come home three days earlier.

"I can't prescribe medication for him," the nurse said. She rubbed her hands on her crisp pastel uniform. She couldn't even *guess* what was wrong with George.

"Should we take him in directly?"

"It's best if you do it. I can stay with Mrs. Wyatt, but I'll phone ahead so they'll expect you. That will eliminate the check-in hassle."

"Thanks," Henry Wyatt said. "I'd better pack something for George. Then we'll leave."

She watched him and shook her head. More and more, he was the one needing hospitalization. His zombielike demeanor told of serious problems. After taking care of his son, he could tend to his own psychic wounds.

"I don't know what to tell you, Mr. Wyatt," Dr. Akhbar said. "I've run blood tests, X-rayed him, done everything I can think of, and nothing seems to be wrong."

"But he's sick. I can tell that." A flare of anger burned away the man's lethargy.

"Without any doubt, but we can't pinpoint it. Leave him with us and we'll keep him under observation."

Wyatt stared at Dr. Akhbar and tried to formulate his inchoate thoughts. They never cured anything. They poked and prodded and vampirically turned their patients anemic with dozens of blood tests a day and they never *found* anything. They always experimented and never cured. Never, never, never.

"He's sick. He's running a temperature. Do something to lower it."

"We're hesitant to use our regular techniques until we find out what's causing his condition," Dr. Akhbar said. "Aspirin is good for lowering temperature but it can trigger viral infections in young children. Acetaminophen isn't quite as good for lowering temperature, and it has other side effects too. If George has a kidney problem, for instance, the acetaminophen can exacerbate the condition."

"I understand," Wyatt said. "Why not reduce his temperature with cold packs?"

Dr. Akhbar's lips thinned. He hated it when patients or family tried to second-guess him.

"We're doing what we can. In some ways a temperature is a healthy sign that the body is fighting off infection. Since we can't isolate the proximate cause, it might be best to let the fever run its course and monitor George's other vital signs. Go home now, Mr. Wyatt, get some rest. Here, take this."

The doctor scribbled a prescription.

"This is a tranquilizer. It'll relax you."

"Thank you," Wyatt said, turning and leaving without even glancing at the slip of paper. He had a drawer filled with them at home. Most he had never bothered to have filled. It had been too much bother, and what did he need with more expenses?

Now he had to face the ugly prospect of losing his only child because modern medical science hadn't a clue why he was sick.

Henry Wyatt sat in the hospital lobby and assimilated what had happened to him. A hard core of anger formed deep within him, a center that he had thought long gone. It bubbled and boiled faster and began to burn his soul. Giving up solved nothing. Fighting was the only way to win.

He stood and walked from the lobby with a purposeful stride. The doctors didn't know anything. It was up to him to track down the source of his son's illness. The best place to start was at the source.

"Peter?" The static on the telephone line almost drowned out his father-in-law's voice. "Can you hear me?"

"Fine," came Peter Stratton's reply. "Is everything all right?"

The anxiety in the man's voice reminded Wyatt that Margie was sick too and that the Strattons worried about their daughter. Peter probably thought he was calling with bad news.

He was, but not about Margie.

"Margie is doing as well as expected," Wyatt said. "She's resting peacefully here at home. The nurse is with her right now."

"Glad to hear it. Did George get home all right? He was throwing up before his departure."

"That's what I'm calling about. He's in the hospital, but he's as well as can be expected."

Wyatt damned himself for falling into the clichés he had been using when friends and relatives called during the past few months asking after Margie's health. What else was there to say about someone who died a little more each day and took a part of you with her?

"We worried he'd have to go in. What does the doctor say?"

"They can't tell what's wrong. They're running all their . . . tests." He held back saying "goddamn" for some reason. Whenever he spoke with Margie's parents, he found himself falling into the same childhood patterns he did with his own parents: children don't swear in front of their elders.

"That's too bad. Is there anything we can do? I'd meant to box up George's telescope and send it along, but I can't find it."

"That's all right. I'll ask him when I see him tomorrow."

Wyatt's mind raced past such expensive baubles as the Celestron.

"I wanted to ask if any of his friends out there were sick too. It would help the doctors if they could find out what he was doing."

"I doubt he had time to make any friends. Let me ask his grandmother."

Wyatt heard the phone hit the hard tabletop. The heavy static kicked in again, drowned out much of the muffled conversation, then vanished with startling rapidity. The telephone line was as pure and clean as if it were a dedicated fiber optic cable strung between New Orleans and Redding.

Peter Stratton's voice came back, as distinct as a silver bell. "She doesn't know. But most of the people here are retired, like us and don't have kids. There are the Devlins, though, a few blocks over. They have a boy about George's age, though I wonder what's happening with them since the police dropped by a few days ago. He's an alcoholic and beats his wife, so that may explain their visit, but I'm not sure . . . The Camerons and the Canfields also have young children, I think."

"If you could ask around and see if any of their kids are sick, that would help out a lot."

"I—" Peter Stratton cut off suddenly. He came back. "Sorry. There's someone at the door. I can't imagine who'd be calling after nine o'clock."

Henry Wyatt heard his mother-in-law go to the door and exclaim, "FBI? Well, I never."

"Better go, Hank. You take care and I'll see what can be done here. Someone needs my attention at the door."

His father-in-law hung up. Wyatt sat and listened to

the dial tone for several seconds before hanging up himself. What was going on? Why was the FBI calling on his in-laws? It made no sense. He didn't think Peter would forget to ask the others in the neighborhood about possible sources for the sickness.

He had done as much as he could for the moment. It was time to turn off his brain and just coast. Henry Wyatt returned to sit in front of his television, lost in its hypnotic wink and mindless hum.

36

John did not like Lisa Taylor as a blond. He watched her rinse her hair for the hundredth time, or so it seemed, and fingered the thick, heavy Mt. Everest Swiss Army knife in his pocket. Then he pulled it out and opened the largest blade. It had seen good service so far. This was the blade he had used on the woman back in Redding. When his superior came ashore in another seventy-two hours, the orders would include removing this annoying blond woman with black roots.

He might use a different blade on her, just for variety.

"Why are you staring at me like that?" Lisa demanded. She looked up from the large wooden bucket she had found in the tumbledown shack. Getting just the right tint had been difficult, but she'd had nothing else to do for the past week except to shop for cosmetics. Getting to this lonely spot in the redwood forests north of San Francisco had taken days longer than she wanted. Why couldn't they have driven there directly, or even stayed at the cabin where they had first checked the cylinders? John had insisted on going back through the mountains toward Redding the following day, northwest to Eureka, then edging cautiously down the Coast Highway. Playing tourist when she was sitting on the U.S. biological-warfare experiment that would put her on easy street both annoyed and bored her.

She tried to fathom what went on inside John's head, and wondered if he harbored any sexual feelings for her. His eyes were colder than a dead fish, and he had a completely expressionless face. She wondered if his nerve endings had died, robbing him of displaying emotions. Playing poker with the man would be hell, she thought. He gave away nothing, except limitless details about American life. He was a walking Trivial Pursuit.

More out of habit than desire, she turned slightly so that the towel around her neck slipped away. Her blouse was unbuttoned to her waist. She flashed him a good look at her naked breasts to provoke a reaction.

Lisa didn't know if she was amused or insulted. John's eyebrows rose slightly, the only hint that he had even seen her maneuver. Was she too ugly to evoke a response? Or should she be pleased to have garnered such a reaction?

To hell with it all. She was going to be rich. They had promised her a cool quarter-million for the two vials she carried in the suitcase. Touching the case holding the bio-death made her uneasy, but she wasn't going to let John hang on to it. He was capable of taking the deadly treasure and vanishing without paying her. More uneasy thoughts intruded on her greed. She had to be sure they paid her. She had done a few drug deals and they had always been between crooked men, all armed to the teeth.

Lisa Taylor wanted to avoid having to fight her way through to get the promised money. It benefited the KGB to simply pay her; what the cylinders held would pay off thousands of times for them. The information that the U.S. had violated biological-warfare treaties would give the Soviets a powerful bargaining lever. Lisa knew their agricultural complex was the pits. They bought millions of tons of grain year after year, even from third-world countries such as India and China. Preferred trading status with the U.S. would feed their population and defuse some of the secessionist pressures.

But the prospect of a double cross existed. That explained the roundabout trip down the coast. John had said that the meeting time had changed, that this was to throw off FBI pursuit, but she had seen no indication that the FBI was on to them. They had worked fast and well. The FBI shouldn't even have been called in, unless the Pentagon had already figured out the experiment was missing from the satellite's wreckage.

John might have been looking for an opportunity to gut her with that damned knife of his, or maybe just to strand her. He claimed that the trawler which would take him farther out to sea and the rendezvous with the submarine had to chug down the coast from Alaska—and he worried that the FBI might follow them. Always the FBI, and this from a man who showed no emotion.

Lisa had seen no evidence of pursuit. Who even knew they had the crystalline cylinders? By now the boy had died and the parents were grieving. Who would ever notice that the tubes were missing from his room when they were making plans for the funeral? Who could possibly tie it to John and her? She was home-free.

"You will catch cold," John said in a level voice that gave her the willies. "You don't want to start your new life with a cold."

"Don't worry about me," she said, disliking him more and more.

"I worry about very little," he said, his eyes drifting toward the suitcase with the test cylinders.

She stood upright, shoulders back, making sure she showed him even more skin. His eyes never wavered from the suitcase. Lisa decided that he wasn't interested in her. But she wished he would put that damned red-handled army knife away.

"Soon," John said. "Soon a raft will come ashore to pick up the American bio-weapon." He paused for a moment and smiled. "And there will be your money."

"Yeah, sure," Lisa said, feeling increasingly uneasy about the KGB.

Fifty-two hours later, in the middle of the night, Lisa stole the suitcase and lugged it into the woods. Carefully marking her path, she buried the case behind a shrub, where John would never find it. This was her sole insurance. John had made a slip that worried her. She had seen the feral look that crept into his eyes. The huge Swiss Army knife flicked menacingly in his grip too, moving from hand to hand, the long blade shining in the bright winter sunlight. He was going to kill her.

She buried the suitcase and got back onto her false trail, moving deeper into the redwoods. Now and then she laid a trap for the unwary with deadfalls and ankle-twisting holes dug into the soft earth. This was to convince anyone trying to follow her that she had carried the suitcase with its precious cargo far away from the shoreline.

"Let the bastards dig up the whole goddamn forest," she muttered as she worked. It took most of the night to hide the suitcase and lay the bogus trail, but it was good insurance.

John's superior would arrive after sunset the next day. If he had the promised money with him, she'd tell them where to find the suitcase and then she'd get the hell away. If they tried to double-cross her, they'd never get the cylinders and all their machinations would fail.

The memory of the knife bouncing from hand to hand sent shivers up her spine. That damned knife.

By dawn she sat cross-legged on a rocky bluff looking down to the ocean. Ross Counter was surrounded by small clusters of rangers' buildings, private homes with dogs ready to bark furiously at any passerby, and a state monument complete with a picnic ground and museum. Lisa wasn't sure this was the best possible place to come ashore for the pickup, but it carried some ironic charm for the Soviets.

A slow smile crossed her face as she remembered with some fondness her contact at Fort Detrick. He had been fun in bed—nothing great, but an adequate diversion—and he hadn't minded that she wasn't a Miss America. Her body attracted and held him—and it had kept him feeding her important information long after she left.

Lisa was glad her control had put her on to Jack Parkessian.

From Fort Detrick to Fort Ross. The stronghold of American bio-war research to an ancient Russian seal and fur outpost. It seemed right to her, appropriate, the way to do it. She had screwed her way to that information, but she wouldn't be screwed out of her due.

The Pacific turned an iron color as the wind picked up and the whitecaps started forming in the distance. She saw the small dilapidated shack she had shared with John. A tiny swirl of smoke rose from the chimney. He was awake, but she wouldn't return until she saw the rubber raft coming in.

37

"Why don't they contact us? They haven't cut us off the payroll, have they?"

Elaine Reinhardt's voice pleaded with Stevenson to tell her everything was going to be all right. He wasn't able to give her the assurance she sought.

"Morningside isn't answering the calls I put to him. I wonder if he isn't in trouble up to his earlobes over us."

"Screw that. *He* left us out here alone. We work for him. We're *his* responsibility. He's got one hell of a lot of explaining to do." Her mouth thinned to a harsh line. When she got this angry, Stevenson knew it was best to stay out of her way. He just wished her anger would do some good. This time, it wouldn't. The people most likely to be worthy of the righteous fury had insulated themselves with security and mountains of paperwork and obsequious aides.

Stevenson put his arms around the woman and pulled her close, while staring at the television set. He hadn't had the time or inclination to dig into its guts for the bug the FBI agents had planted there. The silent exchange between Bartholomew and Dennis had been eloquent. Dennis had fucked up bad and Bartholomew had caught him at it—and worse, the subjects of their bugging had too.

"I shouldn't be like this, Tom. I know it. I just feel so used. I can't contact *any*one."

"You're not alone. I'm tempted to get down to Sacramento and hop a plane for Maryland and home. Then I'll

drive into Fort Detrick and punch out Morningside's
lights. This is where the government and I part company.
Let Parkessian have my job. The ungrateful bastards
think more of covering their own tracks than they do of
rescuing us from a bad situation. They pulled Gorton and
his team back and stranded us. We didn't put that damned
atomic battery in the satellite."

He wondered if he was talking for the FBI's benefit or
solely to comfort Elaine. She knew their predicament,
and she knew they would be forbidden to leave Redding.
Bartholomew hadn't told them to stay, but the special
agent obviously watched them closely. They might not be
suspects in the Devlin murder, technically the Redding
police's worry, but they knew a great deal about the
source of the plutonium that killed Billy Devlin.

That *was* the FBI's bailiwick.

"Bartholomew showed us their report. He's after some
KGB agent. We're in the clear as far as the murders go,"
Elaine said. "Let's get the hell out of here. I'll quit too.
Damn Beaumont and Morningside and all the rest!"

Stevenson said nothing as he gently rocked her back
and forth in his arms. They were both stressed and tired.
One point kept hammering itself through his brain, though.
No one was going to clear them. The Pentagon wasn't
going to admit the satellite's loss—ever. Major Zamora
had cleaned up that mess and removed all trace. Even if
scattered bits and pieces of the KH-18 were located, it
would be publicly denied by clever Pentagon public-
relations teams. Fred Wyman would do anything to keep
from being incriminated, and he would stop at nothing to
protect the president from such humiliation. That was his
job—that first and national security second.

If Stevenson wanted to escape this fiasco with his own
reputation intact, he needed hard facts. He asked Elaine
to follow him outside. She shrugged and grabbed her
coat without questions.

"Let's go to the Devlin house. There's got to be something there the police and the FBI missed."

"You're Sherlock Holmes now, after being Saint Sebastian for a week or so?"

"I feel the arrows piercing my hide," he said, clutching at the mock wounds in his chest. "I also feel the cold winds of publicity blowing past us. There hasn't been any mention of the Devlin murders in the newspaper, not one column inch. Something that bloody and sensational would have been bannered across the front of the New York *Post*, much less a small-town paper. This is the kind of crime that's mumbled about for years in a place like this. Look at Juan Corona and the murders over in Oroville."

"The police? The FBI?"

"The lot of them. I'm wondering if the Pentagon hasn't come into this in force."

"An ugly thought. They're hard at work and aren't letting us know a damned thing. What do they gain by holding back the Devlins' murders? Perhaps they are involved . . ."

"Why would the Pentagon boys have anything to do with the crime? Even if they knew Billy had my experiment, there was no reason to torture and kill his parents. All they had to do was walk in in snappy uniforms, wave some official-looking court order, and seize what they wanted—or just go in and take the cylinders without explanation. How could the Devlins have protested?"

Elaine walked beside him for a while, then said, "This is starting to sound like some paranoid conspiracy. I'd as soon believe the UFO's came down and did it. Everybody knows more than we do, including the KGB."

Stevenson has no easy answer. Pieces of the puzzle floated just beyond the range of his vision. He sensed them come and go. Like Nurse Ratched. Where had he seen her before? He wished he had realized she wasn't a duty nurse right away. They had given away too much information, speaking with Billy. He damned himself for even mentioning the KH-18, much less his experiment.

But what could he have done? Billy was dying, and he had sorely needed information.

They caught a cab to the end of the street where the murders had occurred. Stevenson paid off the driver and bemoaned having so little cash left after his ATM withdrawal. He was allowed only one hundred dollars every twenty-four hours. He didn't even want to think about the bills piling up back home.

"There'll be a police cordon around the house," Elaine said. "It's a misdemeanor to cross the line."

"Are you sure?" he asked with more confidence than he felt. "It hasn't been in the papers, remember. They're trying to keep it quiet. Yellow plastic police banners around the house would make the neighbors wonder what was going on."

"How'd they remove the bodies without anyone seeing? The houses in this neighborhood look like retirement homes, full of old folks spying through their kitchen curtains."

"No plastic warning banners," he said, his confidence rising now that he had predicted accurately what the police would do. Spies might be lurking in the neighborhood. He wasn't sure if it was a myth about the criminal returning to the scene of the crime, but the police might be awaiting them.

"Do we just break in?"

"We did the first time."

And he did again. A window in the rear of the house was improperly fastened. Stevenson jiggled and tapped and finally got the latch to slip just enough to bang hard on the window. It slid up easily; he crept into the house and helped Elaine through the window. They both started for Billy's bedroom.

He had seen something in there before which still niggled at the corners of his thoughts, something that didn't belong in a boy's room.

"Should I chance a light?" Elaine asked.

"Go on. No one will notice it back here." He wondered if anyone had noticed the house was dark for almost a week. Did the Devlins go on vacations around New Year's? Perhaps the neighbors didn't care.

He was momentarily blinded by the bright overhead light. He shielded his eyes, then relaxed. The room was as he had seen it after discovering the murders. Clothes were strewn around and the dresser drawers were pulled out.

"Well, Tom? What are we looking for?"

He didn't have an answer. "What doesn't fit. That's more important than what does."

"Everything looks as if it belongs. Billy wasn't much in the housekeeping department."

Elaine wandered about, poking at items on the dresser, floor, and bed but not picking them up. Stevenson stood in the door and slowly looked from one side to the other.

His eyes kept returning to the Celestron telescope.

"Was this a wealthy family?" he asked Elaine.

"Not from their furniture. Every piece is flea-market quality or worse."

"What is the most expensive thing in the house?"

"The television set is old, but it must have cost a few bucks. I didn't see a VCR or CD player. There wasn't even a stereo, now that I think about it."

"But Billy has a twelve-hundred-dollar telescope. Where did he get the money for it?"

"Hobbyists pay exorbitant amounts for their toys. So the kid was an amateur astronomer."

"There are no books, no star charts, nothing to show an interest in astronomy. Look under the bed."

Elaine got on her hands and knees.

"What's there? Comic books?"

"How did you know?" She looked up, startled at his insight. "Oh, I get it. That's where you keep yours."

"That's where I used to."

Stevenson pushed the telescope around on its fork-mount tripod. It was brand new. A few specks of mud sullied the feet. There were few scratches on the tube itself, and the lens cover had only a few fingerprints. He looked out the window and tried to figure if the boy had used it to spy on neighbors. He couldn't tell if there was a comely teenage girl's bedroom window within sight.

"A Christmas present?" Elaine asked, looking over his shoulder as he examined it.

"Probably," he said, "but it wasn't Billy's."

The engraved name plate on the bottom of the telescope tube read "GEORGE WYATT."

38

"You'll never find the suitcase," Lisa Taylor shouted. John watched her stoically, hands shoved deep into his coat pockets. She wondered if he was fingering that damned knife of his. Probably. The past twenty-four hours had been hell for her. The raft never came, and John had been prowling around the small shack, hunting for the cylinders.

He'd never find them, and she'd go straight to hell before she told him where they were.

"Your masters will kill you for failing. It's damned easy to pay me off for what I've got; it'll be well nigh impossible for you if you try double-crossing me."

"Calm down, please," John said in his level voice. He sounded cool, but Lisa saw the flickers of—what?—in his eyes. Was he actually showing signs of panic? Had they abandoned him?

"Where is he?"

"I don't know," John said. "He was supposed to come last night. I can't contact him to find out if anything is wrong. There was only one message allowed."

"Plenty is wrong. How would you like it if I dumped the contents of those tubes into the ocean? You'd end up with squat then. What would your Kremlin bosses say about that? You'd be sweeping floors in a power station somewhere in Siberia—if you're lucky."

"That's a capitalist myth," John said. "Failure is not respected, but neither is it punished by exile or death."

His hands worked nervously inside his jacket pockets.

Lisa knew he was running his fingers over the Swiss Army knife, opening and closing the largest blade.

"And it's a socialist myth that people betray their country only for money. I *want* to give you the cylinders. What the U.S. is doing with these bio-warfare reagents is a scandal. I just don't want you to double-cross me."

She was out of breath. She stood on a high rocky prominence and stared down at him on the cold, rocky beach. Waves moved out restlessly; they had missed the incoming tide when the head honcho with the money was supposed to paddle in.

"I am not double-dealing with you," John said, a touch of anger entering his voice. "You aren't paid. I'm stranded here. I was supposed to go home. Something has gone wrong. We must contact the trawler again somehow and—"

"Screw that," Lisa shouted. "You get your ass down to San Francisco and that fancy consulate of theirs. Find out firsthand from the KGB agent in charge there."

"There are no KGB agents in the consulate."

"And the pope's not Polish. Go to hell, man. No money, no biological weapon."

"We don't know that is a bio-weapon," John said. He edged slowly toward the face of the bluff. Lisa had seen a narrow path leading up. He couldn't rush her, but he could get a few feet head start up the path before she noticed. Or so he thought.

She turned and bolted for the dark woods. By the time he made it to the top of the bluff, she would be well-hidden. There was no way he could ever unearth the test tubes. She hunkered down behind a fallen log and heard the soft sounds of cloth moving across a tree trunk. Straining against the twilight, she saw John moving through the woods after her. He moved like a ghost.

He passed her, then paused. His nose worked like a rabbit's. Turning slowly, like a lightless beacon, he rotated a full turn, then came back until he stared directly at her.

"Your hair tint is distinctive in odor," he said. "You should not have dyed your hair."

She tried to run, but John caught her after a few steps. The bright blade of his knife rested against her naked throat. A single stroke would sever everything in her neck down to her backbone.

"I don't want to kill you. They have not informed me of the reason for their change of plans. Will you cooperate?"

"All right," Lisa said, frightened for the first time. Until now, she had felt in control. The wicked knife edge changed her mind.

He released her. She knew that running again was pointless. John was too fast, he was too good at hunting his prey. Rubbing her throat, she stood and glared at him. The idea of destroying the vials came and went. If she did that, any hope of collecting her money would vanish.

"What do you think went wrong?"

"The standing order is to wait an extra day," he said.

She heard the lie woven through some small element of the truth. He was supposed to wait, but it wasn't for an entire day.

"Midnight is a good time for them to try coming in again," she said.

John stiffened slightly. That was the truth, not waiting twenty-four hours. She had hit on it by accident.

"Do we try at that time or do we call this entire operation off?"

"We can't 'call it off,' as you say."

"No? I can find others to sell the tubes to. Maybe I can ransom them back to the U.S. government. They thought they were worth something, since they put them in that satellite."

John stepped toward her. She reached up and put her hand against his chest.

"Don't," she warned. "You don't know where I've hidden the treasure."

"We want the experiment."

"You'll get it, if you play fair."

"Standing orders are to wait six hours."

She smiled to herself. Guessing right helped restore her confidence. Dealing with the Russians wasn't so hard, if you understood them.

"Let's wait in the shack. It's starting to get cold outside," she said, smiling. Maybe she could deal with John's boss better than she did with him. They walked slowly back down to the beach. It was over an hour past high tide. The waves looked puny to her now. It was a shame that whatever went wrong had—

Lisa's gaze snapped to the side of the gently curving cove not a quarter of a mile distant. A light flashed on and off.

The knife thrust made her gasp in pain. A tiny river of blood began running down her back, not enough of a wound to do serious harm but enough to let her know what would happen if she protested.

"I was supposed to retrieve the test tubes before they came in. I must now work quickly."

The knife moved into her body a fraction of an inch. Lisa had never felt such pain in her life.

"Tell me where you have put the American experiment."

"Go on, kill me, you stupid son of a bitch."

"First you will tell me where the cylinders are. Torture is not something I relish, but I am very good at it."

She fell to her knees as the knife twisted, carving out a tiny pocket of flesh in the middle of her back.

"The woman would have told me anything I wanted. It was her husband who resisted. He was an alcoholic; his nerve endings had deadened. That is why I had to work on her. He gave me all I needed."

"You . . . t-tortured th-them?"

John's silence was more eloquent than any boasting. He forced her into the shack and shoved her into the only chair. His expression had not changed. He was an entrepreneur and death was his business.

"Wait for the man in the boat. Wait. I . . . I'll tell him everything."

"You will tell me. I must have the cylinders before he arrives."

"They're buried," she stammered. "Far away from here."

"No," he said simply. Then he started to work on her with his knife. Lisa fought, but John was too strong, too expert. She quickly learned she knew nothing about being a spy.

Just as she was ready to gasp out the location of the two cylinders, the door exploded inward. John spun, then moved faster than any human she had ever seen. His hand came up and the heavy knife spun in the air. The man in the doorway, pistol in his hand, stupidly stared down at the blade embedded in his chest. He toppled slowly, a forest giant felled by a woodsman's ax.

Shots rang out and splinters began flying from the walls. John shouted something she didn't understand and raced for his bag. She saw the butt of a handgun before he reached it.

Lisa rolled over, ignored pain lancing into her arms and legs, then drove forward as hard as she could. Her elbows crashed into the lower wall. The shack's rotten wood gave way and let her spill out onto the cold sand. Facedown, she kept scrambling. She didn't know who was doing the firing; she didn't care. A bullet meant for John could as easily kill her.

"Stop, FBI!" came the cry. She didn't heed it. She rolled and rolled and rolled. Then the air filled with bullets, both entering and leaving the shack. John had reached his pistol. The staccato bark of his small-caliber pistol came in counterpoint to the heavier boom from the FBI .38-caliber revolvers.

Lisa knew it was all over. They must have surrounded them. She didn't know how it could have happened. Who had followed them? John had been so careful—too careful, she had thought. But there was no denying the

FBI's presence. More bullets ripped through the night and sought her.

She ducked and dodged and somehow got to the top of the bluff. The wooded area where she had hidden the cylinders was directly ahead. She could make it.

She did.

39

"We're not getting anywhere. Let's just resign and to hell with it all," Elaine Reinhardt said in disgust. "This is as far as we can go without official help."

"I still wonder why Morningside has pulled in his horns and decided to hide," Stevenson said.

They had been in the cheap motel room too long, he knew. By now the Pentagon or the national security adviser or *someone* should have alerted them to work being done in their behalf. There hadn't been any report of the Devlins' deaths, and only a small notice of Billy Devlin's death showed up in the local papers. The KH-18 crash was still a secret.

"They've got it all sewed up, Tom. Zamora got away with what they needed for the cover-up, and the rest? What difference does it make if they leave us to take the rap for the Devlins' deaths?"

"But the police haven't told us to stay in town. We must be free to go."

It rankled him that he hadn't been able to gather the evidence necessary to put him and Elaine in the clear, that he had no idea what was going on with Bartholomew and the FBI investigation, and, above all, that Morningside had deserted them the way he had. So much for loyalty.

"I agree, Tom, let's split. There is no way in hell we are ever going to prove our innocence. Let's make them come after us and formally charge us."

"The plutonium," he muttered. "And the experiment. Why was that stolen from Billy's room?"

"Who can say? Maybe it was a burglar who liked green snow."

Elaine's flip remark drove to the heart of his dilemma. Green snow. What had Billy meant by that? The quartz tubes had contained nothing but gray sludge and clear nutrient fluid. And no simple burglar had skinned Mrs. Devlin to make her—or her husband—talk. Someone had obviously been after the Project Big Hunk test tubes.

"Don't eat the green snow," he muttered to himself.

He shook his head. They were spinning their wheels and getting nothing accomplished in Redding. Returning to Maryland was the best they could do for the moment—return and get lawyers. Stevenson knew that their security clearances needed to enter Fort Detrick had been revoked and that they were out of jobs. Removing this blot from his record would take several years of litigation; the government didn't have to fire anyone from a job. Lifting the security clearances prevented their victims from reporting for work—and they could then be fired for failure to perform their assigned duties.

"Pack," he said. "We'll figure out a way to get to Sacramento. This place doesn't have a direct flight to anywhere."

"That's not true," Elaine said. "I looked it up in the phone book. There's a private airfield north of town. We can charter a plane, get to Sacramento, and then we can figure out where to go."

"What did you have in mind?"

"I've got family in San Francisco. I haven't seen them in a while, but . . ."

"We can stop off in San Francisco, then," he said, wondering if she wanted to part company there. He couldn't blame her—not too much.

"I was thinking we should look for jobs. Silicon Valley might be moribund, but SRI is usually looking for ex-government researchers. There might even be a teaching spot open at Stanford. How long has it been since you worked on that organic semiconductor project?"

"Ten years, but not much has been done in that time. And over at Santa Cruz they're doing interesting work applying chaos theory to cell growth."

They packed their few belongings into a single bag and left for the small private airport, where they started hiking toward the single metal shed housing the charter service. Stevenson's steps slowed and then stopped when he saw the profiles of the two men inside the building. One moved away from the grimy window and came to the door. Larry Bartholomew lounged indolently, scratching himself like a baseball player.

"Howdy, Doc. We got a plane all ready for you."

"I went over the room. Were there more than the two bugs?"

"Something like that. We used a sophisticated approach on you—we had a special agent in the next room watchin' as you came and went. The walls were thin and he overheard you talkin' about how you were comin' this way. Want to do us a little favor?"

"We want to leave Redding," Elaine said coldly.

"Can't stop you. No reason to."

Stevenson hesitated. The FBI agent's tone spoke a volume, but it was closed to him. "Did you catch the Devlins' killer?"

"Reckon we did. That's one reason you folks can come and go as you see fit."

"But?" prodded Elaine. "What's the punch line?"

"We've got a small problem with that experiment you lost. It's been found over on the coast. Seems the little lady who has it is threatenin' to open the valves and spread a nasty biological-warfare bug all over northern California."

"There's nothing dangerous in my experiment, Bartholomew. I told you that."

"We're not too concerned about the gray gunk in the one tube. That looks real innocuous. It's the green material in the other tube that has us worried." Bartholomew picked his teeth with his fingernail. " 'Less I miss my guess, it's botherin' you something fierce too, because it's not supposed to be green or like snowflakes."

Stevenson knew the agent had snared him. No matter what happened, he had to see if his neutral-cell experiment had changed—and what it had changed into.

40

The single-engine Piper Apache made a dangerous night landing on the strip of the Coastal Highway. Stevenson kept his eyes closed and thought his right hand was going to be crushed to dust as Elaine clung to it. The plane hit and bounced twice on the potholed highway; then the pilot applied the brakes savagely, and they came to a screeching halt. Stevenson felt that the plane was hanging on the edge of a cliff, although it was too dark to see more than a few feet.

Bartholomew seemed pleased with the ease with which they had landed. Like a spring, he popped out the passenger door, then turned to help Stevenson, saying, "That's just about the best landin' ole Pete's made in a dozen years or more. I've got to hand it to him. He's real gentle when he has nonbureau passengers. We ought to do it this way more often, Pete."

The pilot laughed without humor. He sounded relieved that he had survived another landing.

Elaine looked sick from the rough ride over the Coast Ranges and the sudden descent to the shore. Thermals had bounced them around until they had touched down. Stevenson, for his part, was glad they had left the other FBI agent back in Redding. The weight in the plane must have pushed it beyond the safety levels allowed by the FAA.

"Here's the problem," Bartholomew said, suddenly somber. "The woman with the jugs of goo is over there in the woods. She is sitting there with the valves open. If we try rushin' her, she's promisin' to spill the contents."

"What about a shot to the head?" Elaine asked sarcastically. Bartholomew didn't take her question that way. The FBI agent's response chilled Stevenson.

"We can't get a sniper into position for a clean shot," he said. "The woods are dark and there are more trees than you can shake a stick at. We figured we would try talkin' her out of it first."

"Or determining whether she poses a threat," Stevenson finished.

"Of course, of course. Now, I know you're claimin' that your experiment—I'm goin' on the assumption that what she's got out there *is* your lost experiment—isn't too dangerous. Would you just verify that for us?"

"If he does, you'll shoot her," Elaine said.

"Not at all. We'd just walk up all nice and proper and take the two cylinders away from her. She wouldn't have any hold over us. But if she's got a bio-weapon that can wipe out everyone from Baja to Alaska, it doesn't look good puttin' that into a report. You don't know how many forms have to be filed if somebody dies, not to mention a few *million* folks. Reckon there must be damned near thirty million people she could wipe out with a good biological weapon. That adds up to more time on the copy machine than Congress has authorized in the last ten years."

"Too bad," Elaine said. To Stevenson she said, "There's no reason to go along with him. We don't know if this woman even has the test cylinders from Project Big Hunk."

"It won't hurt to look," Stevenson said. "If nothing else, we've gotten a free ride to the coast. We can't be more than a hundred miles north of San Francisco."

He didn't hear Elaine's reply. Bartholomew had grabbed his elbow and was guiding him through the line of tight-lipped FBI agents circling the wooded area. Stevenson noticed the firepower they had with them. It was enough to start—or quell—a major guerrilla uprising in a small Latin-American country.

"I want you to look through our Starlight scope and

tell us what you can," Bartholomew said. "We need to know how to handle this here matter."

"I'd need to analyze the green snow in the cylinder. It wasn't there when the experiment was lofted."

"Lab work is out of the question. This little lady's spooked something fierce. She's goin' to jump out of her skin if we don't gentle her along."

Bartholomew's heavy hand pushed him to his knees. Stevenson dropped to his belly as another agent passed over an infrared viewer. The night was impenetrable in the woods. Through the scope, Stevenson saw tiny, eerie movement everywhere. Testing it, he sighted in on squirrels and other small animals moving through the darkness. He almost screamed when he aimed it up and saw talons and serrated beak coming at him.

"That's a spotted owl," the agent beside him said. "We're cutting into his hunting time. He won't harm us."

Stevenson swallowed hard. The Starlight scope magnified as well as amplified available light. He returned to a view closer to the ground. It took several seconds for him to home in on the woman. Her cheekbones burned with dancing red fire. It didn't take an expert to know she was frightened and flushed.

"She's a blond," Bartholomew said. "We don't know much about her other than that. Ugly as mud, but then, most Soviet agents are."

"What's happening here?" Stevenson asked. He tried to steady the scope and get some idea about the condition of the two quartz cylinders she held. He wondered what had happened to the other three containers Elaine had designed and he had used in the Project Big Hunk orbiting.

"The boss man for this spy ring was coming in on a rubber raft. He left a Russian trawler that had sneaked into our territorial waters. The Navy has spotted a nuclear submarine, Oscar class. Nothing unusual. They use 'em for moving personnel as much as they do patrol work."

"And?" Stevenson wanted to learn as much as he could. The FBI had been hard at work while he and Elaine stewed needlessly back in Redding. He might even have a job waiting for him at Fort Detrick, if he wanted it. What he considered to be a betrayal by Morningside and the others might just force him to look for a job down in San Jose, as Elaine had suggested.

"The boss man was coming in. A Coast Guard cutter intercepted him. We held off sending in a man as long as we could, but we knew John back in the shack would take a powder."

"John? Oh, the KGB agent."

"That's the one. We don't know his name, or if it really matters. He was trained and dumped in this country years ago. The Soviets thought he was under deep cover, but we'd had our eye on him."

"So you iced John and now have his boss in custody?"

"Something like that. We don't rightly know where this little filly fits into the picture," Bartholomew said. "What can you tell us about her?"

Stevenson saw her profile and muttered, "Lisa." He did recognize her, and not just as Nurse Ratched in the Redding hospital.

"How's that, Doc?" Bartholomew moved closer.

"She looks like my research assistant's date at a party— not his date, exactly. He pried her loose from another scientist in my department."

"Do tell." The sudden lack of inflection in Bartholomew's tone told Stevenson he had made a mistake identifying the woman as he had. He might be wrong. And he certainly couldn't remember anything more about her— not now. He would have to ask Elaine. Adding a name to the face might jog her memory.

"What's she doing?" asked the agent on Stevenson's other side. "She's moving."

"She's hunkering down behind a log," Stevenson said, interpreting the woman's glowing profile. "She isn't taking her hands off the valves on the test containers."

"The experiment, Doc. You're goin' to have to tell us quick what to do. She's startin' to make demands again."

Stevenson peered through the Starlight scope and tried to make out the containers. The difference in viewing between daylight and shimmery IR prevented him from making a decent decision about the test cylinders' condition.

"I can't tell you anything. I'd have to examine the cylinders more closely."

"So go on over and look at them," Bartholomew said. "She's gonna let one of us look. It's your ball game, Doc."

Stevenson tried to protest, but to no avail. He knew the woman wasn't armed. Her only hold came from the threat of a biological weapon. Stevenson hadn't created it. Project Big Hunk should have had only neutral cells and their replicators. If one container held green snow, it was no longer his experiment.

But what was it? Had someone else added another experiment? He shook off such nonsense. The telemetry from the test had confirmed the contents, at least for a few weeks.

"I'm coming over," Stevenson said, standing. The woman turned and held up a cylinder as if she held a fire extinguisher. "There's nothing to worry about. I want to verify the contents of the quartz test tube."

He almost got to her. In light from distant flashlights, he saw her face more clearly. As he had thought, she was the nurse who had tried to stay in Billy's room during his first questioning session.

And she was the woman Jack Parkessian had stolen away from Basil Baker at the Christmas party. Had Jack leaked the information to her during pillow talk? But what did Parkessian even know about Project Big Hunk?

"You, the scientist. Stevenson. Stand back. This shit is under pressure. I'll spray it all over you."

She shook it hard and held the container so that the valve pointed at Stevenson. He knew the gray gooey gob inside was harmless.

His stomach still knotted up and his hands started shaking. She definitely knew him by sight. What else did she know that he didn't?

"I need to verify the contents," he repeated, his mind turning in circles. He had never faced such uncertainty before. What she had might not be his experiment after all.

Green snow?

"Stay back. You know what's in these two cylinders."

Stevenson heard movement on either side and knew the FBI was moving in. He tried to grab the woman. She let out a shriek of pure fright and opened the valve. Liquid spewed into his face, blinding him.

Stevenson yelped like a scalded dog as he wiped at the fluid in his eyes. Through a blurry right eye he saw her pick up the other cylinder, raised it over her head, and bring it crashing down onto a jagged rock. More liquid spattered everywhere, but Stevenson was already moving to the side.

The FBI had set him up, used him as a decoy, to get to the woman. He wasn't going to stand between them and their target, not while he was still blinded.

He heard the scuffle, then a single gunshot, and he knew it was over.

Stevenson corrected himself as he wiped the sludge from his eyes. It was over for the woman, but if anything had happened to his experiment, this might just be the beginning for them. The contents of both cylinders had sprayed everywhere.

And he had one quartz tube's contents splashed in his face.

41

"Tom!" Elaine Reinhardt's cry rang through the deathly quiet forest. "Are you all right?"

Bartholomew held her back as Stevenson sat on the ground rubbing his eyes and trying to get a good look at the world around him. Things remained black. He tried not to panic. It was night. The world ought to look dark, but should it be this inky? He dabbed at his eyes and gently removed bits of sludge. Blinking hard, he got tears to flow. In a few seconds his cheeks were caked with a gooey mixture of gray sludge and tears. He fumbled in his pocket, took out a handkerchief, and wiped away the grime in his eyes. He heaved a sigh of relief when the world returned to normal.

"What should we do, Doc? We got her, but she released both cylinders." Bartholomew's usually languid voice carried an almost hysterical edge. Everyone feared bio-warfare. Dying from a bullet was a risk every FBI agent accepted; dying from some creepy-crawly bio-warfare experiment was something else.

"Elaine, can you help me? It's only the gray-gooey-gob experiment. There's nothing else in what she sprayed on me."

He heard Elaine fighting with Bartholomew. He smiled slightly: the special agent had no chance against her. She knelt beside him, took the handkerchief, and expertly dabbed at the gunk remaining on his face.

"Without a detailed analysis," she said, "I'd say the replicating cells worked pretty damned well. There must be quite a bit more gray goo than there was when you lofted the experiment."

"Success comes in all shapes and sizes," Stevenson said.

She helped him up. His face felt tight and wrinkled where the gray gooey gobs had partially dried. He looked at Lisa Taylor, who lay sprawled on her back, sightless eyes staring up at the canopy of redwood limbs.

"Did they have to kill her?" he asked Elaine in a low voice.

"I would have," Elaine said. "She shouldn't have fooled around with the experiment as she did. There's not much doubt she was a spy—and that she had a part in killing the Devlins."

Stevenson walked to the rock where Lisa had cracked open the second cylinder. His heart almost exploded in his chest when he saw the green flakes. Billy Devlin hadn't made it up. The test had changed.

"But how?" he asked. "Look at it." He bent down, careful not to touch the sharp edges of the broken quartz tube or the green flakes dusting the pieces. "It's not a neutral cell, not with that color."

"Don't worry about photosynthesis plasmids," Elaine said. "That's entirely out of the question." She paused, then added in a whisper only he could hear, "Isn't it?"

His head bobbed up and down. The original cells for his experiment had been derived from animals. They could not have been altered to duplicate plant cells, even if the replicators had joined the neutral cells to create a viable, reproducing new life form. If he had been successful, he would have moved on to plant cells—perhaps he should have started with plants and argued to keep the experiment earthbound.

"I don't know what happened," he said. He took a twig and scraped part of the green flakes off a sharp quartz spire embedded in the ground. The FBI flashlights illuminated a bright reflective pattern unlike anything he had ever seen. "I need to get this into the lab immediately."

"The mutating effect of the plutonium," Elaine said. "That's got to be the reason. The atomic battery broke open and spilled its plutonium, causing cell mutation."

"That might have happened," Stevenson allowed. "Or radiation from a particularly intense solar flare might have disrupted the function of the replicators. Whatever happened wasn't intentional." He heaved a deep sigh. "A change in the replicators is the cause here."

"There's no way of telling what was being grown if the replicators altered their function," Elaine said. "The green cells don't have to be viable."

"Bartholomew!" Stevenson shouted. "I need the entire area cordoned off. Now!" Then he licked dried lips as he watched the green flakes stir and multiply. The replicators were doing their job well, and they were doing them outside the closed environment of a nutrient-filled test tube. Whatever went on could do so outside a controlled medium. He had no idea how fast it might spread.

"What will the wind do, Doc?" Bartholomew asked. He had cleared out most of his agents, but they had left Lisa Taylor where she lay. Green spots were spreading slowly up her lifeless legs. Stevenson needed to take samples to determine just what was happening. He hoped it wasn't anything more sinister than simple crystal growth on the surface of her skin, but he thought he saw tiny tendrils working down into the woman's dead flesh.

"What's the status on the equipment I ordered?"

"There's a little hang-up on that, Doc. Seems no one can locate a sprayer like you asked for."

"To hell with that. Get me an insect sprayer, a paint sprayer and compressor, anything! I need it to hold this gunk in place."

"It has to have a nozzle large enough to handle an acrylic," Elaine reminded. "We want to saturate the area and cover it with a plastic film. That will keep the wind from blowing any of it away."

Stevenson listened to Bartholomew's excuses for the delay. They meant nothing to him. Let the agent sweat this one out; it was his operation. What bothered Stevenson was not so much the possibility of wind kicking up the green flakes and turning them airborne, as the number of animals roaming the woods. Owls could become contaminated and fly away. Small rodents scurried about in increasing numbers the closer it got to sunrise. Soon the larger predators would emerge, and with them the daytime birds.

Stevenson kept staring at Lisa's leg. Most of the area exposed through her torn pants was kelly green. A contaminated animal might spread the contagion throughout the redwood forests in a few days. From Muir Woods it was only a small jump down to San Francisco—and beyond San Francisco lay the entire world. Stevenson remembered a case of pneumonic plague twenty or more years ago. A young boy had passed through the airport and had missed the period when he was highly contagious by only hours. A few coughs, an incautious touch, and the plague could have been spread worldwide.

The world had been lucky then. Stevenson hoped it would be again now.

What worried him most about his spreading green blight was his ignorance. Where to begin?

"The kid," Elaine said to him. "Do you think he died from this instead of radiation exposure?"

"The plutonium got him," Stevenson said. "I saw the doctor's report. There was system poisoning suggesting plutonium, as well as a bright spot on the X-rays where a tiny speck had lodged in his lung. All symptoms were characteristic of plutonium poisoning."

"You don't know what the symptoms are for this," she pointed out. "Billy could have inhaled a tiny particle from this tube and . . ." Her words trailed off.

"Plutonium," he said positively. The boy had died from the inhalation of radioactive and chemically poisonous plutonium, not from a mutation of Project Big Hunk.

"This wasn't what you expected," Elaine said.

"It's my experiment, my responsibility," he said. He complained to Bartholomew about the delay, but was cut short by four agents who struggled through the forest lugging spray equipment. A fifth agent lugged up cans of acrylic to spray the area and "fix" it to keep even the smallest mote of dust pinned to the ground.

"I'll need power for that," Stevenson said, pointing at the sprayer.

"We're working on a portable generator. We're makin' do, Doc. Don't go frettin' yourself none over this." Bartholomew stayed at the edge of the spot where Lisa Taylor had splattered the green snow, never coming too close, but not retreating either.

Stevenson circled the contaminated area while the FBI agents set up the equipment. They grumbled as they worked. He overheard one complaining that this wasn't in his job description. Stevenson didn't doubt that he would rather be out gunning down KGB spies, but this work was possibly more important to the country.

What *had* happened aboard the KH-18?

Stevenson knew there might never be a good explanation. He had to accept that his replicators had gone wild and produced the green snow—and what else? Did they carry death? He couldn't take his eyes off Lisa Taylor's corpse. He shone his flashlight over it repeatedly. The green had spread beyond the limits of his vision. Until he had the area sprayed down, he didn't want to get any closer.

He wanted to avoid even touching her, but that wasn't likely.

"All ready, Dr. Stevenson," called out the agent who had complained about his task.

Stevenson searched his pockets for a handkerchief. The one he had used to wipe off the gray sludge was securely packaged in an agent's sandwich bag. He ought to have warned everyone to wear coverings on their mouths and noses.

"Here, Tom." Elaine passed over a clean linen handkerchief. "I got it off one of the cowboys." She jerked her thumb toward the dour line of special agents. "The one who drilled her with his thirty-eight. He liked it."

Stevenson said nothing about her lack of enthusiasm for the man. He didn't care for the FBI agents either. Bartholomew was smarter than he looked, no difficult chore, but the others were sociopaths who would kill anyone standing in their way.

"Get back," he called. "All the way to the beach. Everyone. Now!" He tied the handkerchief around his nose and mouth, then began spraying. The acrylic sparkled in the morning sunlight like myriads of spinning, crazy diamonds. He went about his work grimly, starting at the farthest reaches of the green contamination, then working in until he covered Lisa Taylor's body in a half-inch-thick layer of durable plastic. Twice the sprayer clogged and twice he fixed it, only to return to his tedious chore.

An hour later, he scouted the limits of his work, hunting for the smallest speck of the kelly-green particles that might have escaped his attention. Not satisfied, he made a second round and found nothing. He summoned Elaine and let her hunt.

"It's all contained," she said. "Good work."

Stevenson was bone tired. He nodded numbly, knowing the real work was only beginning. Now came the task of determining if the green flakes were dangerous—and what the hell had happened to the remaining three cylinders.

42

"How are you going to explain this?" Stevenson asked, looking around the empty refectory. Bartholomew had evacuated the high school four days after Christmas vacation.

"A piece of cake, Doc. You're an old hand at this top-secret stuff. We just hint at this and do that and flash our badges." Bartholomew smiled. A piece of meat had caught between his front teeth. He seemed unaware of it, and Stevenson wasn't going to tell him. "The kids all wanted an extra day off."

"The teachers did too," Elaine said. "I know. My mother taught high school for twelve years before she got sick of it and found a job that paid better."

"See, the little la—" Bartholomew coughed to cover his *faux pas*. "Dr. Reinhardt hit the nail right on its pointy head. We chase them out with some defense-readiness bullshit and you get three days to putter around in their science room to see how nasty this green snow of yours is."

"It's not well-equipped," Stevenson observed. "Not for the work we need to do. It's only a high school."

"It's a biology room, isn't it?"

"Laboratory, Special Agent Bartholomew, we call it a laboratory in the science biz." Elaine smiled sweetly. She had caught the slip of his tongue when he almost called her "little lady."

"You need anything more, you let me know, you hear?"

"I hear," Stevenson said, his mind already wandering. What did they have in a rural-high-school biology lab that could be useful? A poor glass-lens microscope, some crude handling equipment, and not much else. The chemistry lab might yield up the reagents he needed. There wouldn't be anything in the physics classroom to help him out. This school in the middle of a redwood forest wasn't going to have a scanning electron microscope or an 50kv X-ray generator for a Debye scatter or a von Laue backscatter or a stainless-steel precession camera, and it certainly didn't have a Cray 3 for serious computational work.

He'd have to do with a few eyedroppers and a prayer.

"You need help setting up?" Elaine asked. "Otherwise, I want to catch some shut-eye. It's been hell the past couple days."

"I understand. Go on. I'll get going on the analysis the best I can."

She paused for a moment. "What of Morningside? You haven't tried to contact him recently."

"No," Stevenson said, "I haven't, and I don't think I will. He could have found me if he'd put his mind to it. So could Beaumont and Wyman and all the others. They threw us to the wolves, Elaine. I'm doing this for my own peace of mind."

"And then?"

"Then it's to hell with them all."

"Even if the green snow turns out to be deadly?" She studied him carefully.

"It won't," he said confidently. "And if it is nasty, I'll report it, and then to hell with them. Morningside could have prevented this from happening."

"How? Tighter security at Fort Detrick? I did recognize Lisa as Jack's conquest that night of the party. Or by listening to you in the first place?"

Stevenson laughed without humor. "There are a dozen answers to your questions," he said. "Take your pick.

All of them apply. Mostly, I'm pissed off at how they treated me like an extraneous hunk of equipment."

"I'll be in the nurse's office. There's a cot there, if Bartholomew hasn't already commandeered it."

Stevenson stopped her and turned her around. He kissed her softly. "Thank you for sticking with me. This wasn't your fight."

"I designed the containment for you. That makes it mine, at least in part. Now, get to work, and I'll get to sleep. When I've put a few hours of Z's behind me, I'll check and see how you're getting along."

Stevenson nodded, his mind already ranging to the problems facing him. He was aware of Elaine leaving, but only barely. He had the large biology lab all to himself. The black tops and the curving spotted silver faucets and sinks at every table brought back memories long buried. High school. The lousy times he had had there. The school dances without anyone to take. The jocks calling him a nerd.

He picked up a Pyrex test tube with the green particulate matter in it and stared at it. What would they have said if they knew he would one day hold bio-warfare life and death in his hand?

Stevenson smiled ruefully. Probably nothing. They hadn't been smart then, and they were probably still too dumb to understand that real power meant more than winning the Friday-night football game. He started to work.

Using the fume hood was out of the question. He remembered a high-school chemistry-class experiment that had gotten out of hand. One student had started a bromine vapor generator and had foolishly removed the stopper. He had placed the generator in the fume hood, only to find that the noxious vapors were vented into every room in the wing. The school had to be evacuated. For days afterward, the rooms smelled of heavy metallic bromine.

To vent his green snow accidentally might only spread it. Stevenson contented himself with working behind the protective pull-down glass shield, but without the fan on. A negative air flow kept the tiniest dust particles in place, but he didn't know how to contain the result. Any filter in the fume hood would be inadequate to the task.

Carefully he began his work.

Stevenson jumped when Elaine came in. For a moment he thought she had changed her mind about taking a nap, then saw the clock over the door. He had been working steadily for three hours.

"Well?"

"I hate to admit it, but Morningside would call me an utter failure," Stevenson said. "Preliminary work shows nothing to worry about. The replicators mutated—radiation is my only guess why."

"What changes did this produce in the gray gooey gobs?"

"It made them viable," Stevenson said. "They can multiply on their own because the replicators' DNA joined with the spliced section on theirs, but why they're green is beyond me." He tapped the test tube containing his culture. "I studied the effect on the woman, how the cells spread on her legs, everything."

"What happened?"

Stevenson put the test tube back into the holder behind the protective glass door before answering. "The green flakes can multiply on their own, but they are still neutral cells."

"So they are harmless?"

"I've ordered all the debris collected in the forest burned," Stevenson said, "just as a precaution, but yeah, it's all as harmless as the original. There isn't an ecological niche for the green snow, and it would die out after a while. It serves no purpose I can discover."

"That's a relief," Elaine said. "Now what?"

"I want to find the other three cylinders, destroy them, then go back home, shout at Morningside, and *then* go to sleep for a week."

"Sounds good to me," Elaine said. "Mind if I join you?"

43

"How are you doing, George?"

Hank Wyatt had lost some of the haunted expression that had been his for so long. His wife was still alive, if not in remission, and his only son had slowly struggled back to a semblance of his usual healthy self. In the midst of all this, Hank had even managed to get some needed rest and put away a good meal or two. Things were still wrong in the world, but he was coming to grips with them now. A little.

"I want to go home, Dad," George said plaintively.

"Oh? Aren't they treating you well?"

"Quit teasing. The food's lousy, and this place is boring. There's nothing to do except watch TV, and I've seen everything. I want to go home."

"The doctor agrees," Hank Wyatt said. "How would you like to check out of here right now?"

"You're not joking? You mean it?" George sat up in bed, his eyes bright.

"I certainly do mean it. Your mother misses you, and so do I. Whatever nasty bug you had must have passed through your system. The doctor didn't know exactly how to treat you, so he more or less left you alone. Your fever burned out whatever brand of influenza you caught back in California."

"I'm going home!" George crowed. He bounded out of bed and tried to run around the room. He was weak but the sudden adrenaline rush kept him going. Rather than show his feebleness he grabbed on to the bed and edged around it, still bobbing up and down like a spring, then turned toward his father.

"I've got a present for Mom in my suitcase. I can't wait until she sees it."

"I'm sure she'll be happy with whatever you brought. Get dressed. I don't like this place any more than you do."

George started dressing, but the coughing continued until his face turned red. He sat down, and turned pale from the effort.

"Let's get you home," Henry Wyatt told his son.

The boy nodded dully. Wyatt knew his boy wasn't feeling as well as he pretended. George's suitcase was still at the airport, but they'd pick it up later. There wasn't any hurry. The airline had held it for more than a week already.

Wyatt stared out the window at the side of another building. Everything was too close, and he didn't know how much longer he could hold it at arm's length. But with both Margie and George at home, he could do it for a while. Just a while.

44

"They've what?" Tom Stevenson was astounded at Special Agent Bartholomew's simple statement. "After all this time, they've remembered me? I'm touched. They didn't even bother to send a Christmas card."

"You've got a bad attitude, Doc. You've been around the block more'n once with the government service. I've looked over your record. You know how they work."

Bartholomew ran his tongue around his teeth, pushing his lips outward in a grotesque gesture. "They didn't forget you, they just misremembered you."

"Until now."

"Hey, Doc, look at it from their angle. You're clean again. This gray-gooey-gob experiment, as you call it, is harmless. What more could a news-shy bunch like you work for want out of life? They're worse than the spook groups like the CIA and the NSA about publicity."

Stevenson stared at him in wonder. The man wasn't stupid. Why did he think everything was all right just because the brass hats back in the Pentagon said it was? The answer came to Stevenson in a flash of revelation. Bartholomew thought it was okay because this was the only way he would work. Cast off the dangerous until things resolved themselves, then embrace that which remained valuable. It was a sociopath's delight. What worked out was right. What failed was someone else's problem.

"What did the autopsy show on the woman?"

"What you'd predicted. The green stuff spread on the surface, like spreadin' glue. It wasn't growing. When she broke the test cylinder of yours wide open, she splattered it all over herself."

"You've been watching that patch of forest?"

"Your plastic sheet held everything down just fine, Doc. Cleaned the place up as slick as a whistle. Nothing spread, nothing is wrong, all is right. Why don't you let me go back to chasin' down the spies and you go back to growin' weird globs in test tubes?"

"Did you talk to Morningside?"

"Morningside? I thought it was Ironside." Bartholomew laughed at his small joke. "Reckon that's the name. He's real anxious to get you back in the fold."

"Do I have to hitchhike or is he sending a car for me?"

"He didn't mention that. I suppose you can contact him directly. We've got to get out of this high school. Be sure to clean up and turn out the lights."

Bartholomew walked toward the door of the biology classroom, then stopped and turned.

"I hope to hell I don't have occasion to see you again, Doc. You're a pleasant fellow, but you work with bugs too creepy for me to get a good's night sleep."

With that Larry Bartholomew was gone.

Stevenson began cleaning up, spraying down the work areas with a variety of acids taken from the chemistry lab. Aqua regia took off any oxidation on the surface, then strong disinfectants completed the job of sterilizing the laboratory. When he finished, the laboratory was in better condition than when he found it.

Stevenson heaved a deep sigh and went to find Elaine. He wasn't pleased with this turn of events. He'd as soon have continued being ignored. It would have made walking away from his job at Fort Detrick easier, but General Morningside never made things easy.

Tom Stevenson wasn't going to let the general off the hook this time, though. There would be hell to pay for cutting him loose in the field as Morningside had done.

45

"Fish or cut bait, General. That's the way I see it," Tom Stevenson stormed. "You've had me sitting on my thumb for six weeks. I've given seminars, done debriefings, talked to Pentagon bears, tried to convince Wyman that he shouldn't let the president stick my severed head on a pike outside the White House, I've—"

"Calm down, Tom," Morningside said. The general was ill-at-ease, but Stevenson was losing patience. Morningside had been stonewalling him for more than a month, and he was sick of it.

"You've left me slowly turning over the fire. My research has gone to hell, my suggestions about security leaks haven't been looked into, and now I find that someone's been tapping into my computer files."

"I've been catching hell too, Tom. You're not the only one who isn't happy with the way this came down," Morningside interrupted him.

Stevenson was too furious for words. He had been recalled to Fort Detrick, thinking Morningside would tell him why he had been cut loose and left to swing in the wind for almost two weeks, but the general's curt greeting a month and a half earlier had stunned him. More than anything else, this had gone a long way toward convincing him he ought to quit and find employment elsewhere—anywhere else. Back in California, he had mentioned this to Elaine, but wasn't committed to such a course then. He would have liked to keep his job as department supervisor, in spite of the lack of support on this project. The job carried a measure of prestige, though it now appeared to be a thing of the past, and he had derived more satisfaction from that work than any other job he had held. The papers he presented were thoughtful, studied, and well-researched, thanks to decent funding and the veil of secrecy that allowed him to make progress on a project without fear of usurpation by other researchers. Those were the good points.

Now he swung like a pendulum, between this job and private employment.

Worst of all, the security problems had not been addressed, and he didn't know why.

"I quit, General." He stood up and started to leave the wardroom.

"Tom, you can't walk out on me like this. There's important work to be done."

"The hell I can't chuck it all. I've cooled my heels too long waiting for a simple thank-you or, even better, an apology. I didn't think you were the kind to abandon your troops. After we got back, you didn't even have the courtesy to tell me why you deserted us out there. Zamora and Will Gorton were pulled back, and Elaine and I were left without knowing what was going on. I *still* don't know what end is up."

"Tom, be reasonable," Morningside pleaded. His tone took Stevenson aback. Morningside ordered, he blustered, he maneuvered—but he didn't grovel.

"Reasonable?" Stevenson was past caring about how Morningside manipulated his men. "We couldn't get past O'Connors. He fielded all the calls and shoved us into a box. It was black there, General. Too damned black for my liking."

"The Pentagon," Morningside muttered. "Beaumont called in a lot of markers on this one. He was responsible for stranding you. He made sure Major Zamora had packed up the pieces of the KH-18, and then he dropped a security net over everything. They . . . they ordered me not to contact you."

"They? Who is 'they'?"

Stevenson knew the answer. Wyman had given the order. The president probably knew nothing about it.

"The DCI and Wyman got together to discuss the ramifications. If anything came out of the KH-18 downing, you were to be the scapegoats."

"Were we supposed to be stuck with the two murders too? And why wait this long to tell me?"

"I've just disobeyed orders by discussing this with you," Morningside said, looking drawn and pale. "Losing a three-hundred-million-dollar bird is bad enough. Having it land and scatter plutonium dioxide over the countryside is even worse."

"Worst of all would be having a killer-mutant-germ-warfare experiment go bug-fuck on you, is that it?"

"The press . . ." Morningside now pleaded for forgiveness. It wasn't in Stevenson to give.

"If there had been a biohazard, it would have ripped through the entire state before you'd've admitted it—or would you have done so even then?"

Stevenson doubted that the Pentagon would have accepted any responsibility. The NBC command might have stepped in, trumpets blaring, to "contain" the resulting disease, but would never have admitted to causing the problem.

"The budget overruns, the publicity, Congress," Morningside started. None of the arguments held Stevenson, so the general shifted tactics. "Whom would we have sent? Will Gorton and his men were experts on radioactive spills. You and Reinhardt were the best we had to counter potential biological difficulty."

"Difficulty?" Stevenson shouted. "Others in my division would have been helpful. Basil Baker. Or Donnelly or Forsythe or Richard Chin. Any of them might have been able to help."

"Need to know, Tom," Morningside said. "They didn't have a need to know. This was more sensitive than you want to believe."

"It's been almost two months since I returned, and I've been effectively barred from my lab and from computer access because of all the debriefings you've made me attend. You've written me off as a division supervisor and a researcher. You know how that Lisa Taylor got her information—from Jack Parkessian. He's the one who ought to be kicked out, not me." Stevenson shook his head. He understood none of this. "I'm not able to take it any longer. I said I quit before, and I stand by it."

"As you wish, Dr. Stevenson," Morningside said coldly. "I've tried to explain our position. If you can't be a team player, well, it will be difficult to replace you, but for the good of the research unit and the country's security, it will be done."

"Ask Basil if he wants the job. He's always got his finger on the pulse of what's happening in the lab. He'd never disappoint you as I seem to have done—he's one hell of a masochist for this type of punishment."

As he spoke, some distant memory tried to crowd itself into his brain. Stevenson was too angry to let it burst forth. He shoved a chair out of the way and left the room, conscious of Morningside's hot glare on his back.

Stevenson ran into Basil Baker just outside the man's laboratory.

"Where are you going in such a hurry, Tom? I've been wanting to find out how your trip to Redding came out. What's with Project Big Hunk?"

"Ask Morningside. Or better yet, look it up yourself in my files."

"What's going on?" The man's bulbous nose looked shiny red in the fluorescent hallway lighting. Stevenson wondered if he had been drinking heavily. "You know I can't get into your files without access codes."

"Morningside will let you have them. Or ask Jack. I

think he's been mucking around in my files for months without my approval. I just nominated you to be the new division supervisor."

"What? What's going on, Tom? I don't want your job. Too much responsibility. Too high a visibility, and the pay's the bloody pits."

"I've got to go, Basil."

"Hate to hear you're leaving," Baker said. "But if I am made super, this is the best luck I've had since I found that nurse over in trauma a couple years back."

Again the memory nudged at Stevenson, but he was in too much of a hurry to tease it into full-blown existence. He muttered something inconsequential at Basil Baker and pressed on. He barely glanced into Parkessian's laboratory. The man worked at a transmission positron microscope. The sight of such equipment in the lab brought a lump to Stevenson's throat. The government might not pay as well as industry, but he'd have to find a job with the Japanese to equal the quality of equipment he had at his disposal—and his contract with the U.S. government forbade his accepting a position with any foreign company for two years.

A new job. Maybe it wasn't too bad. The security here was ass-backwards, and the pay wasn't that great, as Basil Baker had said. He came to a branching corridor. His office was at the far end of the left hallway. He turned right and walked slowly toward Elaine's office, hoping to catch her in. The door was closed but he heard the click-click-click of computer keys. He rapped twice and got no answer.

He poked his head inside the small room. Elaine was hunched over her workstation, lost in whatever problem she was working on.

"Got a minute?" Stevenson jumped when she did. She saw him and let out a long sigh of resignation.

"You startled me, Tom. I was busy working on—"

"Never mind that," he said. "You shouldn't be telling

me anything about your work. I no longer have a need to know."

"It finally came down to that?" she asked. She blanked her screen.

"I'd thought we could sort everything out after I got back. It didn't work."

"I haven't seen much of you during the past couple weeks," she said. "I've missed you. What made you change your mind about staying?"

"The Pentagon, the attitude, the way they would have used us to draw fire for the KH-18's crash. If there had been any biologic release, our heads would have rolled and saved Beaumont's and Morningside's and Wyman's."

"And the president's," she said.

"They'd have dropped us like a hot rock." He sat down in her desk chair and stared at the shelves of books.

"You knew it would be like that. From the instant Zamora split, you knew it."

"Yeah, but I'd hoped." He smiled crookedly. "The triumph of hope over experience kept me going for six weeks. No more. I've had enough of this."

"So?" Elaine pushed both hands through her thick black hair and leaned back in the swivel chair in front of her workstation. "What now?"

"I've been grilled and chastised, accused and badgered enough. What bothers me the most is that they've closed all records to me. I wanted to see if Bartholomew followed up on the missing three test tubes. I can't find out."

"They're harmless. Why bother?"

Stevenson shrugged. "Call it symmetry. In a way, I'm responsible for the project. I don't want it running around loose out there with no checks."

"Did you continue your tests after your return?"

"I wanted to, but jurisdictional hassles over the green particulate matter made it impossible. The FBI has it and won't release it; the Pentagon wants it and can't get it. From what has been said, Morningside tried to recover it for more tests inside Fort Detrick but couldn't."

"Where is the debris?"

"It must be in some FBI evidence vault. In Washington, maybe." He shrugged again. He wished he could have continued the tests on the material in the tube. The neutral cells should not have changed color and become viable, even if they organically remained the same basic neutral cells.

"A cell without function, except for reproduction." He leaned back and laced his fingers behind his head. It would have been an interesting experiment, finding out why the gray gooey gobs had mutated, *how* they had changed, and what it meant having a cell with no function except reproduction.

He no longer had a need to know—and hadn't since returning from Redding.

"You should have received a medal, not this," Elaine said.

"Thanks, love. I appreciate the support. But life goes on. I've got to think of the future." He wanted to ask her about her own change of heart, but he knew the answer. In Redding the job had seemed terrible and the betrayal even worse. Back in harness, Fort Detrick was a good place to work, intellectually stimulating. He had never been bored there. It must be the same way for Elaine.

"You're not, though," she said, reading his mood accurately. "You want to find the other three test cylinders."

He smiled sheepishly.

"Why not? No one else does. And truth to tell, I'm curious to see what rumors are flying around that neighborhood concerning the Devlins. The FBI's efficiency in covering up two cold-blooded murders astounds me."

"Makes you wonder, doesn't it?" Elaine said. "What else have they covered up in the name of national security and we've never known?"

"That's something else Morningside is ignoring—a leak inside our division. It's got to be Jack. How else could the KGB have known to home in on the Devlins? We didn't know Billy had the experiment until long after the woman and her contact had gone to the coast to be picked up."

"Jack might have slept with her, but the leak might be somewhere else. Think about it. A downed spy satellite is a hot property. The KGB might have just stumbled on the experiment. Why put a bio-experiment in orbit? Their paranoid conclusion has to be that it's a dangerous weapon."

"We should put all Congress in orbit. That's where the real danger lies."

"Don't get bitter," Elaine chastised. "Where are you going to look for a new job? You can always teach at Stanford."

Stevenson abruptly changed topics. "Do you remember the Christmas party two or three years ago?"

"Not really. Why?"

"Who was Basil's date then?"

"Can't say I remember," Elaine said. "That came from left field. Why do you ask?"

"Nothing." He heaved himself to his feet and said, "You ought to apply for my job. The division can use someone at the helm who knows the ropes."

Elaine's dark eyes bored into his. "I won't be staying too much longer, Tom. It wouldn't be the same with you out on the coast and me here."

He experienced a moment's uneasiness. Quitting his job was a major upheaval in his life. What was happening between him and Elaine unsettled him even more. She wanted to come with him. That meant changing their almost-friends-but-more relationship to something else. He wasn't sure he wanted to take that step.

And yet he did. He was losing his job; he didn't want to lose Elaine too.

Did he love her or was he holding on for the security

she could give him during this emotional and professional upheaval?

"You finish off your work," he said. "It'll be a day or two before I go back to Redding."

"I'll be done here around six," she said. "Your place or mine?"

"Mine," he heard himself saying. Another entity might as well have taken control of his body. Stevenson kissed her and left in a daze.

So much was happening. So much, so fast . . .

46

Thomas Stevenson felt better about returning to Redding than he had about leaving for the northern California city two months earlier. The pressure was off. All he had to do was clear up the mystery of the missing three cylinders, recover them, and his role in the fiasco would be at a final end.

He whistled tunelessly as he drove up I-5 from Sacramento. He had quit his job. Fort Detrick was a good place to work, with good equipment and fascinating projects. In his twelve years there he had worked on isolating human growth-factor hormones, several anticancer projects, and most recently had delved into the use of nanotechnology replicators to manipulate and rebuild animal cells for his own purposes. Utilizing the replicators to fiddle with crystal structures to produce new enzymes and amino acids, define new functions for cells, discover completely unexpected organisms that were neither bacterium nor virus, filled him with a sense of accomplishment.

Project Big Hunk was a part of it—and a part that was in his past, except for the tidying-up he had to do. He just wished he could understand what had happened at Fort Detrick. Parkessian had not been suspended, even after Lisa Taylor's connection with him had been established. It was as if the security breach did not matter. Stevenson knew Parkessian must have violated security measures at other times. He remembered the man bragging about the crypto clerk dispensing classified information to him.

But Jack Parkessian was still at Fort Detrick and Thomas Stevenson wasn't. It didn't make much sense.

He tried to backtrack and figure out when his job had become a chore rather than a challenge. Stevenson couldn't pinpoint a date, but it had to be around the arrival of Jack Parkessian at the lab. In the ambitious research assistant he had seen his own replacement, the wave of the future, the aggressiveness of youth that he had lost—his own obsolescence.

"Germ warfare," he scoffed. "That's what the press thinks it is. I'm better off away from there."

He took a swallow of the coffee from the polystyrene cup in a holder on the dashboard and made a face. It was cold and bitter. He drove past the fleabag motel where he had stayed with Elaine. He had enough money in his bank account and in his pockets to do better than that this time. He found a Holiday Inn and pulled in. When he unpacked and hung his clothes in the closet, he decided it wasn't that much better. Heavy mildew odor clung to the rugs and drapes. The sink in the bathroom had come loose from the wall and stood precariously on two nicked silver legs, and the bathtub tiles had seen better days. Stevenson splashed water on his face and decided the place was clean and adequate for his needs. There was no reason to stay at a lavish five-star hotel, after all. Just a box to sleep in.

Stevenson looked at the hard bed and considered a short nap. He needed the rest, but he decided to do some quick work on his laptop computer beforehand. He pulled it from its case and plugged it in to save his precious batteries. Grumbling as he stared at the twisted-strand LCD display, he wondered why no one had put an atomic battery into a laptop. The Air Force used them in their satellites. Why not here, where he needed it? Each RTG unit produced about 285 watts, more than enough to run his computer.

He snorted and talked to himself as he entered information into the small computer. Maps of the area popped into view. He added the location of the downed KH-18, the scatter pattern showing where they had found the spilled plutonium-dioxide pellets from the on-board radioisotope thermoelectric generator, then finished with the main pod containing his experiment.

The Devlin house was a good four miles away. Billy had intentionally sought out the satellite, Stevenson decided. The presence of the telescope told him the boy had been interested in astronomy—or had a friend named George Wyatt who was. He continued to enter data into his random-relational data base, then pressed the key to let it sort and shift and come to some rudimentary artificial-intelligence conclusions.

He was pleased to see that the computer's coldly logical AI conclusion matched his intuitive one. He leaned back in the hard chair and smiled. This was the way to work. Let the computer come up with an answer, match it with what he had already decided, then proceed from there. If the two answers differed, pick a middle course.

"Find George Wyatt," he said. "Simple and straightforward." He reached over to the bedside table and picked up the telephone book. A quick search revealed four Wyatts in Redding. Ten minutes of phoning made Stevenson frown. He had drawn a blank with all four numbers. No George Wyatt. No teenage sons, for that matter.

Stevenson pored over the map, the addresses of the Wyatts listed in the telephone book, and frowned even harder. None had a home near the Devlin house.

"Time for fieldwork," he said.

His gut-level instinct was that Billy Devlin's friend lived in the area. Stevenson saved his notes, the map with its scatter pattern, and encoded them out of sheer habit. He had worked with classified projects too long not to use rudimentary trapdoor codes, even on his laptop-computer files. He closed the lid on the computer and put it back into its case. He had developed complex methods in his undergraduate days.

It was time to put them to use in Billy Devlin's neighborhood.

Stevenson stretched and yawned. He remembered how tired he had been when Major Zamora had found the KH-18 and worked them around the clock. He was as tired now, and he was his own taskmaster. The Devlin house was still sealed tight. He had spent the afternoon asking neighbors about the Devlins but hadn't learned anything important.

The government still hid the details of their deaths. As far as anyone nearby knew, the Devlins had gone on vacation and had never returned. One woman ventured a guess that they had left Redding because of Billy's death. The others didn't show even this much inventiveness. They shrugged their shoulders and looked blank before closing the door in Stevenson's face.

He slowly walked up and down the streets, taking careful note of the mailboxes and the names on them. He wished he had been able to read Special Agent Bartholomew's final report. The FBI must have blanketed the area with agents searching for the Devlins' killers. Names and relations would have been recorded, and this could have given him the lead he needed.

Few of the people fitted the pattern Stevenson sought. Most were older, retired, or without children. Retirees might look after grandchildren, though. It had been Christmas. George Wyatt might have come to visit. That would be the way to proceed, but Stevenson lacked the resources to follow up on the idea.

And who wanted to answer personal questions when a stranger knocked at the door?

Stevenson changed his tactics when he went to the next house. An older woman peered through the chain-locked door at him.

"What do you want?"

"I'm conducting a survey, ma'am," he said. He prepared himself for the big lie. "I'm with the city, and we're talking with residents about teenagers and whether they've been disturbed by their activities."

"Not many children in the area," the woman said. She paused, and Stevenson's heart sped up. She wanted to say more.

"We've had complaints," he said, letting his voice trail off. She would finish for him if he gave her enough opportunity.

"There was that Devlin boy, but he died."

"He and his friends did raise a ruckus," Stevenson said, pretending to check his notebook. "Especially one named George Wyatt. Broke a window and . . . other things."

"Do tell?" the woman said, interested. "I never met the boy, but he seemed a decent sort. Never knew why they let him hang out with that Devlin boy. *He* was a troublemaker, and little wonder, with his parents."

"An alcoholic father," Stevenson said, remembering what Bartholomew had told him.

"And his mother wasn't much better. But Peter didn't see anything wrong with letting the boy out with Billy."

"Peter? Is that George's father?"

"No, his *grand*father. Peter Stratton."

Stevenson checked his list of names and addresses. "Is that the Stratton over a street, 523 Herring Road?"

"Don't know the address, but they live on Herring Road."

Stevenson spent a few more minutes skirting the issue, asking pointless questions about gangs and teen violence more appropriate for a big city than a suburban area of Redding. He dutifully made notes and left, letting the woman think he was keeping the streets safe for her.

He made a beeline for the Stratton house, then hesitated for a moment as he stood in front of the house. It looked the same as the other tract houses, but something stirred within him, telling him this was the place. He was close to recovering his lost cylinders.

A pleasant-looking woman with a small smear of flour

on her cheek answered the doorbell. She had been in the kitchen cooking.

"Mrs. Stratton?"

"Yes." She wasn't as hesitant as the other woman. She didn't bother leaving the door on a chain lock.

"I'm looking for George Wyatt. I've been told he's your grandson."

"He is," she said. A suspicious light clicked on in her eyes. "What do you want with George? He's a good boy."

"I'm not a policeman, ma'am," Stevenson said. "I am with the government, however." This lie came out easily. For twelve years he had been, and he was still doing work that they ought to have done. "We have reason to believe your grandson saw a meteorite one night and investigated it with a friend named Billy Devlin."

"Billy's dead," she said. "I read it in the paper. What a tragedy, being killed by a hit-and-run driver."

Stevenson paused when he heard this. The cover-up had been thorough.

"Is anything wrong?" Mrs. Stratton asked.

"Not really. Your grandson's an amateur astronomer, isn't he?"

"Why, yes. He got a fine telescope for Christmas."

"May I speak with him?"

"He . . . no." The woman started to close the door.

"He's not ill, is he?" Stevenson asked. If Billy Devlin had died from exposure to plutonium, it was likely George Wyatt was similarly contaminated. By now, he might be dead. Had the government covered up his death also?

He decided against it. Mrs. Stratton was worried, but not angry at opening old wounds.

"How did you know he'd been ill?"

"Had been? Is he better?"

Before she could speak, Peter Stratton pushed past her. "I heard the questions. Do you have some ID?"

"Your son left his telescope with Billy Devlin. It's over at their house. You can get it back if you contact Special

Agent Bartholomew. He's with the San Francisco office of the FBI. Sorry I bothered you." Stevenson backed off and started to go. Peter Stratton would have stonewalled him if he had kept pressing with his questions. Now he had sparked the man's curiosity.

"Wait a second, mister."

"Stevenson, Tom Stevenson. Pleased to meet you." Stevenson thrust out his hand. Peter Stratton shook it with restraint.

"Mr. Stevenson, George was ill. We put him on a plane and sent him back to his parents in New Orleans."

Stevenson wanted to jump for joy. His detective work had paid off. All that remained was to be sure the boy hadn't left the cylinders here—or buried them somewhere. As the thought crossed his mind, his elation evaporated.

"I'm interested in three quartz containers the boy had. Billy had two and George had three."

"I don't remember seeing anything like that," Mrs. Stratton said.

"He might have packed them in his luggage. He was secretive about it, even as sick as he was."

Stevenson described radiation poisoning symptoms.

"Did he have any burns?"

"No, but he did have symptoms something like you described. How did you know?" Peter Stratton was growing wary again.

"He recovered, you say? I'd like to speak with his doctor, or with his parents."

"That's impossible." The curtness of the answer told Stevenson he still didn't know the full extent of the problem.

"I'm with an agency of the public-health department. Billy had a communicable disease."

"He died in a hit-and-run accident."

Stevenson nodded. "True, but the autopsy showed traces of a disease that would cause the symptoms I've outlined. If George has recovered, then everything is fine. I would like to speak with his doctor to confirm his diagnosis. George might not have the same virus at all.''

"Peter, what harm can there be in giving him the name of Margaret's doctor at Tulane? He was the one who treated George.''

Again Stevenson almost smiled. Their daughter's name was Margaret and she and her husband lived in New Orleans. He wasn't sure he wanted to pursue the matter any further.

Stratton asked, "What's this about quartz containers?''

"If your grandson is well, I'm happy. I'll make a notation of it.''

"He's fine. He spent a few days in the hospital and then he was released. He's been fine.''

"Thank you for your time.'' Stevenson left quickly. He had learned that they didn't have the experiment. They hadn't even known what had happened to their grandson's telescope. That meant George Wyatt had been shipped back home in a hurry.

"Little wonder," Stevenson muttered, "if he had radiation sickness. But it couldn't have been too bad.'' He finished making a few notes in his spiral book and headed back for the hotel for a long hot shower and a good night's rest. The Strattons didn't have the experiment, but Stevenson now knew that George had it in New Orleans and that his mother's name was Margaret.

If he ever got ambitious enough, he could recover the three cylinders. But why bother? The green flakes weren't dangerous, even if the boy swallowed them.

Symmetry, he told himself. He had to get them back for the sake of symmetry.

47

Thomas Stevenson was torn between pursuing his hunt to its conclusion and quitting. Calling General Morningside and telling him what he had discovered about the stolen experiment—that should be good enough. Given the way the Pentagon bears, including the president, had treated him, he wasn't sure if he ought to do even this much.

He smiled wryly. Calling the FBI agent and telling him what he had found might be more fitting. Bartholomew was a pig, but a brain worked overtime behind that corpulent, oafish exterior. Let it look as if the FBI had retrieved the missing test elements. That would cause waves all the way up to Wyman. Stevenson didn't kid himself that the president would hear of it. The national security adviser would squelch it the instant such news hit his desk, but it would occupy a day or more of his time.

The Director of Central Intelligence would have to call the FBI director. They would have to discuss the matter. The Pentagon would be informed. General Beaumont would be called on the carpet. He would kick and scream to both the secretary of defense and the Joint Chiefs of Staff, who would chew Morningside's ass for his failure.

It was a long and complex chain of red tape, but Stevenson knew it would be followed just as he had mentally outlined. But was this secondhand revenge even worth doing?

Stevenson trudged up the steps to his second-floor room at the Holiday Inn. He paused for a moment when his key touched the lock. Something was wrong. Tense, every sense straining, he unlocked the door and opened it slowly.

He heard his intruder before he saw him.

"Hello, old chap. How's everything going out on the frontier?"

Basil Baker sat in the room's only comfortable chair, his feet hiked up to the corner of the bed.

"How did you get in?"

"A jolly bother, it was, but the room clerk actually came around to believing my story. I told him you were my American cousin, and he saved me from the beastly cold. It's true, in a way, that we're cousins. You and I always were closer than most. Too many of the scientists at Fort Detrick resent a foreigner in their midst. Not you, Thomas. You always made me feel right at home."

Stevenson would have disputed that. He had found Baker to be too much the gossip for his taste and had grown used to editing everything he said in front of the biologist. He wondered if Basil Baker had ever finished an assignment without quizzing a dozen others for their opinions.

"What are you doing here?"

"I told you. I wanted out of the cold."

"What are you doing in Redding?"

Stevenson hated it when Baker played coy. He was as tired as he was elated at having discovered where the three cylinders were. All he needed now was time to work out his options. He could fetch the three test tubes, he could tell Morningside, or he could give Larry Bartholomew a call. Either of the last two courses held promise; he was dog tired.

"Didn't the general tell you? He shipped a team of us out to give you a hand."

"The hell you say. I don't work for him anymore. I resigned."

Basil Baker's eyebrows rose at this.

"Morningside never mentioned accepting your resignation. He bloody well hinted that you were out here on a secret mission and that you needed backup. So he sent me and Chin and a couple others."

"Where are they?" Stevenson asked.

"They've got rooms across town. It was hard tracking you down. Morningside didn't see fit to tell me where you were lodging. Can't bloody well understand his reasons."

Stevenson pulled his laptop from its case and plugged it in. A few quick keystrokes got through the encoding and brought up his file holding all he knew about the downed KH-18 and the loss of his experiment. Half-listening to Baker, he typed in his most recent findings.

"He told us your public resignation was a smoke screen. You had come back to the wild west to . . ." Baker's words trailed off, as if he expected Stevenson to fill in the rest of the sentence.

Stevenson worked on his computer, then saved his material, certain it was encoded once more. Only then did he turn off the laptop and give Baker his full attention.

"It wasn't one of those damned security ploys. I *did* quit, and Morningside knows I meant it. What are you supposed to be doing to help me?"

"That's wasn't too clear," Baker said, frowning. "Morningside hinted that we would get out here and then you'd brief us on your progress. The crashed satellite and all that."

Stevenson no longer worked for the government, but his contract had forbade him from discussing classified matters for a period of ten years.

"Ask Morningside," he said. "I'm a civilian again. What I do is my own business."

"Most peculiar," Baker said. "This isn't what I was led to expect from you. You say you *have* resigned?"

"It's not a British TV show, either," Stevenson said. "I've resigned for good, and Morningside knows why."

"But Elaine remained behind." Baker's bulbous nose wiggled as he frowned even harder than before. "I really do not understand this. Not one bit of it."

"Too bad." Stevenson had decided on his own course of action. The cylinders had to be recovered, but Morningside was sneaking around behind him, sending out Basil Baker and others from his division. He could retrieve the quartz tubes, but his interest was rapidly waning. He was too tired of this to fly to New Orleans.

Agent Bartholomew could do as he pleased with the information.

This simple decision made Stevenson smile. He had figured out the chain of woe it would cause. He had nothing against Morningside, not personally, but professionally this would put five or six pounds of demerits into his service record. It might even cost him another star when the DCI, the JCS, and the national security adviser finished with him.

"What have you found out? You were certainly busy with the computer," Baker said.

"Haven't found out anything that would interest you or Morningside. Sorry," he said insincerely. "If you don't mind, I'd like to get some rest. It's been a long day."

"Very well," Baker said, heaving his feet off the bed. "Just remember, we're here to help however we can. Do call on us. Cheerio."

Stevenson waited for Basil Baker to leave, then closed the curtains and dropped onto the bed. The more he thought about the biologist being sent to Redding, the more furious he got. Stevenson reached for the telephone book, found the number he wanted, and called the local FBI office. It took another ten minutes to reach Bartholomew in the San Francisco office.

"Special Agent Bartholomew, how may I help you?" came the crisp voice. For a moment, Stevenson was taken aback. It held none of the Southern drawl he had come to expect from Bartholomew.

"This is Tom Stevenson."

"Hey, Doc, how're they hangin'?" The abrupt change convinced Stevenson that much of what Bartholomew did and said was for effect.

"I'm in Redding, tracking down the remaining cylinders."

"Do tell. We've been havin' some second thoughts about closin' this case ourselves. You have any luck tracin' down those puppies?"

Stevenson considered telling him about George Wyatt and the three test cylinders in New Orleans. Something made him hold back.

"Some luck, yes. I'd like to discuss the matter with you in person."

"Reckon that's possible," Bartholomew said. "There's a matter I need some consultation on. Can you drive on down to San Francisco by tomorrow morning?"

"Make it tomorrow afternoon. That's quite a drive. As I said, I'm in Redding."

"Three o'clock sharp, in my office. You know where the Hall of Justice is? I'm in the government annex next door, down in the catacombs. Just ask. Everyone knows where it is." Bartholomew paused, then added, "There anything you needin' to tell me right now?"

"Tomorrow," Stevenson said. This was working out better than he had thought. He wanted to go to San Francisco and start his inquiries about jobs. Elaine had mentioned a possible post at Berkeley. He could talk with Bartholomew and then get across the bay before rush hour and make an appointment for an interview with the medical-sciences department in the Donner Laboratory before they closed for the day.

Who knew? He might be done with the KH-18 experiment and have a new position all in one day.

Basil Baker watched him come down the black-metal-and-concrete stairs and go toward the restaurant. He waited until Stevenson was out of sight before following him. A slow smile crossed his lips as he saw him place his order. Service was slow here, and Stevenson always took his time eating. It paid to note the odd habits of those around you. Basil Baker knew he had time enough.

He returned to Stevenson's room, pulled out the lock

picks, and got to work. It had taken him ten minutes to get in before. This time, with his "touch memory," he was able to pick the lock in only six minutes. He slipped into the room and went directly to the laptop computer.

"Ah, yes, this is the little darling I've come for," he crooned to himself. He powered it up and began typing slowly when he got the cursor on the screen. He broke Stevenson's code in minutes. It took even less for him to scan the information Stevenson had entered.

Baker turned off the computer, replaced it in its case and, before leaving the room, checked the bug he had put into the telephone. It was still functioning. Now he needed to replay the voice-activated recording to find out if Stevenson had used the phone—and whom he had called.

Basil Baker slipped from the room, taking care to relock the door behind him. He didn't think Stevenson would notice, but it never paid to take unnecessary risks.

48

Stevenson fumed. The rental car was costing him a young fortune; he had already gone beyond the limited mileage and was now paying by the mile. It seemed to take a hundred miles just to find a parking place near the Hall of Justice, south of Market Street. The only thing he didn't have trouble with was locating Bartholomew's office. Huge arrows pointed to the basement annex used by the FBI agent.

Stevenson went into an office that was twice the width of his shoulders but as long as the corridor on the other side of the cinder-block wall. One particle-board-partitioned alcove after another showed to his right. The third one held a battered gray-metal standard government-issue desk with Bartholomew's name engraved on a fake gold plate. The special agent was nowhere to be seen.

Stevenson stood to one side and read the papers strewn over the agent's desk. Most had to do with crimes that were of little interest to him. A notification about a kidnapper being caught in West Virginia lay atop the stack, a wanted poster on a husband-and-wife team wanted for mail fraud poked out from the bottom, and a man who had crossed state lines to avoid prosecution in Arizona completed the pile. The few knickknacks on the desk were more interesting than Bartholomew's mail. The baby alligator swallowing its tail and holding a cheap glass ashtray testified to Bartholomew's taste for the outrageous.

"There you are, Doc. I was wonderin' what happened

to you. This town'll eat you up if you let it. I saw a guy carryin' an Uzi out in plain sight the other day, and another guy in a skull mask takin' a baseball bat to some son of a bitch ridin' a bicycle. And to top it all off, there's no parking. Everyone uses the BART or the damned cable cars or trolleys to get where they're going."

"What's wrong with that?"

"The cable cars are filled with tourists, and the trolleys have hordes of senior citizens on them usin' the discount fares. Never figured out how to take the BART north and south, and the buses have a route that reminds me of a drunken cow staggerin' through a meadow. Sooner or later they'll get to where you want, but it might take a while."

Bartholomew indicated the single chair beside his desk. Stevenson sat down, waiting for Bartholomew to get the down-home homilies out of his system. The agent surprised him.

"There have been three deaths," he said suddenly. "All at the airport. How's this tie in with what you've discovered?"

Stevenson was taken aback and had to rethink what he was going to say.

"Nothing that I know of. I just wanted to find the last three cylinders."

"Did you find them?"

"Not exactly." Stevenson watched the FBI agent close his eyes, then open them as if hoping a major annoyance would have evaporated.

"What have you discovered?"

"If I'm taking up valuable time . . ."

"Spit it out, Doc. This is a thorn in my side. I don't like it, the special agent in charge does not like it, and, so help me, the director himself isn't tickled pink with it either."

Stevenson hesitated, confusion tangling both tongue and thoughts. Everything had been crystal clear to him back in Redding. Basil Baker's intrusion had galvanized his thinking. Put it to Morningside. Let the bastards in the Pentagon squirm. And if he could reach all the way to Fred Wyman, so much the better.

Bartholomew's attitude changed his feelings of vengeance to something more akin to confusion.

"I may know who has the other test tubes from the experiment."

"So?"

"Nothing, Bartholomew, nothing. Forget I ever came here."

"Wait, Doc." The words snapped like a whip. "I did some calling around after you contacted me. You quit your job back at the germ factory."

"Fort Detrick," Stevenson corrected absently.

"They've cut you loose, and this is all on your own stick, right?"

"I like seeing a project through to its finish. Having three of the five cylinders unaccounted for bothers me, even if they are harmless."

"Yeah, right."

"What are you saying, Bartholomew? Are you telling me they aren't harmless?"

"You did the field testing on the one Lisa Taylor busted open. You're the expert on the stuff. It's your experiment, after all. You tell me if they're nontoxic."

"From all the work I did immediately afterward, I can say they seemed harmless." Stevenson damned himself for falling into the CYA mode, but he felt the steel-jawed trap closing around him again. What did Bartholomew know—and Basil Baker and Morningside?

"Tell me all about it. Then you can clear out of here. You won't have to sully your hands with it again."

"Why did you mention that three people died?"

"Coincidence," Bartholomew said. He rocked back in his chair and laced his fingers over his paunch. "I *hate* coincidence. The three died and the autopsies came back negative. Nobody could figure out what croaked them. They just . . . died. One wit with the M.E.'s office suggested germ warfare. The papers picked it up, we had a couple dozen people marching on this building, shouting about government spooks. That stirred up everyone in the office for a month or so, but there wasn't anything to show any connection with Fort Detrick's primary product." Bartholomew smiled without humor.

Stevenson went cold all over. "You said they died at the airport?"

"They were baggage handlers."

"Did they load baggage for a flight to New Orleans two days after Christmas?"

Bartholomew blinked. "How the hell should I know that? What do you know that I ought to?"

Stevenson revealed what he had discovered about George Wyatt, finishing in a rush that left him exhausted. He still had a premonition that George Wyatt's sickness might not have been plutonium poisoning. If he had been exposed to as much radiation as Billy, he should have died too.

"So you're sayin' he might have come down with some berserk mutant germ from your Project Big Hunk?"

"It's possible, but I'd be inclined to doubt the gray gooey gobs did anything, or the green flakes, for that matter. I ran tests on the green particles, and they weren't too different from the originally gengineered experiment; they were innocuous. And this George Wyatt is still alive—your baggage handlers are dead. Why didn't he die?"

"Good questions, Doc."

Bartholomew sucked on his gums, then fished in a drawer for a toothpick. He began digging away at his molars, the toothpick pulling his lip back to the breaking point.

"Let's hop a bureau plane back to Redding and do some official digging. You got time?"

Stevenson had the time. His stomach produced acid whenever he contemplated the possibility that his experiment had caused the three men's deaths. And what of a fourteen-year-old boy in New Orleans? Stevenson had to recover the three missing cylinders and know for certain he wasn't culpable.

49

"The bureau spends a fortune every year on junkets like this," Bartholomew said, hunched over the wheel of the expensive rental car. Stevenson tried not to appear apprehensive about the hell-bent-for-leather way the agent drove. Bartholomew wheeled in and out of traffic on I-5 recklessly, swearing the while.

"You've got a charter plane on call all the time?" Stevenson asked, more to keep his own mind off Bartholomew's driving than through any desire to know how his tax money was spent by the FBI.

"Special rates this month. The bureau's in a new high-visibility drive against drugs, so we can flit anywhere we want on a second's notice. We'd better not tie up the plane longer than a couple hours. The boss gets real mad if I do. Somebody might actually have to use it for something important."

Stevenson couldn't bear to look forward any longer. The cars whipped past, some just inches away from their fender. He turned in his seat and looked at Bartholomew's partner. Dennis slept noisily in the rear seat and provided no hint of conversation to take Stevenson's mind off the perilous trip.

"What about your partner?"

"Dennis? He's all tired out. Been through the wringer the past couple weeks, and he's only just back from administrative leave."

The way he cut off discussion told Stevenson not to

pursue the matter. "Administrative leave" was a bureau-cratic euphemism for screwing up and being placed on leave until blame could be assigned. Dennis' presence indicated that the matter was closed. Otherwise the FBI agent would be guarding federally owned paper clips in Icebox, Alaska.

Realizing that Dennis was not one for conversation at that time, he reluctantly faced forward once more, trying to occupy himself with thoughts other than imminent death. Stevenson tried to figure out the roads Bartholomew took, but he lost track within minutes of leaving the freeway. The FBI agent seemed to know Redding well, shooting up residential streets and across thoroughfares, missing both stoplights and the small traffic jams that plagued even this small city at five-o'clock rush hour.

"There it is," he said.

"Why check out the Devlins' house again? I thought you'd gone over it with a fine-tooth comb."

"The lieutenant in the local police force I was dealin' with kept buttin' in where he wasn't wanted," Bartholomew said. "I had our boys go over the place, but they didn't turn up squat. That KGB agent we got over on the coast was good at what he did."

"So why are we coming back here? Wouldn't you rather check out the Strattons?"

"In a while," Bartholomew said. "I put a stopper on this place, hopin' something would turn up. The business with the telescope is it. We take the gadget back to the Stratton place and see if they can make a positive ID on it."

"But it has their grandson's name on a brass plate. The scope is too expensive to belong to Billy Devlin."

"Never considered that. Must be slippin' in my old age. Maybe it was that lieutenant takin' my mind off business. Can't work with too many people breathin' down my neck all the time. That's why I don't mind havin' him as a partner." The agent jerked his thumb over his shoulder to indicate the still-sleeping Dennis.

Stevenson clutched at the dashboard as Bartholomew pulled into the driveway, braked fast, and hopped out before the car had come to rest on its springs. Stevenson followed, unsure why they had returned here. He had to be right about the telescope. As Bartholomew had said earlier, he didn't like coincidence, and it would have been an unbelievable one if Billy had somehow acquired the telescope with George Wyatt's name without direct contact with the boy.

"Got equipment with you, Doc?"

The question took Stevenson by surprise. "What sort of equipment?"

"You know, stuff like you used out on the coast. Biology stuff."

"No. What you see is what you get."

"WYSIWYG," Bartholomew grumbled, pronouncing the acronym as "wizzy-wig."

"Sorry. I didn't know we were making a forensics assault on the house."

"Not that. We went over the entire place for fingerprints and the like. I wanted a biological scan."

"You've dodged telling me about the three dead men at the airport. What happened to them?"

Bartholomew shrugged. "We called in the big guns for those autopsies. That's why they came up with the germ-warfare scenario, though they drew the line at suggesting it was *our* germs. One pencil-neck from San Diego suggested, in writing yet, that this was a clandestine Iraqi assault on our shores." Bartholomew snorted in contempt. "I'm more inclined to believe it came from the satellite that got spirited away. Didn't that strike you as odd, Doc?"

"That Zamora took everything and vanished? Of course it did. They didn't bother telling me a damned thing. Hell, General Morningside sent part of my former division out to follow up on the crash." Stevenson smiled wryly. "They didn't even tell them I no longer work at Fort Detrick."

"Left hand, right hand," Bartholomew said, disgust in his voice. "One never knows what the other's doing." He rapped hard on the back window and woke Dennis. The other FBI agent stirred and came out of the car like a bear leaving winter hibernation.

"Get your bones moving," Bartholomew ordered. "We're going over the house one last time. Look for green snow."

"Wasn't there before," Dennis said, stretching and yawning mightily. "I couldn't have missed it if it looked like the shit the Taylor broad had at the coast shoot-out."

"We look again, this time with a magnifying glass."

Bartholomew scratched his crotch and strode up to the house. Stevenson noticed two neighbors peering out their windows. He hurried after the two agents, feeling uncomfortable and not knowing why. This time he had authorization to search the house, but it still irked him.

"You want to go to work out in the area where the two were snuffed?" Bartholomew pointed Dennis across the living room and toward the den, where the Devlins had been murdered. "The Doc and I'll check out the kid's bedroom. I want to take the telescope."

"Got it," said Dennis.

Bartholomew turned and started for Billy's room. Stevenson was just behind him when he stopped and stiffened. He had heard something out of the ordinary. Before he could ask Bartholomew what the soft sliding and snapping noise was, a shot rang out.

"Damn," came Dennis' muffled cry. Two more shots followed. Then Stevenson found himself too caught up in action to understand what was happening. Bartholomew shoved him out of the way so hard that he smashed into the wall.

Stevenson turned awkwardly, lost his balance, and dropped to his knees. Bartholomew roared like a charging bull, ripping his service revolver from its holster. More shots echoed down the hall.

"Bartholomew!" Stevenson tried to get to his feet, but a cascade of plaster from a passing bullet drove him back down.

"Shut up and stay down," came the agent's sharp command.

Dennis called out something that vanished in a roar of gunfire. Stevenson fell flat on his belly and wiggled for the bathroom.

50

Stevenson kicked the bathroom door shut behind him and struggled to sit beside the toilet, using it as a porcelain shield. Panting hard, he heard continued gunfire out in the house and wondered what the hell they had blundered into. Dennis had caught the brunt of the bullets, of that he was certain. The sound of lead striking bone was unmistakable, and Stevenson had heard it twice before in his life: during a bank robbery, and during an ill-fated hunting trip his brother had organized.

The gunfire died down for a few seconds; then came a single shot that made him jump. He knew he couldn't stay here. If Bartholomew and Dennis were the victors, he was relatively safe. They were professionals and wouldn't shoot at any movement, no matter how keyed-up they were. But he couldn't count on their victory in this shoot-out.

CYA. That's what he had to do. Stevenson looked around and saw an access panel to the attic above the toilet. He dropped the lid, jumped up, and pushed hard against the panel. It had been painted into place. This would take more work than he had thought—was it worth the effort?

He went to the bathroom door and opened it a crack. He saw Bartholomew lying facedown in the hall. Beyond him, in the living room, Dennis lay sprawled on his back, arms akimbo. Of their attacker he saw nothing. Stevenson let out the breath he had been holding and started to explore. A sixth sense made him freeze.

A dim figure dressed in gray flitted across his field of vision. He got a clear look at the plastic pistol clutched in the man's hand. Stevenson had heard two of the gun nuts in his division talking about the Glock 17. One biochemist had shown detailed pictures from a magazine to Stevenson, gleeful about the weapon's ballistics, heft, and ability to slip past most airport metal detectors.

Stevenson knew he could not leave the room without being seen—and ending up like Bartholomew and Dennis. He gritted his teeth as he closed the bathroom door, acutely aware of the slightest creak and squeaking. One quick look at the small frosted window over the bathtub told him he would never get his broad shoulders through it in time. And he had no idea who might be waiting outside the house. Anyone willing to gun down two FBI agents would be clever enough to post sentries outside to cut off retreat.

He jumped back to the toilet lid and almost fell off in his haste. Stevenson stopped, took a deep, calming breath, then began working on the access panel to the overhead crawl space. The paint chipped and flaked and came off with protesting screeches loud enough to awaken the dead. Stevenson tried not to think of the noise or the sweat pouring down his forehead and into his eyes.

He paused when he heard the soft padding of steps outside. The killer was coming after him, checking the rooms to see that he had eliminated all opposition. Stevenson redoubled his efforts; the small plywood panel popped free.

He wanted to collapse and thank his lucky stars but knew he had to keep going. If he tried to celebrate too early, he'd end up dead like the FBI agents. He got his hands into position on either side of the opening, positioned his feet on the toilet-seat lid, then jumped and pulled. The narrow opening caught at his clothes and tore strips off his heavy coat. Frantic at being caught halfway through the aperture, he kicked furiously. The ripping of cloth sounded louder than gunshots to him as he wiggled flat into the attic.

Heavy dust assailed his nostrils, threatening to make him sneeze. Stevenson forced down the urge as he rolled across the uneven beams and moved the hatch back into place. He wanted to look past a lifted corner and see if the killer came into the bathroom, but he restrained the impulse and instead began making his way through the dust-filled space toward a sluggishly turning vent fan placed at the far end of the house. The cold wind rejuvenated him. He could make it. He had come this far. He was going to escape.

Stevenson almost screamed when a bullet ripped through the thin plywood panel behind him. He bit down hard on his coat sleeve to keep from making any sound at all. A second bullet tore away a hole larger than his thumb and sent splinters flying through the attic.

He waited for the panel to lift and an eye to appear—an eye sighting along the automatic's barrel.

It never came.

He pressed his ear flat on the wallboard serving as ceiling and listened. He didn't know what room lay below him. It might have been one of the bedrooms. A distant, dull thump sounded. He thought it was the front door closing. He moved toward the vent fan and peered out past its corroded silver blades.

Straining, he managed to see the edge of the driveway. The only thing parked there was the FBI agents' rental car. Stevenson turned and looked into the backyard. He saw a gray blur moving slowly toward the waist-high chain-link fence. The man stopped for a moment, buttoned his coat, and turned back to look at the house.

Stevenson got a good look at the man who had just murdered two federal agents.

Basil Baker smoothed out the wrinkles in his coat, easily vaulted the fence, and walked off as if he were out for a Sunday stroll.

51

Stevenson leaned against the attic wall and tried to collect himself. His emotions ran wild. Working at Fort Detrick made them all murderers in some people's minds. Still, there was a world of difference between genetically engineering microbes that might be turned into offensive weapons and pulling the trigger on a pistol.

Or was there?

Stevenson shuddered and tried to calm himself. He couldn't just sit here and shake. Making his way back to the ceiling access, he looked into the bathroom, irrationally expecting to stare down the barrel of a smoking automatic. The room was empty.

Shivering, he moved the panel aside and dropped back to the toilet lid. He was grateful for the cursory examination Basil Baker had given the room. A more careful inspection would have shown the footprints on the wooden toilet seat and the broken paint around the plywood hatch.

Stevenson looked up and saw the two holes Baker had shot through the ceiling. Had the biochemist known he was up there, or had the shots been merely cautionary? Or had they been intended to flush him out like a frightened bird? If that was Baker's intent, the two bullets had almost succeeded. Only biting down on his coat sleeve had kept him from crying out in fear.

He wobbled into the hallway. Bartholomew lay face-down, not moving. In the living room, Dennis stared sightlessly at the ceiling. Stevenson stepped over Bartholomew and examined Dennis. Three bullet holes leaked sluggish black-red blood: one in the shoulder, one in the leg, and one squarely between the agent's eyes. His gorge rising, Stevenson turned, went to the front door and threw up. Every time he entered this house, dead bodies appeared.

Struggling, he tried to decide what to do. If he went after Basil Baker, he might be able to track the man down and find out what was going on. Had Morningside sent him to Redding as an assassin? Or was it something else?

Coldness welled in his gut when he remembered Elaine's theory of a security leak at Fort Detrick. In the vacuum left as controlled thinking fled, Stevenson remembered where he had seen Lisa Taylor before the night with Jack Parkessian. Two, maybe three years earlier, at a staff Christmas party, she had been Basil Baker's date. A nurse with the trauma unit, she had quite a reputation as an easy lay. Stevenson hadn't thought anything about it at the time, meeting her in passing before leaving with Elaine for a night of revelry.

"Why didn't I remember this earlier?" Stevenson held his aching head and shook. The weakness passed and his gorge settled. He couldn't go after Baker. If the man had been with Taylor for more than two years, that meant he was a KGB informant—or worse. He might be a spy, a mole burrowing around within the Army's research division. Lisa might have worked for him.

Stevenson stood no chance against him. Baker was armed and willing to kill. He had shown that all too clearly.

"Call the police," he told himself. "Get out from under this. Let the authorities handle it. They're able to do the right thing. They can track Baker down. They know what to do."

Stevenson babbled as he turned and went back inside. He expected to hear the whine of police sirens even as he made his way back to the living room. Why hadn't the neighbors called in the shooting? Didn't anyone notice? It puzzled him no one had heard the shots.

He sat down and reached for the telephone. He froze when he heard movement behind him.

Heart in his throat, he turned and stared. Larry Bartholomew leaned against the wall, looking pale but otherwise unhurt.

"You're alive," Stevenson whispered, not trusting his voice. "How?"

Bartholomew moaned and straightened. He pulled back his torn jacket to reveal a flat black vest underneath his shirt. He sucked in air again and winced. "Composite material, Kevlar, the best bulletproof jacket on the market, but it can't soak up the bullet's momentum. Hurts like hell under here."

Stevenson got to his feet and helped the agent strip off the pliant vest. Bartholomew's chest was a huge bruise. One bullet had hit above a rib. Probing produced such pain that Stevenson guessed a rib had been fractured. The bullet hadn't ripped the agent apart, but its impact against the vest had been damned near enough to do him in.

"Dennis bought it," Bartholomew stated flatly. "He hated wearin' his vest, even though it was regulation. Stupid fucker."

"It might not have helped him much," Stevenson said. "The bullet to the head . . ."

"Call an ambulance, will you?"

"I was going to call the police first."

"No, this is bureau business. Murdering a federal officer goes beyond local-police jurisdiction. Damn, there's gonna be a ton of paperwork on this."

"I know who he was," Stevenson said dully. "I know him."

This snapped Bartholomew out of his shock. "Who was it? Nobody kills my partner and . . . Who?" The demand was sharper than the edge of a hunting knife.

"Basil Baker. He worked in my division as a biochemist. I don't know what's going on. I talked with him yesterday."

"You know why he was here?"

"He told me General Morningside had sent him and a few others out to help me."

"You told him about this place?"

"He would have known," Stevenson said dully. "He and Lisa Taylor must have worked together. But he knew I was doing more checking here. He had followed me."

"Chances are good he waited for you. Did you leave any notes around that he might have gotten a good look at?"

"My laptop," Stevenson said. "I encode everything, but I've had problems for months with unauthorized tampering. He might have broken my code and accessed my notes while I was out of the motel room."

"Let's hope he was working solo on this, though it's unlikely. If he was a KGB agent, he has a control he reports to, no matter how high his rank." Bartholomew moaned and touched his rib. He turned white with the pain. "Definitely busted. You call this number and tell 'em what happened. It's going to take an hour or more. I'll be all right until they get here."

"Who is it?"

"Special task force out of San Francisco. We've got access to a lot of planes, thanks to the drug smugglers. Just get on with it. I'm not gonna die, but it damned well feels like it."

Stevenson argued with him about calling a local ambulance, lost the argument, and called the number. He helped the man sit in a chair. Bartholomew insisted on talking; this kept Stevenson occupied with wild tales and improbable arrest stories. A half-hour after he made the call, Stevenson saw three cars roll up in front of the house. Silent men dressed in matching plain blue serge suits marched in. One man, shorter than the others, took out a first-aid kit and began wrapping Bartholomew's ribs. The others prowled the house, measuring, recording, digging bullets out of walls.

What bothered Stevenson the most about their quiet efficiency was the way they ignored Dennis. He lay undisturbed in his rigor mortis in the center of the living-room floor.

"We've got to figure out if this Basil Baker of yours found anything," Bartholomew said. "We never made it to the boy's room, did we?"

"I checked the room before. There wasn't anything in it. Certainly nothing that came out of the satellite."

Bartholomew motioned for Stevenson to follow. Together with the third man giving support, they entered Billy's room. As soon he walked in, Stevenson knew what was wrong. The valuable telescope had been dismantled, its lenses carelessly dropped onto the floor.

"In the tube. Check it out, will you, Doc?" Bartholomew was wheezing slightly. He braced himself as he watched Stevenson finger the telescope components.

"The tube is large enough to hold one of the cylinders from my experiment, but there's no telling what was in it. Why would Billy hide one cylinder here and keep the other two where Lisa Taylor could find them?"

He stared at the telescope parts. The screws holding the corrector plate to the baffle tube where the mirror moved in and out had been removed. The visual back had come off, and foam rubber padded the interior. The space inside was large enough for one of his experimental cylinders.

"You know kids. Secretive cusses. I should have *really* searched this place when I had the chance. Chalk it up to that lieutenant sniffin' around and distractin' me whenever I tried to get down to work." Bartholomew spoke quietly to the man helping him. The other agent nodded briskly and hurried from the room.

"What now?" Stevenson asked.

"It gets rough. We find Basil Baker and retrieve the tube."

"And if we don't?"

Bartholomew laughed without any hint of humor. "We will, Doc. He killed my partner. I want him—so does every FBI agent in the field. And then there's the other thing."

"The cylinder?"

"I think it's got pure death in it. No matter what you say: pure, unadulterated, painful death."

Stevenson wished he could argue, but he was past knowing what was true.

52

Larry Bartholomew sucked in his breath and let it out slowly. Stevenson watched as the medic wrapped the FBI agent's ribs with quick, firm tugs on the two-inch-wide adhesive tape. One had been broken, and the purple-and-green bruise spread like wildfire across his broad chest. Still, he was in better condition than his former partner. The FBI crew that had swept through hadn't even bothered to close his eyes. He stared sightlessly at the ceiling, his pistol still clutched in his hand.

"You never get used to it," Bartholomew said, seeing Stevenson's morbid fascination with the dead body.

"I'd better. I'm stumbling over more and more bodies these days."

"Yeah, that seems to be true. You found the Devlins, didn't you?"

"Elaine Reinhardt and I did." Stevenson's voice came out hollow, empty. He was drained inside and wondered how much more he could tolerate.

"Why don't you give her a call? That's what you're thinking about, isn't it?"

Stevenson nodded. Even injured, the FBI agent was a careful observer. Stevenson went to the phone and picked it up, then hesitated. He looked at Bartholomew.

"We've been paying the bill, just in case someone tried to phone in. Your call's on the U.S. taxpayer."

Stevenson hadn't thought before that the telephone—all the utilities in the house—should have been cut off by now. It had been almost three months since the Devlins had been murdered. The FBI must have kept a surveillance on the house, waiting for something to happen. He shook his head. That couldn't have been right. They would have known Basil Baker was already inside if they had. It was too complicated for him, and his headache had returned with a vengeance. Stevenson dialed Elaine's work number at Fort Detrick.

For a second he was too relieved to say anything when she answered.

"Who is it? I'm very busy," came Elaine's irritated voice.

"This is Tom." He hesitated. The Defense Intelligence Agency monitored all calls in and out of Fort Detrick for security violations. Whatever he said was going to be recorded.

"Good to hear from you, Tom. Really. But I've got a meeting with Morningside in fifteen minutes and—"

"Is Basil Baker on assignment?" he asked suddenly.

"What? Basil? He's not around here. I don't know where he is."

"Ask Morningside about it. And who else is gone from the division?"

"Nobody. Wait a sec, there's Jack. He knows everything. Let me ask him."

Stevenson heard Elaine shouting at Jack Parkessian, but he couldn't hear the answer until Elaine came back on the line.

"Tom, the best Jack could figure is that Basil is on vacation, but he's the only one gone. The rest of us are working our tails off now that we're shorthanded. There are new budget hearings, the money estimates for next year's research have to be submitted by the end of the week, equipment purchases have to be placed now, and—"

"All the usual March hassle," he finished for her. His mind raced. Basil Baker wasn't there; he was on vacation. If anyone knew, it would be Parkessian. But was he a dupe or was he in this up to his ears with Basil Baker?

"Things are getting complicated out here. I'll talk to you soon." Stevenson paused, again aware of the silent recording. "I love you, Elaine."

"Love you too," she said. "Got to run."

The line went dead, then the dial tone came back, a haunting litany of buzzing and static. Stevenson tried to make sense of the conversation. Elaine was caught up in the spring appropriation rituals—and so were the others. This wasn't a good time to take a vacation. Scientists who didn't file their requests and fight for them tooth and nail during interminable budget meetings had their funds siphoned off to other projects. Basil Baker's funds would be cut to the bone if he was absent.

Stevenson had the gut-level feeling that Morningside hadn't sent him to Redding.

"You want to help us on this one, Stevenson?" Bartholomew was still pale, but some color had returned to his cheeks.

"What else can I do?"

"We're working on a file for your Basil Baker."

"He's not *my* Basil Baker," Stevenson protested. He didn't like the way Bartholomew lumped him with everything that went wrong.

"He works with you."

"Worked."

"You're getting touchy. Did the little lady put you in a real bad mood?" Bartholomew knew everything that had been said. Stevenson closed his eyes for a moment and tried to make the pain welling up behind his eyes vanish. Of course the agent knew what he had said to Elaine. The FBI had the line bugged, just as it was on the Fort Detrick end.

"You want me to do the routine with the spray again if you find Baker," Stevenson guessed.

"*When* we find the son of a bitch, not if. And yeah, he's got another tube of the green stuff."

"Tell me about it. Why are you so sure it's dangerous?"

Bartholomew looked at him for a moment, then

frowned. "You're not playing a game, are you? You really think it is harmless."

"As far as my tests ran—and you watched them while I did them—the green snow was as innocuous as the gray gobs. If you had let me use better equipment than the high school had . . ."

Again Stevenson worried that he had been too cursory in his evaluation, but with the equipment at hand, he had done the best he could. It had been Morningside's job to demand the return of the mutated biologic material for a complete evaluation. He had been given the runaround for more than six weeks and had never had the chance to do comprehensive tests.

"We've got it in our lab back in Washington," Bartholomew said. "They've not come up with anything more than you did, except for some weird results in dying test animals."

"Dying? What was the cause?"

"That's the weird part. They keep dyin' and there's nothing much wrong with them."

"Just like the airport workers?" Stevenson didn't need the agent's answer. He read it on the man's face. Men had died, just as the lab animals had—and there wasn't any obvious cause. Stevenson remembered what Bartholomew had said about coincidence. Men died all the time. Medical science wasn't up to determining the exact cause in all cases, but having three men die mysteriously was too much to score against coincidence. Coupled with lab animals that just died, the green snow looked like the culprit.

"It's just a replicating neutral cell," Stevenson protested.

"I don't know all the fancy words. I don't rightly know your experiment *is* the cause of people dyin', but your Basil Baker sure is interested. So were two KGB agents. That's enough circumstantial evidence for me to start worryin'."

"Baker is KGB, is that what you're saying?" Stevenson remembered the Christmas party and Basil Baker being with the woman KGB agent, Lisa Taylor. That meant nothing, but it did establish a link between them and Jack Parkessian. Baker and Parkessian might have been nothing more than informants, but Stevenson was coming around to believing Basil Baker was something more—something evilly more. And Parkessian? He doubted his former research assistant was a spy.

He coughed. The facts were incontrovertible. Stevenson knew he was in over his head. Worse, the water was filling his lungs and suffocating him.

"Looks good to us. He's a limey, and it's damn hard gettin' good intelligence background on them. Their government is friendly with ours, except when it comes to tradin' real information. Can't blame them much, I guess," Bartholomew said.

Stevenson wasn't interested in the agent's reasoning. Before he could put his own thoughts into better order, an agent signaled to Bartholomew. The two men exchanged soft whispers that Stevenson couldn't hear.

"Well, well, well, we got that son of a bitch cornered. He didn't get too far. He was hightailin' it for the Oregon border, and we spotted him from the air. He took off for a cabin in the hills just west of the interstate. Why don't you come along and give us some expert advice?"

53

The pilot banked sharply, dropped the nose, and landed on a dirt road. Stevenson hoped he hadn't chipped his teeth too much on the bumpy landing and taxi to the edge of a wooded area.

"Here it is," Bartholomew said, looking none the worse for the rough landing. If the broken rib bothered him, it didn't show. He was fired up to get his partner's murderer.

Stevenson followed the agent, glad to be back on the ground. A dozen men were gathered just inside the copse. Most carried shotguns, but two had sniper rifles with long black telescopic sights.

"He's trying to negotiate," one sniper told Bartholomew. "He claims he will release the bio-agent and kill everyone in the countryside if we don't let him waltz on out of here."

"The usual?" Bartholomew asked. "Money? A plane? Free passage to somewhere far away?"

"To Libya," the sniper said, taking off his Giants baseball cap and running his hand through thinning hair. "He hesitated too long coming up with the country. He had somewhere else in mind. If we give him a plane, he'll divert."

"He won't get into Russia. No matter what he's got for them, they couldn't take the publicity right now," Bartholomew said. "He's likely to ask for Libya and settle for Cuba. The new regime is cozier with the Kremlin than Castro ever was."

Stevenson let them talk. He walked through the woods

along a poorly defined path until he came to the edge of a clearing. A car was parked to one side; a single bullet hole through the front showed where a sniper's bullet had put an end to the engine's usefulness. Around the edge of the clearing were arrayed a half-dozen agents. Stevenson had no idea how they had arrived, since he didn't see any ground vehicles. From all Bartholomew had said, they might have parachuted in, being trained as a quick-strike antidrug task force.

"It'll kill all of northern California!" Basil Baker called from inside the cabin. "You can't let me do it, but I will if you try rushing me."

"He's blown' hot and cold right now," Bartholomew said. Stevenson jumped. He hadn't heard the FBI agent come up behind him. "He's alternatin' threats with pleas for us to let him go. He might be a KGB agent, but he's not a good one."

"He's good enough, if he's been working at Fort Detrick for five years without giving himself away. There are annual security checks."

"Yeah, sure," Bartholomew scoffed. "I've seen what the DIA does. They may take forever authorizing access, but once it's given, they don't care. They never do an adequate recheck. Lazy."

"I need to get the cylinder intact—and I need to analyze it with good equipment."

"Next thing you know, you'll be wantin' to see our Washington lab's analysis. You're gettin' real pushy, Doc." Bartholomew was in better humor now that he had Basil Baker trapped in the cabin. No matter what the treasonous biochemist threatened, he wasn't getting a free ticket out of the U.S.

"Where's my armored car to take me to the plane?" Basil Baker appeared briefly at a cabin window, then ducked back, as if tempting the snipers to open fire.

"That wasn't Baker," Stevenson said. "Not directly, I mean. It was a reflection. He held up a mirror."

"He was testing us to see if we'd fire at him. He's a bit

smarter than I thought." Bartholomew turned to the sniper and issued more orders. The sniper pulled a small microphone down from his shoulder and spoke into it for almost a minute before giving Bartholomew the high sign.

"This is interesting," said Bartholomew. "One of our men thinks Baker is injured. They got a few shots at him when they drove him off the road and into the cabin. He might not be able to move enough to show himself. The mirror trick might be his way of lookin' out rather than a method to keep us from shootin' him down."

"What about the cylinder?" Stevenson asked. "Was it damaged?"

Bartholomew looked at the sniper, who only shrugged. No one knew the condition of the quartz test tube.

"Dr. Baker," Bartholomew called out in a booming voice that belied his own injuries, "would you let our expert in to see if the bio-weapon is intact—or if you even have it?"

"I have it." Baker flashed a quick look out, using his mirror, this time holding it directly up to the window and making no attempt to hide the tactic. "It's deadly, and you know it."

"You want me to go see?" Stevenson asked, startled. "He—"

"Yeah, he might kill you. Are you game, Doc? You don't have to. We can send someone else."

Stevenson's thoughts turned to the lack of containment available to him. The best he could do was tie a handkerchief over his face.

That wouldn't stop a truly virulent bio-weapon, he knew.

Stevenson shook himself and tried to drive such thoughts from his mind. The FBI laboratory might be good for forensics work, but they lacked his knowledge of recombinant DNA techniques, replicators, and nanotechnology. Project Big Hunk hadn't been a weapons experiment, and he couldn't believe it had mutated into one. If it had, the entire country would have been reporting deaths by now. George Wyatt's cylinders must have leaked at the airport.

"This isn't like your nice clean lab where nothing can happen. Scary stuff, dealing with life-and-death situations in the field, isn't it?" Bartholomew asked.

"I'll do it," Stevenson said angrily. He knew the agent was goading him into meeting with Basil Baker, but that didn't matter. He was going in to see after his experiment and nothing more. Stevenson kept telling himself this over and over, and each repetition came up that much more a lie.

Bartholomew was manipulating him, and he was letting him.

"Dr. Baker, we've got a colleague coming in. Don't shoot." To Stevenson he said in a low voice, "Stay to the left of the door if he tries anything. Let the snipers work if he shows himself. Otherwise, enjoy yourself." Bartholomew slapped him on the back.

Stevenson failed to appreciate such bonhomie.

He stepped into the clearing, aware that he was unarmed and didn't even have one of the bullet-proof vests that had saved Bartholomew's life. Stevenson started toward the cabin. Visions of the slain FBI agent flashed through his mind. A head shot; one in the arm; another in the leg. What good was a flak vest against a brainburning round?

"Basil? It's me, Tom Stevenson. I'm coming in." He walked slowly, his heart racing. Sweat beaded on his forehead. He hoped he was enough to the left, as Bartholomew had requested, to give the snipers a clean shot. He kept walking and it soon became a moot point. He'd have to go through the door.

"Basil?"

Stevenson looked over his shoulder. He couldn't see Bartholomew or the snipers. Two other FBI agents were in view. He thought they might be decoys to keep Basil Baker occupied.

He pushed the door open with his foot, expecting a comet of hot lead to rip through him. Nothing. Not even a sound from inside the cabin.

"Basil, I'm coming in. Don't shoot. I just want to talk. We can work this out together." Stevenson edged into the dim, dank cabin interior. As if he had developed radar, he pivoted and squarely faced Basil Baker.

The man was slumped on the floor. Without going to him, Stevenson knew he was dead. He was becoming an expert on the subject. In the past few months he had seen more than his share of corpses.

An explosion from behind enfolded him, carried him forward with irresistible force. Heavy weight pressed him to the dirty cabin floor, crushing his lungs, preventing him from breathing.

"It's all right, Larry. He's out of action."

Stevenson struggled under the FBI agent pinning him down. The man moved enough to let Stevenson swing away and sit up, his back against a wall. Three other agents had followed him into the cabin, their shotguns trained on the silent Basil Baker.

Bartholomew came in, his face drawn. Stevenson saw that the man's ribs hurt him, but he kept going to arrest the man who had killed his partner. Stevenson was never sure if Bartholomew had even liked Dennis, but pride entered into the equation. No FBI agent could lose a partner without demanding retribution, if not justice, for the loss.

"Don't go near him," Stevenson said. "There's something wrong. You shot him, but there's no blood."

"Earlier, yeah, we plugged the bastard," Bartholomew said. He motioned for the others to stand back and let Stevenson have a closer look.

As he crept forward on hands and knees, Stevenson was acutely aware of the huge bores of the agents' twelve-gauge shotguns pointed past him. He forgot them entirely when he grabbed Basil Baker's coat and heaved. The biochemist rolled over, his arms clutched to his chest. His face was contorted in a grimace of stark pain.

"Be careful, Doc. He looks like the three baggage handlers at the airport."

Stevenson's curiosity began to get the better of him. Had Baker died from the green snow? How? The cells were neutral, not virulent. They weren't plague carriers or botulism bacteria or bizarre viral vectors. Stevenson gingerly opened the coat and saw a large flower of blood staining the lining. An FBI bullet had struck Basil Baker in the center of the chest.

A small clinking sound alerted him to more damage than was apparent from a cursory examination. Baker had hidden the quartz cylinder inside his coat in a zippered pocket. The same bullet that had buried itself in his chest had also nicked the cylinder.

Taking a pen from his pocket, Stevenson poked and prodded and moved the test cylinder. Some of the green flakes held in suspension in the nutrient solution had oozed out and into Baker's open wound.

"Well, Doc? What's the good word?"

"I don't know, Bartholomew. The bullet may have killed him. It's a nasty wound. He must have been running on nothing but adrenaline."

"He was still strong when he got to the cabin," the sniper said.

"The experimental cells must have entered his chest," Stevenson said, more to himself than to the FBI officers. "What did they do there?" He shivered. He wouldn't know for certain until an autopsy had been conducted, but he didn't think Baker had died from the gunshot wound. It was serious but not fatal.

The mutated cells from Project Big Hunk had entered his body and killed him. But how? Stevenson just stared at his former colleague.

54

"This is the most isolated area we could find," Bartholomew told him. Hot wind blew across the arid land, kicking up sand from the alkaline desert soil. Above flew two huge black bombers, still in their low-level testing phase. The shadows from the vulturelike airplanes passed over him and blotted out the hot sun. Stevenson shivered and tried to tell himself this was working out just fine.

He tried it and knew deep down that he was lying. Nothing was right. Bringing Basil Baker's body to Edwards Air Force Base had been the best compromise under the circumstances. General Morningside had demanded that the body be returned to Fort Detrick and that the investigation be conducted there. The FBI was reluctant to let go of either the body or the investigation of the potential cover-up the Army NBC command might try. They had a bona fide KGB agent who had stolen an illicit bio-weapon and had possibly died as a result. Such a coup was not likely to be given up lightly.

"Air Force doctors will do the autopsy," Bartholomew said. "We get to watch."

"Why are they letting me in?" Stevenson asked. "I don't work for the government. I can't imagine Morningside wanting me within a thousand miles of this place."

"We know you quit, Doc. But it's pretty simple reasoning on our part. You've been involved in this from the beginning. The director thinks you're the perfect expert to watch. Who knows more about Project Big Hunk than you?"

"No one," Stevenson admitted. It had been a single-man experiment and had never been intended to be such a major catastrophe. He had asked Elaine to design containment cylinders, but she had no real idea what had gone into them, other than the snippets he had passed along to her on the damned need-to-know basis.

"See? The FBI wants you to watch as our expert witness and take notes and let the Air Force doctors know what they're up against."

"May I assist?" Stevenson wasn't eager to help cut Basil Baker open, but he wanted a closer look at the effects of his experiment. He could perform the proper biopsies needed and suggest procedures a medical doctor might not consider.

"We'd like it. In fact, we want you to design the operatin' theater for this. You know more about containment procedures than they do. They're sawbones, not bug doctors."

Bartholomew had a point. Stevenson knew how to design a work area that wouldn't leak the green particles —if they would give him the equipment and personnel to construct it.

To his surprise, the Air Force cooperated fully. Two days later they began the autopsy. Bartholomew stood behind the glass and peered into the operating area. Fans and filters kept the section at a lower air pressure than outside. Particulate matter that tried to escape would have to flow against strong air currents. In addition, Stevenson had insisted on a two-room air lock. The inner one had scrubbing equipment and UV lights to detect fluorescence of the green snow and to kill the neutral cells, should any escape a chemical bath in the operating area. Beyond this, Stevenson doubted they could do anything without going to a P-4-level containment building specifically constructed to accommodate biohazardous recombinant DNA material.

"They're supposed to be good," Bartholomew said. "Both are flight surgeons who look after the test pilots.

They know all the weird shit to hunt for. Heard a couple pilots talkin' between themselves. Those two have down-checked more pilots than have crashed here." Bartholomew shook his head. "From all I've heard, that's a whale of a lot of dead bodies too."

Stevenson donned his rubber gloves and settled a filter mask over his nose and mouth. It took only a second to pull up a hood covering his ears. He let an orderly fit the goggles firmly over his eyes. He was too distracted by what had to be done to listen to Bartholomew's mumbling. He indicated his readiness to go in. Bartholomew stopped him with a hand on his shoulder.

"You keep that radio workin', you hear? We're recordin' everything that goes on in there. Don't worry about gettin' too technical. I may not understand, but there are experts back in Washington who will."

"Color me Judas," Stevenson said. He had come to feel like a human sacrifice. Morningside had already shown his willingness to cut him loose and dodge responsibility. The Air Force certainly would never admit culpability in the KH-18's crash.

Stevenson kept digging himself deeper and deeper.

"Tell us how he died. That's all we need to know," Bartholomew said.

Stevenson snorted angrily, pulled away, and went into the first room of the makeshift air lock. That was the least of what they needed to know. Was the green matter able to infect others through aerosol excursion? Through injection? Was there an infectious potential? He had more than just one question to answer.

He waited for the air pressure to build. The next door opened. He felt the gentle push of the air shoving him inward. The second door closed and vacuum pumps started working to lower the pressure in the second air lock to nearly match that of the work area. Stevenson finally opened the door and joined the two Air Force flight surgeons. They stood anxiously next to the stainless-steel table holding Basil Baker's body in a slight depression to catch and funnel any liquids. They had yet to remove him from the airtight body bag that had been his final resting place for almost three days.

"Please, gentlemen," Stevenson said. "Start your procedure."

The doctors grunted, turned, and started their autopsy. Stevenson ignored the steady drone of their voices as they commented on the incisions made, the condition of the organs exposed, their progress toward a resolution about how Basil Baker had died.

One doctor stopped as he worked on the heart. Stevenson saw the man with a bloody organ in his left hand and his right buried in the open chest cavity. A moment's giddiness passed. He wasn't a medical doctor. Cutting open frogs in freshman biology was as bloody as it had ever gotten for him during his training. Stevenson belonged to a generation of scientists content with computer simulation and development. Most of what he did was theoretical or done at the genetic level. Micromanipulation of biochemical systems rather than gross anatomical change was his goal. He played with the basics of life rather than the results.

"There's something . . . odd in his intestines," one doctor said. "There has been extreme hemorrhaging."

The other doctor bent over and examined the gut more closely. He pried and poked and began pulling. Part of Baker's large intestine crumbled under his inspection. The doctor stood and took a step back and just stared.

"What do you make of that?" he finally asked.

"I've never seen such deterioration." Both doctors turned to Stevenson. It was time for him to pass judgment.

He took scrapings of the intestine and prepared a slide. He took the cells to a visible light microscope and turned on the transmission light. Working for a few minutes got Stevenson a decent view of the cells from the dead man's gut.

"Could you . . . ?"

Stevenson moved aside to let one doctor in.

"Intestine cell," the doctor said. "The gut is only one cell thick at this point. But it's unlike any intestine cell I ever saw. Cell parts are missing."

"Get me a section from the liver," Stevenson said. He fought down a moment's dizziness.

"What do you think happened?" asked the doctor still at the microscope. "The cells have altered. From the lack of a well-formed nucleus, that cell couldn't possibly function."

"The large intestine's epithelial cells secret mucus, don't they?" Stevenson asked.

"Yes, but—"

"These cells can't. As you said, they're lacking important parts. No mitochondrion, and the nucleus is deformed."

"You're right," the doctor said, looking once more at the slide. He studied the new cross section taken from the liver, then looked up. "The liver cells are similar. There's no way the dipeptides can be absorbed and transmitted."

"Are you saying the man starved to death? Impossible," the other doctor said.

Stevenson took a deep breath. The cotton-and-plastic mask suffocated him. "That's not why he died. Cells in his body were replaced by neutral cells. He would have starved to death eventually. Or he might have drowned in his own poisons, since the liver wasn't able to transport blood wastes. I suspect we'll find nerve ganglia replaced by the neutral cells too."

"What's all this talk about 'neutral cells'? What the hell are they?"

Stevenson didn't answer. His Project Big Hunk had gone from a harmless gray gob to green snow capable of replacing the human body's cells—and turning them into nonfunctional blobs. Replace one here or two there and the body could continue living. Replace enough, and systems began stopping: digestion; gas transport in the blood; nerve impulses; brain function. It might not be possible to ever assign an exact cause to Basil's death.

Important organs had simply ceased working because of the cell replacement.

One thing was perfectly clear. He had died from an experiment designed by Thomas Stevenson.

55

"I don't have a choice, do I?" Stevenson asked Bartholomew.

The FBI agent smiled crookedly, worked a fingernail between his front teeth and picked a moment, then shook his head. A hint of a smile crossed his lips.

Stevenson sighed. It was always like this. He had resigned from his post, but the government still had irrevocable claim to his soul.

"We're goin' to see you get to the White House safe and sound. Dr. Wyman insisted on me bein' the one to escort you."

"You've met Wyman?" Stevenson stared out the window of the twin-jet Grumman Gulfstream. The FBI seemed to have any number of aircraft on tap. He wondered if they needed them or if they only padded out a strained federal budget. Grow or die was the maxim he had always heard. Any agency holding its budget constant was likely to vanish—and no one ever asked for less then they received the year before. That was fiscal suicide.

"Never had the pleasure. The national security adviser travels in circles way above my head."

"Big wheels turn in small circles," Stevenson said. He wasn't happy with the idea that he had to brief the president on the autopsy findings. He had yet to work out the meaning of the results. Basil Baker had died from the contents of a Project Big Hunk test cylinder. Stevenson couldn't come to any other conclusion, but *why* had Baker died? The neutral cells had been responsible, but they should never have been able to compete with existing cells to perform their task of . . . doing nothing.

The neutral cells had replaced working ones and done *nothing*. And the replacement had come within hours, once the neutral cells were introduced to his bloodstream.

"I won't be able to give him any good answers," Stevenson said. "The way I designed the experiment, the cells should never have been viable outside their nutrient environment. The radiation from the radioisotope thermoelectric generator's spilled plutonium dioxide altered the genetic structure, but I can't tell you how."

"This might be just the kind of weapon the Army's been lookin' for," Bartholomew said slowly. "The body just sorta stops working. Who's to say it's a weapon? Imagine using your fancy techniques and puttin' that into some camel jockey's lamb chops."

"It wasn't intended to be used as a weapon." Stevenson almost choked on the lie. He knew Morningside had been interested in the project as an attack against foreign foodstuffs. Replace nutrient proteins with a neutral cell and all food value was gone. The bulk was there, but slow starvation was the result for anyone eating the grain or meat.

"So why did you want to run the experiment?" Bartholomew fastened his seat belt as the small jet banked and started down for a landing at Andrews AFB.

Stevenson hesitated to give the answer Morningside would. He considered the other purposes he had designed into the experiment.

"I'd thought it might be used to mitigate cancerous growths. Replace the wildly reproducing cancer cell with a gengineered neutral cell and you've found a safe way of saving patients where surgery or other therapy is impossible. Both chemotherapy and radiation therapy have dangerous side effects."

"Sure, sure, Doc. Replace the cancer cell—and about every other one in the body. You'd end up with a patient looking like this gray gooey gob you're always talkin' about."

Stevenson said nothing. Bartholomew was right. If the neutral cells couldn't be restrained to a small area, if they spread like wildfire, the entire organism was at peril. What horrified him most of all was the rapidity of replacement of the functional cells with the neutral ones. The green particles had entered Basil Baker's body through a chest wound. This must have sped up the process immeasurably. There might also have been other reasons the cells spread so quickly. It hadn't been more than four hours between the neutral cells' entry into Baker's body and his death.

"How long between Christmas and the deaths of the baggage handlers?" he asked.

Bartholomew frowned as he recalled the details. "They started dying in mid-January. The last died toward the end of February."

"Two weeks to two months," Stevenson muttered. None of the three must have been infected through an open wound, as Basil Baker had been. Airborne? Skin absorption? Why would it take longer for the neutral cells to kill if they were inhaled rather than injected directly into the bloodstream? Cilia in the nose? Did mucosa filter out the no-longer-gray gooey gobs? Was there a mediating mechanism in the nasal cavity he knew nothing about?

"You got it all worked out now, Doc?"

"What? The mechanism for transfer and contamination? Hardly."

"You'd better. It looks as if Dr. Wyman is conducting you personally to the White House." Outside the plane, parked and waiting on the tarmac, was a long black limousine. Stevenson couldn't help thinking of it as a hearse: his hearse.

Wyman grunted at him as Bartholomew opened the door of the limo. The FBI agent started to get in with Stevenson, but the chauffeur slipped past and closed the door. Through the dark window glass Stevenson saw Bartholomew arguing to no avail. The chauffeur turned his back and strode around, leaving Bartholomew alone. The limousine roared off, pressing Stevenson into the soft cushions.

"Well?" he asked Wyman. "You've seen the autopsy report. What is going to be done about it?"

"That's your domain, Dr. Stevenson. The president will want to know your course of action in stopping this plague."

"It's not a plague, dammit," Stevenson flared. He was tired of being used as a pawn. "The Air Force didn't tell me it had an atomic battery in the satellite. That's what mutated my experimental cells. There's no telling how long the experiment was in contact with the RTG pellets."

"This has set a bad precedent. I hate to admit it, but those fools a few years ago protesting the Galileo probe's RTG might have been right. Plutonium dioxide scattered all over the country." Wyman shook his head sadly, as if deciding on the proper facial expression to wear when he met reporters. Stevenson saw the man wasn't likely to listen to anything being said.

But he had to try.

"The atomic battery was safe enough, even on impact. You couldn't have foreseen that kids would have found it and broken open the platinum-rhodium containment or the radioactive elements."

"So why would you have protested the placement of your experiment if the atomic battery was that safe?"

"I didn't want it in orbit at all." Stevenson sighed in exasperation. Talking with a bureaucrat always ended up with a circular argument. "I wanted to keep it on Earth, where it could be watched carefully. That doesn't address another issue, though. I am no longer employed at Fort Detrick."

"You quit," Wyman said, "but your resignation has been rejected. Therefore, you still work for the federal government. The president does not want to hear of such trivial matters. The real concern is the plague you've unleashed and how we will contain it."

"I haven't unleashed any such thing," Stevenson said, growing angrier by the moment. He calmed himself a little. Losing his temper with this officious menial employee of the president was useless. The truth of the matter was that Stevenson no longer knew what was important. Stopping the spread of the green particulate matter he had found in Billy Devlin's cylinders was important, but it was hardly a plague.

"We've run more tests," Wyman said, staring straight ahead. "It takes less than a microgram of your so-called neutral cells to kill an advanced organism."

"You know more than I do, then," Stevenson said. "How big an organism are you talking about?"

"Human. We introduced cultured cells from Baker into test animals."

"How?" Stevenson asked. This was the crux of his real concern.

"Both intravenously and through the respiratory system. Intravenous infection resulted in death within hours. There is some evidence that breathing this shit takes much longer, but it is nonetheless still deadly."

"The three baggage handlers must have inhaled the dust at different times—or does the rate of growth depend on temperature?"

"We have no data to confirm or refute that contention," Wyman said.

"You don't need me. You've got more information than I do." Stevenson paused, then asked, "Do you have the data with you?"

"No."

Wyman lapsed into silence the rest of the way to the White House. Stevenson fumed and turned over and over the meager information Wyman had doled out so grudgingly. The limo pulled into a back entrance and the chauffeur escorted them directly into a ground-floor conference room adjoining the Oval Office. Morningside. and Elaine Reinhardt sat at the far end of the table.

Before Stevenson could speak to them, Wyman motioned to the general. Morningside growled like a bear, heaved himself to his feet, and left with the security adviser.

"Tom, they said you'd be here. I didn't think you would." Elaine threw her arms around his neck.

"I didn't have a choice. I'm not under arrest, but Wyman made it clear that they're going to pin the entire thing on me."

"They can't. The Air Force . . . The KH-18 had an atomic battery in it. The crash wasn't—"

He silenced her with a quick kiss. "I know all that," he said. "And so do you and Morningside. It is just a matter of finding someone to crucify in the press."

"I'll say that I was a co-researcher."

"You didn't have anything to do with Project Big Hunk, except designing the cylinders for me. And you had no idea what was going into them."

"But—"

Stevenson silenced her again. "This is my cross. I don't want them to nail you up alongside me."

Elaine swallowed hard and nodded. Stevenson thought she looked pale, drawn, as if she had been under immense pressure. He wanted to ask her about the repercussions of Basil Baker's ties to the KGB, but he had no time. And what had been done about Jack Parkessian?

"I've got to follow up on the brass nameplate," he said. "That's important now."

"On the telescope? You mentioned it, but—"

"Wyman said they had done some quick work on the green snow from Billy Devlin's cylinder hidden in the telescope."

"I know about it. Morningside mentioned it, at any rate. They didn't show me the results."

Stevenson looked at her. The way she said it meant she knew the contents even if Morningside hadn't revealed the file's contents to her. He didn't want to ask how she had gained access.

"This stuff is really bad. As little as a microgram can cause immediate death if it enters the bloodstream. I think it takes up to two months if you inhale it."

"As little as a microgram?" she asked, startled.

"Probably so. Larry Bartholomew said the FBI was investigating the deaths of three airport workers. I think some of the experiment was inadvertently spilled at San Francisco International and—" Stevenson bit off the rest of his sentence. The president and Wyman came back into the room. General Morningside was not with them. Wyman motioned for Elaine to leave. She looked back at Stevenson with saucer-wide eyes, then turned and hurried out of the room.

Stevenson had never felt more alone in his life.

"It's time to assess this matter," the president said.

It went downhill from there.

56

Stevenson paced back and forth like a caged animal. It had been four days since his meeting with the president. While in the presence of the president and Fred Wyman, he hadn't been allowed to say a word. They had taken turns outlining how Stevenson was going to take the full blame for anything that filtered to the press. He was ready to take the entire sordid account to the news himself when the president had dismissed him.

He knew firsthand how the shuttle pilot, Colonel Jensen, had been treated when his mission went sour.

In the intervening time, Stevenson had been unable to contact Elaine. He had left message after message on her answering machine, but she was not at home. Reaching her at work was out of the question. He had taken to sitting outside her apartment to wait for her, but he had begun to develop paranoid fantasies of being followed. As he waited for her, someone was waiting for him.

In his home, he tried to work on the vector for what he had once considered a neutral-cell experiment. He used his desktop computer, but it lacked the sophistication and number-crunching power of the workstation at his Fort Detrick laboratory. Giving up on the problem for lack of data had done nothing for his disposition.

He pulled back a curtain in his front room and looked out. A late-model blue American-made sedan was parked across the street. Two men sat inside drinking coffee and eating sandwiches, joking and looking as if they were having a fine time. Stevenson watched the misty tendrils of smoke stream upward from the hot polystyrene cups and wondered if this was FBI-issue. Or if the pair worked for the FBI. The DIA wanted a piece of him, as did the Air Force and just about every other intelligence agency in the government.

Soon someone would leak the story of the downed KH-18 to the press. With it would come the revelation of the plutonium-dioxide-powered RTG and Project Big Hunk. Illicit recombinant DNA experiments. Children dying from radioactive debris. KGB spies. When the story hit, it wouldn't leave the front pages of the major papers for a week, and months from now his name would be vying in the tabloids with people who saw three-meter-high three-eyed space aliens and neutered Elvis clones at the corner Burger King.

He had to act. Waiting would ruin his career, his life, those of the people around him. Elaine would be dragged into it. He had given up caring about Lucien Morningside. Basil Baker was a spy, Parkessian might be, and what did Donnelly and Chin and the others in his division matter? To them he was a tyrant, an unrelenting slave driver who would never give them enough appropriations money or time or equipment to work on the projects they wanted.

He had to act _now_.

Stevenson glanced at his tapped telephone. That would be the FBI's first order of business—find out whom he called, cut him off from his contacts, spook him enough to make him run and betray himself.

He went to his closet and selected several shirts and a large pair of pants. After donning them all, he looked roly-poly, but he might be able to get the hell away from Washington and surveillance without carrying a bulky suitcase.

He stuffed what money he had into his pockets. Using a credit card would be risky; the computer authorization would immediately flag it and relay usage to the FBI. Stevenson thought of contacting Bartholomew, then decided against it. He knew a few details the agents had missed. He would have a stronger bargaining lever if he retrieved the missing cylinders by himself.

If he could. Unless something else with a higher priority had come up, Bartholomew would be on the trail of the cylinders by now. He might already have found George Wyatt and recovered them. Stevenson wished he knew what the hell was going on. He hated being in the dark.

He glanced out back and wondered if he could just leave down the alley. A slow smile came to his lips when he saw the garbage truck coming down the alley. Two men clattered and banged the cans as they worked. He hurried to the alley and got to the far side of the huge, dirty white garbage truck. He kept it between him and the men in the blue sedan when the truck emerged from the far end of the alleyway.

From there he turned the corner and heaved a sigh of relief. It would be a few minutes before they knew he was gone. He had to make the most of his time.

"Or am I just being silly?" he said aloud to himself. The men might not have been staked out to watch him. The government might not care. If anything, they would be off the hook if he panicked and ran. That would make him appear all the more guilty when this mess broke in the news.

That thought convinced him. He had to retrieve the remaining cylinders if he wanted to deal with Wyman and Morningside and all the others in the Pentagon and the White House.

Quick steps carried him to the bus stop. From the bus, he transferred twice in downtown Washington, and by two o'clock was at National Airport. The crush of people kept him safe from outright detection. He went to a telephone and stared at it, undecided about his course of action. He knew enough—almost.

Sitting down, he fished out his dialing card and dragged the magnetic strip down the acceptor. He quickly got information, asked for the telephone number of George

Wyatt's grandparents in Redding, and placed a call to them. Peter Stratton answered.

"Hello? Hello? Who is it?"

"Mr. Stratton, I spoke to you a couple weeks ago about your grandson and his astronomy hobby, do you remember?"

"Yes." The frostiness of the answer told Stevenson he wasn't likely to get much information from the man.

"I was wondering if any of my . . . colleagues had been by since then."

"No, no one," Stratton said. "Not even anyone selling magazines, except that woman who got lost and asked directions a couple days back. It's damn cold here for such nonsense."

"Yes, yes, I know." Stevenson fought to get his questions formulated. The FBI had not been asking after George; Bartholomew had not followed up on the name engraved on the brass plate on the telescope. That was good. It gave him a head start. "I wonder if you could give me your grandson's address in New Orleans. I might be able to make him an offer on a . . . on a different telescope."

"No." Stratton hung up abruptly. Stevenson stared at the telephone, then replaced the handset. How long would it be until the FBI knew he had used his telephone credit card? Not long, if the president had built a fire under them.

He leaned back and wiped sweat from his forehead. They thought he was a KGB agent too. That had to be it. They were flushing him out to see where he would run.

They were doing a dangle on him. Prod and goad and poke enough, until he bolted, then follow and get the goods. That was an accepted technique. All that had been missing were the long hours of intense interrogation and random arrests. Stevenson snorted. The president's little speech had been substituted for being booked repeatedly.

And it had worked.

He had to get to New Orleans right away. From there he could find George Wyatt and the cylinders.

Stevenson stopped at a rest room and peeled off a layer of sweat-soaked clothing. He kept a jacket and two shirts on and discarded a pair of pants and a shirt. As he was throwing the shirt away, he experienced a pang of regret. Elaine had given him that shirt for Christmas two years ago. It hardly seemed possible, but they had just started seeing one another then. Two years was both an eternity and a split second. He couldn't reconcile the disparity of feelings.

He hurried from the rest room to find the video monitors displaying departures. If he used a credit card and got on the next flight to New Orleans, he would be picked up when he landed. He had to be more clever than that. It would push his credit to the limit, but he could buy a half-dozen tickets to different destinations, on assorted airlines. Let "them" tie up personnel in all the cities, whoever "they" were.

He wasn't going to be in any of the places the computer would kick out.

The first four ticket purchases went well, including one to London. Only the fifth and last purchase before he exceeded his credit limit proved difficult. He had to change from Minneapolis to Chicago to keep within his limits. Then he spent two hours finding people willing to pay him cash for discounted tickets. Only then did he make his way to the American Airlines terminal to buy the ticket that would take him to his real destination.

As he slowly made his way forward in a long line, he saw dozens of young men and women in bright holiday dress. They were joking and jostling. He thought it might be a college get-together when he heard the nineteen-year-old in line in front of him tell the ticket agent, "I'm going to New Orleans too. Just like a million other people from my school. It's going to be a great party."

Stevenson sidled up to the counter and laid his cash down. "New Orleans, please. Tourist class."

"You're lucky, sir," the harried woman behind the counter said. "Only four seats remain on the next flight."

Stevenson didn't mind being surrounded by the college kids. They would give him plenty of cover.

"It's my lucky day, then," he answered. "You'd think their university would have blocked enough seats for them."

The woman smiled tiredly. "Hardly. Most of them don't even know they're going until a day or two before they leave."

"That's they way kids are," he said. "They just don't plan ahead."

She nodded absently as she finished entering the ficti-tious name he had given her into the computer. His ticket was spit out. She handed it to him with the board-ing pass inside the envelope.

"Flight nine-oh-three leaves in forty minutes, green concourse, gate fifty-four. Enjoy the Mardi Gras, sir. Next, please."

Fat Tuesday. Mardi Gras. Millions of people in New Orleans. Millions of drunken revelers who might become infected with his gengineered plague.

57

The swarming, shoving throng at the New Orleans airport made Stevenson claustrophobic. Everywhere he turned there were more celebrants, all come to the Crescent City to drink and crowd the streets and enjoy themselves before Lent. He pushed his way to one pale green wall, then followed it as if he were blind and it was his Seeing Eye dog. How many might die if either of George Wyatt's cylinders spilled more of the mutated green particles? Stevenson couldn't begin to estimate the number. If a mere one-millionth of a gram was sufficient to kill a laboratory test animal, it was also enough to kill a human being.

He shivered. He had to believe the last two cylinders were in the boy's possession. That was the only explanation for the three deaths of the San Francisco baggage handlers. George had left northern California and returned to New Orleans because he was ill.

The twin cylinders might contain enough death to slaughter the entire city and the two million partygoers from all over the country.

Stevenson pressed his forehead against the damp, warm wall and thought of something else. New Orleans was the third-largest seaport in the world. What if some of his mutated experiment got aboard a ship? If inhaled, it took weeks to grow inside its victim and kill. The victims could end up spreading the plague throughout the world.

The only consolation Stevenson could see was that the neutral-cell quality seemed to prevent growth outside a human body. One human wasn't likely to infect another with it unless it could be spread like AIDS.

He shuddered with dread. That might be possible. He just didn't know enough about the cells.

"Even if person-to-person contact isn't possible, that leaves airborne contamination of about three million people. Wonderful." Stevenson had never thought of himself as a mass murderer. This would rank him with Stalin and Hitler, if it came to pass.

Again he considered trying to reach Larry Bartholomew, worrying that George Wyatt might not have the two quartz tubes at all. If the teenager didn't have them, it might require an army of field agents to find what had happened to them. Billy Devlin had hidden one. He might have hidden the other two also. Only the deaths at the San Francisco airport hinted that George Wyatt had the others. The FBI agent was as close to honest as anyone Stevenson had come across, but he knew the man would have pressure on him from his superiors. He had mentioned speaking with the FBI director, who was susceptible to political suasion. And such pressure was at a maximum from the President of the United States.

Stevenson wiped sweat from his face and continued down the concourse until he got to the airport lobby. He went past banks of telephones until he found one with an intact phone book. Stevenson leafed through the pages looking for listings of the name Wyatt. He hoped that George was a junior, but he found no George Wyatt, Sr.

He started counting the number of Wyatts and stopped when he reached forty-seven. He slammed his hand down on the book, tearing a flimsy page. Why couldn't George's grandfather have given him more information? A phone number, an address, something.

Stevenson replayed in his head everything Peter Stratton had said. The only scrap of information he had was the hospital's name where his daughter—George's mother —was a patient. He struggled to remember it. Then it came to him as easily as pulling his own fingernails with vise-grips.

It hadn't been Peter Stratton but his wife who had inadvertently mentioned it. She had said Tulane. Their daughter was a patient at the Tulane University Hospital.

He pulled his wallet out and counted his cash. Sweat popped out on his forehead, and this time it wasn't from the oppressive heat inside the terminal. He had less than thirty dollars. If he tried to buy an airline ticket on a credit card and then resell it, the computer would flag his location. He thought he had been clever to this point. He would just have to make do with the little money he had.

That ruled out taking a taxi to the hospital. Stevenson considered calling, but rejected it. Hospital staffs were notorious for their lack of cooperation with telephone questions, even teaching hospitals. He would have to be present to get the most from this trip—or start calling the Wyatts listed in the telephone book. Stevenson considered this again and decided against it. The Wyatts might not even live in the city of New Orleans. Like any other major urban center, the city proper was ringed with bedroom communities. The hospital remained his best chance of tracking down George Wyatt and the remaining cylinders.

He looked up the address of the hospital in the telephone book, checked its location on a map of the city, and then picked the nearest large hotel near it. A shuttle van from the airport for eight dollars took him to the hotel, although the driver looked askance at him when he told him he had no luggage. By the time they arrived and Stevenson hopped out, the driver knew not to expect a tip.

Stevenson disliked drawing attention to himself in this fashion, but he had no other choice. He was increasingly cut off from everyday conveniences he had come to take for granted.

The crush of Mardi Gras revelers multiplied the closer he got to the Riverwalk or the French Quarter. The hospital, thank God, was in the opposite direction, out to the west by Tulane University. By walking up Canal Street a few blocks, he was able to get a trolley car for a seventy-five-cent fare. He rode the picturesque trolley along St. Charles Street, through the Garden District, and past Tulane. He sat apprehensively, worrying about a dozen different things. Stevenson wondered if his rampant paranoia was necessary. He didn't even know if he was considered a fleeing felon, escaping from punishment for crimes he had never committed. Every rider on the trolley was a potential law officer wanting to arrest him. The black man sitting in the seat in front had that look. Stevenson finally shook himself free of the notion that everyone sought him. He glanced down at his map and saw that he had gone four blocks too far. Jumping up, he attracted even more attention. He forced himself to stay calm and walk back toward the rear door. He pulled the tattered black cord and signaled that he wanted off. The ancient, creaking car ground to a halt, the door opened, and he hopped off the green trolley.

He trooped back the four blocks and found the proper street. He fancied he saw the hospital less than a quarter-mile to the north down a tree-lined lane. Stevenson marched like a soldier, eyes ahead, his mind racing to come up with just the right arguments to convince the Wyatts that he was the proper one to take custody of the cylinders. Without their cooperation, he didn't know how he was going to get the experimental tubes back.

The hospital facade dated back to the nineteenth century. He walked up the antebellum-South steps and entered the lobby, acutely aware of how little authority he had to do anything. Whatever he accomplished had to be by bluff and pretense of a confidence he didn't have.

"May I help you?" a nurse asked in a heavy Southern accent. It took Stevenson a second to decipher the simple phrase. He cleared his throat and tried not to sound desperate.

"I'm looking for a boy, George Wyatt. His mother is—was—a patient here."

"Wyatt?" the nurse asked, her head cocked to one side. She looked thoughtfully at him and said, "I remember. I'll refer you to his doctor. One moment."

"That's all right . . ." Stevenson started, but the woman had already completed a connection and was speaking softly into a telephone. She looked up, her eyes holding just a trace of sadness.

"Dr. Delacroix will see you. Mr. and Mrs. Wyatt are in the chapel, down the hall and to the right. But you might want to speak with the doctor first—second floor, turn right, and his is the third office on the left."

"Is George . . . ?"

"I'm afraid I can't say anything more." The nurse turned the word "more" into a two syllable "moe-ahh."

Stevenson hurried upstairs, wondering if he ought to approach George's parents and ignore the doctor. Intuition told him the doctor would be a better source of information. He left the elevator, found the office, and paused for a moment. Then he pushed inside.

A middle-aged, dark-haired man with the look of someone deprived of sleep for three days looked up. The circles under his eyes matched his hair color. Double chins quivered as he cleared his throat.

"You're inquiring after George Wyatt?" he asked. "Are you a friend of the family?"

"A relative," Stevenson lied, knowing friends received very little information. A relative might get a more comprehensive rundown. "From Redding, in California."

"You must be from Mrs. Wyatt's side of the family."

"She has parents in Redding too," Stevenson said.

"I know. She's mentioned them. George even went out for a week before Christmas."

"He came back mighty sick," Stevenson said. "A friend of his, Billy Devlin, came down with a virulent flu and died."

"Then it might not come as a surprise if I tell you that

George has also died." The doctor watched his visitor's reaction carefully. Stevenson didn't have to feign the hopelessness he experienced. His chances of finding the cylinders diminished with every passing second, if George had hidden them as Billy had done. And why not? The boys had known they were stealing government property —or *someone*'s valuable property. Guilty consciences had a way of inventing pursuers.

Stevenson knew. He had the feeling of FBI agents hot on his heels.

"I . . . I didn't know he was that ill."

"Right after he came back from northern California he was admitted. Curious mixture of symptoms. Nothing I've seen before. Just as I was about ready to call a conference with several specialists to discuss his case, he started improving. He was released a week after admission —the first time."

Stevenson thought the first bout had been from radiation poisoning from the spilled contents of the satellite's atomic battery. "When was he readmitted?"

"Four days ago. The symptoms this time were entirely different. He hemorrhaged internally, bleeding from his intestines. There was some evidence of liver and kidney failure also. I've ordered an autopsy to be more specific. I am sorry, sir."

"Yes, sorry," Stevenson said numbly. "I'd like to send flowers."

"The boy just died this morning. You will have to see his parents about the funeral arrangements. The university will release the body in a few days."

"The university?"

. "Yes," Delacroix said. "This is a research hospital and we want the most complete autopsy possible. There is a chance he had an infectious disease, and we're treating it as such." Delacroix frowned, as if trying to remember something. "You said another boy died?"

"Yes, Billy Devlin," Stevenson said, knowing the doctor might unravel the facts so carefully hidden by the government. "In Redding. Can I send flowers to their home? I hate to bother them."

Delacroix wrote down Billy's name and underlined it. He looked up, hardly listening to Stevenson. "Their home? I suppose."

"They still live just off St. Charles?" Stevenson asked, naming the first street that came to mind.

"I don't think so. They live on the other side of town, out near the city museum." Delacroix flipped back a few pages in the folder open on his desk. "Thirteen-sixty-seven St. Anne."

"They've moved since I was here last, but that was a long time ago," Stevenson said, hoping his explanation didn't sound too lame. He hurried on to keep Delacroix's mind on other matters. "The nurse said they were in the chapel. Is it wise to see them now?"

"I'd give them a little time to themselves. With your sister's illness—it's responding, but not in remission—life has been difficult lately. No one expected George to die so suddenly."

Stevenson said nothing to correct the doctor's mistake about his identity. Let them chase down imaginary brothers to their hearts' content. He had the address, and he knew he had to search the Wyatt home if he wanted the cylinders.

"May I have your name?" Delacroix started as Stevenson reached the door. "For the records. I can't seem to find any notation of you in Margie's file."

"Thank you, Doctor. I'm sure you've done all you can." Stevenson left before the doctor stopped him.

He took the stairs down to the lobby, reflecting on how much time he had spent in hospitals over the past two months, and how many had died already. Stevenson wasn't a betting man, but from Delacroix's description, the neutral cells had replaced functional ones in the boy's intestines and excretory system, and probably in his lungs. The interval between infection and death resembled the baggage handlers' in San Francisco.

He couldn't call it a plague, but he could call it damned dangerous, especially in a town filled with Mardi Gras revelers. Stevenson spent most of his remaining money on a cab across town.

Stevenson walked past the Wyatts' modest whitewashed clapboard house a dozen times before he settled his nerves enough to go to the front door. He felt like a thief—he *was* a thief. He was going to break into the house and hadn't a clue how to begin. He was a biophysicist, not a cat burglar.

His trips up and down St. Anne Street convinced him no one was paying any particular attention to the Wyatts' home. He rang the bell and waited, wanting to be sure a neighbor wasn't house-sitting for them while they were at the hospital. The pressure of time weighed heavily on him—the Wyatts might return at any instant—and more than that, his concern about the cylinders, always the damned cylinders. He had to retrieve them.

He waited impatiently for what stretched to an eternity, then put his hand on the doorknob and rattled gently. Stevenson looked around the small courtyard for some easy way into the house. He didn't worry about a burglar alarm. A house as unpretentious as this one wouldn't contain anything worth stealing. He had seen a detached garage in the back and wondered if there might be tools he could use.

He laughed ruefully at that notion. He didn't need anything more complicated than a big rock to break a window before reaching in to unfasten a catch. He walked around the courtyard, hoping to find a carelessly unlocked window. He didn't.

A circuit around the house might be dangerous. Neighbors would notice if he pried at the windows and rattled the back door, but he wanted to be sure of getting in quietly. He decided it was better to take the chance of being seen than to create a loud ruckus that would definitely draw unwanted attention.

And he had to hurry. It was late afternoon and the Wyatts would be back soon. He wished he could wait for nightfall, but that was out of the question. There might be a gathering of the Wyatts' friends and family before too long to help share the grief. He had heard of deaths in the South attracting hundreds of people over a week's span, each family bringing food and turning the death into a Roman holiday.

Stevenson got to the side of the house and tangled himself up in discarded barbed wire. He cursed and hoped he didn't have to get a tetanus shot. But he stopped cursing when he got to the door leading from the kitchen to the garage. It stood open a full inch.

"Luck, at last," he whispered. He pushed the door open, then looked back over his shoulder to be sure there wasn't a legion of police aiming their revolvers at him. He was alone.

Alone and in the Wyatts' house. He had no time to waste. He hurried through the house, giving it a quick once-over. He stood in the small living room and looked around, then moved swiftly down the hall to what had to have been George Wyatt's bedroom. A mobile of the solar system hung from an overhead light fixture. On the pale green walls were thumbtacked dozens of pictures of space shuttles and computer-enhanced colorized photos of different nebulae. Stevenson knew this was the boy's room from those items, even if he had not seen the rest of the clutter that was so distinctively a teenager's

Ten minutes later he gave up his search for the cylinders. If George Wyatt had had them, he had hidden them too well.

Stevenson chewed at his lower lip as he went through the house again, this time working his way methodically from room to room. He didn't dare miss finding his test cylinders.

And once more he failed to find them.

He sat down heavily on the bed in the master bedroom and put his head in his hands.

"Not here. But where? The boy died from the green particles. I know it, but where are the cylinders? They had to be with him, or the men at the San Francisco airport wouldn't have died. Where?"

Stevenson sat up and looked around.

"A suitcase. Where is his suitcase? I remember his grandfather saying they'd checked his bag at the airport." Stevenson searched the master-bedroom closet, George's closet, and the entire spare room laden with medical supplies for Margie Wyatt. Nowhere did he find a suitcase.

Hope mounting, Stevenson left the house and ran back to the detached garage. The door into it was open. He slipped inside and fumbled around until he found the light switch. His gaze lifted to the rafter overhead. Three suitcases lay on a plywood sheet balanced precariously on two of the supporting beams.

Using a stepladder, Stevenson crawled up. His heart was racing and his hands shook as he pushed aside minor debris to get to the suitcases. He looked inside each one, even though he knew none had accompanied George back from Redding. The layers of dust on them showed none had been used in long months.

"No suitcase," he muttered to himself, hoping the sound of his own voice would bring out the truth. "Where would it be? Still at the airport?"

It seemed unlikely, but the routine at the Wyatt household had been severely disrupted. George might have returned to New Orleans too ill to wait for the luggage. Or it might have been lost or delayed.

"A claim check. He'd still have a claim check—or his father would."

Stevenson didn't like returning to the house, but he had no choice. Once more he entered the tomblike home, and this time sought the boys' airline ticket. He found it thumbtacked to a corkboard in the kitchen.

He took it down. His heart sank when he opened the paper envelope. Inside was George's canceled ticket and only the torn stub of his luggage-claim check. The bit of purple-and-black cardboard mocked him.

Before he could force down his disappointment and start a new search through the house, he heard a car driving down the alley out back. He glanced out the kitchen window and saw an eight-year-old white Chevy with massive rust spots on the fenders making the sharp turn into the garage.

The Wyatts had returned from the hospital.

Stevenson quietly closed the kitchen door and locked it, then went through the house and out the front. He had failed, and the experiment cylinders were still missing—still missing and a deadly threat to the city's millions of Mardi Gras revelers.

58

Stevenson clutched the portion of the baggage-claim check outside the Wyatts' home. He glanced back over his shoulder as lights winked on inside the house. There was no joy there. And he took no pleasure in knowing he had yet to recover the missing experimental cylinders. Even if the Wyatts knew where the two remaining test tubes from Project Big Hunk were, he doubted they would speak to him.

Even Bartholomew and his clever FBI wiles wouldn't work on a grieving family. The Wyatts had seen enough woe; no need to tell them that their son was responsible for bringing back two tubes of slow death with him.

Stevenson didn't intend to explain his part in this fiasco to them either. Let them come to grips with their sorrow in their own way. If he couldn't get a lead on the cylinders at the airport, he was going to have to give up his search and call Bartholomew. With Mardi Gras reaching full swing, Stevenson doubted that the FBI could do anything. But something had to be done.

Soon.

He built up hope as he walked south, thinking that the boy's bag was still at the airport. It had been months, true, but the Wyatt family had been occupied with so much.

"George came back sick," Stevenson said to himself. "His father might have left the bag at the airport for any number of reasons. And he might not have had time to go back after it. George was sick, his wife was sick, who cared what happened to one suitcase? Not even George would have complained about missing his possessions, since he was in and out of the hospital." Stevenson went on to construct an elaborate theory based on the boy caring about nothing but the telescope he had left in northern California with Billy Devlin. Contact with the other teenager would have ceased—and there was no way this side of hell anyone could communicate with the elder Devlins.

Stevenson worried over this scenario. It didn't ring right. If George had tried to contact Billy to arrange delivery of his telescope, the FBI would have intercepted the message and homed in on him. Or would they have kept a low profile after Lisa Taylor and the KGB agent John were killed?

His head began to ache and throb. He tried to squeeze it back into shape before realizing that the pulsing came from the outside, not from within. He had touched the fringes of the French Quarter, and the raucous merriment of the Mardi Gras. The pull of the crowd was magnetic. How he wanted to simply slip into the mob and let the festivities carry away all his worries.

"What does it matter anyway?" he asked himself. "I'm not going to find the damned suitcase and the cylinders at the airport. The claim check was used."

Something about George Wyatt's father keeping the ticket gnawed away at the edges of his mind, however. Why had the man thumbtacked the ticket to the board unless it was useful? Why hadn't he tossed it into the trash?

But the gaiety of the Mardi Gras crowd—dozens of men and women in costume who snake-danced on their way through the French Quarter—kept Stevenson off-balance. George Wyatt had been the only victim of the green particulate neutral cells in New Orleans, as far as Stevenson knew. He might have infected himself back in Redding. The cylinders might never have made it this far.

The young teenager's bag might have been lost by the airline. If so, that made it an impossible task for Stevenson to track it down by himself.

Let the FBI do it, a small voice inside his head kept saying. Let them do it; it's their job. Project Big Hunk is theirs, not yours. It always had been. If millions died from the mutated effects of the supposedly neutral cells, that was the government's fault. That was Morningside's fault, and the fault of Beaumont and a dozen others in the Pentagon and Congress who had forced the test to be conducted in orbit rather than under careful watch in an Earth-bound laboratory.

The voice kept telling Stevenson to let it be, but resolve hardened within him. He hadn't come this far to simply fade into the crowd and eventually fall down in a drunken stupor. No one knew he was in New Orleans. He had been too clever by far for them to follow.

Them, he snorted. The paranoid "them" of every psychotic's nightmare.

That decided him. He would see it through. If the cylinders weren't in a suitcase at the New Orleans airport, he would return and try to enjoy the Mardi Gras. A day and night of partying wouldn't be a bad reward for all he had gone through. Maybe no one was on his trail, as he imagined. He could call Elaine and have her meet him here.

Who needed a hotel room? He could sing and dance and watch the parades and the people and do just fine on the street.

He went and caught the hotel shuttle back to the airport, the cardboard stub firmly in his grip.

Stevenson opened his wallet and almost came up empty for the shuttle driver. He had exhausted the little cash he had. He looked at the four dollars he had left after paying the fare and thought that it didn't matter. Not much of anything mattered to him anymore, other than finding the cylinders. He gave two dollars to the driver as a tip, then watched him dart back into his van and screech off to the next curb site where Mardi Gras revelers waved and made fools of themselves. Turning, he crossed two lanes of traffic from the concrete island and went into the terminal.

Glancing at the ticket stub a final time, he tried to work up a plausible story about the suitcase, how the claim check had become damaged, how he just wanted to look inside the bag to be sure it was his son's.

"No, no," he said to himself. This wouldn't do. They'd ask for ID. George Wyatt must have some name tags in his clothing. That would force Stevenson to invent a spur-of-the-moment lie to account for the difference in names. "A stepson," he decided. "I'm George's stepfather and have been sent to retrieve the bag. That'll let me look disgusted, and they won't think anything's wrong if I can't quite pull it off."

Stevenson became aware of people stopping and staring at him as he talked to himself. He nodded politely and kept walking. In the Mardi Gras crowd, attracting this much attention required an act of God—or a madman. It didn't take divine intervention to know which camp those watching put him in.

He wandered through the terminal until he came to the lower-level baggage carousels. Off to one side was a passenger-assistance office with "Luggage Claims" neatly painted on the door. This was his new stage. He hoped the pitch carried some conviction. He was too tired, hungry, and disappointed to put his all into it.

Stevenson's hand froze on the doorknob. He took a half-step back and stared at the reflection in the glass. He spun, eyes wide.

"Elaine!" he called. The dark-haired woman stood with a short, stocky man near a baggage carousel. He paused before shouting out her name again.

The man was dressed strangely for Mardi Gras. He wore a long overcoat, far too heavy for the mild New

Orleans weather. His face was turned away, but the greasy black hair strongly hinted at a swarthy complexion. He stood uncomfortably close, almost face-to-face with Elaine, arguing over something worth pounding a heavy fist against a plaster pillar. His anger spilled over to Elaine.

Stevenson had seen her angry before, but not like this. Fire blazed in her dark eyes. She maintained her distance and did not back down while disputing whatever the man had just said. Her clothing was nondescript, not like the flashy, bright patterns she favored. If Stevenson hadn't been so hesitant about going to ask about the suitcase, he would never have noticed her reflection. She faded into the crowd surging and boiling through the baggage-claim area.

His eyes moved from the arguing pair to their feet. Between them was a battered cloth suitcase neatly wrapped in a heavy clear-plastic drop cloth.

Stevenson knew whose suitcase it was. Before he could move away and observe them more carefully, Elaine Reinhardt saw him. She turned back to her companion, grabbed him by the coat lapels, and swung him around. The expression on the man's beetlelike face chilled Stevenson's soul.

The man reached under his coat and pulled out a long, thin black tube. As he lifted it, Stevenson realized it was a weapon. He tried to move, to dodge, to avoid the inevitable, but just stood frozen with fear.

The barrel of the weapon lifted. Stevenson thought he was looking down a fire hose, it seemed so large. A tiny *pft!* sounded and a piece of plaster from the wall behind him exploded. The weapon recoiled slightly, and the beetle-browed man aimed again.

This time Stevenson dropped to one side. His knees turned to rubber and let him fall bonelessly. A second silenced shot ripped away at the plaster behind him.

Elaine was shouting at the thickset man in a guttural

language Stevenson didn't recognize. All he knew was that staying alive had gotten immensely more difficult.

The man with Elaine got off a third shot. This time the report was louder. Stevenson hoped it would attract someone's attention. It didn't. He rolled behind the silver-metal carousel and came to his knees, peering over the top. The man had left Elaine with the suitcase and was stalking his prey.

Stevenson looked around, hoping to find a policeman. He didn't see anyone in uniform except for a skycap. He lifted his hand and yelled to attract the man's attention.

The skycap's eyes widened when he saw the problem. Then they closed suddenly as a tiny red star blossomed on his chest. He slumped into a pile on the floor and brought dozens of people running to his aid.

Stevenson tried to put people between him and the gun-wielding murderer—and failed. The man had rounded the carousel quickly. If Stevenson had tried to go to the skycap's aid, he would have died instantly, a bullet shattering his spine.

"Elaine!" he shouted. "Elaine, it's me." Stevenson saw the woman bend over and hoist the plastic-shrouded suitcase. She didn't even glance in his direction. She walked away as unconcerned as if she were in New Orleans for the Mardi Gras and nothing in the world mattered.

Stevenson saw that he couldn't run without being cut down. That left him only one option. He roared like a bull and attacked, arms flailing and legs kicking. He wasn't a skilled fighter, but the attack took his would-be assassin by surprise. A wild arm caught the weapon's sinister black barrel and knocked it to one side. Then Stevenson's other arm circled the stocky, sweating neck of his adversary and pulled hard. Their foreheads crashed together.

Who was more stunned by the collision was difficult to tell. Stevenson recoiled and almost fell. The assassin jerked sideways and crashed onto the slowly rotating carousel, his weapon's barrel exposed and aimed upward. Recovering somewhat, Stevenson got his feet under him and jumped, crashing down on the man.

It was like landing belly-first on concrete. The assassin didn't have an ounce of fat on him; everything was muscle and mean. Short fingers raked Stevenson's face, seeking his eyes. Stevenson squinted and tried to avoid the attack while both of his hands closed on the man's thick right wrist. The peculiar weapon was again lowered and seeking a target on Stevenson's body.

"Don't do this," Stevenson grated out between clenched teeth. "I'm a friend of Elaine's."

The man might have replied in his guttural tongue, but Stevenson didn't know what he said. From the short, staccato burst, it had to be a curse.

The barrel moved between them; Stevenson was losing his battle. The man's right arm was stronger than both of Stevenson's—and the left hand still gouged at his eyes. Thin rivulets of blood sprang from his cheeks and eyebrows, threatening to blind him.

"Stop it! Stop!"

Stevenson's pleas availed him nothing. The stocky man's efforts doubled, and the biophysicist was lifted upward and dropped to one side on the revolving carousel. The weapon came up. Stevenson jerked spasmodically, trying to turn aside. Again the dull *pft!* sounded.

All struggles ceased. The burly man flopped onto his back, unmoving. His sightless eyes stared at the chute starting to drop baggage from a New York flight.

Stevenson looked from the dead man, to the bags piling up, to the slender, silenced weapon beside him on the carousel. He began to understand what had happened. This wasn't standard issue for any law-enforcement agency he knew. A crowd was beginning to push back from the skycap.

He tried to think. How long had the fight been going on? Hours? Minutes? Reaching over, he pulled out the man's wallet and flipped it open. A photo ID card matched the dead man, but he couldn't read the Cyrillic lettering. Frantically leafing through the documents in the wallet, Stevenson found a card in Russian and English proclaiming that Dmitri Borskin was a Soviet trade delegate to the New Orleans legation.

"A trade representative?" he muttered. Stevenson tumbled off the carousel and crawled away quickly as the crowd approached to observe the new disturbance. When he got to the pillar where he had seen Elaine and Borskin arguing, he halted and looked back. Small holes dotted the wall, hardly larger than .22 caliber.

Whistles sounded and the pounding of booted feet told him the police had arrived.

It was time for him to leave.

59

The roar of disbelief and fear rose from the crowd when they realized Borskin was dead. Stevenson slipped around the pillar and leaned against it to catch his breath. It was then that he saw the slender black weapon in his hand. He had picked it up and had forgotten that he held it.

Cold fear jabbed into him. He would be accused of murdering the Russian. Borskin was a poor trade representative, his consul would cry, murdered in the most corrupt of cities in America. No one is safe! We demand justice! We demand the head of Thomas Stevenson!

Stevenson slipped the weapon under his left arm and tried to walk away without drawing attention. He felt hot gazes on him. He sweat until it ran down his forehead and mingled with the blood still oozing from the shallow grooves Borskin had torn in his face. But he kept walking, and no cries for him to stop sounded.

On the curb outside the baggage-claim area, Stevenson heaved a sigh and sucked in the fetid New Orleans air. He looked for Elaine. There had to be an explanation for all that had happened, one that didn't depend on her sending a KGB killer after him.

Stevenson closed his eyes and tried not to shake. No argument now convinced him that she wasn't a KGB agent too. Or an informer.

"An agent," Stevenson decided after arguing with himself. "She was in command. She sent Borskin after me. He wouldn't have listened to an informer."

He wanted to be sick but held down his gorge. The

bile burned in his throat and mouth and blurred his vision. He spat. It didn't help. From behind came a new surge of Mardi Gras celebrants. They rushed past him toward shuttle vans and busses. He was buffeted by their passage, and had to fight to keep the KGB agent's pistol hidden.

When the crowd had passed, he started walking. A pair of pillars provided enough privacy for him to examine the weapon more carefully. It was a rudimentary device. It had a trigger that snapped flat after being pulled. Stevenson looked at it and saw how to manually cock the pistol. A short handle held several .22 rounds. Stevenson guessed it had a capacity of eight shots, but the bullets were odd. He peeled one off the clip and stared at the hollow point. It had been filled with a brown, waxy substance.

Stevenson replaced the bullet and avoided touching the filling. From the quickness of Borskin's death, Stevenson guessed the cavity held a fast-acting poison. A single round of such a small-caliber bullet, even at close range, wouldn't drop a husky man unless it had been doctored.

Stevenson tried to keep calm. It wasn't possible. His hands shook as he tucked the strange weapon into his waistband. He pulled his dirty jacket around it. As disreputable as he looked, he wasn't likely to get far without being stopped for questioning. Getting away from the airport took on new importance when he saw two uniformed policemen exit the baggage area. They looked up and down the street.

He found himself torn between protecting his own safety and performing a heroic and stupid action. He saw Elaine Reinhardt getting into a car at the far side of the concrete island. The maroon sedan pulled away from the curb smoothly, only to slam on its brakes as a tour bus pulled out in front of it and stopped.

If he went after Elaine, the police would see him. If he didn't, there was no telling what she might do with George

Wyatt's suitcase or the Project Big Hunk test cylinders inside. She had wrapped the suitcase in plastic because she wanted to contain a leak, a leak responsible for the deaths of three San Francisco International Airport workers.

"Finish it," he said to himself. "Do it now."

Even as he argued with himself, he stepped off the curb and started toward the distant car. The bus continued to block the sedan's escape. Stevenson saw Elaine in the front passenger seat, another of the swarthy, stocky men at the wheel. When he caught sight of the license plate, he knew he was spitting into the wind. The diplomatic plate allowed the driver to get away with murder behind the wheel. He had listened with some envy to the stories floating around Fort Detrick about the foreign diplomats and their scorn of parking tickets and other minor American annoyances. Not being required to pay parking tickets would be a gift second to none, but the diplomats didn't stop at this. In Washington one attaché had been guilty of the hit-and-run killing of a seventy-year-old woman; he had been ordered from the country, and nothing more was said about the incident.

When Stevenson was only halfway across the first street, still more than ten feet away from Elaine's car, he saw he was not going to stop her. The bus was pulling out. Her driver jerked the wheel savagely to the left and pulled in front of a van. Horns honked and drivers cursed, but the maroon sedan went on. In seconds it would be swallowed up by the heavy traffic flowing from the airport into New Orleans.

In desperation Stevenson sought a way to follow. A line of taxis stretched along the far curb, their drivers yelling to new arrivals that they knew the best places to celebrate Mardi Gras. At this time of year, the drivers didn't bother taking turns. There was more than enough business to go around.

"Hey, buddy, want a ride? I know this great place down in the French Quarter where the women don't wear no—" The cabby's eyes widened when he saw Stevenson draw the pistol.

"Let's go. You drive. I'll tell you what to do."

"Wait a minute, buddy, I—"

"Now!" Stevenson was frantic. Elaine's car was halfway down the long access road leading to the freeway. If she got onto the interstate, he would lose her for certain.

"You can't do this," the driver protested.

Stevenson considered driving the cab himself. The police would be on him like flies. He wouldn't stand a chance of explaining all that had happened in the last few minutes. He couldn't even discount the chance that Wyman and his Pentagon cronies had brought formal, public charges against him. He might be a federally wanted fugitive.

"In, or die on the spot," he said coldly. More than individual lives were at stake. If Elaine released the green particulate matter in the cylinders now, millions could die. It might not spread infectiously, but that would be small comfort for a dead victim. Basil Baker had perished quickly; George Wyatt and three others had taken weeks before the neutral cells replaced functional ones in their bodies and important organs ceased working.

"I got a wife and kids."

The protest fell on deaf ears. Stevenson couldn't leave the cabby behind. An added bonus in forcing the man to drive was his knowledge of the city. The streets were narrow, and many turned into one-way nightmares for the uninitiated. It was better if Stevenson kept Elaine's car in sight and let the man tend to the driving.

"You'll have great stories to tell them if you do what I say. Drive!"

The man hopped in and tried to pull away before Stevenson crawled into the passenger side. The slender black silenced pistol rested easily on Stevenson's left forearm, aimed directly at the man's face.

"Try anything like that again and you won't be telling anyone anything."

"What do you want me to do?" The man's pudgy face had turned pasty white. He clutched the wheel so tightly that the plastic quaked and threatened to shatter.

Stevenson almost laughed when he said, "Follow that car."

The taxi accelerated and pressed Stevenson into the hard cushion. He tried to keep his attention on the distant car, but he knew he had to be careful. The nervous driver would wreck the cab if he let his attention wander too much from the job of keeping his captive in line.

"Twelve years I been a driver," the man muttered, "and this is the fuckin' first time anyone's asked me to follow another car."

Stevenson did laugh at this. It broke the tension a little and made him aware of how close he had been to squeezing back on the trigger and putting a round through the driver. He had no idea about the pressure required to fire the pistol. Since it had belonged to a KGB assassin, Stevenson thought it would be sensitive—a hair trigger: he remembered the phrase from watching all the cop shows when he was a kid.

"She's pulling onto the expressway. Don't lose her there," Stevenson said sharply.

"She? That your wife you're trailing? Look, mister, there's better ways. Divorce ain't *that* bad. Me, I been divorced twice and—"

"Shut up and drive."

Stevenson became uneasy as he realized that Elaine was heading into New Orleans, into the Mardi Gras-crowded French Quarter. The cylinders were leaking, and she knew it. Who was this woman? Certainly not the one he'd thought he knew, and whom he had dated for two years. She had used him. For years, she had used him. Had she felt anything at all for him, or had she only been interested in spying?

He had loved her. Had? Stevenson shook all over. He

still did. There might be an explanation for this. There had to be.

As the taxi weaved and bobbled through the heavy traffic, his mind raced through all the possibilities, and he knew he was only kidding himself about her. There wasn't any other answer: Elaine was a Soviet spy. The only consolation—and Stevenson hardly thought of it as such—was that the green-flake neutral cells in the experiment didn't cause an infectious disease.

Just replacing viable cells with dysfunctional ones in millions of people was enough, though. If this was her intent.

"It's gettin' harder to avoid the people, mister. You want me to run them down?" The cabby had lost some of his nervousness. "Get five and I'll make you an ace."

The revelers were beginning to bang against the sides of the cab. They had driven almost to the heart of the French Quarter. Two- and three-story buildings, decorated with fancy wrought-iron railings and gaily strung banners of flowers and crepe paper, rose on either side of the street. The people peering into the cab wore Mardi Gras costumes, ceramic or cloth masks with colorful peacock feathers, and outrageous costumes—or almost nothing. Stevenson felt as if he had slipped into the lowest level of Dante's hell.

The cabby came to a complete halt when a crowd burst north across their street.

"It's getting thicker, mister," the driver said. "Bourbon Street's two blocks down there. We might get stuck here for an hour if the crowd decides to come this way."

Stevenson craned his neck and saw Elaine's car turning north at the next corner. They were having the same problems with the crowd. He looked up at the old buildings with their picturesque design and saw only looming monsters.

"Listen and listen good," he said. "I'm letting you go. Don't call the police."

"Anything you say, mister," the cabby said, fear returning to his face. His jowls began to tremble.

"No, no," Stevenson said irritably. "Don't go to the police. Go straight to the FBI. Tell them to contact Special Agent Bartholomew. Tell them Thomas Stevenson has found the lost cylinders. But be sure they let Bartholomew know. He's with the San Francisco office. Do you understand?"

"That woman wasn't your wife?"

"Do you understand?" Stevenson jabbed the pistol into the corpulent driver's ribs. He paled again and let his head bob up and down as if it had been put on springs.

"They must be going to the park nearby. You know the car. Here's the license number." Stevenson scratched it on the man's clipboard with a pencil stuck through the silver clip. "Special Agent Larry Bartholomew. Got it?"

The man's head almost came loose as he nodded.

Stevenson shoved hard, got pedestrians out of the way, and burst out of the car. He was instantly swallowed by the circulating Mardi Gras revelers. He fought to get his back to the wall of a house and used it to support him as he forced his way to the distant corner. He hoped that Elaine wasn't having any luck getting through the crowds. He reached the corner of Battalion Street, looked up and saw the brightly lit arch of bulbs over the entrance to Louis Armstrong Park, but of the maroon sedan he didn't see a trace. Stevenson pushed through the people intent on nothing more than getting drunk and having fun. He hid the KGB assassin's pistol under his coat. This made working through the crowd even more difficult.

Halfway down the block, Stevenson realized that Elaine couldn't have gone too far. The crowd was even thicker toward Bourbon Street than it was here. He stopped struggling and let the motion of the crowd carry him into the center of the street. Vine-covered walls hid the inner courtyards of four houses. Two had entrances hardly larger than his shoulders. Stevenson knew the sedan hadn't gone in either of them. They might be spies, but they weren't magicians. The other two homes had intricate wrought-iron gates guarding inner courtyards. Stevenson hopped up and down and tried to get a good look inside the nearest, hoping to see the maroon car.

"You've got cute buns. Wanna dance?" a nearly naked woman dressed only in a cape of feathers asked him. He jerked when she pinched him on the rear.

The request shook him out of his near-panic. He had to keep his wits about him or the cylinders would be lost. But before he could answer, the woman was gone, off to pinch another, more receptive butt. The sounds of jazz rose in the distance and grew louder, closer. A band was approaching.

That would draw even more of the Mardi Gras partygoers. Stevenson hopped up and down again and failed to see a car inside the nearby courtyard. He twisted and turned and got to the opposite side of the street, then followed the whitewashed wall of the house to the second set of iron gates.

Parked inside was the maroon sedan, but he saw nothing of Elaine or the car's driver. He rattled the gate, but a heavy padlock prevented him from opening it. He glanced up and saw sharp steel spikes fastened to the iron decoration. Whoever owned the house didn't want the curious getting in unscathed.

Stevenson had no choice. He began climbing. He was almost at the top of the ten-foot gate when the crowd started chanting and cheering. He looked back over his shoulder and saw that he was the center of attention. They were rooting him on.

"No, no, go on, go away!" he shouted. They couldn't hear over their own chants and cries. Stevenson knew he was dead meat if anyone inside the house came to investigate the disturbance. His only salvation lay in the continual roar from the streets. This was a city that never slept for days and days during Mardi Gras celebration.

He was saved by the approach of the jazz band he had

heard earlier. It rounded the corner and gave an im-
promptu concert for an appreciative, if drunk, audience.
Stevenson felt the eyes swing off him and focus on the
band. He almost slumped in reaction. He regained his
composure and continued climbing, avoiding the razor-
sharp spikes on the top of the gate.

Stevenson winced when a careless move caused one
knife-edge to cut through his left forearm. He paused,
almost over the top, and let the pain slide through him
like an icicle. By the time he dropped safely to the inner
courtyard, he saw that his imagination was running wild.
The cut might require stitches, but the blood caked quickly
over the four-inch cut to seal off the flow.

He looked around and froze. Outside in the street the
crowd danced to the music of the band. Men and women
yelled and cheered and enjoyed themselves. Inside the
courtyard Stevenson faced a man half-hidden in shadow.
The man's features might have been cloaked, but the
drawn pistol in his steady hand reflected blue and cold
from the streetlight. The man's finger squeezed the trigger.

60

The bullet ripped Stevenson's left sleeve and sent new waves of torment through his body. He jerked around, bringing up his own pistol. He fired twice before he even realized he had triggered the weapon. The two small *pfts!* were drowned out by the cheers from the crowd just a few feet away, on the other side of the wrought-iron gate. The roar from the pistol facing Stevenson rocked him again, almost as much as the lead tearing at his leg.

This slug went through the fleshy part of his calf. Stevenson dropped to his knees. He had never been fired at before. Now, in a single day, two professional killers had tried to assassinate him. The slender pistol in his quaking hand rose, and he fired a third time.

Stevenson wasn't sure what happened. The louder reports stopped. The other man wasn't firing at him any longer. In disbelief, Stevenson stared at the shadowy doorway. The man had fallen backward. Only his feet stuck out into the pale light cast by the streetlight. The small-caliber bullet didn't have much stopping power, but Stevenson kept forgetting about the gummy substance poured into the hollow tips of the bullets. Whatever poison the KGB used, it was potent, instantly fatal—and it had saved Stevenson.

He pushed himself to his feet and hobbled over to his fallen assailant. He pried the heavier pistol from the man's lifeless fingers. Stevenson didn't know how many rounds he had left in the assassination special in his right hand. He needed a backup weapon, and this would do just fine. He checked the 9mm Beretta and found four rounds remaining in the clip. With the one in the chamber, he had more than doubled his firepower potential.

Only after he shoved the Beretta into his waistband did it hit him that he had just killed another human being. The KGB agent—was he even a Soviet spy?—had tried to gun him down, but Stevenson had prevailed. The sound of the jazz band, the smell and roar of the Mardi Gras celebrants, the slow trickle of blood down his arm and leg, Elaine's betrayal—it all made him sick to his stomach. How far he had come from his laboratory!

He sucked fetid air deep into his lungs, hoping this would calm him. It didn't. His heart pounded furiously, and his hands shook even harder. His mouth had gone drier than a desert, and weakness rose from within, replacing any suggestion of strength. But he had to keep going. He had come too far to stop now.

"Arthur, what was the disturbance? Another of the drunks?"

The voice coming from deeper inside the house made him raise his pistol. His eyes adjusted to the dim lighting inside the small room. He stepped over the fallen man—Arthur? —and worked his way around to the inner door. Waiting was more than his ragged nerves could stand.

"Arthur?"

Another man appeared suddenly in the doorway. Stevenson swung his pistol around and shoved it under the man's nose. Surprise flickered across the swarthy face, then vanished. Stevenson had seen the trick work countless times in the movies. The mere presence of a gun made other people cave in to the wielder's demands.

He found himself flying through the air. Landing hard on his back on the cold linoleum floor, he stared up. The man who had come searching for the now-dead Arthur towered above him, the slender black assassination pistol in his hand aimed squarely at Stevenson's chest. There wasn't any doubt in Stevenson's mind that this man knew the weapon's deadly potential.

"Who are you?" he bellowed.

"KGB," Stevenson said, "First Directorate."

"What?"

The brief pause allowed Stevenson the chance to slide his hand to his waistband and pull out the Beretta. He had left it cocked. He fired, not caring if he hit a vital portion of the other man's anatomy. Blind luck favored him this time. The 9mm slug tore upward under the man's chin, through his mouth, and into his brain. He died instantly.

Stevenson had no time to react to yet another killing. From the house came stirring sounds. Others had heard the commotion and were coming to investigate. He had no doubt now that he had found the right place. He retrieved the slender black pistol and quickly searched the fallen man for another weapon. He found only a pocketknife. Stevenson dropped it. He wanted firepower if he was going up against professional killers. The one he had just killed had reacted with a judo move when the gun had been shoved into his face.

"Keep your distance," he warned himself. "Keep back so you can use the gun and they can't grab you. Keep cool, don't panic." The urge to turn and run almost overwhelmed him. The cabby must have alerted the FBI by now. They would have dozens of agents on the way to help him. A single call to Bartholomew would confirm the seriousness of the situation.

Stevenson didn't kid himself further into thinking the FBI would respond instantly. Even if they got the authorization to make an attack, they had to find the house through the crush of the Mardi Gras crowd, they had to fight through the KGB agents, and then they had to find and arrest Elaine before she could hide the cylinders.

He was here. They weren't. And if they stopped to ask questions, they might never show up.

Stevenson slipped around the doorway and into a narrow hall. He had started toward the front of the house when a fusillade of bullets ripped the floral wallpaper and plaster off the wall around him. He fell forward onto his belly, trying to figure out where the shots had come from. Through the daze of all that had happened, he finally realized he hadn't been attacked by an army. A single man with a small machine pistol stood at the top of a flight of stairs.

Squeezing off three shots brought the man down. It also emptied the pistol he had come to rely on. The Beretta's recoil bothered him; the smaller-caliber pistol had hardly any recoil to cause him to miss with a second shot.

Stevenson dropped the empty weapon and pulled the Beretta from his waistband. Only then did he start up the stairs, limping. Every time he put his weight down, he heard the ancient risers protesting loudly. If the gunplay hadn't awakened the dead, moving up the stairs would.

He got to the top of the landing and pulled the machine pistol from the man's hand. Stevenson had to work to pry the fingers loose. Death had frozen the muscles. He stared at the new weapon. He had seen similar ones in the movies, but he had no clear idea how they worked. He pulled back a toggle and wondered if he had chambered a round. The small Mac-10 balanced well, in spite of an almost empty clip in the handle.

Small ripping sounds forced him to postpone his examination. Stevenson dropped the weapon in favor of the more familiar Beretta. He hadn't scouted this house properly to know how many KGB agents he faced. Three were dead. Were there more? He had no way of knowing. And he still had to find Elaine.

Stevenson took a deep breath, then let it out. "Elaine?" he called softly. "Where are you?"

The ripping sound grew louder. He walked down the narrow corridor, between *belle epoque* decorations. He sidled around an ornate carved wood table with a heavy white marble top and painted *biscuit* knickknacks. His shoulder brushed against a painting on the wall and knocked it to the floor. The clatter echoed louder than the gunfire had.

"Elaine?"

The ripping sound stopped. He pressed his ear against a heavy door. From within came scurrying sounds more like those of a rat rather than of a human. No matter who or what was in here, he had to flush it out before proceeding. He didn't want a gun in his back if he found Elaine in a room farther down the hall.

He turned the cut-glass doorknob slowly. The door wasn't locked. Stevenson slammed hard into it, the Beretta preceding him.

He blinked, and everything within the room moved as if caught in a stroboscopic light. Elaine jerked and recoiled as she threw open the French doors leading to the balcony. He saw the suitcase on the bed. It had to be George Wyatt's. The clear plastic had been stripped away and lay discarded on the floor next to a roll of heavy tape. The clothing inside the suitcase had been tossed aside. Some was matted with a green growth.

The legacy of Project Big Hunk's original gray gooey gobs had soaked into the boy's clothing.

Stevenson saw all this and the wardrobe and the bed and the porcelain basin on the sideboard in a flash. But his concentration focused on the fleeing woman. In her hand she had one of the quartz cylinders. Green flakes caught the pale light from the street outside and told Stevenson all he needed to know.

George Wyatt's containers were filled with the mutated neutral cells too.

"Stop!" he called, expecting her to disobey. She did. He rushed through the room, stumbling on the plastic torn from the suitcase. His leg gave way, and Stevenson landed facedown on the threadbare rug, the wind almost knocked out of him. Gasping, he crawled forward, the automatic still in his hand. He had to stop her.

He got to the door leading to the balcony. Below in the streets were thousands of Mardi Gras celebrants.

"Stay back, Tom. I don't want to do this." Elaine stood at the far end of the balcony, one leg hiked over the wrought-iron railing as she readied herself for the two-story drop to the busy street. Her plain dark dress had caught in the rough ironwork and prevented her from jumping.

"Don't," he warned, aiming the pistol at her. "Come back onto the balcony."

He could barely speak. His mouth had turned to cotton. He was threatening the woman he had loved—and she held the upper hand. Her fingers were wrapped around the release valve on the bottom of the cylinder. Her intention was clear. If he didn't let her go, she would release the deadly mutated recombinant DNA experiment into the crowd below.

"There are hundreds here," she said in a mocking voice. "How much does it take to kill? A gram? Less? How much killed Basil? Someone mentioned a microgram in the report. Don't force me to do this, Tom. And they won't all die. It'll get on their costumes."

He glanced down involuntarily. The ornate apparel would hold most of the green particles. Feathers and ruffles, lace and intricate folds would catch and carry the green dust to others. Hundreds of others. Thousands. He didn't want to think that millions might die if Elaine released the valve.

"Don't, Elaine. It's not worth it."

"Oh?" She raised her eyebrow and mocked him. "Why isn't it? I've been paid well for secrets before. They'll pay even better for this."

"It wasn't intended as a weapon. It was a research—"

"Grow up, Tom. What difference do your intentions make?"

His aim steadied. His finger tightened on the trigger.

"You can't kill me. We mean too much to each other. I do love you, you know. And you love me too much to murder me in cold blood."

"Put down the cylinder."

"No, Tom, you put down the gun."

He saw her wrist begin turning. He imagined he heard

a hissing. Were the contents pressurized? Probably. There had been too much going on in the gengineered cells not to release some gas. Carbon dioxide, maybe. It didn't matter. The lethal contents would spray over the crowd below, and they would become Typhoid Marys carrying it to others, friends and strangers alike.

"All right, Elaine," he said, lowering the Beretta. He stepped back and closed his eyes. The world spun around him.

"I knew you couldn't do it, Tom."

He opened his eyes. She had turned to pull her dress free from the wrought-iron railing. The cylinder was no longer over the crowded street. If she dropped it, Stevenson saw that it wouldn't fall into the throng below.

He raised the pistol and fired without even trying to aim.

The bullet hit Elaine high in the chest. She straightened and almost fell over the railing. A look of surprise crossed her face.

"Tom . . ."

She fell to the balcony, but she wasn't dead. She muttered something he couldn't hear, then rolled so that the virulent spray from the experimental cylinder would shower through the railing on the crowd below.

Stevenson moved faster than he ever had in his life. His hands closed around her wrists, trying to keep her from opening the valve all the way. He failed. He heard the hissing and knew the death-giving green dust was spraying into the Mardi Gras air.

"You lost," she said, staring up at him.

"No!"

He wasn't even aware of reaching the decision. He dropped the useless pistol. Killing Elaine meant nothing now. Saving the multitude below did. He wrestled the cylinder from her and tried to close it. She had either jammed it or in the struggle the valve had stuck open. Stevenson had no time to study the problem.

The valve whistled with its release of pressure and

green particles. Stevenson spun the test vessel around and crammed the valve into Elaine's open mouth. She tried to force it away. He was stronger. She clawed and kicked and tried to force him back. Stevenson rose slightly, then dropped, his knee driving hard into her sternum. All the fight went out of her.

But he saw another problem. The green ooze from her nose, a mixture of mucous and green mutated cells, would contaminate the balcony. He tried again to twist the valve off. He failed.

Frantic, he dragged her inside. The cylinder continued to spew forth its stream of death. He grabbed the roll of tape off the floor and quickly pulled off a strip and used this to close Elaine's nostrils. The last sign of life fled from her. Stevenson worked more methodically now, taping shut her eyes and ears and fastening the valve firmly in her mouth.

He sat and watched for ten minutes until the pressure inside the vessel had been released. He didn't know how much of the green particulate matter from the experiment had gone into the woman's lungs and belly, but the bloating indicated that it was a considerable amount.

What the cells would do to her corpse, he didn't know. Elaine Reinhardt had died preventing the horror she had tried to release. It was fitting, but Stevenson was past caring about right or wrong. He was too drained to feel anything at all.

61

"I'll give you this, Doc, you sure leave one hell of a mess to clean up."

Special Agent Larry Bartholomew worked on a bit of shrimp stuck between his front teeth. He picked it free and flicked it across the room. Stevenson cringed at the action.

"It's lucky for you I was already on my way here. We finally pinned down that Mr. Stratton about where his grandson was." Bartholomew chuckled and shook his head. "The old man was fed up with everyone bangin' on his door. Seems Elaine took some time off and followed the track from there to here. I don't know what story she used. Door-to-door magazine saleswoman or something."

Bartholomew smiled even more broadly. "Yes, sir, Doc, you're damned lucky I was on my way here to get you out of this mess."

"What's the difference? The Pentagon will throw me to the wolves," Stevenson said. He leaned back in the hard wooden chair, trying not to look at Elaine's body. The FBI had covered it with heavy plastic, then used acrylic to spray it down to the floor. Stevenson had heard one forensics specialist say they were bringing in saws to cut through the floor. Everything in the room would eventually be sterilized, using formalin, but they would start with Elaine, the plastic shroud, and the floor around her.

"Been talkin' to some of them boys. There's a change in the chain of command. Somebody named Beaumont got kicked upstairs for all the pressure he put on your Morningside about pullin' Zamora and your cleanup team back in Redding without tellin' you. They gave him a new star and made a new command post for him."

"He was promoted to major general?" Stevenson shook his head. In the government, if you screwed up they either shot you or promoted you. He doubted he would come out as well, even if Beaumont ended up in charge of the Far East command's doorknob-supply-and-repair division.

"Might not be too bad. We're workin' on the crowd down below. They're mostly too drunk to notice what's goin' on around them. There's not much danger."

"Probably not," Stevenson said. "I stopped her before she sprayed too much." He flashed back to the way he had killed her. The bullet hadn't taken Elaine's life. Stuffing the spewing nozzle in her mouth had suffocated her. What massive organ failures would have resulted if she hadn't died?

"We're tryin' our best to check on them," Bartholomew repeated. "And we swept through the university autopsy records and put an end to speculation about George Wyatt's death. They aren't happy, but they're listenin' to Fred Wyman tell 'em how they might be in line for a brand-spankin' -new wing chock-full of research gizmos."

Stevenson hardly listened. Just as Major Zamora had been able to hide the nuclear spillage from the downed KH-18, Bartholomew was doing an able job of keeping what might have been a nightmare to an acceptable level. People would be curious, but greed would quench that quickly. If no one went to the press, the government would be able to sweep all this under a rug and hide it forever with a need-to-know, top-secret classification.

"What about the Wyatts? They racked up considerable medical bills because of George's exposure."

"You are a do-gooder at heart, aren't you, Doc?" Bartholomew perched on the edge of a sofa, seeming to float over it without actually touching it. "You ever eat at K-Paul's Kitchen? Best damn food in New Orleans. Menu changes every day or two, dependin' on what he finds over at the market."

"How nice. What about the Wyatts?"

Bartholomew acted as if he hadn't heard. "Wyman tells me some strange and little-known bureaucrat in HUD is gettin' a call. The Wyatts are eligible for a few bucks in aid from the government. Catastrophic-loss insurance they didn't know his employer had taken out on him. Or something like that. They're experts at putting it all in legalese so nobody'll figure out where the money really came from."

It was small compensation for a boy's curiosity, but no amount of money could ever remove the loss. Stevenson wondered what George Wyatt and Billy Devlin had been like. Had they wanted to be scientists? Had they known curiosity had to be coupled with conscience for real research? He would never know.

"What about me?" Stevenson's eyes locked with the agent's.

"What about you? You never existed. The fewer who know that your mutated gray gooey gob fell from the sky, the better. That's the official word. Go on back to Fort Detrick or wherever you want."

"How can I? I quit there." Stevenson looked squarely at the FBI agent. "What about Jack Parkessian?"

Bartholomew cleared his throat and looked around, as if he were giving out a secret not meant to be overheard. "It's like this, Doc. Your boy's been bad. We grilled him good about his affair with Lisa Taylor."

"Basil Baker orchestrated that, didn't he?" Stevenson closed his eyes and wished this was all over. But it would never be finished in his mind.

"He surely did," Bartholomew said. He pulled out a minted toothpick, peeled the paper wrapper off it, and started on his teeth. "Jack was real contrite about what he'd leaked to her. Between him and your boy Basil, that got the wheels turnin' to get the Russkies to Redding.

We think there was another leak, maybe at Colorado Springs. That was probably John's hook that got sunk into meat there."

That made sense to Stevenson. How else could they have arrived so quickly at the crash site?

'But Parkessian. What of him?"

"He was a bad boy, but he decided to cooperate with us to redeem himself. He's quite a snoop. We thought there was someone more than Baker leakin' to the Soviets. Turned out we were right."

Elaine Reinhardt. Stevenson took a deep breath and winced when he tried to stand. His leg hurt like hell and his left arm was almost useless, but the pain wasn't comparable to the one he felt in his belly.

"Yep, we had a notion she was a spy for some time—or someone in the department. We checked back and found she had cracked your computer codes a long time back. She dipped into your files and sampled stuff all the time, and you never noticed. Seems she thought more of your project than you did, but she had a different perspective on it."

Bartholomew stared at him. Stevenson didn't know what the agent expected.

"What am I supposed to do? I quit at Fort Detrick." Chills racked him. Elaine was dead. He had killed her because she was going to slaughter hundreds—thousands! —of innocent people for a propaganda victory for the Soviets. He didn't even understand how the Russians intended using the leverage.

As if reading his mind, Bartholomew said, "New round of talks out on a carrier in the Mediterranean start next month. All about your gengineered weapons. Gas. Germs. Nuclear dust. The whole spectrum. Our official position is that we don't have anything like that. This 'accident' would have put us in a bad light with our allies, not to mention the poor folk in the LDC's."

"They aren't mine. The germs and all that," Stevenson said. He stood. "Not now. I'm free to go?"

"Free as the wind. Go enjoy Mardi Gras. You've been through hell."

Stevenson laughed bitterly. How he was going to enjoy anything was beyond him. He left the KGB house and melted into the crowd, accepting any drink offered to him. He got roaring drunk, but it didn't help.

ABOUT THE AUTHOR

Born in Mineral Wells, Texas, in 1947, Bob Vardeman obtained a master's degree in materials engineering and spent five years at the Sandia National Laboratories before becoming a full-time writer. His numerous novels include the MASTERS OF SPACE, and BIOWARRIORS series, as well as *Ancient Heavens, Road to the Stars,* and the recently published *The Screaming Knife.* Bob has served as vice-president of the Science Fiction Writers of America, has been nominated for the prestigious Hugo award, and has attended more than forty conferences and seminars as guest of honor or featured speaker. He now makes his home in Albuquerque with his wife, Patricia, and his son, Christopher.